Max Kinnings lectures in Creative Writing at Brunel University in London. He lives in Oxford with his family.

MAX KINNINGS

BAPTISM

MAX KINNINGS

Quercus

First published in Great Britain in 2012 by

Quercus
55 Baker Street
7th Floor, South Block
London
W1U 8EW

A CIP catalogue record for this book is available
from the British Library

ISBN 978 1 78087 181 3

10 9 8 7 6 5 4 3 2 1

Typeset by Ellipsis Digital Limited, Glasgow

Printed and bound in Great Britain by Clays Ltd, St Ives plc

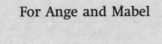

For Ange and Mabel

10:02 AM

*Tunnel between Leicester Square
and Tottenham Court Road stations*

From the train, Glen could just make out the faint sound of voices, passengers talking most probably. Sweat dribbled down his face and his heart thumped against his sternum. *Remember the training.* It was like a mantra that had been instilled in him. If he remembered the training, everything would be all right. As a member of CO19, he was at the sharp end of one of the world's most elite police special operations groups. They had earned a bad reputation in the past due to a couple of high-profile mistakes. The media had made a lot of those while playing down the successes. Glen felt proud to be a member of CO19, proud that he had passed the psychological tests and been invited to attend the eight-week training course at the Metropolitan Police Specialist Training Centre to learn about firearms, methods of entry, fast rope skills, scenario intervention, rescue techniques and potential terrorist attacks. His colleague, Rob, was one of the top specialist firearms officers in the country and by being chosen to be on operation alongside him, Glen knew that he too must be held in high regard by the powers-that-be.

The voice was relayed into his headset: 'Can you see anything?'

'Nothing,' said Rob.

'OK then, move in closer and keep talking to me.'

Rob stood up first and moved past Glen, who followed him, aiming his 9mm Glock 17 pistol at the train. This was not the most dangerous part of the mission but it was close to it; they were in the open, approaching a static target, with no cover. But they had darkness and the enclosed space of the tunnel on their side. It was unlikely that a night scope would pick them up at this distance. A few feet further on, Rob crouched down on one side of the tunnel and Glen did the same a few feet behind him, careful not to touch the live rail.

'OK, we're about twenty feet away from it now,' said Rob into his mouthpiece. 'There's nothing moving and all is quiet.' But just as he said these words, something did move. There was a flash from the cab and a soft popping sound. Glen felt a spray of warm liquid and grit on his face. He glanced at Rob but there was something wrong with him. The upper right-hand quadrant of his head was completely missing, leaving a jagged fringe of shattered bone fragments and ruptured brain in its place from which blood sluiced freely as his legs gave way and he collapsed to the ground.

'Rob?' Glen didn't know why he said it. It wasn't as though Rob could hear anything.

'What is it?' came the voice over the headset.

'Shit.' It wasn't an exclamation. Glen spoke the word softly. He looked at the train and suddenly felt very lonely. The rules of engagement seemed so far away now. He knew what he had to do but he also knew what would happen when he did it. He raised his pistol and took aim at the rear cab of the train, from where there was another flash followed by a pop. Before he could fire off a shot, the entire top of his head, from the bridge of his nose upwards was sheered off and he fell backwards onto the sleepers between the rails.

'Someone talk to me.' The calm, flat voice came from the bloody remains of two radio headsets. But no one was listening.

12:04 AM (TEN HOURS EARLIER)

Inside Madoc Farm, Snowdonia

It sounded like laughter. It came from along the corridor. Varick looked up from his book and squinted into the darkness beyond the bubble of light thrown by the candle on his desk. Why would someone be laughing so loudly after midnight? The Church of Cruor Christi didn't forbid such things, didn't trouble its flock with rules and regulations. They weren't needed. The brothers and sisters at Madoc Farm were there because they wanted to be there, they wanted to live the life. They had chosen it, just as they themselves had been chosen by God. But laughter, so loud and unrestrained at this time of night, was odd.

When Varick realised that what he was hearing wasn't laughter, he picked up the candle from his desk and made for the door, shielding the flame from the onrush of air as he made his way down the corridor towards the source of the sound.

All the doors to the bedrooms were shut apart from the one next to the bathroom, Father Owen's room. The sound wasn't coming from there but the bathroom itself. Brother

Alistair was on his knees by the side of the bath. He had succumbed to some sort of hysteria, tears streaming and his mouth stretched wide, emitting the sound that Varick had mistaken for laughter.

Varick was about to drag Alistair to his feet and slap him to his senses when he saw what was in the bath. Trembling, naked, his gnarled hands gripped around the sides of the bath as though trying to prolong his life through sheer force of will alone was Father Owen. Sticking out of his throat was the handle of a carving knife. The bath water was the colour of rosé wine.

The candle dropped from Varick's hand and went out. The only light came from the candles burning in Owen's room next door. Varick reached down to the old man, this kind old man who had taken him in and saved him when he was lost, and he half-lifted, half-dragged him from the bath and laid him down on the stone floor in the hallway.

'Who did this to you?' asked Varick. There was more light in the hallway and Varick could see the old man's face as he tried to speak. The only sound that Owen could make, however, was a faint whistling from the wound in his neck as his tongue churned blood in his mouth. Owen made another attempt to speak before his body went limp and his head cracked back against the floor as the blood bubbles around the blade in his neck popped their last.

'Who could have done such a thing?'

Alistair managed to find a gap long enough between his sobs to provide Varick with a response. 'It was Tommy.'

As Varick took in the implications of Alistair's statement, the growing sense of unease that had plagued him
all day came into needle-sharp focus. Of course it was
Tommy. It could only be Tommy. The day before Father
Owen had come to find Varick in the vegetable garden,
where he was digging, to tell him that he had found something 'most distressing', as he had described it. Worried
about Tommy's recent behaviour, Owen had done something that Varick disapproved of and searched the young
ex-soldier's room. There he had found a notebook in which
Tommy had written about his mounting frustration
relating to his faith and the state of the world in general.
Nothing unusual in that, particularly amongst the younger
members of the church of Cruor Christi, but Owen had
read something in the notebook that had alarmed him,
something that he felt compelled to impart to Varick. Hot
from the sun and tired of digging, Varick had been angry
with the old man and told him it was wrong to go into
Tommy's room and read his diary.

'Do you know where Tommy is now?'

'I heard him run,' said Alistair, sniffing. 'There were
others too.'

This was the final confirmation that Varick needed.
With Father Owen dead, responsibility for the church's
future had devolved to him. He knew where Tommy was
going. The details of what he wanted to do were all laid
out in his notebook. If Tommy was serious about carrying
out his mission – and Owen's murder could only suggest
that he was – this was more than just an attack on the

church of Cruor Christi, it was an attack on everyone who failed to share the insanity of Tommy's grand designs. Varick knew what was happening. God was testing him.

12:07 AM

They were on their way. The moment she had been waiting for for so long had arrived. Her flesh tingled. She felt strangely intoxicated but also completely in control. It was a spiritual feeling. Never once had she doubted her brother, never once had she found cause to concern herself regarding the legitimacy or morality of what they were embarking on. Tommy was a prophet. She was a prophet too. Tommy had told her she was.

She hadn't liked watching what Tommy had done to the old man. It reminded her of her mother and father. It wasn't nice. But if she was honest – and she always was because God knew when she lied – she was pleased with herself that she had been strong enough to witness it. It made her realise that she would be able to do what had to be done later in the day. This was something that she had given great thought to in the past few weeks. She didn't want to let Tommy down.

While Tommy put his bag in the boot of the car he had stolen earlier, Simeon said, 'What's happening? Why now?'

'Just practising,' she said. She didn't like lying to Simeon but he would find out the truth for himself soon enough. Of course they weren't 'just practising'. Why kill the old man if they were practising? Not that Simeon knew that Father Owen was dead. Tommy had made sure that Simeon was in his room when they dealt with Father Owen. But there was no more time for Simeon to ask further questions; Tommy climbed into the car, started the engine and they set off.

It reminded Belle of when she was little, when their parents were still alive and they went out in the car for the day. She didn't care where they were going; it was the journey she loved, sitting there in the back seat looking out of the window at the scenery going past. She felt the same excitement now, sitting next to Tommy as he steered them along the mountain roads. Their destination was still a few hours away and she could enjoy the journey, safe and secure in the car with the two men she loved most in all the world: Tommy and Simeon.

Tommy had kept telling her to expel all doubt from her mind and sometimes she found it hard. Many people – most people probably – would find it almost impossible to understand what they were going to do but that didn't mean that it wasn't right. Jesus had been misunderstood, had been persecuted for his beliefs. Suffering was all part of the process but, now that they were on their way to London and the waiting was over, she felt sure that her suffering was nearly at an end.

12:09 AM

Inside Madoc Farm, Snowdonia

Varick hurried back to his room, the familiarity of his surroundings allowing him to navigate in almost total darkness. He went to the desk in the office next to his bedroom, opened the drawer and took out a large metal torch and a Smith & Wesson revolver. Never had the gun's chequered stock felt so reassuring in his hand. It always supplied him with strength of purpose. Clicking on the torch, he headed towards Tommy's room at the other end of the corridor. The door was open and he could see from the light of the torch before he even stepped inside that the room was empty.

Varick went to the shelves above the bed and dragged down the shoeboxes in which Tommy kept his personal possessions. The boxes' contents spilled open on the bed. There were letters, postcards, athletics badges from school, diaries, notebooks, computer disks and a pack of playing cards. Varick didn't know what he was looking for but, as he looked through Tommy Denning's possessions, he realised how little he had really known him.

Cruor Christi was an evangelical Christian order that welcomed troubled souls. Varick was a troubled soul himself. His own personal experience gave him vision and understanding. Tommy had been something of a special project for him. Fiercely intelligent yet damaged, when Tommy had first come to Madoc Farm he had been like a coiled spring. Varick thought he could save him; he thought that Cruor Christi could succeed where other institutions had clearly failed. It was a struggle but he had known that it would be. Tommy's childhood traumas and his time fighting in Afghanistan had left him in a dangerous state of mind, one in which he would surely have ended up in prison if Varick hadn't taken him in. Owen, however, was convinced that Tommy and his sister Belle, who had joined the church before Tommy and had encouraged him to join too, would be disruptive influences at Madoc Farm. Owen and Varick had clashed over this a number of times. Now it looked as though the old man had been right all along.

Feelings of dread and fear came to Varick just as they had done in the old days, the days before he was born again. He looked at himself in the mirror on the wall. He looked old. He would be fifty next birthday. But he was still big and strong, still resolute. He would do what had to be done.

With the door to Brother Thomas's room closed behind him, Brother Varick walked back along the corridor. There was no point knocking on Brother Simeon's door; he knew the room was empty before the beam of the torch on the empty bed confirmed it. He closed the door and continued to Sister Belle's room. Empty. Tommy had his two foot-soldiers with him.

Varick could hear other brothers and sisters stirring in their rooms, awoken by the disturbance, no doubt, and reaching for candles and matches. At the end of the corridor, kneeling next to Father Owen's body, Brother Alistair continued to sob, but more gently now. Looking up as Varick approached, he said, 'Tommy's gone hasn't he?'

'Yes,' said Varick. 'He's gone. All three of them have gone.'

'What are we going to do?'

'We're going to London.' This was enough to stop Alistair crying. He looked afraid as Varick continued. 'We're going to give Father Owen the last rites and then we're going to London.'

'Me too?' Alistair shook his head as he asked the question, as though willing a negative response.

'Yes, you too. We've got to find Tommy and the others and we've got to make them stop.'

06:45 AM

Inside 14 Highfield Road, South Wimbledon

George Wakeham's radio alarm clock clicked on and the voice of the travel-news presenter filled the room. It was the Scottish one with the sing-song tone who spoke cheerfully of industrial action by baggage handlers and security staff at Stansted which had affected outbound flights. The 43 bus route was diverted in Muswell Hill; a lorry had shed its load on the A40 in Acton causing eastbound delays; the Strand Underpass was closed and the Hangar Lane gyratory was 'snarled up through sheer weight of traffic'.

'And now to the tube . . .' George listened more intently. Of the two hundred and seventy-five stations on the network, one was closed due to construction work – Southfields on the District Line – and one – East Acton on the Central Line – was shut due to staff shortages. Aside from these flies in the collective ointment, all remaining stations were open for business as usual.

'London Underground has issued a travel warning, following predicted daytime temperatures in excess of ninety-five degrees Fahrenheit. Travellers are advised to take a bottle of water with them on their journeys and people who are susceptible to heat-related disorders are advised to stay at home.'

There he was, the Scottish bloke, sitting in some air-conditioned office explaining that it was going to be the hottest day of the year. George could have done without that. He had been awake since four. His insomnia had no specific cause. It was just the standard issue middle-aged paranoia that gives you a shove in the middle of the night and sits with you, prodding you until any thought of sleep is futile.

The sun was already beating down on the roof of George's small terraced house in South Wimbledon. He could feel it coming through the ceiling and the walls, ceiling and walls in need of paintwork, his paintwork, work that he kept meaning to get round to but never seemed to manage.

They would issue a warning for just about anything nowadays. Like people were too dumb to realise it was hot and they should behave accordingly. They needed someone to warn them, patronise them. Like the posters cautioning against reckless drinking, paid for by the drinks companies. Treat people like morons and they'll behave like them.

The electric fan at the foot of the bed blew gusts of warm air across George's body, a body pretty much unchanged from his days at school when he played on the wing in the first eleven. His arms and legs were still muscular but around his middle was proof of his sedentary lifestyle, proof that was beginning to creep over the edge of his belt.

His hair needed a trim too. The spiky cut he had gone for in the spring was long grown out and his sideburns were bushy and accentuated – or so he feared – his full cheeks, depriving him of a face that had led a former girlfriend to comment that he looked like a young Albert Finney, an observation he had proudly mentioned a number of times since, long after said girlfriend had become someone else's. He sometimes wondered if his Albert Finney similarity might have continued with age so that he now looked like Albert Finney at forty, after a few too many pies.

George enjoyed the breeze from the fan but the time on the radio alarm kept niggling at him. It was always the same. As soon as he felt like sleeping, it was time to get up. Maggie didn't have that problem. She was asleep as soon as her head touched the pillow and she only woke if Sophie or Ben stirred in the night. It was like she had a sixth sense as far as the children were concerned. But neither of them had woken and Maggie slept on with her back to him, the sheet pulled tight around her shoulders.

When he and Maggie had first met and started seeing each other, he had struggled to believe that a woman so good looking could find him attractive. She seemed to like the fact that, unlike her friends from college who studied business and marketing and wanted to get on and do well for themselves, he wanted to lead a more – he hated the expression – alternative lifestyle. The fact he had no money – he was the bass player in a band called Crawlspace at the time – was not a problem. Maggie had a good job in the West End working for a theatre market-ing agency and she could afford to indulge his artistic ambitions.

What had kept him going as a young man while he trawled from one low-paid job to another was a supreme confidence that there was some great creative achieve-ment awaiting him just round the corner. At varying times, he had planned on being a pop star, a writer, a comedian and an actor, but every time he tried to establish himself within his chosen field he gave up at the first taste of rejection. If he had concentrated on one specific vocation he might have made it; perhaps he spread himself too thinly – an expression he had overheard his parents use about him when he was a boy.

Ten years before he had seen a notice in the *Evening Standard* for staff at Morden tube station, the most southerly station on the Northern Line and not far from where he lived. He applied for a job and he was successful. It was a stopgap, he told himself, until something else came along. But after a few weeks, he saw an advertise-ment in the weekly *Traffic Circular* and applied for a posi-tion as a train operator. Again, he got the job and after a short training course, he was 'on the handle' – a London Underground train driver.

It was a novelty at first; it made him feel like he was breaking away from his middle-class roots to work with 'the people'. It appealed to the left-wing principles he had developed at college, where he had briefly studied psychology before dropping out. He joined the union,

ASLEF, and went along to a few meetings with the intention of trying his hand at politics but found that he was too shy to assert himself among the shop stewards. What was that Smiths song about shyness stopping you from doing things in life that you'd like to do?

All that music he had listened to over the years. All those records – he still had them in boxes, all those bands with integrity and passion and fire in their soul, all those manifestos for a different life he had believed in as a young man, all now pushed to the back of the cupboard on the landing. What use rebellion when you've got storage requirements for bumper packs of Pampers? It was funny how life sanded down the corners of your idealism. One minute you're a spiky young guy in black clothes with a dedication to the pursuance of cool that is as serious as your haircut, and the next you're an overweight dad with a receding hairline and a scary mortgage.

He still harboured dreams of artistic endeavour. He still wanted to be the guy who wrote that book – it's really good – did you know he was a tube driver? Or the bloke who played guitar for that band – he used to drive a tube train, you know? Anything so long as he wasn't just George Wakeham, tube driver.

When Maggie worked for the agency in Soho, he sometimes accompanied her to the first nights of shows. There were all the comedians, the television personalities and the celebrities of the day – the ones only too eager to accept free tickets to the opening of another bloody musical – and he convinced himself that deep down he had more talent than they had. He just needed to find some outlet for it. This yearning for artistic success was motivated by vanity, pure vanity, he knew, and this self-knowledge helped fuel the creeping anxiety that he was wasting his life, wasting his potential driving a tube train all day.

If only he could accept his lot like the other drivers and station staff. That would make life a whole lot easier. But he couldn't. Maybe they couldn't either. How depressing was that? He envied people who enjoyed their work, people for whom the job was enough, people who were happy. There was a time when driving a tube train was just a day job, something to pay the bills while he tried to pursue a creative career. But now he was a tube driver – that alone – and nothing more.

The red diodes on the clock radio were taunting him: it was time to wake the children. He pulled at the clammy sheet that had become twisted around his waist but he was lying on it and it stuck fast. For a moment he felt a twinge of claustrophobia before he managed to release himself.

Sometimes he could go for days without feeling anything but then he would be held at a red light in the middle of a tunnel for a couple of minutes and the sweating would start. If he was stationary for anything longer than a few minutes he knew he would be in trouble.

All was well when he was moving. The fact that he was locked in one of the deepest and narrowest railway lines in the world meant nothing. When he was motionless in a tunnel, on the other hand, that was something entirely different. Every two or three months there would be a lengthy delay. Perhaps five or six minutes. He could deal with that. He would feel wretched but he could cope. Only once had he nearly come unstuck. A passenger had run amok with a knife at Elephant and Castle and the station was closed down. George's train was stuck in the tunnel for nearly an hour.

The discomfort had come in waves, each wave peaking that little bit higher, sustaining itself that little bit longer, until it broke. Each time the claustrophobia had struck, he knew that the only way to deal with it was to move even if the train itself was stationary. There were only two ways to go, either through the J door, as it was known, between the cab and the passenger area, or out of the M door at the front of the train leading out onto the track itself. To make a run for it in either direction would have meant the end of his career as a tube train driver but during the final few minutes of his ordeal it seemed like an increasingly small price to pay. Finally, the all-clear was given and he was saved. Never had he been so relieved to see a green light and he set off once more, sweating, hyperventilating, but safe.

He knew it was ridiculous, comical even. Did you hear the one about the tube train driver who suffered from claustrophobia? But George didn't find it funny, not today, the hottest day of the year.

06:58 AM

Highfield Road, South Wimbledon

Simeon sat in the back seat of the car outside the train driver's house and ruminated – as he had for the past few hours – on why they were proceeding with the plan a week early. If it was a rehearsal for the real thing then why bother waiting for the driver? He might not even be on the same shift rota this week. But whatever the truth, Tommy wasn't saying. He was in one of his moods where it was almost impossible to get any sense out of him, fielding all questions with his usual enigmatic bullshit.

When Tommy had come to fetch him just after midnight, he was wiping blood from his arm. Simeon asked him whose blood it was. What the hell was going on? But Tommy had told him, whispering, that they were on their way to London and they had to leave immediately with Belle. When Tommy had said that he would explain everything later, Simeon immediately had a bad feeling about the whole thing, which was compounded when he heard what must have been Brother Alistair sobbing. He didn't have a chance to make further enquiries, just collected his things and left with Tommy and Belle.

It was Belle who led him to believe that it might just be a dry run. As they waited in the car outside Madoc Farm while Tommy loaded his things into the boot, Simeon had asked her what was going on.

'Just practising,' Belle had said, and before he could question her further Tommy was into the driver's seat, and they set off down through the mountains in silence. From where he sat in the back, Simeon could see Tommy's face reflected in the rear-view mirror. Tommy stared ahead at the narrow winding roads lit up in the flare of the headlights but his thoughts were clearly elsewhere.

As they made their way along the M4, Tommy said that he and Belle should try and get some sleep. Simeon didn't want to push the questioning but he tried again: 'So we're going early? Or is this some kind of rehearsal?' His and Tommy's eyes met in the rear-view mirror. Even though Simeon couldn't see Tommy's mouth, he could tell that Tommy was smiling. He could see from the wrinkles in the corners of his eyes. The bastard was enjoying this. Tommy didn't even answer his question, just went right on smiling.

As they sat in the car outside the train driver's house, Simeon could sense Tommy's and Belle's nerves. They weren't behaving as though it was a dry run. Tommy was alert, acutely focused. Belle watched her brother intently and waited. Simeon felt compelled to speak.

'So we're going to go this morning?' He tried to sound hopeful, like this was something that he had dreamt of.

He never was much of an actor, always avoided drama classes at school.

'Surrender,' said Tommy, turning around in his seat and smiling right at him.

'What do you mean?'

'Surrender to God's will.'

As soon as he heard Tommy say this and saw the mobile phone and headset in his hand, Simeon knew that today was no rehearsal.

Inside 14 Highfield Road, South Wimbledon

George made his way through to the bathroom. Maggie was still asleep. Being the first one up, he could avoid the rush. He looked at himself in the mirror. He was forty years old. His parents used to say of the passing years, 'Where does it all go?' and he didn't know what they meant. Not until now. The name of a Charles Bukowski poem summed it all up, although he had never actually read the poem itself. He was reading a Charles Bukowski book, *Post Office*, and one of Bukowski's other works listed at the back was called *The Days Run Away Like Wild Horses Over the Hills*. And it was true, they did. Bukowski was right on the money.

As he had grown older, he had found himself becoming more emotional, more likely to tear up at a sad moment in a film or a tragic incident on the news. It might have had something to do with his recent 'one under' – his first suicide on the job. For a while, he had been appalled but also strangely intrigued by the prospect of seeing someone jump. It wasn't as though he was chasing a perverse thrill, far from it, but if he had to come to terms with its likelihood then what better way to do so than with an air of mild curiosity? Some of his colleagues were traumatised by the experience while others didn't seem to give a damn. George often wondered how he would react when his time came. It would come eventually – there were over a hundred incidents every year. He wondered how it would feel to watch someone die. It happened to most tube drivers if they drove for long enough. Then, one day, sure enough, it happened to him.

He was pulling into Warren Street station six months previously. It was about five o'clock. The platform was full of the usual late-afternoon crowd, people trying to beat the rush – and failing. He was about halfway into the station when one of the faceless hordes, a smartly dressed woman in her early fifties, launched herself off the plat-form edge straight in front of the train. As an exercise in efficient life termination, it was spot on. She timed it perfectly. Her body slammed into the front of the cab and dropped down under the wheels. She was killed instantly. George was lucky in that respect. He guessed the woman was too if she was serious about her desire to die, and he could only presume from her very definite leap that she was.

Colleagues of George had told him about instances where people had jumped and were only injured, trapped under the train. That could be harrowing for all concerned. So he was thankful that his one under, when it came, was mercifully quick for both himself and the jumper.

Giving evidence at the inquest was more difficult than he had anticipated, especially seeing the woman's grieving relatives. After the verdict of suicide was returned, the woman's husband had approached him outside the coroner's court and apologised for his wife's actions. George had found the experience extremely moving.

He took the leave he was entitled to and accepted an offer of counselling, not because he felt he really needed it but because he had never had any counselling before and wondered if it might help him with his anxiety and corresponding insomnia. It didn't.

As George showered, he enjoyed rinsing away the sticky glaze of sweat coating his skin. It was getting on for half past by now, it had to be. Time to wake the family. He pulled a towel around his waist, squeezed some toothpaste onto his toothbrush and started on his teeth as he made his way back towards the bedroom.

'I thought you were going to wake me,' said Maggie as he appeared in the doorway.

'I am waking you,' he said with a mouth full of white foam. 'That's what I'm doing now.'

'Well there's no need because I'm already awake.'

'So why are you digging me out for not waking you?'

'I'm just teasing.' That tone of voice. She was in a good mood. He liked it when she was happy.

'What time is it?'

'About twenty past seven.'

She yawned and stretched out her arms. George smiled at her and she smiled back. He was just about to say something affectionate, something about how she looked nice with her new hair – and she did, the short bob suited her – when she said, 'God, you look rough.'

'Thanks.'

'Don't mention it.'

George turned back towards the door.

Maggie said, 'Can you wake Sophie and Benji?'

He grunted yes as he headed back towards the landing.

Sophie was fast asleep. George watched her for a moment, hoping that the sound of him brushing his teeth would bring her round but she didn't stir. She was lying on her side sucking her thumb, her dark brown hair – the same colour as her mother's – lay across her tiny pixie face. She looked so helpless. Her future lay in his hands and as much as he wanted the best for her in all things, the best wasn't always possible on the salary of a London Underground train driver. He reached down and rubbed her back. Her eyes opened and she frowned at him for a moment, squinting into the light. 'Hello, little one. Have you had a nice sleep?' The question was phrased in that tone of voice that he reserved for his children only. It was a high-pitched version of his normal voice and it made him cringe when he heard himself talking like that on family videos. Seeing himself on them was bad enough.

'It's hot, Daddy,' she said.

'It is, darling, it's very hot.' He lowered the tone so it was more like his normal voice, his Maggie voice, as opposed to the more blokey guttural one he used with colleagues at work. Lifting Sophie out of bed, he gave her a squeeze before setting her down on the carpet, where she tottered a little sleepily and yawned.

Ben was already awake, playing with his Action Man as George entered his room and said, 'Morning, fella.'

After a series of energetic vocal simulations of gunfire and explosions, Ben said, 'Morning,' and proceeded to question George about the pros and cons of machine-guns as though they were already mid-conversation on that very topic.

'Is it my birthday today?' Ben asked as George tried to steer him from the battlefield into the bathroom.

'It's tomorrow,' said George. 'And where are we going, fella?'

'Mr Pieces!' He shouted it and Sophie joined in, the two of them running and jumping as they cheered and sang out, 'Mr Pieces! Mr Pieces!'

Mr Pieces was in reality a restaurant called Mr Pizza, but Ben had mispronounced it when he was little and forever more it was known as Mr Pieces in the Wakeham household. Mr Pieces was a family favourite.

Having corralled his two children in the bathroom, George supervised Ben's morning wash – 'Dad? If you shot a man a hundred times, would he die?' – and helped Sophie sponge her face and clean her teeth. While Ben pulled on his jeans and a Spiderman T-shirt, George brushed Sophie's hair and dressed her in the clothes Maggie had left out on the chest of drawers outside the bathroom, a pair of pink jeans with a flower patch on the knee and a stripy top. To save time, he carried Sophie down the stairs behind

Ben, whose stream of consciousness had re-routed from machine guns to breakfast cereal. When George arrived in the kitchen doorway, however, Sophie still in his arms, Maggie's face collapsed into an expression of annoyance.

'George, it's about a thousand degrees out there and you've put her in long sleeves.'

'Well that's what was on the chest of drawers.'

'Leave it to me.' She said it with that long-suffering tone as though he was forever dressing his children in inappropriately warm clothes on hot days. George looked at Sophie and Ben and rolled his eyes as Maggie made her way back upstairs.

'Silly Daddy, eh?'

'Silly Daddy,' mimicked Sophie, grinning.

George watched Ben and Sophie sitting at the kitchen table and even though he had kissed them both earlier, felt compelled to bury his nose and lips in their hair and kiss them again, relishing the smell of them, a smell somewhere between honey and freshly baked biscuits with just a hint of shampoo. God, he loved that smell.

Sitting on the work surface next to the microwave oven was Sophie's favourite doll, Poppy.

'Look! Here's Poppy Doll. Look, Poppy's saying hello. "Hello Sophie!" she says. "Hello Sophie!"' He was back to the high-pitched voice again. Sophie took the doll and gave it a squeeze as Maggie returned and George beat a hasty retreat, grabbing his bag from the banister rail and making for the front door. Turning back to the kitchen, he waved to Ben and Sophie, said, 'Bye bye!' – high pitched

– and then back to his normal voice for Maggie: 'See you later.'

He blew her a kiss and she kissed the air and smiled. George closed the door and hurried off along the pavement. As he climbed into the car, put his bag on the passenger seat and was about to put the key in the ignition, he heard an unfamiliar ring tone nearby. He reached into his pocket for his phone. Perhaps Sophie had accidentally reprogrammed the ring tone from the opening bars of 'Train in Vain' by the Clash which he had uploaded to it a couple of weeks before. He had always loved that track. When he took his phone out of his pocket, however, the screen was dark. Then he realised that the ring tone was coming from the glove compartment. He snatched it open and there was a mobile phone – a much higher specification model than his – along with a wireless headset. As he picked up the phone, he looked at the name of the caller on the screen: Maggie. His Maggie? What did it mean? His wife was calling this phone – a phone that wasn't his.

And then it occurred to him: Maggie must be having an affair and her secret lover had left his phone in the car and now she thought she was calling him. It had to be that. She had been caught red-handed and he wanted her to know it. He pressed the Call Answer button and held the phone to his ear.

'Maggie?'

'Look at the window, George . . . of the house . . . look at the window.' Her voice sounded weird, like she'd been crying. Maybe she'd realised her mistake, a mistake of marriage-wrecking proportions. He looked at the window. Perhaps he was wrong about the affair. Maybe she was going to wave to him? Or maybe Sophie and Ben were. But why? They didn't normally and why the strange phone in the glove compartment?

Suddenly a man stepped into view in the living room window, a slim man dressed all in black, wearing a balaclava. With one hand, he held Sophie, crying and struggling, and with the other, he held a gun to her head.

07:45 AM

Inside 14 Highfield Road, South Wimbledon

Any lingering doubts that perhaps today was a practice run had been dispelled when Tommy had opened the back door of the house and they had made their way inside. Tommy behaved as though he had done this a thousand times before. He didn't even seem to be nervous. Simeon, on the other hand, felt sick as he pressed his gun into the woman's back as Tommy explained what she was to say into the phone.

'Please don't hurt them,' the woman had shouted when Tommy approached the children.

'Keep quiet and everything will be fine.' Simeon felt as though he was reciting lines from a script. He had no idea whether anything would ever be fine again. There were times in the past few weeks when it felt as though Tommy's and Belle's plans were fantasy. That wasn't to say that the two of them weren't serious and meticulous about every-thing but, as with the po-faced religious observance at Madoc Farm, it felt as though they were all involved in something that wasn't real, something make-believe.

Obsessing over every minor detail was something that Tommy and Belle clearly relished. But Simeon had suspected that when all the strategising was at an end, they might then start preparing for another hypothetical attack. As though that was how they liked to amuse themselves during the long boring nights. The events of that morning, however, had proved him spectacularly wrong.

Tommy scooped up the little girl with one arm and pointed his gun at her head. Simeon pushed the gun into the woman's back, her cue to tell her husband on the phone to look at the window where Tommy stood. It was an audacious way of ensuring the train driver's compliance. What if someone had been driving or walking past the house and had seen what was going on? But they didn't. If Tommy could do this and get away with it so easily, Simeon was in no doubt that he could do everything else that he had planned.

07:46 AM

Highfield Road, South Wimbledon

It felt like a vent had opened up in the quiet suburban facade, allowing George Wakeham a glimpse of hell. But just as soon as the image was branded on his memory, the man holding Sophie stepped away from the window.

'Maggie! What the fuck is going on?' On the phone, he could hear Sophie and Ben crying.

'Don't get out of the car!' Maggie screamed so hard it hurt his eardrum. George had the door halfway open already. He slammed it shut. 'If you get out of the car they'll kill us.'

'What do they want?'

No reply.

He heard Maggie talking to Sophie. She said, 'You're all right now. You're all right, Mummy's got you.'

'Maggie!'

'George, I've got to read something to you.' Her voice was trembling. 'You have to listen to it very carefully, OK?'

'OK.'

'Unless you do exactly as instructed, the three of us will be killed. Any attempt to raise the alarm will result in us being killed. Any attempt to deviate from the implicit nature of any instructions given to you, however minor, will result in us being killed. Do you understand?'

He couldn't speak. His mouth was devoid of saliva and he felt sick.

'Do you understand? George!'

'Yes, yes.'

'You must take the headset that is with the mobile phone. Can you see it?'

'Yes.'

'It has an on/off switch on the side. Put on the headset and turn it on. Do it now.'

George picked up the headset. With shaking fingers he found the switch, flicked it on and hooked the earpiece around his ear.

'Can you hear me?' asked Maggie.

'Yes, I can hear you.'

'You must keep the headset on at all times and keep this line open until you are instructed to do otherwise. Have you got that?'

'Yes.'

Norman, a bespectacled oddball of a man who lived with his mother at the Bates Motel, as George and Maggie called the house, stepped out from behind his brown front door and made his way along the street. Maybe George could communicate with Norman and have him raise the alarm? Maybe he could write something on a piece of paper and hold it up? Norman saw him in the car and waved.

George looked away as though he hadn't seen. Trying to raise the alarm was a stupid idea. It would never work.

But Norman had stopped almost level with the front window of George and Maggie's house. George gestured to the mobile phone to show Norman he was on a call.

'George? You're not trying to do anything are you?' Maggie sounded desperate. 'You're not trying to signal to anyone are you?'

'No.'

Still Norman stood there. George looked away.

'Then why can they see a man on the pavement looking at you?'

'He's just going.' But he wasn't. Norman was watching him.

'George! For God's sake! They've got a gun against Ben's head!'

In the background, he could hear Ben shout, 'Mummy!' George had to do something, anything. So he held up two fingers to Norman, flicked a 'V' at him and mouthed, 'Fuck off,' as unmistakably as he could muster. Norman frowned and blinked a few times, bemused. He went to say something but thought better of it and walked away.

'Tell them he's going away,' said George.

'Christ, George, OK, OK.'

'Maggie, I want to speak to them.'

Pause.

'They won't allow it, all communication must come through me. Now you must continue with your day, exactly as normal. You must go to work and you must keep the headset on with the line open until instructed otherwise.'

'Maggie, ask them what they want.'

'They can hear you. They're listening.'

'So? So what is it? What's this all about?'

Dead air for a moment and then: 'They say that you'll find out everything in due course but now you should do as you are told.'

'In that case I want them to know that I will do whatever they want, on the condition that they don't harm you or the children in any way.'

'They can hear you, they want you to know that they agree but you must now proceed as you would on any other day and they want you to know that they will be watching you and listening to you at all times. If you do anything . . .'

'I know, I know, you'll be . . . I know.'

'George, you'd better get going.'

He started the car and set off, his foot trembling against the accelerator pedal. As he drove past his house, he looked into the living room. There was no one there but he could just make out Sophie's doll, Poppy, on the arm of the sofa.

As he pulled out into the traffic on the main road, his eyes filled with tears and he listened intently to the faint hiss from the headset during the ten-minute journey to the depot. When he pulled up at traffic lights and zebra crossings, he watched people as they went about their business, oblivious to the horror in which he was cocooned. Could he signal to one of them? Could any one of them become his family's saviour? The answers to these and every question he might ask of himself regarding possible solutions to his predicament went unanswered. Any attempt to raise the alarm, to alert the world to his situation was a potential reason for his family to be harmed. Such was his fear and dread that turning the car into the car park at Morden, he retched.

'Maggie?'

'Yes?'

'Is everything all right?'

'George . . .' She was cut short and he could hear a man muttering something. He couldn't make out what he was saying. George felt the need to keep speaking, to say anything.

'I'm at the depot.'

'George, listen to me.' There was an intimacy to the way she spoke that George hadn't heard in a long time. 'You've got to keep quiet. Please. Don't speak unless you really need to.'

'OK, I just want you to know that I love you.' He needed to say it. It made him feel better.

No reply, just the hum of the open line. How long did they intend to utilise this communication channel? It was all well and good above ground but if they wanted to talk to him once he was in the tube tunnel then they would need to use some other method. They had to have thought of that, hadn't they?

Parked up in the station car park, he took his bag from the passenger seat. Holding the mobile phone in his hand, he climbed out, locked the car, and walked towards the depot building with his head down.

'Hi, George!' Panic stabbed him. He looked up. It was Louisa. She worked in the canteen. They had developed a friendship over the past couple of years. George found her attractive and sometimes, he couldn't help but fantasise about how things might be if he was about ten years younger and unmarried. Louisa smiled at him, the sort of smile that, until today, had the ability to make him blush. Now, he felt nothing.

'Hi, Louisa. How are you?'

'Fine, thanks,' she replied. 'You?'

'Yeah, I'm good.' My wife and children are being held hostage by an armed gang was what he wanted to say. He didn't; he couldn't.

It was still early but already the heat was in the high seventies. Louisa looked as cool and fragrant as ever but George could feel the perspiration forming on his upper body.

Louisa fell in beside him as they climbed up the steps and in through the front door of the depot. His conversations with Louisa usually followed a certain pattern. He would tell her some anecdote, try and make her laugh. Impossible now but he knew he had to say something.

'Another hot one.' It was all he could think of.

But she didn't get to reply as Neville, a fellow driver, a big ungainly Scot who prided himself on his irreverent humour, came bounding down the corridor with a big grin on his face. He and George were friends. They some-times went for a beer together after work.

'Georgie-boy! Finally embraced the new technology, I see!' He pointed at the headset George was wearing. Neville had only recently joked about George's phone being not just last year's model but last century's.

'Yeah, I thought it was time I took the plunge.'

'Give us a look then.' Neville held out his hand.

'Neville, I'm speaking to someone.'

As soon as he said it, he realised how ridiculous it would sound to Louisa, who was smiling, preparing herself to enjoy Neville's good-humoured ribbing of 'George the technophobe'. She looked confused. They had just walked across the car park and George had made no indication that he was on a call.

'Come on,' said Neville. 'You can still talk, I just want to have a look at the handset.' He made another grab for the phone.

'Just fucking leave it!'

The ferocity of George's response was glaringly inappropriate to those who didn't understand his unique predicament. Louisa was taken aback. She muttered, 'I'll see you later,' and hurried off.

Neville froze, eyebrows raised in surprise.

'I'm sorry, Nev, but I'm on the phone, all right?' George pushed past him.

When George went to sign on with the duty manager, a round pink man who was sweating through his shirt, he was told that the city branch of the Northern Line had just been closed due to a 'security incident'. This would normally have been enough to prick George's curiosity. A security incident was fabulously vague. It was the sort of thing announcers said to punters over the public-address system in a station, not the sort of explanation given by a duty manager to a driver. But George had more important things on his mind.

He made his way to his train, number 037, in Bay 12 of the shed. The mobile phone had become slippery with sweat and he slid it into the top pocket of his shirt slowly, being careful not to knock any buttons or keys and making sure he could still hear the open line humming in his ear from the headset.

'They want to know what time you leave from Morden,' said Maggie as he approached the train.

'Eight seventeen.'

'OK.'

George hung up his bag and his jacket in the cab. The temperature being what it was, he made sure the heating was turned off. Then he checked the lights and changed the destination blind to 'Mill Hill East via Charing Cross'. He was so used to the procedure he could sleepwalk through it. He checked the PA handset was working, and the saloon lights were on and he tripped out the motor alternators and overloads and reset them. Turning on the radio, he heard the bronchial wheeze of the depot shunter as he called other trains out of the depot.

George checked the wipers and whistle, the air-pressure gauge and the brakes. Satisfied there were no faults with the train monitoring system, he carried out a lamp test followed by a traction test and checked the heat and vent system, the doors, and the passenger alarm. It was a few minutes before he was due to be called so he wandered through the six cars of the train checking that everything was as it should be.

A group of maintenance engineers were working on a section of track in the shed. They were laughing at something. George had never felt so alone in all his life. He returned to the cab, slamming the J door – the door between the passenger area and the cab – after him. Usually he just sat and did the crossword in the *Metro* newspaper that he picked up on his way to the shed until the depot shunter called him down to leave the depot. Sometimes, as he waited to be called down, he played a game on his mobile phone called Snake. But as he thought of his own mobile phone, all thoughts of the game were forgotten. Why hadn't he thought of it before? Reaching into the side pocket of his jacket, he took out the phone and looked at it. He couldn't call anyone for fear of being overheard but he could send a text. Who could he send it to? Was it possible to text 999? Could he text a friend – Dougie perhaps? My family are being held hostage – call the police but tell them not to do anything for fear of alerting the hostage takers. Dougie would think he was joking, taking the piss. Even if he did believe him and raised the alarm, his actions might inadvertently cost the lives of George's family.

George slid his phone back into his jacket pocket and sat with his legs bouncing up and down on his toes, his nerves jangling out of control. He felt like a condemned man. It was a struggle to keep the panic at bay. After years of mundanity and routine, something so frightening and profound was happening to him that he felt as though if he allowed himself to think about it with any clarity his brain would run away with itself. Because in whichever direction he looked, it was too much to take in. The people who had taken his family were armed and, more frightening than that, they were clever. There was no point trying to raise the alarm because he knew for a cold certainty, from that one-second image in the front window of his house that kept replaying over and over in his head, that if he did and they found out, they would kill his family without compunction.

On the radio, the depot shunter called him forward to the outlet signal. George took hold of the dead man's handle, pushed the lever into drive and the train moved off out of the shed. When the signal cleared, the train headed down the track to Morden station and he heard the radio switch across from the depot channel to the line channel.

He pulled up to the signal in the station and opened the doors. Usually he would lean out and watch the punters climb aboard. He enjoyed people-watching and often, to try and dispel a crushing sense of boredom, he would weave little stories about his passengers and where they were going. Sometimes it might be nothing more than trying to work out someone's name from their appearance. With some people it was tricky but for others – a total Jeremy for example – he liked to feel he could spot one a mile off. But today he didn't indulge this interest; he stood in the cab and looked at the two tunnel entrances at the end of the deep man-made gorge up ahead, where the train would enter London Underground's longest network of tunnels.

George wasn't an anorak like some of his colleagues but he did know that from Morden to East Finchley on the Northern Line was – at over seventeen miles – one of the longest and deepest railway tunnels in the world. And once inside it, all phone signals would die. So, in approximately two minutes, he would be left all alone with only the radio channel linking him to the line controller. The people who had kidnapped Maggie and Sophie couldn't listen in to him on that, could they? Would this present him with an opportunity to raise the alarm – if he felt it was safe enough to do so? Would he ever feel it was safe enough to do so?

When the signal changed, George pressed the buttons to close the passenger doors, checked the pilot light was out and turned the dead man's handle. The train moved forward out of the station into the shadow thrown by the high sides of the gorge leading to the tunnels. George slid the mobile phone out of his top pocket and watched the reception bars down the side of the screen collapse to nothing as the train was swallowed by the darkness. As the line went dead, he took off the headset and put it in his pocket with the handset.

It was a strange feeling being suddenly released from the surveillance that he had been subject to. It afforded no relief from his all-pervading sense of dread, however, and now he felt himself consumed by indecision. Was now the time to attempt to communicate his unique predicament to the authorities? Turning off the main light in the cab as he always did, in order to see more clearly in the tunnel, he reached for the radio handset on the console. But as his fingers touched the moulded plastic, he heard an unexpected sound. Someone was opening the door into the cab.

08:17 AM

Northbound Northern Line platform, Leicester Square Tube Station

He loved the rain in the Welsh mountains. It wasn't like the rain in Louisiana, which was cleansing and ferocious, sometimes even biblical as it had been with Hurricane Katrina. Snowdonian rain could be powerful too but what he loved was the gentle patter that often went on all day.

As Brother Varick of the church of Cruor Christi stood on the northbound Northern Line platform at Leicester Square tube station, he wondered whether he would ever feel the Welsh rain on his face again. He wished it would rain today – it might cool things down. But there was little chance of that. When he and Brother Alistair had entered the station, the sun was high in the sky and there wasn't a cloud in sight.

After they had bought their tickets and made their way down onto the Northern Line platforms, Alistair had caught the first southbound train on his quest to find the children. Both men had a mission. When they had set out from Madoc Farm that morning in the Land Rover, Varick had anticipated that Alistair would join him in his efforts to stop Brother Thomas and the others from completing their vile deeds, but after their discussion on their way into London, it was clear that one of them would need to save the train driver's children. Alistair was hardly a man to whom heroics would come naturally but, on this occasion, he wouldn't necessarily need to be. He just had to find them. It was imperative that amidst all the other potential loss of life, the lives of two of the youngest and most innocent potential victims weren't forgotten.

Travellers sweated as they rushed around Varick, climbing on and off trains, while he stood still on the platform peering over the top of the free *Metro* that he had picked up in the ticket hall earlier. He pretended to read it as he watched the front cab of each of the trains that rattled into the station.

Varick knew that in one of them would be Brother Thomas; he also knew that his unmoving presence on the platform, watching the trains – it was at least an hour he had been standing there now – might arouse suspicion.

Another train entered the station with a solitary driver in the cab. Varick knew that it had to be this line and it had to be this station. That was the plan that Owen had found in Brother Thomas's notebook, the information that had cost him his life. So Varick stood and waited. His patience would be rewarded. He didn't know exactly when but Tommy Denning would be there soon enough.

08:19 AM

Northern Line Train 037, driver's cab

London Underground procedure states that all staff entries into a cab should be made while the train is in a station but whoever was entering the cab had the standard issue London Underground J door key – so named on account of its J shape. The intruder alarm went off – beeping away – until the door was shut again, deactivating it, as George turned to see a slim, muscular man dressed all in black and carrying a large canvas bag. Although clearly not wearing London Underground livery, his bomber jacket was of a sort a night-club bouncer might wear and leant him an official air. George thought he might be a member of staff, after all, even though he had not been informed of anyone scheduled to be joining him in the cab. The man was in his mid-twenties, his head shaved to the length of the thick dark stubble on his face. The eyes that stared into George's were a light blue, almost aquamarine, with pupils the size of a teenager's on ecstasy.

'Hello, George,' he said as he put his bag in the corner of the cab. The voice was British, almost accentless, with just a hint of London and the south-east – what's known as 'Estuary'. It had a soft, almost intimate tone.

'Maggie and Sophie are fine.' George felt the relief flood through his innards. The guy was special forces, SAS possibly. They had taken out the bad guys and he was here to tell him that all was well and George was now free to sell his story to the papers, maybe even appear on a reality TV show. But the words that followed were like torpedoes that sank George's hope: 'And rest assured, they will continue to be fine so long as you do exactly as I tell you.'

'What's this all about?' asked George.

'Just keep quiet, carry on with your job and we'll get along famously.'

George looked him up and down. He was only a kid. Maybe he could take him in a fight. George was taller than him by a good three inches after all. But the kid had that supple wiry physique that hid unexpected strength. That and he was about fifteen years younger.

'I need to know what this is all about,' said George attempting to convey an air of authority.

'Why?' It was said with a smile.

'Because this train and all its passengers are my responsibility.'

'Good.' The smile remained. 'Then I suggest that you carry on being responsible for them.'

'What do you want?' George allowed a hint of desperation to enter his tone which he regretted.

The smile was gone. 'I want you to allow your wife and children the opportunity to survive this situation and I want you to know that if you try to stop me from doing what I've come here to do then they won't. You have to trust me on that one, George. If you try to do anything to stop me, they *will* die. Have you got that?'

'Yes. But . . .'

'Ssssshhhhh . . .' It was a soothing sound, the sound a parent might use to calm a baby with troubled sleep.

'The next station is South Wimbledon.' The voice came from CELIA, the Complete Electronic Line Information Announcer, and was relayed throughout the carriages as the train entered the station. At the far end of the platform, gathered together in a tight group in the midst of the commuters was a party of schoolgirls aged no more than seven or eight, George guessed, all dressed identically in blue blazers, pink dresses and straw hats. As the train came to a halt, George opened the doors and the sound of excited little girls' voices could be heard as their hassled teachers ushered them on board the train.

'This train terminates at Mill Hill East via Charing Cross,' said CELIA.

There followed a station announcement on the platform: 'Please be aware that there are currently no Northern Line trains running via the Bank. Customers are advised to take the first available train and change where necessary.' This sent some more of the punters who would normally have waited for a 'via Bank' train hurrying on board, leaving the rest of the platform empty. George closed the doors, checked the pilot light and turning the dead man's handle sent the train rattling into the tunnel.

George's need to establish what was happening was irrepressible, his compulsion to speak impossible to resist.

'Can I ask you something?'

'Looks like you just did.'

'Why me?'

'Go on.'

'I'm asking you, why me?'

'And I'm asking you to get all the questions out of the way now before this goes any further. Come on, you can do better than "Why me?", can't you?'

'OK, so how did you know who I am, where I live, who I live with, what time I go to work, what car I drive – how do you know so much about me?'

George's sense of unease felt like an abscess, throbbing, poisonous, agony. And when the kid spoke he felt it erupt.

'It's you, George, because you were the one who responded. You were the one who told me everything that I needed to know.'

For a frustrated dreamer like George, the internet provided a release. It allowed him to connect with people the world over. He enjoyed the immediacy and anonymity of chat rooms but he also liked the sense of community provided by message boards and those in particular that were hosted on the site that had been established by one 'Piccadilly Pete' some ten years previously. The message boards on Piccadilly Pete's site had become the central community forum on the internet for London Underground staff and anyone interested in discussing the mechanics, society and culture of the tube. Many of the discussion threads were overtly technical and George didn't bother with them but often there were discussions of day-to-day procedure and working conditions which he found of interest. Sometimes a writer or journalist would post a message eliciting information for their research; sometimes prospective LU employees would ask for advice about finding work or request details of various aspects of the job.

It was via Piccadilly Pete's message boards that George had started an ongoing email correspondence with a member of the community who posted under the name of 'Pilgrim'. Here was a young man who clearly had a burning interest in becoming a train driver. When George had replied to his initial question regarding the best way of getting a job 'on the handle', George offered him the benefit of his own experience and a sort of internet friend-ship had developed. George had found himself strangely flattered by Pilgrim's attention and the reverence with which he treated him. George had opened up to him prob-ably more than he should have done, more than was strictly safe. But George was a big boy; what possible harm could come of it? He hadn't even stopped to consider when Pilgrim had gradually made his enquiries more personal. Now, however, George could see that he had been the subject of an ongoing grooming process.

'You're Pilgrim aren't you?'

The question received a smile.

'I thought you might have figured that out before now.'

George felt the bile rise in his throat, hot and stinging.

It was a strange form of betrayal that he felt. Pilgrim's smile faded as he said, 'We can talk more later but now, I need you to concentrate on the job in hand, so let's keep quiet. OK?'

The threat was implicit and George nodded, trembling, returning his gaze to the darkness of the tunnel up ahead.

The stations passed by, each one announced by CELIA's automated monotone. At Stockwell, about a third of the passengers left the train to change to the Victoria Line. But others climbed aboard George Wakeham's train, train 037, and sat down or stood holding the yellow handrails and read newspapers, books, tablet computers, listened to music or played games, nursed hangovers, sipped coffee, cast surreptitious glances at someone attractive or just stared into space.

'OK, zero three seven,' said the line controller as George waited for the signal to clear. 'There's a trainee driver at Kennington going up to East Finchley, wants to watch how it's done. All right?'

It was common enough, trainee drivers riding in the cab or 'riding on the cushions' as it was known by LU staff. There was no way George could decline the request without arousing suspicion. Pilgrim clearly knew this because, when George glanced nervously at him, he nodded his assent.

'Fine,' said George into the radio handset. Once clear of Oval, George saw the tiny point of light at the end of the tunnel grow larger and he felt his panic intensify as he worried about how to explain away his existing passenger to the trainee driver.

As the train pulled into Kennington, George could see him in his uniform standing at the end of the platform. He was about thirty, of medium height, slightly overweight with a ponytail. He waved to George as the cab pulled past and George waved back. Stationary at the signal, George opened the offside door to the cab and the trainee driver stepped aboard.

'All right, mate,' he said, seemingly unfazed by the extra passenger in the cab.

'All right,' said George, closing the offside door.

The trainee nodded at Pilgrim, who nodded back, expressionless. The signal cleared and they moved off into the tunnel, all three of them in a line, George in his seat and the other two standing.

It sounded like a pool cue striking a pillow. George looked around to see the trainee driver's legs crumple beneath him as he fell sideways and a jet of blood pumped from a hole in the side of his head. As he landed on the floor of the cab, his legs kicked out in the death throes. Pilgrim looked down at him impassively, holding an automatic pistol with a silencer attachment from which there curled a wisp of smoke.

'Oh Jesus!' George gasped, breathless and numb with shock.

'Keep your hand on the handle, George.' Pilgrim's voice betrayed some urgency for the first time before it resumed its confident purr. 'Nice and steady, that's it.'

The trainee's legs spasmed a couple more times and then he lay still, the blood from his head wound squirting across the cab floor, the trajectory of its arc decreasing with each dying pulse.

George glanced down at the body; blood was lapping from side to side in the little gullies on the floor beneath the poor bastard's head. He looked away. This was the second dead body he had been in close proximity to in the past two months. The one under and now this. But they could not have been more different. The one under was something he had been not exactly anticipating but something for which he was at least prepared. This wasn't.

His limbs felt as though they were made of rubber and it took all his strength to hold the dead man's handle. He stared ahead through the glass into the tunnel. Colourful kaleidoscopic patterns danced in his peripheral vision; his head felt like it was way too big for his neck, which felt reedy and unsteady. As the train passed a green signal, CELIA's now echoing voice announced: 'The next station is Waterloo.' George's head began to tip forward. The thought came to him that maybe he had been shot too. Perhaps these were his dying moments. Someone was holding his hand.

Pilgrim stood beside him with his hand on top of his own, maintaining the pressure on the dead man's handle. With his other hand, he slapped George on the cheek repeatedly while cradling his head in the crook of his arm.

'I'm OK,' said George, his face stinging as the fog started to clear.

'Don't go passing out on me, George.'

'I'm sorry.' An apology for his tormentor.

The train pulled into Waterloo station and a crowded platform. George pulled the train up to the signal and opened the cab door to look back along the cars. The air that he sucked up was warm and metallic and offered little oxygen. As he stood there watching people embark and disembark, he thought it might be possible to step out of the cab and make a run for it. But the thought never made it past the planning stage. His legs were too shaky. He knew he would never make it.

'This is Waterloo station, change here for the Jubilee Line, the Bakerloo Line and national rail services.'

The platform was busy with tourists pulling suitcases on trolleys, commuters, day-trippers and backpackers, businessmen, schoolchildren and students, pensioners, women with babies.

'Please stand clear of the doors, this train is ready to depart.'

The signal cleared and as George propelled the train into the tunnel once more, moving beneath the Thames towards Embankment station, he chanced a couple of glances at the man he knew as Pilgrim. There he stood still and stiff-backed – the pistol was nowhere to be seen – and he stared out of the front window, deep in thought, the corpse of the man he had so recently murdered at his feet.

08:46 AM

Northbound Northern Line platform, Leicester Square
Tube Station

Varick knew that in a little room somewhere he might be framed on a CCTV security monitor. If Tommy Denning didn't come soon, someone would come for him. Impatience joined his other strained emotions. But the waiting had also given him time to think and when he wasn't contemplating Tommy's arrival, he thought about his journey from New Orleans to the mountains of Snowdonia. It had been a trial, a test that Varick had finally passed. God had given him a task and he had carried it out. During those lawless days back in September 2005 after the levees had broken, it was as though the world had been turned upside down. He had done some things – firing on looters being one of them – which troubled him deeply. He had tried to justify it: society had broken down. What else were he and his colleagues in the New Orleans Police Department – those who hadn't already deserted – expected to do? But however he tried to explain away his actions, they had continued to prey on his mind.

After Katrina, his drug consumption had increased as though he were attempting to blot out what he had done and what he had seen.

It was not long after he had last been here, in the West End of London, that Jesus had spoken to him and shown him the one true path. He had made the London trip with a girlfriend. Frieda, her name was. She was half-German. She loved to party. It was the first vacation he had been on since Katrina. It was meant to be a week's sightseeing, although the only sights they really got to see were the inside of the hotel room, where they fornicated energetically, and the inside of numerous night-club toilets in which they snorted lines of cocaine from the bag he had smuggled through customs up his ass.

The devil had stalked him, waited for him in the shadows. Varick could see that now. But at the time it had felt as though it was how life was meant to be. A couple of months after he had returned from his trip to London with Frieda, Jesus had steered him towards Father Owen at Madoc Farm. There was no other explanation as to why he had found himself on the website of a sect of British evangelical Christians by the name of Cruor Christi. Despite thinking of himself as a Christian since birth, other than funerals and weddings he hadn't been to church since he was a teenager. Yet there he was, late at night, sitting at his computer with a head full of cocaine, searching for something, searching for meaning and it was the simple reassuring words of Father Owen that had struck a chord in his heart. Owen was a man who genuinely wanted to help those less fortunate than himself. Here truly was a Good Samaritan and Varick felt that altruism that had made him want to serve his fellow man in the NOPD, that selflessness that had laid dormant for so long, stir once more beneath the corrosive effects of his debauchery.

Initial emails to Father Owen had led to a series of phone calls and, within a couple of months, Varick had turned his back on drugs and alcohol, resigned his position with the New Orleans Police Department and been on his way to Wales and Madoc Farm in Snowdonia. The rest was history, pre-ordained just as surely as his immediate future was now as he set out on his mission to find Brother Thomas. Some things were meant to be.

The first few months in Snowdonia had been tough. It was winter and the farm was in a terrible condition. He had set about rebuilding part of the roof himself and fixing the plumbing. Gradually, as God decreed, he and his fellow brothers had rebuilt Madoc Farm and Varick had allowed himself a little pride in his achievements.

Madoc Farm in Snowdonia was now his true home. It was a home where he could go about the work that Jesus had seen fit to bless him with, the saving of troubled young men and women, prising them from the clutches of the devil and returning them to the path of righteousness. Many of those who made up Cruor Christi's flock were from military backgrounds, like brothers Thomas and Simeon. Others were ex-drug addicts like Alistair. The world was full of casualties from the wars on drugs and terror. Cruor Christi, however, was there for them and would be for ever. Those poor spiritual refugees were not alone – he would make sure of that – and he would do all in his power to stop Brother Thomas from destroying the special bond that united the brothers and sisters at Madoc Farm. Responsibility lay with him now and him alone. The authorities would have no cause to trouble the good people of Madoc Farm if the members of the church of Cruor Christi could be seen to have averted this potential cataclysm themselves. Father Owen's death would not be in vain. Varick would ensure that his good work continued.

He had had a bad feeling about Tommy right from the start. Tommy's hot-headed, almost sociopathic charisma was something he had seen in other young men during his years working for the NOPD. The police often attracted that sort of person. But there was something different about Tommy. It was as though he was just watching and waiting, biding his time. He only really came alive when he was talking about personal sacrifice.

Tommy was fascinated by radical Islam and Jihad. He believed that the promise of virgins in heaven supposedly given to would-be suicide bombers was all just propaganda by Western media, a way of trying to discredit their steadfast purpose and strength of will. These people knew what they were doing. Their vision should be admired. They were dying for what they believed in. Christianity did not have that strength. Christ had displayed it but his followers had failed him. Christians had always fallen far short of

the example that Christ had set them. It needed someone
to come along and show the way. To make a statement.
To stand side by side with his Muslim brothers.

Tommy often spoke about the values and commitment
of the suicide bomber. Sometimes Varick decided to draw
him out on the subject, but when he did the ex-soldier
was reluctant to open up and gradually Varick's concerns
faded as other more pressing day-to-day matters arose from
everyday life on Madoc Farm. Then came Owen's discovery
of Tommy's notebook. Much of what it contained was indecipherable, just rambling notes and ideas and quotations
from the Bible. But alongside his plans for the train driver's
family and the occupants of the train, there was much
mention of the river which played such a part in his sick
idea. One biblical quotation that appeared to refer to it
had stuck in Varick's mind. It was Revelation 22:1. 'And
he shewed me a pure river of water of life, clear as crystal,
proceeding out of the throne of God and of the Lamb.'
This was written out a number of times as though mention
of the 'pure river' in the scriptures seemed to offer Tommy
some sort of divine confirmation that what he was doing
was right.

Another train pulled into the station. Varick watched
it over the top of his newspaper, dreading a solitary driver.
But this one was different. The driver was a large man
with a serious, worried expression. Standing next to him
was a younger man, wiry and muscular, leaning forward
and peering out onto the platform. Even before the light
caught his face and confirmed it, Varick knew that it was

Tommy Denning. He didn't like to think of him as Brother Thomas any more. He was no brother of his.

The train stopped and the automated voice started up once more: 'Please allow the passengers to leave the train first. This is a Northern Line train to Mill Hill East.' Varick had positioned himself in the middle of the platform so as to join the train well away from either end, which he knew from the plan would be occupied by Tommy and his team.

As Varick entered the carriage, he felt a strange sensation of destiny unfolding. This was how it was meant to be. He might have become a man of God but he still knew how to use a revolver. Especially the one he had tucked in his belt beneath his shirt. He had used it thousands of times during target practice and he knew all its little nuances. It pulled to the right slightly and he knew exactly how much he would need to aim left to compensate. The Smith & Wesson was the only possession that he had kept from the old days back in Louisiana, from before he was born again. Smuggling it into the UK was easy; he had dismantled it and hidden its individual components throughout his possessions in the packing crate in which they were shipped. He wasn't the only one who loved guns. Almost all the members of Cruor Christi had weapons. Some of them were more than just handguns. In the armoury at Madoc Farm – where Father Owen insisted that all weapons were kept – there were semi-automatic assault rifles, most of which were now in Tommy's possession. There was even a small quantity of plastic explosive.

One of Cruor Christi's members, 'Big Bob' Wilcox, had been involved with ordnance and explosives in the army and had managed to 'liberate' it – as he put it – from a depot where he worked. It did trouble Varick, all that fire-power. But he concluded that amongst the members of his unique flock, paranoia often came with the territory, and if they felt safer with their weapons – and didn't use them irresponsibly – then so be it. He was hardly in a position to preach on the subject what with his own back-ground and firm belief in the right to bear arms.

After finding Owen dead the night before, Varick had checked the armoury and it was all but empty. What guns had not been taken had been rendered inoperable by having their firing pins removed. Tommy had obviously expected Varick to come after him. But Varick had his Smith & Wesson with him and it was all he would need. He knew that he could finish this when the time came. Just so long as he could get within range, Tommy Denning would be – as he might have described it in his former life when he wore the powder blue shirt of the New Orleans Police Department – a dead man walking.

08:54 AM

Northern Line Train 037, driver's cab

George had to do something, not just for his family and the hundreds of people on the train, but for himself. If he died and did nothing then his life was a waste. It wasn't as though he was a religious man. If pushed, he would have claimed agnosticism as his faith. Some people called that a cop-out. If you're going to deny God then at least have the guts to be an atheist; agnosticism is spineless, nothing more than sitting on the fence. It was usually the religious types that came out with stuff like that. Like a taunt. To George, agnosticism was the only rational reaction to religion: I don't know. I don't know because no one can know. Some things are unknowable. But it wasn't something that he had ever given much thought to. He and Maggie had been married in a church; the children were christened. If there was a god then they were covered. It was insurance. George thought it was like that for most people. What he did feel, however, was a sense of destiny, regardless of whether there was or wasn't a god, and he could feel that destiny now compelling him to act. He would have to try and stop these people. Never before had he felt so protective towards others, but never before had he felt so afraid that his own emotional frailty would let him down.

'Oh Jesus.' He said it so softly under his breath it was inaudible. Blasphemy was a constant in his life. George was a hardened blasphemer. Bang his toe: Jesus Christ. Slam his finger in a door: fucking Jesus. And far lesser sources of grievance, everything from the sub-standard driving of his fellow road-users to the poor state of the weather he greeted with blasphemous profanity. Today was no exception. But today, during those moments when the emotion and fear became too much for him and he needed some form of release, he found his muttered blasphemies were altogether more pleading, as though attempting a dialogue with a god whose existence he doubted.

George was no stranger to panic. He was one of life's worriers. And often that worry manifested itself as panic. Usually it was late at night, when he woke up consumed with the fear that he was wasting his life. All his great heroes, all the writers and musicians who informed his outlook, were people who had a handle on existence, who knew who they wanted to be – or seemed to. He had considered therapy, but felt squeamish at the thought of opening up to a stranger. Besides, there were more important things to be spending his money on. More benefit might be derived from a few drinks and the odd joint here and there. At least then he could look at life and laugh at the absurdity of it all. At least then the panic would lift, or be reduced to a vague sense of unease. But even on those rare occasions when he did manage to attain a state approaching contentment, his mind would conjure up some image for him, some bold and incontrovertible fact about the state of humanity and the nature of the world that would cast him back into the gloom. Somewhere a child was being abused; somewhere an unspeakable act of cruelty was being committed and there was nothing anyone could do about it. The horror never went away.

A song was playing in George's mind, continually repeating on his psycho-juke box. It was 'London Calling' by the Clash. The band's front man, Joe Strummer, was one of his heroes and he had been lucky enough to see him play live when he was a boy. Strummer was passionate and uncompromising, everything that George aspired to be and feared he wasn't.

George and his best friend, Dougie, another lifelong Clash fan, had a private expression between the two of them for when a situation appeared desperate: 'What would Joe Strummer do?' It came to him now as 'London Calling' repeated once again in his mind.

When Joe Strummer died, George and Dougie had met for a drink, and every so often during the evening they would break off their conversation to raise a glass to Joe. By closing time, they both had tears in their eyes.

What would Joe Strummer do? What would he do now? Driving a busy tube train into a tunnel with an armed hijacker in the cab with him. What would he do?

The only comfort that George could manage to derive from the situation was that this man he knew only as Pilgrim didn't look like an Islamic fundamentalist. He was white Caucasian for a start. That had to mean something. Didn't it? But any hope this shoddy racial profile might have offered was immediately snuffed out by his awareness of the dead body on the floor of the cab. Whatever else this man was, he was also a killer.

As he sat in the train cab moving through the warm air in the tunnel, George wavered between *déjà vu* and *jamais vu* – everything was strangely familiar one moment and terrifyingly new and hyper-real the next. When he had pressed the buttons at Leicester Square to open the doors, it was as though he had never seen them before. He once dropped some acid when he was at college. Objects that he had looked at and handled a million times in his life felt new and vibrant. As now. But when he looked at the hijacker it was as though that face had loomed in his subconscious all of his life. It was like an ugly spirit made flesh.

When George had shut the doors at Leicester Square, checked the pilot light and driven into the tunnel, the train was carrying a little over half its passenger capacity. Not far out of the station, George was told to 'Slow down now.' George did so. Now was not the time for heroics. He needed to choose his moment.

'Slower . . . slower . . .'

The train moved to walking speed. The man was alert, his turquoise eyes darting around as he looked into the tunnel up ahead. It was as though he was searching for something.

'OK, now really slow. That's it, George, that's lovely. Now . . . stop.'

George stopped the train but he kept the dead man's handle in the 'coast' position out of habit.

George was told to, 'Take your hand off the handle now.'

'But it'll set off the alarm,' said George.

'That's fine.'

George let go of the handle and they both stared into the tunnel as the motor idled. The line controller came through on the radio: 'Zero three seven, is there a problem? You appear to have stopped. Zero three seven? Hello? Is everything all right?'

What would Joe Strummer do?

Pilgrim looked at him and smiled. 'OK, George,' he said, 'this is the end of the line. This train terminates here.'

08:56 AM

Northern Line Train 037, rear cab

As soon as the train came to a halt in the tunnel between Leicester Square and Tottenham Court Road stations, Simeon knew that the first part of Tommy Denning's plan had been concluded successfully. It may have been a week early but everything else was to the letter. It was four minutes to nine by his watch. Tommy had said it would be nine when they reached the target – give or take a few minutes. In the passenger area on the other side of the rear cab door was the train driver's wife. The three of them – Tommy, Belle and Simeon – had debated long and hard about whether to take her on the train or not. Belle had said she thought the woman might be a liability, but Tommy had said it was worth having her along in case the driver needed some mental support or further emotional arm-twisting and they could put her on the walkie-talkie and have her talk to him. Simeon had said that he would keep an eye on her, make sure that she didn't cause any trouble. He had already put the frighteners on her – if she did anything to raise the alarm, her kids would die. As far as the children themselves were concerned, they were all in agreement that they shouldn't be brought onto the train. It was rough on the train driver's wife but the trauma and fear engendered by her separation from them would mean that she would be thoroughly compliant. You only had to take one look at her to see that she was going to do whatever it took to see them again. You had to hand it to Tommy, it was a hell of a plan, twisted but brilliant. There was only one flaw in it and that was him, Simeon. If it wasn't for him, Tommy and Belle might have been able to get away with all this. But he was there to make sure they didn't. The children would be OK. He would have them out of there soon enough. First he had to let Tommy make his intentions known to the wider world. Once that was done, he could proceed as planned and all the hard work would be over. But despite all that he had had to endure in the past few weeks, there was one good thing to come out of it and that was getting to meet Belle.

There she was sitting next to him in the rear cab of the train, so cute, so damaged. Despite the extreme, almost insane beliefs that Belle shared with her brother Tommy, Simeon couldn't help but feel attracted to her. Her lithe, supple body had a vibrant energy to it that was palpable. Even sitting here in the rear cab of the train, having come here to do what they had come here to do, he couldn't help but find her intensely arousing. This made his emotions all the more conflicted when he considered that, before the day was finished, he would have to kill her.

Flat 21, Hyde Park Mansions, Pimlico

He clicked up his speed another kilometre per hour. This was the time that he liked most on the treadmill, about fifteen minutes in, when he was all warmed up, and the blood was pumping; it felt as though the serotonin was being released. That sense of disappointment that he often felt on waking could only really be lifted by a run. He ran miles every day, here in the corner of his bedroom. It stimulated him on so many levels. It kept him fit, kept his weight down, provided him with 'flow' – allowed him to think with more clarity than at any other time of the day. Some mornings were harder than others. It depended on what time he had gone to bed the night before, whether he'd had a glass of wine. Some mornings it just felt right and this morning it felt as good as ever. In a couple of hours, it would be too hot to run. Now, he could really fly.

When he had lived in Muswell Hill back in the old days, he used to run through Alexandra Park. His favourite section was along the front of Alexandra Palace with its views over London. He imagined himself back there now as his trainers thumped out their mesmeric rhythm. And for a moment, it was as though he had achieved some sort of transcendence and could forget the truth. The sun was shining down on him from the north London sky. To his left was the huge, round, stained-glass window of Alexandra Palace; to his right London stretching away to the horizon.

Ed reached for the remote control console for the hi-fi and clicked on the radio. It was tuned to a classical station. He used to fool himself that it was soothing. An admission that he needed to be soothed, however, didn't help and besides, he wasn't angry any more. Anger had given way to resignation just as all the psychologists said that it would. Acceptance would be next. He hadn't got there yet. Not by a long way.

The nine o'clock news. 'This is Marsha Wilson.' Ed often wondered what Marsha Wilson looked like. He listened to her every morning. He liked her voice; he liked the way she could switch from a serious tone, something she employed when telling you about an earthquake or a paedophile, to sounding smiley and upbeat at the end of the bulletin, when she was reporting a giant marrow or someone building their own space rocket in their garage. There was nothing in the news. Nothing interesting. They used to call it the silly season. Everyone was on holiday. The news was cancelled for a few weeks. Ed didn't wish ill on his fellow man but sometimes he yearned for a major incident somewhere, a story in which he could immerse himself. Not today though. All that was on offer today was the weather. It was going to be hot, possibly the hottest day of the year. And next up the first move- ment from Bach's Brandenberg Concerto Number Three in G Major. Not one of his favourites so he brutalised it with the rhythm from his trainers on the treadmill.

He wasn't exactly dressed for running – boxer shorts and trainers – but no one could see him and it was hot. Twenty minutes previously he had thrown some cold water on his face in the bathroom and stepped straight onto the treadmill to warm up with a brisk walk that had devel- oped into a jog and then this, not exactly a sprint but not far off. Running was an effective distraction. Waking up was always a reminder of what had happened just over thirteen and a half years ago. The events of that day might be receding into the past, but they were still as painful as if they had taken place yesterday.

Due to a media blackout, the Hanway Street siege never made the news. But the fact that what happened went unreported did nothing to lessen the torture of its memory.

Conor Joyce was spoken of as something of a legend amongst Ed Mallory's Special Branch colleagues. An explo- sives expert, he was thought to have constructed and deployed a number of devices as part of the IRA bombing campaign. During the late nineties, however, he had found that his services were no longer in demand. What's more, he had met and fallen in love with a Protestant woman and renounced his fierce Catholicism and accompanying republicanism in order to be with her and subsequently marry her. This fundamental change in his life had meant that when the British secret service came knocking, he turned. MI5 were interested in his knowledge of potential arms caches as they tried to ensure that the IRA complied with the decommissioning terms of the Good Friday agreement. Yet despite Conor Joyce's apparent readiness to provide certain limited pieces of information, he was considered slippery and his service handlers were never convinced that his co-operation was not a meticulously constructed false front and that they were the ones being handled rather than the other way around. Nonetheless, some of his intelligence had proved valuable and he was shrewd enough to drip-feed it gradually, thus prolonging his time on the payroll.

As part of the deal that Joyce struck with the service, he was provided with a flat in Kensal Rise in north-west London complete with a panic alarm, in case his cover was blown and a former colleague in the Provisionals came looking for him.

It was Boxing Day morning when the panic alarm was activated. A Special Branch counter-terrorism unit was dispatched to Hanway Street but when they approached the address and tried to enter the building, shots were fired at them and they were forced to withdraw. The entire street was evacuated and sealed off.

It was only Ed's second official assignment as a hostage negotiator. The first assignment had involved an elderly husband armed with a cricket bat barricading himself and his much younger wife in their home. The man was convinced that his wife was having an affair with a neigh-bour, but Ed soon realised that he was dealing with someone suffering from mental health problems when it became apparent that the neighbour in question had been dead for a good ten years. After a few minutes of gentle coaxing, the old man put down the cricket bat and the crisis was resolved. Hardly a tough gig, so as soon as he heard the details of the incident in Hanway Street that Boxing Day morning, Ed knew that his training and apti-tude would be tested for the first time.

Due to the sensitive nature of the situation, Ed was only one of a larger team made up of Scotland Yard nego-tiators and MI5 counter-terrorist personnel. But he arrived on site first and quickly took up position in the hastily established command centre in a flat above a row of shops directly opposite Conor Joyce's no-longer-safe safe house. It was apparent that Joyce's cover had indeed been blown and he was being held hostage by an IRA hitman who had come to kill him.

Whether or not the hitman had succumbed to an attack of conscience when he found the target of his hit with a heavily pregnant wife was never established, but the subject – as he had now become in the language of crisis intervention – was using his hostages as bargaining collat-eral. If he was granted safe passage with them, he would allow them to go free once he was at his chosen destina-tion. If not, they would both die. He had a hand grenade from which he had removed the pin and he made it known that if a marksman were to try and take him out then everyone would wind up dead.

There was no way the British government would allow the escape of a known IRA hitman from the scene of a hostage-taking, so Ed settled in for a long negotiation. The subject, however, wanted to play things differently. He was impatient to talk. Ed was nervous but also excited. He would play it by the book, maintain an ongoing dialogue, calm the subject, establish trust and gather information through active listening, all skills he had acquired through his extensive training.

But the subject was like no other hostage taker that Ed had ever come across in the case studies. He was a hardened Provo who would stop at nothing for what he believed in, and what he believed in, caged in that small flat in north-west London, was his need to escape.

'My name is Ed Mallory, I'm a negotiator and I would like to help.' Name, role and intention – a standard opening gambit once telephone contact has been established with a subject.

The heavily Irish accented voice on the other end of the line came through loud and clear.

'Fuck off, you stuck-up cocksucker, don't give me any of your psychology shit.'

And from that moment on Ed knew it would be a tough negotiation, one that would require all his guile and ingenuity to resolve. It was unlikely this subject would respond to the standard crisis-intervention techniques. The man was working from a totally different set of moral values to those subjects Ed had studied up until then. But Ed was young – not yet thirty – and he was confident that he could get through to him. He was ambitious and he wanted to show his colleagues and superiors that he had what it took.

Ed tried to find out the subject's name but got nothing but obscenities. He tried to calm the subject down by telling him that he felt uncomfortable with his use of profanity. Bollocks, fuck you – more profanity. Whatever he said, he could not get through to him. The guy was completely unreadable and his behaviour followed no accepted pattern. He went from anger and frustration to a calm psychological detachment with no apparent transition. Ed had never come across anything like it. He was one of those rare subjects that an FBI crisis intervention trainer had told him and his fellow students about in a seminar once, one who was completely impervious to all negotiation methods. Freud had said of the Irish, 'This is one race of people for whom psychoanalysis is of no use whatsoever.' Maybe the same applied to them in hostage negotiation.

The subject issued a demand and a deadline. Unless he had a call from Ed by four o'clock to say there was a car to take him and his hostages to a light aircraft, which would deliver them to an unspecified location in the Irish Republic, he would let off the hand grenade.

Ed knew all about deadlines. They held a central place within the study of hostage negotiation. He also knew that there was no way the subject was going to be allowed to go free. Ed was sure the subject knew it too. So he decided it was a choice between two distinct paths of conduct: he could either stall him, tell him that four o'clock was unrealistic and he would need more time, or he could try and gain the subject's respect by acknowledging that his demand was never going to be met and try to resolve the situation in a spirit of brutal honesty. He opted for the latter, told the subject straight. There was no way the authorities would let him go free.

'You've got until four,' came back the reply and the line went dead. Ed told his superiors and the other members of the team who were now in situ that he thought the best thing to do would be to call back the subject a little before four to negotiate a new deadline just as the existing deadline was expiring. An effective tactic that he had learned in his training. Everyone agreed.

Ed was nervous as he picked up the receiver at five to four and dialled the number. He looked across to the first-floor window of Conor Joyce's flat only thirty feet away. The narrow street was deserted. All the properties were empty, apart from the snipers staring through telescopic sights at the same single window as Ed.

He could just make out the sound of the telephone ringing in the flat across the street. The call was answered and Ed started talking.

'What you're asking for is proving very difficult. I'm doing my best but you're going to have to give me more time.' Ed had prepared himself for objections but the response from the subject was surprising: 'OK, mate, that's fine. At least we know where we stand.' He sounded calm, almost cheerful. For a moment Ed felt a surge of confidence before he realised he was being reassured by the subject for no tangible reason, a characteristic often displayed by potential suicides when they have finally decided to kill themselves. Ed knew he had to act fast, had to establish a new line of negotiation. But he didn't get the chance. It was discovered subsequently that the subject had spent fifteen years in the Maze Prison. He wasn't going back. The sound of the explosion relayed into Ed's ear through the telephone headset gave him tinnitus for a fortnight.

It wasn't his ears, however, that were the problem. He hadn't even considered the potential force of the blast. All that separated him from the exploding hand grenade were two panes of glass and one of those panes was only inches from his face. His face would be scarred for life but, as with his ears, it was a small price to pay compared to the blast's primary damage. Glass fragments were embedded in the orbital tissue of both eyes. His left eye had a prolapsed iris; both eyes suffered multiple perforations of the cornea. The facial lacerations healed. People told him that the scarring wasn't too bad, which meant that it probably was. He would never know. According to the doctors who ran the tests, his left eye retained about thirty per cent light sensitivity. He could see shadows but little else. The trauma his right eye suffered was such that for a couple of days after the injury, it was felt that it would have to undergo enucleation – complete removal. As it turned out, it ended up staying where it was, although it was totally redundant.

The grenade explosion killed the subject and Conor Joyce's wife and unborn child. Conor Joyce survived the blast but with multiple injuries. He was conscious – in great pain but still lucid – when they brought him out of the building.

Conor Joyce kept shouting, 'You fucking let her die!' over and over again as he was loaded into the ambulance next to the one in which the paramedics worked on Ed. And in a way, he was right. Maybe Ed had let her die. For a long time afterwards he blamed himself for what happened. Joyce's wife was the first person he would ever lose during a negotiation. There were others after her, both hostages and subjects. During his career, he had been involved in over forty-five crisis situations throughout the world, from the United States to the Middle East. Forty-three of those had been as a blind man. By the law of averages, he was bound to lose a few and he had learned to accept that sometimes, ultimately, you cannot take responsibility for someone else's behaviour. People do what they want to do and even if you are armed with an acutely intuitive understanding of how individuals react to crises, sometimes you are unable to stop them.

For the most part, when subjects and hostages had died on his watch, Ed had dealt with it in his own way. Even when he had spent hours and sometimes even days in intense negotiation and really felt that he was getting somewhere with a subject and they had gone on to kill themselves or others, even then he had been able to assimilate it. But not so Conor Joyce's wife and it was to her that his thoughts always turned, her death coinciding with the exact moment when he lost his sight. She was the only one he felt he had let down, just as he had let himself down in the process. He had been too cocky and self-assured, too keen to impress his superiors. If he had intervened with the subject earlier, if he had stalled more effectively, if he had encouraged the subject to open up more. If if if. Conor Joyce's wife haunted him every day of his life. It was as though he had been imprisoned on the day she died. Over and over, he was told he would finally come to terms with his sightless existence. Thirteen years now and he was nowhere nearer to accepting it. Maybe if he could then he could get on with his life.

After an initial desire to pension him off, the force had been good to him, realising that his ability to listen and intuit potential behaviour patterns in hostage takers' voices was enhanced by his blindness. His stock as a hostage negotiator had certainly risen after he was blinded, although at his most cynical and self-loathing he suspected he was only there to ensure that Scotland Yard achieved its disability quota. That was unfair, although he knew he wasn't being paranoid when he detected a sense amongst his colleagues that he was in some way to blame for what had happened to him. During the negotiation, his active listening was not what it should have been. He should have discerned more in the subject's voice, should have encouraged more dialogue. So, despite his injuries, it was not as a hero that he returned to work and he couldn't help but feel as though he had been kicked upstairs. His rank sounded fairly grand – Detective Chief Inspector – but most of the time, it was nothing-work. Government liaison. Bullshit. His hostage-negotiation work had developed into something of an obsession but it was an obsession that found little release. There were only so many situations with oil company executives being kidnapped and held for ransom in Nigeria that he could advise on; only so many distraught Fathers 4 Justice to be talked down from on high. To save the lives of innocent people caught up in impossible situations was what he lived for. But as more and more people took the training and became involved in the world of hostage and crisis negotiation, he felt as though he was being squeezed out, marginalised. His special talents, his ability to listen and hear things that others might miss, didn't seem to count for as much any more. Months could go by and his only involvement in negotiation would be some lecturing and the odd seminar. Perhaps now it was time for a career change? Although job prospects probably weren't that great for a forty something blind policeman.

Ed clicked up his speed another kilometre per hour on the treadmill and sprinted through the park. The sun shone down on him from a clear blue sky. It felt good. London looked so beautiful today.

08:59 AM

Northern Line Train 037, driver's cab

George glanced at Pilgrim, who stood and stared into the tunnel, deep in thought. The Line Controller's voice came through on the intercom once again: 'Zero three seven, please confirm your situation.'

'Can you turn him off?' asked Pilgrim.

George was thankful for something to do even if it was something as basic as turning down the volume button on the intercom console.

'That's better, couldn't hear myself think. Oh, and you can turn on the light too.'

George flicked off the radio and clicked on the light in the cab. There was no way of reading this guy. He spoke with the generosity of a genial host who wants to make sure that his guest is happy and at ease. But George was very far from at ease. As the seconds ticked by, he felt his claustrophobia intensify.

George knew exactly where it came from. For many claustrophobics, the phobia's trigger is a traumatic experience relating to a confined space, like being trapped in a lift perhaps. For him, on the other hand, it was reading a short story when he was eleven years old. It was in a book he had borrowed from the school library, a collection of short stories by Edgar Allan Poe. To his young mind the stories seemed very old-fashioned, with a dense almost impenetrable prose style that had to be deciphered rather than read. He was just about to give up on the book and exchange it for something else when he came across a story called 'The Premature Burial'. As he waded into the arcane narrative, he felt an acute discomfort. To be buried alive and to know with every desperate futile scrape at the wooden coffin lid that there was no escape was a concept which haunted him. He couldn't get it out of his head. The more he tried not to think about it, the more it invaded his mind. And it was from this that his claustrophobia sprang. But, like all phobias, his didn't follow a pattern. He would be fine in an enclosed space so long as he was moving – hence his ability to drive a tube train – but as soon as he was rendered stationary, the sick feelings, the dry mouth, the sweating and the breathlessness would descend on him. Only renewed movement or escape from the enclosed space would save him from a panic attack, the strength of which he had no way of gauging, having always managed to avoid prolonged exposure to the requisite stimuli in the past.

When trawling for possible cures for his condition on the internet, he had found a website that suggested that one of the best ways of counteracting the effects of claustrophobia was nothing more than a type of positive mental thought. It stated that the claustrophobic does not fear the situation itself but the negative consequences of being in that situation. It suggested that a form of self-hypnosis which would infuse the consciousness with comforting 'neutral' imagery might be of benefit, along with a repetitious mental refrain that 'Everything will be OK.' And when he had tried this method, when held at a particularly long red light in a tunnel, it had worked. To a degree. But this potential cure was not available to George now. At his feet – although he had managed to avoid looking – he knew there was a man with his brains leaking out all over the floor of the cab. He could smell the blood. Everything was most definitely not going to be OK. Not today.

Such was the heat, it was difficult to work out whether he was sweating more than usual, but he could feel his heart pounding in his chest and his mouth felt leathery and dry. Worse still, was the breathlessness. This was what always brought on the worst feelings.

'I'm a claustrophobic.' He said it without thinking. And as he said it, he knew that it was probably the first time that he had ever articulated the truth so bluntly. Maggie knew that his working environment sometimes made him feel uncomfortable but they hadn't spoken about it for some time because he knew that, under normal circumstances, he could control it. But these were not normal circumstances and something in his subconscious had forced him to speak.

Pilgrim turned to look at him and smiled. 'You're joking.'

'No, I wish I was.'

'You never told me that on the message boards.'

'I never told you a lot of things.'

'Plenty of things you did tell me though, George.'

George winced at the thought of the incontinence of information that Pilgrim had managed to elicit from him. This intense young man had flattered him, massaged his ego and he had responded. George could remember almost word for word what he had said about how he would do anything for his kids. Pilgrim had intimated that he had had a troubled upbringing. This had made the email exchange become all the more personal. George had enjoyed the role of the comforting older brother. And now this. George had been played.

'So, you're a tube driver who suffers from claustrophobia?'

'Yeah, I'm fine so long as the train's moving.' The words came out quickly, breathlessly. 'I can cope for a few minutes but anything more and I . . .' And just as suddenly as the words had flowed, they dried up again. The fact was he didn't know what would happen after a few minutes. He was in unknown territory.

'The thing is we're not going anywhere.' Pilgrim said it as though he felt genuinely sorry about it.

'Oh God.'

'That's just the way it is, I'm afraid.'

There was no point trying to act normally. It was impossible. George could feel his heart rate rise; the sweat was pouring off him now and he felt various parts of his lower body, his thighs and his buttocks, succumb to a chill tremble. But it was his breathing that was the biggest problem. There wasn't enough oxygen to sustain his hungry lungs.

'Deep breaths,' said Pilgrim and, stepping over the body of the trainee driver, he took hold of George's hands and held them in his. His hands felt rough. The complexion of the palms belonged to a man who was no stranger to manual labour. He stared into George's eyes, unblinking.

'In,' and he took a deep breath and indicated for George to do likewise. 'And out,' and he blew out the air and George tried to copy him. For the first few breaths, George felt no better but, as he surrendered to the slow deliberate rhythm, he felt himself calm down. The fear remained but the panic subsided. There was something about the man's demeanour, as though he genuinely had George's best interests at heart. More than that, it felt as though there was some sort of affection in his actions. It gave George hope and this helped calm him even further. This man genuinely wanted to help him, to ensure that he was OK. That he did so because he had a purpose for George was a good sign because if he had a purpose for him then he was not expendable. He would stay alive. And that was all that mattered, that and the fact that his family stayed alive too.

They breathed together for a couple of minutes.

'You're going to be all right, George. Everything's going to be fine. I'm not going to do anything horrible to you. Quite the opposite in fact. So don't despair, don't be afraid.

All you've got to do is keep breathing slowly and deliberately and keep happy. This is going to be a big day. Not
just for you and me and everybody on this train but for
the peoples of the world, who will see it as a sign. Just
put your faith in Christ and all will be well.'

George shrugged and exhaled, shaking his head.

'Don't tell me you don't believe.'

'Believe in what?'

'Who. Believe in who.'

'I don't know what you mean.'

'Jesus Christ. Who else?'

'No, I don't believe. Is that what this is all about, religion?' George turned and looked the man in the eyes.
They didn't look like the eyes of a terrorist. Not that George
had ever looked a terrorist in the eyes to know. But there
was something kindly and benevolent about the way
Pilgrim looked at him. It was as though he felt pity for
George – and more so now that he knew that George was
a non-believer.

'You must believe in something, George.'

'I believe in nature, evolution, science. I don't believe
in the supernatural.'

The man was nodding at him; the smile had given way
to a thoughtful expression.

In the past, George's lack of belief had provided him
with comfort. No cosmic disappointments for him. No self-
delusion. There was no God. He knew it; he had always
known it. So what was that part of his psyche, that part
of his human make-up, that now made him reach out to

a god in which he did not believe? Where did the compulsion come from? Was it born of desperation? Some sort of psychological clutching at straws? Whatever the reason, he couldn't help himself from pleading for someone, for something, anything, to save him.

'You don't feel claustrophobic any more, do you?'

The question caught him off guard.

'Not as much, no.'

'You might not believe in God, you might never have believed in him, but hear me when I say that, before today is over, you will.'

George wanted to say, 'Never.' He nearly did. But something stopped him. He knew it would sound childish, petulant. There was no point in antagonising this man.

'The thing is, George,' Pilgrim continued, 'we're going to start a revolution today. Just you wait and see. And when you see the beauty and the truth of what we're going to do – you and I – then you'll be a sinner no more and God's love will fill your heart, now and for always.'

09:16 AM

Northern Line Train 037, sixth carriage

Seated at the end of the carriage, up against the door to the bulkhead separating the passenger area from the rear cab, Maggie Wakeham sat on her hands and stared at the floor. The sick feeling wouldn't lift. It was like a constantly peaking wave. Maggie felt as though part of her had been amputated with no anaesthetic and no concern for her well-being and ultimate survival. Her children were gone, her little ones taken. It was more than an amputation, it was as though the very core of her being had been ripped out and burned in front of her. She hadn't eaten anything before they came. So there was nothing to throw up, not that she felt she could have retched even if she had wanted to; her teeth were clamped together so tightly, it made her jaw ache.

They were going to Mr Pieces the night after. It was Ben's birthday treat. He'd be six. Six years before, she had been in labour. She was in labour for a day and a half. It was horrendous. That's what she told people when asked to describe the experience. But it had all been worth it.

Ben was a beautiful baby boy, and life for her and George was never the same again. Neither was their relationship. It wasn't necessarily worse – if a marriage can ever be judged on a scale with good at one end and bad at the other – but it was different. More fraught. Less affectionate, somehow. She wished that sometimes he'd just take control, just take her in his arms and let passion take over. But maybe he didn't feel any passion. Maybe it had gone. She hoped not. She still loved him.

They had gone to Mr Pieces the year before for Ben's fifth birthday. It was just an ordinary Italian restaurant but it was nice, it was cosy, run by a family. When the waiters – four Italian brothers – wanted to commence the ceremonial singing of 'Happy birthday', they threw their metal serving trays on the floor, which made a noise like a cartoon thunder clap. Crayons were provided in a little tin bucket in the middle of each table and diners were encouraged to scribble and doodle on the paper table-cloths. The best tablecloth was chosen at the end of each week by the waiters, scraped clean of any surplus food and mounted on the wall.

There was a group of schoolgirls further down the carriage. They were about seven years old – a little older than Ben – and wore pink dresses and straw hats. Their teachers were doing their best to be reassuring. Seated in their midst was a blind man in a linen suit. A couple of the girls stroked his guide dog. Opposite Maggie was a woman with black hair and black sunglasses. Her casual attire was expensive, fashionable – and all black. Her skin was pale and the only colour on her was a slash of red lipstick. She was nervous, kept taking deep breaths and exhaling very precisely through her lips as though it was some sort of breathing exercise. Maggie knew she was a New Yorker. When the train had started out above ground at Morden station, she had spoken into her phone to tell someone that she was running late for a meeting. For a moment, Maggie had considered wrenching the phone from her and telling whoever was on the other end of the line that she was hijacked on a tube train on its way into central London. She didn't do it of course. All she could think about was her children. She wouldn't do anything that might expose them to harm.

Next to the slim New Yorker was a man of fifty or so in slacks and a sports jacket. Although contriving to make it look as though he might have been on his way to the golf club, the briefcase and trade magazine spread out on his lap gave away his office destination. Clearly troubled by the long delay in the tunnel, he dabbed at the sweat that trickled down his forehead with a white handkerchief. He looked around at the other people in the carriage. It was as though he was trying to catch someone's eye. The passengers had remained silent up until now but, as the delay lengthened, people's nerves got the better of them and the man in the sports jacket was the first to speak.

'How long's it been?'

The question hung in the intense heat of the carriage. Next to Maggie was a large West Indian man wearing a business suit, his short dreads immaculately dishevelled. He looked up at the man in the sports jacket and said, 'About fifteen minutes.'

'Oh Jesus,' came the reply. Maggie could tell that his anxiety was clearly being exacerbated by some underlying condition – claustrophobia perhaps. Now that he'd spoken, he needed to speak some more.

'Maybe we should do something.'

'Like what?' said the New Yorker.

'Oh, I don't fucking know.' His angst made him raise his voice more than he had intended. 'I'm sorry.' He looked around nervously as social embarrassment was now added to his anxiety. The New Yorker returned to her breathing exercise and the sports jacket closed his eyes and rested his head back against the window behind him. But he misjudged the distance and the back of his head thumped against the glass. He didn't acknowledge the pain. When he reopened his eyes a few moments later, he looked at Maggie and she looked away.

The children loved Mr Pieces. When they'd been there last year on Ben's fifth birthday, everything had conspired to make it happy and memorable. The children were excited and she had watched their little faces and enjoyed their attempts to order their food from the waiter. Even George, who had become less talkative of late, especially when called upon to shell out for a meal for the four of them that they could ill afford, had opened up and been at his most amusing and charming, playing games with the children and making them laugh. She had watched him and been reminded of the time they went out to dinner together on their first date. That was an Italian restaurant too. They were both nervous and had drunk far too much. Two bottles of wine and a couple of Irish whiskies each. But George had been a gentleman and put Maggie in a cab back to her flat in West Kensington, where she was living with some old friends from university. He had called the next morning to ask how she was and ask her if she'd like to meet up again in a few days' time. She was relieved, having spent an agonising morning, worrying about having drunk too much the night before and whether she had made a fool of herself. Of course she wanted to meet up again. When you know, you know. And after that first night out with George, she knew.

She laughed at his jokes. She liked the way that he didn't take himself too seriously. He wasn't one of those pushy types that poison London with their ambition and their avarice. He wanted to do something artistic – make a success of his band or maybe write a book – and she respected him for that.

However much their relationship might have changed in the past few years, she still loved him. She just wished she could love him more, wished that they could both love each other more. George's problem was that he didn't much like himself at the moment. He felt guilty for not bringing in enough money. He felt as though life was passing him by and his dreams of artistic expression had come to nothing. It was during the aftermath of their last row, one of those moments when the truth comes tumbling out, that he had told her about his lack of fulfilment and unhappiness. His day job on the tube – while presenting him with plenty of time for dreaming his dreams – also gave him plenty of time to examine what it was that he was doing with his life. She wished he could feel more self-respect. That would make everyone's life in the Wakeham household that bit more easy.

Though he'd been nervous and frightened, the man in the sports jacket had broken the ice and social barriers started to come down. Conversations started up and down the carriage interspersed with the hollow clatter of forced laughter. Maggie kept her head down. She didn't want any form of social contact. She feared that if she so much as caught someone's eye her facade would crack and she would tell them everything, starting with the fact that on the other side of the door to the rear cab of the train were two terrorists, hijackers, kidnappers, whatever they were, and they were armed and dangerous. But she couldn't risk it. Whoever these people were – whatever they wanted – their plan with regards to her and George was brilliantly simple, based as it was on their natural parental obsession that nothing bad should befall their children. George, as a tube train driver, was obviously integral to the project's success. They needed him alive and willing to take orders and it was therefore imperative that it appeared as though Sophie and Ben were cowering somewhere with guns against their heads.

Not knowing her children's whereabouts was the cruellest torture she had ever known. Sitting there in a tube carriage, surrounded by people who might be able to help save her children, but also, in the worst case scenario, unwittingly cause their deaths, was just an extra little horror. She glanced up at the spyhole in the door to the cab. It looked like it had some sort of fisheye lens in it like those in the front doors of houses or apartments, so that even though she was sitting below it and to one side she would still be visible. For all she knew, she was being watched at that very moment.

Before they had boarded the train, she had been told by the younger of the two men, the one with the shaven head, that Sophie and Ben – he had even known their names – would be fine just so long as she did nothing to communicate to other passengers.

Her mind scrambled around trying to find something solid, something safe and reassuring to cling to. She closed her eyes. She was sitting with George, Sophie and Ben in the corner of Mr Pieces almost exactly a year before and the jolly waiters were throwing their metal trays on the floor. It was time. She watched Ben. He had been looking forward to his birthday for months and he could barely contain his excitement. Sophie giggled, a string of mozzarella hanging from the corner of her mouth which Maggie pinched away. As the clanging of the metal trays against the stone floor receded, they began to sing:

Happy birthday to you . . .

Sophie and Ben could barely articulate the words, their grins were so wide. Other diners in the restaurant joined in . . .

Happy birthday to you . . .

Maggie looked up into George's face and he was staring back at her, smiling, affectionate, his eyes sparkling. He reached across the table and took her hand in his. This was happiness. This was safety.

Happy birthday dear Be-en . . .

They were in there, behind that door, they'd taken her children, they'd defiled her family. Her hands on which she sat were sweating into the seat. She wanted to scream. She wanted to claw at her face with her nails, slam bloody hands against the door, she wanted to lose control.

Happy birthday to you!

Sophie and Ben were shrieking with delight as one of the smiling waiters approached their table with a birthday cake. The lights were dimmed and Ben blew out the candles.

'Make a wish!' Ben screwed his eyes up and thought hard.

George squeezed Maggie's hand and smiled.

Make a wish.

When George made an announcement over the PA once again, as he had a few times over the past hour, to reassure the passengers that everything possible was being done to move the train either forward or backwards and 'we'll have you out of here as soon as possible', she could hear the emotion in his voice.

His claustrophobia would be really bad by now. He would be close to cracking up and then what would happen? If the man with the shaven head was in the cab with him alone there might be a struggle. George was a little out of shape, probably didn't take enough exercise, but he was strong. If it was just the two of them in the cab together and no further accomplices had joined them, then he might be able to overpower the kidnapper. It was a possibility. It was something.

George's voice cracked when he said, 'I'll keep you up to date with any information as and when I receive it.'

Could the other passengers not hear that he was being forced to lie? She tore her gaze away from the floor of the carriage and looked around at the people. She was shocked by their expressions of willing acceptance. They were buying it. All except the man in the sports jacket. Why couldn't more of them be like him? People wanted to believe they were held in a tunnel because of a security incident at Tottenham Court Road station, as George kept telling them. To them it was the truth; to her it was a sick joke.

She wiped away a tear that made its way down her cheek but no one noticed. All eyes were on the man in the sports jacket as his panic got the better of him.

'It just doesn't make any sense at all. There's something wrong.'

'Calm down,' said the black man in the sharp suit sitting next to her. 'I'm sure they're doing all they can.'

'Don't tell me to calm down.' It was loud enough that even the little girls stroking the guide dog were distracted.

The man in the sports jacket looked around at the faces turned towards him. He took a deep breath and retook his seat. 'It's just so bloody hot,' he said. 'And there's no reason for keeping us locked up like this. They could just turn off the power to the track, open the doors at the back or the front and let us walk between the rails to the next station. That's what they should be doing. It's just appalling customer service, as always.'

'There's nothing we can do about it,' said the woman from New York, taking time out from her breathing exercises. 'I'm sure we can all write letters of complaint as soon as we get out of here.'

The sports jacket looked around at her, went to say something, but thought better of it and shook his head as he emitted a series of exaggerated sighs.

From the other side of the door against which she sat, came the faint sound of static from a walkie-talkie radio. Maggie could hear muttered voices but nothing she could actually decipher. She was the only one remaining in the carriage who had actually seen them enter the cab at Morden station. Before they went in, the male one had leant towards her to whisper in her ear, close enough that she could feel the stubble on his chin scrape against her cheek. To someone who was watching – and no one was – it might have seemed like he was telling her a joke or even sharing an intimacy. But there was nothing loving about what he said.

'I'm just going through that door there. If you do anything to draw attention to me or try to raise the alarm in any way, you will never see your children again. Got it?'

She wanted to be in Mr Pieces with her family. She wanted to hear the laughter as Ben blew out the candles on his birthday cake. She wanted George to be squeezing her hand and smiling – just as he had squeezed her hand and smiled at her on that first date.

They had come in through the back door just as George was walking out of the front. They must have had the house under surveillance. It was the young female one who frightened her the most. With her pretty gamine looks and pixie bob haircut, she looked so normal, in every way except the eyes. They looked as though they were emotionally switched off and she contemplated Maggie with all the humanity of a wolf.

The man with the crew cut was quiet, calm even. It was like he had done this before and he was clearly the one in charge.

When they first appeared through the back door she almost soiled herself. The door was open in a moment and there they were, guns pointed, telling her that so long as she co-operated with them in every detail they would let her live. It was something George used to say – I nearly shat myself – he would say. He was joking, talking about some horror film he had seen perhaps. But she really did think she might do so – or urinate at least. It was as though all her muscles had relaxed, slipped into a catatonia born of fear.

She used all her powers of persuasion to try and reassure Sophie and Ben that everything would be all right. But she could see it in their eyes. Their mum was telling them everything was OK but something else, something instinctive, was telling them it wasn't.

George had told her he loved her when he was on his way to the depot earlier. Her kidnappers had heard it on the speaker phone. The female one had smiled when he said it. A smile of derision. The man with the crew cut had told her to tell George to be quiet and continue with his normal routine.

Never in all the years that she had been with George had she wanted to see him as much as she did now. She wanted to see him and she wanted to tell him that she loved him too.

09:18 AM

Flat 21, Hyde Park Mansions, Pimlico

It wasn't only his sense of hearing that had improved after he lost his sight. His sense of smell was, if anything, even keener than his enhanced auditory perception. He'd never been a big one for aftershave, either on him or on others – the same went for perfume. The soap he used and the deodorant he wore were both unscented. The moisturising cream that he applied to his face every morning to prevent the scar tissue from becoming dry and flaky was only very slightly perfumed – jojoba, aloe vera or some such – and he liked the smell. He might have been known as 'the blind guy with the fucked-up face' – a description of himself that he had overheard once – but he insisted on his personal grooming being the match of any sighted colleague. He always wore black; colour no longer played a part in his life. A woman who he had almost become romantically involved with a couple of years before had asked whether he wore black out of mourning for his sight. He could tell from the tone of her voice and the way she said it that she had given this question much thought, believed that she was providing some psychological insight by asking it. Their nascent relationship ended soon afterwards.

Romance didn't play much part in his life. There had been a couple of women since he was blinded; the one who had made the comment about his black clothes was one of them. A drawback to being more sensitive to people's tones of voice was that he could tune in more clearly to latent emotion, like sympathy. There were some women – men too – who were drawn to people who had disabilities, who were damaged in some way. The last thing he wanted was that someone should be attracted to him, even partially, because he was the blind guy with the fucked-up face. He was overly sensitive to it, possibly unfairly so at times, but he couldn't help himself; as soon as he felt, or even suspected, that someone was with him because they felt sorry for him, any potential there might be for an ongoing relationship was shot down in flames. That over-sensitivity meant that he was probably doomed to being single. But, on balance, he could live with that. It was probably something to do with his lifelong bloody-mindedness but he liked to prove his independence, liked proving that the loss of his sight had not compromised the quality of his life, liked proving to himself and others that he could cope.

Ed planned on spending the next half hour answering emails via his speech reading and recognition software on his PC. He sometimes got more done in a half hour at home than during an entire morning at work. His car was booked for ten. Not for him, the white stick or the guide dog, the awkward accident-prone navigation of pavements and steps; not for him the reliance on the kindness of strangers to take his arm and help him across the road. It was stubbornness and pride that prevented him from doing what other blind people did – and it curtailed his personal freedom, no doubt about it – but that was how he wanted it to be and because of his job a car was provided for him on all official business.

As Ed finished applying the moisturiser cream to his face at the bathroom sink, his phone let out a soft beep, denoting an incoming call. He walked through to the bedroom and answered it.

'Ed Mallory.'

'Ed, this is Serina Boise.'

As soon as he heard the name and heard that unmistakable posh girl, with the hint of West Midlands accent so often imitated by his Special Branch colleagues, he knew there was work to be done. If it was an admin issue then an assistant would have called him. The fact that Commander Boise was calling him direct meant that, whatever was going on, things were moving fast.

'Hi, what can I do for you?'

'We've got a situation on the Underground; we don't really know anything at this stage – it might be nothing – but there's a train in a tunnel and it won't respond to any radio contact. I'm putting together a team just in case. I'd like you down at the incident desk at the LU Network Control Centre in St James's.'

She spoke quickly – she was nervous – and the 'it might be nothing' was a clear tell. She didn't for one moment think that it might be nothing. As far as she was concerned – according to the intelligence she had – it was very definitely something.

'OK, no problem,' said Ed.

'There's a car on its way to you with Mark Hooper in it from G Branch at MI5. We're going to be collaborating on this.'

There was the faintest hint of derision in her voice when she mentioned G Branch at MI5. It was not uncommon – he had come across it before, particularly in Special Branch. There was bound to be friction between two agencies so closely linked in terms of their common goals in counter-terrorism and yet so far apart in their approach.

'Hooper is heading up any potential negotiation at this stage, but I want you very closely involved.'

'OK.'

'DI Calvert and DS White are also on the team. They'll meet you at St James's.'

Serina Boise told Ed that they would 'speak soon' and rang off. Ed pushed the phone into the top pocket of his shirt and, realising that he still had some stray spots of moisturiser between his fingers, rubbed his hands as he went across to the dressing table, opened a drawer and took out a pair of his favourite Ray-Bans. Sunglasses were his one concession to vanity. He kept his eyes closed most of the time – not much point in opening them – but when he did, he didn't want the sightless lumps of jelly in his eye sockets to be on display to the world.

When the intercom buzzed, Ed answered it and heard the voice of an ex-public schoolboy who introduced himself as Mark Hooper. Ed went down in the lift and came face to face with the man who would be his partner in any potential hostage negotiation.

'Hi, Ed, good to meet you.'

'And you.'

They shook hands. Ed thought Hooper was probably about thirty-five. His hand was manicured and smooth and his handshake was firm enough to suggest that he was somewhat physically insecure. Ed was just under six feet and it didn't sound as though Hooper was speaking from a lower trajectory so maybe it wasn't his height that he felt sensitive about. It could be anything, from facial appearance to an under-sized penis but Ed was certain there was something. And he wore too much aftershave. It smelt soapy and alcoholic.

Hooper cupped Ed's elbow in his hand and led him across the street to the waiting car, which mercifully was chilled enough to dry up the perspiration that he could feel forming on his body after the short walk from the door of his apartment block. Once seated in the back of the car, a Jaguar judging by the smell of it and the sound of the engine, Ed said, 'So, Mark, what's the latest on this train?'

'Well, it might be nothing.'

'That's what Commander Boise said.'

'What we've got is a tube train on the Northern Line between Leicester Square and Tottenham Court Road. It's stationary in the tunnel. London Underground are spooked because not only is the driver refusing to communicate but it would appear that he has tampered with the onboard computer so they can't even check from the control room if there are any technical faults with the train.'

Ed couldn't resist needling Hooper with his next question: 'So how come MI5 appears to have operational control of what appears on the surface to be a fairly minor incident?'

'There's been some chatter for a while about a possible attack on the tube. We've been monitoring it closely after last time.' Hooper paused, tongue-tied by indecision about how much he should divulge.

Ed couldn't pinpoint why it was that he felt a certain amount of animosity towards Hooper. No doubt it had something to do with his perception that Hooper was a new breed of MI5 personnel, a product of human resource management, behavioural profiling, knowledge flow, mission statements and performance appraisals. Gone were the days when young men and women at Oxford or Cambridge universities were approached by some old bloke in a tweed suit who asked if they would like to do some secret work for the government. For the likes of Hooper, the secret service was as viable a career choice as any other.

'So maybe the driver's passed out,' offered Ed. 'Or suffered some sort of seizure.'

'Well, that's just it. They say he must be conscious because he's deliberately blocking radio signals.'

'They?'

'The Northern Line Control Centre. You see, there's a safety feature on the 1995 train stock that they use on the Northern Line. It's called a one person operator alarm and it alerts the control centre if the dead man's handle is not activated for ninety seconds. Well, the alarm has gone off and, as would normally happen, the control centre have tried to make contact with the train. Usually they would make a request over the PA in the carriages for someone to use the emergency handle and go into the cab to check the driver is OK. But the radio has been tampered with and they can't get a message through.'

'So what would they normally do if the driver had passed out or died?'

'They would evacuate all the trains behind and pull them up end to end, open all the doors in the cabs and evacuate the passengers through the trains to the nearest station – in this case, Leicester Square.'

'And they don't want to do that.'

'Not until they know exactly what's going on and what the driver's playing at.'

'Presumably the Northern Line has been closed down.'

'They're in the process of doing just that. The City branch of the line was closed down earlier on because of a bomb warning.'

'I heard the line was closed on the travel news. I didn't realise it was a bomb warning. Was it coded?'

'No, just the threat of a bomb on a train at Bank but it was taken seriously enough to close down that section of the line.'

'How many passengers are on this train?'

'It's a rush-hour train, so maybe three, possibly even four hundred at that stage of the line.'

The numbers jolted Ed out of his comfort zone. 'We've potentially got four hundred people sitting in a tunnel in this heat? How long have they been down there?'

'About three-quarters of an hour so far.'

'Jesus,' said Ed, enjoying the cool breeze of the car's air conditioning, 'I hope they've got plenty of water.'

At the LU Network Control Centre in St James's, Hooper once again took Ed's arm as he steered him through the labyrinthine corridors. Ed could feel his hand trembling. This coupled with something that Ed could hear in his voice – a certain breathy nervousness – made him suspect that Hooper knew considerably more about what was going on than he was prepared to divulge.

'So,' asked Ed, fishing a little as they walked along, 'who do you answer to on your side of things?'

'Howard Berriman.' Hooper said it with a certain amount of pride in his voice. Howard Berriman was the recently appointed Director General of MI5 and someone whose meteoric rise to the head of Britain's security services Ed had followed with interest.

When they arrived at what Hooper described as the gold control desk, which had been established as the operational hub of any potential negotiation, they were met by DI Calvert and DS White from Special Branch. Hands were shaken, Nick Calvert's big and muscular as befitted a six foot four inch seventeen stone bear, and Des White's, smooth and smelling of the alcohol handwash that he insisted on smothering his hands with, which had gained him the reputation of being something of a hypochondriac. Shaking hands between colleagues in the force wasn't something that Ed had been much aware of before he lost his sight but, robbed of his powers of visual recognition, it had become his way of saying hello. Those who worked with him on a regular basis always knew to shake his hand when they met.

It felt good to be working with White and Calvert. Ed knew that there were plenty on the force who had wanted to see him pensioned off after the Conor Joyce siege and even now there were those who felt that a special case had been made of him – and they were right, it had. But he had earned his place and it was people like Calvert and White who accepted that and let him get on with what he was good at. They weren't necessarily the best front men in a negotiation but they were solid, reliable and also inventive and thoughtful. Calvert was one of the most tenacious, dedicated and intuitive coppers he had ever come across and White's technical abilities had almost condemned him to the sidelines as a technician until his abilities as a listener during a negotiation had been spotted by Ed, who had championed him as an asset to any negotiation team. The respect between the three men was mutual but it was clear, however, that this was not purely a police operation – Mark Hooper was calling the shots – and the mood in the room was awkward.

'Ed,' said Hooper, 'this is Paul Hinton, the network operations manager for London Underground. He's got a full
breakdown of the train's movements up the Northern Line
since it left Morden this morning.'

Ed shook Hinton's hand – sweaty – and, taking the seat
that was offered him in a cluster of chairs at which they
all sat, he listened while the man described how train
number 037 had proceeded up the Northern Line from
Morden that morning with an operator by the name of
George Wakeham on the handle. Hinton spoke with a
strong, almost caricature, London accent and his breath
smelt of coffee and cigarettes.

'Anything unusual about Wakeham?' asked Ed.

'We've looked at his files and there's nothing I can think
of.' *Nuffink arcan fink uv.* 'He's a good driver. No disciplin-
aries. Anyway, when the train got to Oval station, the
controller had a request from the training department to
let a trainee driver ride on the cushions—'

'Ride on the cushions?' asked Ed.

'Sorry, it means that another driver was getting a lift
in the cab – up to the East Finchley depot, as it happens.'

'And he definitely entered the cab?' asked Hooper.

'Yeah, he was seen going in by another member of station
staff.'

'Is that normal procedure?' asked Ed.

'Yeah, nothing out of the ordinary. And we've checked
him out too.'

'We're already digging deeper, running both drivers
through the database,' said White.

The incoming call alert went off on Ed's phone. It was the call alert he had dedicated to Serina Boise earlier.

'Serina, hi.'

'Hi, Ed. I take it you're now at St James's?'

'Yes, I'm with the team.'

'Good, all communication links with the train are being patched through to you there. Just to say that we've approved the plan to send the two CO19 officers into the tunnel.'

'What CO19 officers?'

'I thought Mark Hooper would have briefed you about it. It's just a standard approach to see if we can make physical contact with the train in the tunnel.'

It sounded crazy to Ed but he tried to mask the tone of exasperation in his voice as he said, 'Why don't we send the train behind number 037 into the tunnel to connect up with it and have the CO19 officers enter the train via the connecting doors in the cabs? That would provide them with much more cover.'

'We've taken the view that it would also destroy the element of surprise. Our thinking is that if we can get our men on the train without alerting anyone to their presence and have them mingle with the passengers then we have a much stronger advantage.'

'The chain of command here seems . . .' Ed pretended to be fishing for the word, inviting Boise to offer one, which she did.

'Weird, I know. It is but we're going to have to go with it for the time being. I want you to talk the officers into and out of the tunnel, OK?'

'I don't have a problem with that, but I just want to ask whether this is the best course of action at this stage before we even know what sort of threat we're dealing with.'

'It's a decision that's been made in consultation.'

'With who? MI5?'

'Yes.'

Ed had hoped when he took the call that the others in the room might have continued speaking so he could question Commander Boise without an audience but it was clear that he was centre-stage.

'OK, I'll talk them in and out but I'd like this on record that I'm not convinced that this is the safest course of action at the present time.'

'Noted, Ed.'

Despite his misgivings, Ed knew when he had been given an order. He and Commander Boise agreed to speak later and she rang off. Ed turned to Hooper and asked, 'How do we know that a bomb hasn't gone off down there?'

It was clearly something that Hooper had given some thought to and his answer came out fully formed. 'There'd be survivors on the track. We'd have picked up something on the radio. There'd be smoke in the tunnel. We've had none of those things.'

There was a moment's silence as the team gathered their thoughts in preparation for further talk of strategy and potential solutions. Before the chatter began again, however, Ed could feel something in the vibrations given off by the men in the room. There was no mistaking it; the fear came off them in waves.

09:52 AM

Leicester Square

They were told it might be nothing, a tube train in a Northern Line tunnel between Leicester Square and Tottenham Court Road. It might be that the driver had lost his marbles. That's how Rob had put it. Glen was glad it was Rob. Glen was the youngest member of CO19, the Specialist Firearm Command; Rob was the oldest. Not that Rob was that old. Forty-two to his twenty-eight. But there was something father-like about Rob and, if Glen could have chosen anyone to buddy up with on his first official assignment, it would have been him.

Rob drove them over to Leicester Square in the armed response vehicle. He could tell that Rob was deliberately trying to keep the atmosphere calm and Glen was thankful for it. Even though it might be nothing, Glen was nervous. But nerves were important; they kept you on your toes. It felt wrong, he knew, to be thinking like this but he kind of hoped it wasn't nothing. He felt like losing his cherry. He wanted to prove to himself he was up to the job. All the training and theory in the world can only teach you so much. He wanted to face a real-life situation and deal with it, do whatever needed to be done.

The streets around Leicester Square had been hastily evacuated. They looked odd being empty, the pavements that were normally so busy, offices, shops, restaurants, coffee bars, theatre-ticket agencies, their doors usually flapping continually and now standing still.

When they came to the cordon around the tube station, Rob showed his ID to a couple of uniforms and they drove through and parked up. From the boot of the car, they took the flak jackets and Rob took the silver flight case containing the two identical 9mm Glock 17 pistols.

As they went down a flight of steps into the ticket hall, Glen tried to match Rob's nonchalance even though his heart was racing.

'You would,' said Glen.

Rob frowned for a moment before he saw a large illuminated advertisement on the wall opposite showing an attractive young woman in a bikini. It was advertising sun cream.

'And you would,' said Rob.

Glen had passed through the circular ticket hall only the week before with his nephew on their way to the latest Pixar movie in Leicester Square. But it was busy then, there were people everywhere.

At the control room, they were met by a Special Branch techie who wired them up with walkie-talkies and headsets through which they could keep in contact with each other and, via a three-way link, with DI Ed Mallory at the

Network Control Centre at St James's. They checked the equipment and everything was working fine. Mallory came through on the radio to run through the details of the operation.

'You're to go into the northbound Northern Line tunnel and approach the train, taking care not to touch the two live rails. We're going to leave the power on so as not to alarm the passengers by throwing the train into darkness. Once at the train you must try and gain entry to the rear cab using the appropriate key, which will be provided. Having holstered your weapons so as to reduce passenger anxiety and also to give the appearance of being passengers yourselves, you should make your way through the train. If there appears to be nothing untoward, you should proceed to the front cab and try to establish contact with the driver.'

'Why don't we approach the front of the train from Tottenham Court Road?' asked Rob, his words being relayed with a tiny delay into Glen's headset as he said them.

'From a psychological point of view,' said Ed Mallory, 'it would be better if you approached the driver from within the train itself rather than from outside. If the driver is in a state of mental trauma, he might be alarmed by the sight of figures in the tunnel. Now, once you've made contact with the driver, you should evaluate whether he is in a state whereby he might potentially cause harm to himself or to others, and if he is, then restrain him and call for paramedics. His name – and I want you to use it if you can – is George Wakeham.'

'George Wakeham – got it,' said Rob. 'Are we under standard ACPO rules of engagement?'

'ACPO rules, that's right,' said Ed. 'But remember the bit about "unless this risks serious harm", all right?'

Ed Mallory knew his stuff and he was clearly trying to prise away the sticky fingers of the state firearms legislation to give them some more autonomy, should they need it. The Association of Chief Police Officers rules of engagement stated that they 'must identify themselves and declare intent to fire, unless', as Mallory had pointed out, 'this risks serious harm'. Secondly, they 'should aim for the biggest target (the torso) to incapacitate and for greater accuracy'. And finally, they 'should reassess the situation after each shot'. It was made to sound so bloody simple.

'Hopefully, you won't need the guns,' said Ed. 'The best-case scenario is that the driver's had some sort of breakdown and when he sees you guys walk into the cab with him, he'll probably crumble. But we can't be too careful.'

'OK, you're the boss,' said Rob and rolled his eyes at Glen, who smiled, thankful for any excuse to escape his nerves.

'If you see anything, however, that leads you to believe you may be in imminent danger – anything at all – then I want you out of there straight away. This is no time for heroics. What you're doing is purely fact finding, got it?'

'OK, sure.'

Rob opened up the flight case, took out one of the two pistols and passed it to Glen along with a clip of ammunition. Glen loaded the gun and slid it into the holster mounted under the left armpit on the side of his flak jacket. Rob holstered his gun and they walked down the stationary escalators and made their way through the deserted corridors, digital advertising panels on all sides vying for the attention of the 250,000 people who passed through the station every day, ads for theatre shows and magazines, films, books and music, all of them now redundant, seen by no one, ignored by the two men walking past.

They made their way down a second bank of escalators and followed the signs onto the northbound Northern Line platform. There they were met by a group of uniformed officers and an over-enthusiastic London Underground engineer who was clearly excited to be involved in the operation. He shook Rob's hand and then Glen's before he reached into the side pocket of his jacket and took out two metal objects that looked like oversized Allen keys.

'This', he said, taking hold of a T-shaped key, 'will let you open the door into the cab. And this' – he held up a J-shaped key – 'will get you through the J door between the cab and the passenger area.'

Rob took the two keys and slid them into his pocket. Then the engineer gestured for them to follow him down a metal ramp that had been placed between the platform edge and the middle of the track, between the two sets of rails.

'These little buggers here,' he said, pointing at two rails mounted on white porcelain insulators, 'are the live rails. Keep away from these and you'll be fine. Now, you got a torch, ain't you?' Rob took out his torch and switched it on, briefly dazzling the engineer. 'Ah, right you are then. Well, good luck to you, boys.' The man's cheeriness would have been funny if Glen had not been so tense. As the engineer made his way back up the ramp onto the platform, Glen and Rob walked into the mouth of the tunnel, light from Rob's torch flashing around the dark cable-lined interior.

They moved slowly between the lines, their trainers crunching against the grit on the narrow sleepers. About fifty feet from its mouth, the tunnel went into a slight bend and descended through a shallow gradient for another fifty feet or so before it levelled out. With any residual light from the station now left far behind, they trudged through the cone of white halogen thrown by the torch. Mice scurried about playing tricks with their peripheral vision and hinted at the movement of something much larger and more sinister.

They made their way towards the red light of a signal up ahead and as they passed it, they could just make out the two lights on the rear cab of a train about a hundred yards further up the tunnel.

'I've got a visual on the train,' said Rob. Silence. Static on the headset. Then Ed Mallory's voice: 'OK. Are the lights on or off in the rear cab?'

'Off.'

'Approach the target with care and keep me updated.' Glen drew his pistol from the holster and, holding it in a double grip, he raised it up and pointed it at the train as they moved forward, Rob shining the torch. The air was hot and smelt rubbery, like bumper cars at the fair.

Closer still and they could see well enough from the lights on the train that Rob no longer needed the torch.

'We've got movement on the train,' said Rob.

Glen squinted and could just make out the window in the door in the middle of the cab as it was lowered. He felt Rob's hand on his shoulder, a signal for them both to crouch down.

'What is it?' asked Mallory.

'The window in the cab door is being opened,' said Rob.

'Wait and observe,' came the reply.

They waited.

10:04 AM

Network Control Centre, St James's

'Maybe the radio link has gone down,' said Hooper. To Ed, it sounded as though he was in need of reassurance, desperate for anything to contradict the reality of what they had all just heard. Maybe that was how they did things at MI5 nowadays, it was acceptable for operatives to give a loose rein to their emotions. Or maybe Mark Hooper genuinely felt scared and couldn't conceal it.

'No,' said Ed. 'The line's still open, I can hear it.'

White's fingers clicked a computer mouse and keyboard nearby. 'Yeah, the line's still open,' he said and Ed heard Calvert sigh. Had it really come to this so soon, that people were dying?

'It's too early to speculate on what's happened to them,' said Hooper, sounding to Ed as though he was masking his nerves with bluster.

'Is it?' said Calvert. Ed could detect some of his own feelings towards Hooper reflected in Calvert's voice and he was glad that it wasn't just him who found the man's manner irksome. Ed was also aware, however, of the morale within the team and how imperative it was to safeguard it, especially if this situation was as potentially complex and exacting as it was shaping up to be.

He couldn't get it out of his head, the thudding sound that he heard on the radio and the strange way that the CO19 officer had said, 'Shit.' It kept replaying over and over. His guess was that the two men were indeed lying dead in the tunnel. There was no point considering whether he should have suggested a different strategy. It had been agreed that sending two armed officers into the tunnel to make contact with the train was the right course of action. That he had had reservations meant nothing now. It served no purpose analysing what they might have done differently. The inevitable enquiry that would take place afterwards could look into all that. From now on it was essential that he kept a clear head, unclouded by emotion. The two CO19 officers were out of the equation; his years of training and experience would have to take over as he pursued potential resolutions.

The balance of power in the room had shifted. Whatever MI5's involvement in this – whatever they might have been doing up to this point – this was now a police operation. Hooper was clearly feeling emotionally bruised by the outcome of this first collective initiative. Ed wasn't. Someone needed to take control while the negotiating cell was being put together and all the corresponding roles assigned.

Ed could feel the nervous expectancy in the room as the others waited for him to speak. All the bureaucracy

and the seminars and meetings and lectures, all the inces-
sant talking, all the bullshit, all of it was in preparation
for this moment. It was no time for petty vendettas or
posturing, so when he addressed Hooper, he used his first
name.

'OK, Mark, I'll leave you to brief your people but, as far
as our side of things is concerned, we'll report back that
we've got what looks like a terrorist hijack situation on a
Northern Line tube train.'

10:05 AM

Northern Line Train 037, sixth carriage

It was over an hour since the train had stopped in the tunnel between Tottenham Court Road and Leicester Square. All soft drinks and bottles of water had been drunk. Heart rates had increased. Claustrophobia – whether apparent and articulated or suppressed and internalised – was rife. Panic stalked the carriages.

As the voice came over the train's public address system, people stopped talking; those listening to music turned off their audio devices or pulled out hissing earpieces; eyes flicked up from books, newspapers and magazines.

'This is George, the driver, back with another progress report. Apparently we're still here because they can't evacuate us down the tunnel in either direction on account of security incidents at Tottenham Court Road station and now Leicester Square station as well. They're telling me that everything possible is being done to resolve the situation but, in the meantime, rest assured that you're perfectly safe down here and everyone should relax and await further news. Sorry, folks, I know it's been a horribly long time but that's where we are at the moment. As soon as I hear anything else, you'll be the first to know. Oh, and if anyone towards the front or rear of the train can hear voices and movement, it's just some maintenance engineers who are down here with us and can't get evacuated either. But don't worry, they're perfectly harmless and getting on with some work.'

Maggie listened to her husband as he lied to the passengers. It was the sort of reassuring banter that everyone wanted to hear. But although it was unconvincing to her – she could hear the terror in his voice – it seemed as though most people were buying it. But not all. The man in the sports jacket on the opposite row of seats muttered, 'Bollocks,' under his breath. Another panic attack was just below the surface and it didn't look as though his fragile psyche could contain it. Maggie watched the faces of the other passengers as he said, 'Either this dick of a driver is lying or he's being lied to by people further up the chain of command. There's no way there are two separate security incidents at consecutive stations at the same time. No way.' His stream of consciousness was delivered in a hissed monotone. 'There's something going on.'

This was too much for the black man in the sharp suit sitting next to Maggie. The lack of oxygen in the air and the withering heat had crippled his morale. 'Listen, mate, keep your opinions to yourself. You heard the driver.' He gestured up the train. 'They're doing what they can to get us out of here.'

'That's what the people on the planes that went into the twin towers were made to believe.'

'It's not like that.'

Mention of 9/11 had the woman from New York rolling her eyes and tutting.

'Look, can we just keep the histrionics to a minimum here?' she said. Maggie could see from her demeanour that she felt as though she had said too much and now she needed to explain her outburst.

'I was in SoHo when it happened, saw the whole thing. So let's not even suggest . . .' She looked down at the floor. As she looked up again, she caught Maggie's eye. 'I'm Daniella,' she said, holding out her hand. Her spontaneous introduction was a way of coping, a way of distracting herself from the tension of the situation. Both their hands were clammy and trembled as they touched.

'Maggie.'

'Adam,' said the black man in the suit, holding his hand up in greeting.

The three of them looked at the fourth member of their group. It was a group now. Because of their close proximity, these four people were a unit of sorts – all adults over the age of thirty – just one of a myriad of pockets of humanity thrown together at random by the London transport system.

'I'm Hugh.' Confessing his name appeared to calm him a little but Maggie thought he still looked unhinged. If only this creep had stayed at home, or been delayed by a few moments, enough to mean that he had missed this train, or even just ended up in another carriage. She wanted everyone to know the truth about their predicament but this guy was not the right conduit for the information. He looked as though he might succumb to full-blown hysteria at any moment.

'I remember 9/11 really well,' said Hugh. 'I guess everyone does. I was due in hospital on September 12th to have a lump removed from my testicles. They thought it might be cancer – it turned out it wasn't – but before the operation I'd convinced myself that it was. So I had a kind of end-of-the-world feeling already, which perfectly complemented what I was seeing on the television. All those people trapped in the towers.' Hugh looked up from his hands in his lap. 'Maybe we're trapped down here. What's that expression? Just because you're paranoid, it doesn't mean they're not after you.'

It was the first time that Maggie had actually thought about the fate of the other passengers on the train. Her own personal circumstances were so horrific and her thoughts so tightly focused on Ben and Sophie that she hadn't considered that everyone else on the train was someone's son or daughter, mother or father. Her predicament was only different from theirs because she had knowledge. She knew they were all victims – of what exactly she couldn't be sure – but they were victims all the same.

'The atmosphere's getting worse,' said Hugh.

'It's so bloody hot,' said Adam.

'No, I don't mean the temperature, I mean the mood.' Hugh's voice sounded petulant and whiny. 'At first, everyone accepted the situation. It was just a delay. This is London Underground, for God's sake. There are always delays. But it's too long now. People can feel it. As for the driver, well, he's saying just what you'd expect a driver to say under the circumstances. But there's something about the way that he's saying it. Can't you hear it?'

Hugh asked the question of Maggie, looked straight at her. Maggie nodded. He was right. More right than he might ever imagine.

'He sounds afraid, as though he knows something more than he's telling. Whatever's going on up there is serious, you mark my words. Look ...' He gestured along the carriage. 'You can see it in their faces.'

'That's enough now, mate,' said Adam, failing to hide the anger in his voice.

'I know you don't want to hear it but I'm telling you, we're in serious shit.' Hugh leant forward and buried his head in his hands.

'Mind your language,' said Adam. 'There are kids present.'

'Yeah,' said Hugh, 'and they're not going to make it to adulthood at this rate.'

'Look, just take it easy.'

'And just accept it like a fucking sheep?'

'Look, we're all feeling anxious – just calm down.'

'Yeah, just cool it for Chrissakes.' This from Daniella, her New York inflection sounding stronger than before, enriched by emotion. Her outburst silenced Hugh for a moment and Adam took his chance for further placatory words.

'Come on, mate, it's going to be fine. Trust me.'

Hugh's voice had gone up an octave when he said, 'Oh Christ!' and pulled himself to his feet. Conversations halted as people turned to watch him. If she had had the emotional strength, Maggie would have tried to intervene herself, but all she could do was hope that the arrival of Hugh's panic attack could be delayed in some way. Hugh cracking up would do none of them any good. Maggie felt too close to cracking up herself.

Adam stood up opposite Hugh and put his hand on his shoulder. 'Come on, mate.'

Hugh seemed to deflate. 'I hate the tube. Always have. I have nightmares about something like this happening.'

Maggie thought of George and how he might be coping with his own demons.

'It's going to be all right,' said Adam, gesturing for Hugh to retake his seat. But Hugh had other ideas and as his emotion took hold he flung his arms around Adam, who clearly decided that the best way to respond was to reciprocate and the two men stood embracing each other in the middle of the carriage.

On the opposite row to Maggie three seats along was a mother with a little girl on her lap, about Sophie's age. She had covered the little girl's ears with her hands when Hugh had started to swear. Maggie saw the concentration on the little girl's face as she tried to decode the meaning of what she was witness to.

'It's all right, darling, those two men are happy to see each other,' said her mother by way of explanation.

'Happy?' asked the little girl.

'Happy,' came the reply.

Through the door to the rear cab came the sound of laughter. No one else seemed to hear it. It came from the woman who was part of the reason for all this. To Maggie it sounded like the coldest laughter she had ever heard.

10:06 AM

Northern Line Train 037, driver's cab

'They're not going to believe me for much longer,' said George.

'Don't put yourself down,' said Pilgrim. 'I think your acting abilities are commendable. If it wasn't for the fact that I know what you're telling them is a lie, I'd probably believe you myself. You can be very convincing, George, especially when you consider that it wasn't so long ago that you were hyperventilating rather spectacularly.'

There was that smile again and George couldn't help but reciprocate.

'Look, you're even smiling at me. We're going to get along just fine.'

'Maybe I'm suffering from Stockholm Syndrome.' Pilgrim said nothing, just stared at him. 'In the early seventies some hostages in a Stockholm bank began to feel sympathy and even loyalty for the two men who held them hostage.'

'I know what Stockholm Syndrome is. I read papers. I went to school.'

'I'm sorry,' said George, 'I didn't mean to—'

'Some victims of abuse maintain loyalty to their abuser. They think that it has something to do with the way that newborn babies form an emotional attachment to an adult figure in close proximity because that adult figure is their best shot at survival. It's like baby animals forming an almost unbreakable bond with the first creature they see when they are born, regardless of the species.'

'Looks like you know more about it than I do.'

'Maybe I do. Then, again, maybe you're being compliant so that you can choose your moment and try to escape.'

'Do I need to try to escape?'

The smile on Pilgrim's face was well and truly gone now. He put his head on one side and narrowed his eyes as he scrutinised George.

'I hope you'll come to realise that what we're doing here – the situation that we're creating – is not something that you should want to escape from.'

'What's your real name?' It was a question George had considered asking a number of times over the past hour. Knowing the man's name might help. He was convinced, however, that the question would go unanswered, so the response surprised him.

'My name's Tommy Denning.'

Tommy Denning extended his hand and George shook it instinctively. The irony of the situation was not lost on him, that he should be shaking hands with the man who presented an enormous threat to him and his family. But now that this introduction had been made, George thought he might try and capitalise on it. George remembered from a film he had once seen on television the importance of a hostage continually confirming his character and humanity in order to make himself into a person rather than just an object with which to be bargained. If he could arouse some empathy in Tommy Denning then he was less likely to wind up dead.

'So what is this situation that *we're* creating?'

'You'll find out, I promise you that. You will find out.'

'And what about my family?'

'As I told you before, they're fine, they're absolutely fine. You do what you're told and you'll see them again soon enough. You have my word.'

There was a long pause while George thought about how to phrase his next question but then he gave up on his verbal deliberations and just said it as it came to him.

'So, are you some sort of terrorist?'

'To be a terrorist, you've got to terrorise someone, haven't you? And before you say that this bloke here on the floor might see things differently, I'd just point out that he was dead before he got to feel any terror. Why are you so inquisitive?'

'I think you'd be inquisitive if you'd had the morning I've had.'

'Fair enough.' Tommy Denning pulled down the window in the M door set into the front of the cab. He peered out into the tunnel that climbed away from the train at a slight gradient towards Tottenham Court Road station. The pistol hung from his fingers. It was less than five feet away from George's hand. If he was quick, he could lean across and grab it.

'So where did you get the J key from to get into the cab?'

'Why do you want to know that?'

'Well, it's not something that you can just buy in a shop.'

'If you must know, my dad did some work on the Underground. He had a couple and I sort of inherited them.'

Denning dangled the gun by the trigger guard from his forefinger. Five feet. If George leant forward in his seat it was only four feet. Was the safety catch on? Did it even have a safety catch? He looked along the black metal body of the gun. Nothing. Not that he knew what he was looking for but nothing all the same. One lunge and he was there, he could pull the gun from Denning's finger. The handle was pointed towards him at the perfect angle.

'So why here, why now?' asked George, his eyes fixed on the gun.

Denning sighed as he stared out of the window. 'That's a big question. It needs – deserves – a big answer, and if I thought I could do it justice for you right now then I'd have a go. But I'm saving myself. Be assured, you'll get your answer soon enough and, believe me, when you do it'll all make perfect sense. This whole thing hasn't been easy. It's taken a lot of time and effort.' He said it like he'd organised a day at the seaside. 'But it will be worth it. For all of us.' He said the words with conviction and still the gun hung from his forefinger. Four feet away. Four feet.

'Do you have any idea', said Denning, 'what it feels like to wake up in the morning and know that of all the thousands of days that you've spent on this earth, that today of all days you will make a difference, that today is the day that you will truly come alive?'

George stared at the gun. He'd grab it and kill him if he could. There was no point even trying to take him hostage. He was too athletic, there might be a fight and George didn't fancy his chances. So he would have to be quick. Grab the gun, point it at his head and pull the trigger, hope to God there was no safety catch and, if there was, that it was off. But what if he failed? What if Denning was offering the gun to him as some sort of test?

As Denning turned to look at him, George tore his attention from the gun and met his stare.

'You ever done anything remarkable, George?'

'Depends on what you mean by remarkable. If you mean, have I ever climbed Mount Everest or swum the English Channel then no, but I've had my moments.'

'I'm sure you have.'

'We had children. Me and Maggie. Ben and Sophie. You met them.'

'And very cute they are too.'

As Denning turned back to the darkness in the tunnel, George wanted to kill him now more than ever. The satisfaction of pumping a bullet into this bastard's head would be almost sexual in its intensity.

The gun dangled from the finger. It might not be there for much longer. He had to take the chance.

'You're right, bringing life into the world is remarkable.' Denning's voice was softer now, little more than a whisper, as though he was speaking to himself.

George leant forward and the gap between his hand and the gun closed even further.

Do it now, George, do it now.

He lunged forward, arm outstretched but, as his fingers approached the chequered grip of the stock, Denning stepped back and spun around. Before George could register the lack of anything solid within his hungry grasp, the end of the silencer was pressed against his forehead. All the nervous anxiety of the past five minutes was spontaneously evacuated from his lungs in a gasp.

'Ssssshhhhh, George, keep it down,' said Denning, his voice steady and measured and betraying no sign of his sudden exertion. 'We don't want to alarm the passengers, do we? Now, on your knees.'

George stood his ground. If he was going to get a bullet in the head there was no way that he was going to kneel for it. Denning pressed the gun harder against his skin.

'Kneel, or I'll shoot you where you stand.' There was no anger in his voice. It was calm and measured and George knew that if he allowed his natural cussedness and rebellious nature to get the better of him then he was a dead man. As he knelt, he felt the trainee driver's still luke-warm blood soak into his standard issue navy London Underground trousers. The end of the gun barrel remained pressed against his forehead.

'You've got a nerve.' Denning's tone of voice had changed. Though still hushed, it was more high-pitched, angry, as he forced the end of the silencer against George's skin.

'Did you read the scriptures when you were at school?'

'Yes.'

'Remember any?'

'None in particular. I've never had much time for religion.'

'Come on, you must remember something.'

'The Lord's Prayer, I suppose.'

'Everyone knows the Lord's Prayer. How about the psalms?'

'I don't know, I don't think so.'

Terror made George's voice high-pitched too. It was a child's voice. He was a boy again, frightened and alone in the playground as the bully approached. But whatever might happen to him in these next few moments, he was determined that he wouldn't give this creep any satisfaction in seeing his fear.

'Come on, everyone remembers Psalm 23.' Denning's voice hissed with fury, although its volume level was still low enough that anyone on the other side of the door to the carriage would hear nothing more than a whisper. 'Everyone knows it. Come on.'

'The Lord is my shepherd? That one?'

'The Lord is my shepherd, that's right. Now say it.'

'I don't know it all the way through.'

'Then say as much as you can remember.'

'The Lord is my shepherd; I shall not want . . .'

'Excellent, the King James version. That's good, now keep going.'

'He maketh me to lie down in green pastures; he leadeth me beside the still waters . . . erm . . .'

'Come on, George.'

'I can't remember any more.'

'Try!' Denning's breath blasted into George's face. It smelt sour and earthy.

'He saveth my soul?' It was something to do with soul. But Denning remained silent. So maybe this was it. He had got it wrong so now he must die. He thought of the trainee driver, how the life had gone out of him and the muscles in his body had relaxed as the first jet of blood pumped from his head and he dropped to the floor.

'He *restoreth* my soul.' Denning had the voice of a petulant schoolmaster now.

'He restoreth my soul . . .'

'He leadeth me in the paths of righteousness for his name's sake. Now you must remember the next bit, George, you must.'

'Something to do with the valley of the shadow of death.'

'Got it in one. How apt. Yea, though I walk through the valley of the shadow of death, I will fear no evil: for thou art with me; thy rod and thy staff they comfort me.' He was into his stride now. His voice was back to its soft purring best. 'Thou preparest a table before me in the presence of mine enemies: thou anointest my head with oil; my cup runneth over. Now George, I want you to say the next bit with me. OK?'

George was going to die. These would be the last moments of his life; his last glimpse would be the blood-caked interior of a 1995 stock Northern Line tube train. When it came, he wouldn't even know he'd been shot; he'd be dead by the time his body hit the floor. Just like the trainee driver, blood spraying around the cab.

'If you're going to kill me, do it. Don't make me recite all this shit.'

'Shit, is it? Some of the most beautiful and poignant words ever committed to paper. You're such a disappointment. Aren't you going to beg me for your life?'

'No.'

'Right, well let's finish the psalm.'

'Not if you're going to kill me at the end of it.'

'I'll definitely kill you if you don't. So repeat after me: surely goodness and mercy shall follow me all the days of my life. Say it.'

'Surely goodness and mercy shall follow me all the days of my life.'

'And I will dwell in the house of the Lord for ever.'

'Just kill me if you're going to.'

'Say the words, George.'

The end of the silencer broke the skin on George's forehead and he felt warm blood mingle with sweat.

'And I will dwell in the house of the Lord for ever.' Every nerve in his body was jangling, waiting for the bullet. For the first time all day, he felt cold. A ball of ice in his abdomen radiated a feverish chill through his body.

'Do it,' said George. 'Just fucking do it.'

'You almost sound as though you want me to. Things not going well at home?' Denning took the end of the silencer from against George's forehead. 'The fact is I'm not going to kill you. You're my accomplice, my man on the inside, my confidant.' His voice gave no hint of the violence that was to follow. Denning grabbed a handful of George's hair and forced his head downwards, crushing it cheek to cheek against the trainee driver's bloody face. The skin was cold meat against George's sweating face. He could smell the blood.

'That's what'll happen to you if you try to stop me doing what I need to do. Take a long, hard look. I didn't do this lightly. You think I can just drill a hole in a man's head without batting an eyelid? It's hard, George. I'm not a murderer. Have you ever considered the strength of will it takes to do this? Have you?' George's cheekbone was grinding against the corpse's beneath it. 'Have you?'

'No.'

'Have you ever stopped to think that perhaps the Jihadis are the greatest embodiment of human endeavour and they are right to do what they do? Maybe America *is* the devil. Think about it. Shopping malls, happy meals, fat people, TV evangelists, Mickey Mouse with extra fries to go. The banality of evil in glorious Technicolor.'

Tommy let go of George's hair and George pulled himself into a kneeling position once again, clawing at the blood smeared on his cheek.

'Now I want you to get back on the radio and speak to the passengers. They are still your responsibility, I believe. Are they not?'

'Yes they are.' George stood up and looked down at his blood-soaked clothes. 'What do you want me to say?'

Denning opened up the M door set into the front of the train and manoeuvred the trainee driver's body through, letting it drop onto the track outside. As he slammed the door shut again, he said, 'Let's give them a lift. They've been very good, very patient. Let's tell them you've had the all-clear to proceed to Tottenham Court Road station from where they will be able to make alternative travel arrangements. And on behalf of London Underground, you're sorry for any inconvenience caused.'

'Even though it's not true?'

'Even though it's not true.'

'What if they don't believe me?'

'Oh, come on. You know as well as I do that people will believe anything if they want to badly enough. Now hurry up and put them out of their misery. For the time being at least.'

George picked up the handset and held it to his mouth. Denning watched him, smiling.

10:10 AM

Northern Line Train 037, rear cab

There was no turning back after Belle had killed the two men in the tunnel. The thud of the shots and the crimson mist that hung in the air for a few seconds after the two bodies had fallen felt like a demarcation line. Simeon watched her as she sat back down in the driver's seat of the rear cab after her expedition to retrieve the two Glock pistols from the bodies.

'Seventeen 9mm rounds in the handle,' she said, admiring the guns.

'I know.'

He did know. He liked guns. Not as much as Belle did, of course. Although it was more than like with Belle. It was love. She was obsessed.

'A brace of Glocks,' she said and smiled. 'Like a brace of pheasant and brand new by the looks of them.'

She didn't look disturbed. She didn't look as though she could kill two men as easily as that and then sit there and smile about it. Her dark hair was tied back. Earlier on, when they took the driver's wife and children, she had worn a black woollen skull cap but she had taken it off as they entered the rear cab of the train at Morden. She was pretty, almost elfin-like. He liked petite women. They accentuated his masculinity, made him feel more in control. He had suspected that all her gung-ho assurances that she was ready for this mission were just false bravado and, when it came time, she would bottle it. But he was wrong. She had maintained her composure throughout and had shot the two men in the tunnel and then gone to fetch their guns with all the excitement of a child on a shopping trip for a new toy.

It had been a tough few months. Looking back now with the benefit of hindsight, prison would have been preferable to his time at Madoc Farm with the brothers and sisters of Cruor Christi. But it was a deal that he had struck. He was working for British Intelligence now. It sounded grand. He had even told his mother – told her to keep her mouth shut about it – and she had been impressed. She thought it was like James Bond, poor mad cow. It was the beginnings of Alzheimer's. Maybe if it went well today, her final few coherent memories might be of him as a hero. But it was a fragile hope. He had a bad feeling about all this.

Say what you like about Tommy Denning. Extremist nut job maybe, but he was clever. The kid was forever reading. There was the internet as well during the hours when the generator was up and running. There was an unspoken rule that Tommy would get priority when using the single desktop PC that catered to Madoc Farm's IT needs. It was as though the others realised that it was a form of release for him and without it he would become even more highly strung and opinionated than usual. That ramshackle old farmhouse on the side of a mountain was bad enough without Tommy Denning being upset.

Some of the brothers seemed to enjoy the spartan existence. It was all in the name of God and therefore all part of the deal. What do you need nice food for when you've got God? Why bother with hot water to wash in when you've got God? What use home comforts when you've got bone-chilling drafts, fluttering candles, and God? God lived amongst the brothers and sisters of Cruor Christi as surely as the rats did. Sometimes he was everlasting and almighty, sometimes gentle and all-knowing, but he was always there.

When she had raised up the Heckler & Koch PSG1 sniper's rifle she had fitted with a home-made silencer, he hoped she was just using the telescopic sight to see who was approaching. She had a name for the gun. She called it the Pulveriser because of what the high-velocity dum-dum bullets – which she customised herself by filing a cross into the end of each lead cap – could do to the pumpkins that she used for target practice around the farm. And the men she shot might as well have been vegetables for all the remorse she showed for having shot them.

When she opened fire, it sent Simeon's rising sense of panic off the scale. He was frozen to the spot as she calmly muttered, 'Bingo!' and then resighted on the only remaining shadow in the tunnel and fired the second shot, congratulating herself on her marksmanship with a whispered, 'Gotcha!' It would all be worth it – he had to keep telling himself that – it would all be worth it in the end. Besides, what choice did he have?

'So go on,' she said with a Glock in each hand. 'Tell me about Helmand.'

'I've told you loads of times.'

'Tell me again. I need to hear it again today.'

There was no point denying her. If he did, she would become agitated and it was essential that she remained calm. Until the time came. Maybe telling the story might help him stay calm too. He looked down at the floor, at the bloody footprints that Belle had left there after she had collected the guns from the tunnel, and he cast his mind back to Afghanistan.

'What you've got to bear in mind is that our softly-softly approach with the locals had all been forgotten – there was none of that hearts and minds bollocks.'

'Bollocks, yeah,' said Belle like she knew.

'We were on a routine patrol. One minute there we are, two Land Rovers, a few kids playing on a dirt track, every-thing nice and calm. I'm in the second vehicle, sitting in the back, and I'm miles away, thinking about my little boy, Josh – he was just two then – and thinking about what I'm going to get him for Christmas. Something from Hamleys – you know, the big toy shop in London.'

There was no hint of recognition on Belle's face and she looked as though she found this diversion from the narrative annoying.

'Anyway, suddenly there's a bang up ahead. The first Land Rover had taken an RPG ...'

'Oh yeah, er, erm, a prop ... a, prop ...'

'A rocket-propelled grenade.'

'Oh yeah, I've read about them.'

Maybe she had; he had seen her reading some old military hardware magazines that her brother had given her. She had coveted them as though they were religious texts.

'Two of the guys were dead. One of them was a bloke called Jakey from Tyneside. We were quite close. Another guy lost an arm and the rest of them had blast injuries, burns and stuff.'

'You could smell it, yeah?' asked Belle.

Once when he was telling the story, he had mentioned the smell of cordite and burning flesh after the explosion, and ever since then she liked to have this detail included and would remind him if need be.

'That's right, you could smell it,' he said. 'It was disgusting.'

'Yeah, disgusting,' she confirmed. 'Horrible.'

'It was obvious where the RPG had come from. There were some houses off to one side. Someone said they could still see the smoke from the launcher. So we went for it – we could have called in an air strike and flattened the place – but we were so fired up we thought we'd just go straight in.'

'You'd never seen action before, had you?' She was keen to prevent any attempts he might make to abridge the story.

'That's right, and I was scared. I was the first through the door into the house. Everyone was shouting – we were going to kill the bastards – and there was this old woman standing in the doorway to one of the rooms. She was shouting something. I didn't know what it was. I shot her in the chest. She dropped to the floor and didn't move. Then we were in the front room and I just stuck her on automatic . . .'

'You were using an SA80, right?' The type of gun was important to Belle.

'Yeah, that's right.'

'Did 'em up good and proper, yeah?'

She watched him, relishing the story.

'There were about six of them in the room. An old man, a couple of women and some kids. So I'm standing there, firing.'

'Took out the lot of them,' said Belle with satisfaction.

He took a deep breath. The cathartic effect he had hoped for by telling the story had not materialised. If anything, the telling of it had made him feel worse.

'Belle, you know what happens from here on in.' It was a lame attempt to bring the story to a close. Of course she knew what happened and that was why she wanted him to tell her. It was her favourite story.

'Come on, Sim, I want to hear it today. It's important.'

The way she spoke, he could tell that if he refused, she'd become upset. So he continued with the story and told her how he couldn't cope with what he had done, about the investigation that was launched into what was now being described as a massacre; and he told her about the patrol they went on the following day and how he had managed to separate himself from the other men in a street market and had spoken to a local man, a community leader who he had met a few days previously, and how he had pleaded with the man to help him escape.

'Obviously I didn't tell him I was involved in killing that family. I just told him I was sickened by it and couldn't go on. He said he would help me. It wasn't as though I was turning against my country, I was just turning against my country's government. I had seen with my own eyes that what we were doing there was wrong. I had been part of the problem and now I wanted to be part of the solution.'

Simeon didn't expect her to understand – and didn't care whether she did or not. It was just that whenever he told the story he needed to reassure himself that what he had done by deserting was somehow noble and not the behaviour of a man who felt guilt for an atrocity of which he was the primary architect.

As he had told Belle so many times before, his Middle Eastern appearance, inherited from his mother who was Egyptian, made it possible for him to pass himself off as an Afghan and join a group of refugees who were fleeing the country. Once in Pakistan, he managed to make his way through the Middle East, Europe and finally back to the UK.

'I needed to get home. I needed to see my boy. That was all that mattered to me. I didn't really care if they arrested me and put me in prison for what I'd done. I just needed to see my boy first.'

As Simeon looked through the window into the tunnel, he questioned his own motives in prolonging this situation. Why didn't he just shoot Belle and get it over and done with? Perhaps it was because, despite thinking she was a psychopath, there was no getting away from the fact that he found her attractive and it was an attraction that he knew was mutual. There had been a few opportunities in the past to consummate the lust they felt for each other but each time fear had made him draw back. If they had started sleeping together at Madoc Farm, she would have found it impossible to keep it secret and that might have opened him up to reprisals from Tommy. It was much easier to enjoy the flirtation and bide his time. But today was the last day they would ever spend together. He knew what he was meant to do – and he would do it – but the sight of her watching him made him realise that before he killed her he wanted to have her, and if it had to be on a tube train with only a thin door between him and the hundreds of hostages for whom he would soon be a hero, then so be it.

10:17 AM

MI5 Headquarters, Thames House

Howard Berriman shifted in his chair but the movement only intensified the shooting pain down his left leg. So he opened the bottom drawer, reached inside and with practised efficiency popped two more Nurofen from their foil dispenser and tossed them into his mouth, chasing them down his gullet with a mouthful of water from the glass on his desk.

'Headache?' enquired Yates, his assistant.

Berriman had noticed he was making a habit of this, breaking off from whatever it was they were talking about to enquire about medical trivia.

'Bad back, actually. It'll be fine.'

'Trapped nerve?'

'Sciatica.'

'You should see an osteopath,' said Yates. 'A friend of mine could barely walk with back pain and he went to see this chap in Harley Street and he's as right as rain now. I'll find out his details for you, if you like.'

He wished had a pound for every time someone had recommended an osteopath to him. He had seen plenty of osteopaths and plenty of osteopaths had seen him. Didn't do any good.

'That would be great. Thanks. Now what time am I due at Westminster?'

'One o'clock.'

'OK, well I'll catch up with that report from the Met and give you a shout when I'm ready.'

'Right you are,' said Yates, turning to go.

Despite his sometimes irritating little foibles, one thing for which Yates could not be faulted was his intuitive understanding of that tone in his boss's voice which meant that he wanted to be alone. It was a good quality for an assistant to possess. Commendable. Berriman watched him leave the room. Yates was tall, slim and athletic, and moved with a physical grace that never ceased to make Berriman feel inadequate in comparison, waddling about, overweight and hunched on account of his back. What the hell. It said nothing in the rules about the Director General of MI5 having to be a fabulous physical specimen. Good job too.

What he had omitted to tell Yates was that it was highly unlikely he would be going over to Westminster at one o'clock. Not after the news that Mark Hooper had given him earlier, news that had sent his anxiety levels off the scale.

Why didn't Hooper ring back and update him? He had his direct line, a secure line, and he had asked him to call him back in half an hour. That was forty minutes ago. There he was, a fifty-five-year-old man behaving like a teenager waiting for a girlfriend to call.

Come on, ring.

Twenty-eight years in the security service, working his way up through the ranks, respected by colleagues and politicians alike and it had come to this.

Ring, you bastard.

The only voices of dissent that had greeted Howard Berriman's appointment to the top job had come from left-wing elements in the media. Nothing he couldn't handle. That bloke at the *Guardian* had insinuated that he was a government stooge. But what the smart arse didn't realise was that he was locked in an ongoing battle to ensure that government funding for the service was sufficient to enable it to protect the nation. It was a time of war and if people appreciated what lengths the service had to go to to keep them safe, they would not spout off quite so much with their liberal, touchy-feely bollocks. But he could take it. Someone in his position was never going to be universally liked. It was an impossibility.

He couldn't wait any longer. Picking up the telephone, he pressed the speed-dial button for Hooper's mobile.

Hooper answered, said, 'Hi, bear with me a second.' Berriman could hear voices in the background which faded as Hooper clearly moved somewhere more private. 'Sorry about that,' he said in a low voice.

'You said you'd call back in half an hour,' said Berriman, unable to hide his frustration.

'I know, I'm sorry. It was difficult.'

'So is it him?'

'Possibly.'

'What do you mean "possibly"? You must know by now whether it's him or not?'

'Not exactly.'

'Have there been any demands?'

'Nothing, we've had nothing at all through from the train.'

'So it might still be something else?'

'It might be but, let's face it, it's unlikely.'

'Why?'

'We lost radio contact with the two CO19 officers who went into the tunnel.'

Berriman felt a sharp stab of sciatica in his left buttock. Only the weekend before he had congratulated himself on the fact that he had been in the job for all of four months and not once had he lost his 'legendary' temper, as that bastard in the *Guardian* had described it. But that was about to change.

'For Christ's sake, Mark. Are you telling me that he's killing people down there?'

'It's possible.'

'How did this happen? How did we get to this point? What was it you said the other day? "It's as tight as a drum." Well, it doesn't feel that way now, does it?'

'Everything will be fine.'

Berriman could tell from Hooper's tone that he didn't believe what he was saying. He sounded increasingly like a creepy schoolboy whose cunning plan to ingratiate himself with the headmaster had been found wanting.

'Listen, Howard, we don't know anything at the moment.

We don't even know if he's on the train.'

Howard? He was pretty sure that Hooper had never called him by his first name before and he wasn't sure that he liked it. It hinted at a certain level of disrespect.

Hooper continued, 'I'm sure that all Denning wants is his moment in the spotlight and once he's had that then he'll come quietly. He'll spout off with all his delusional shit, then we'll lock him up and no one gets hurt.'

'No one gets hurt?' Berriman gasped the words in a shouted whisper imagining his sciatic nerve as a vicious, blood-red snake writhing and snapping within his vertebrae. 'I'd say it was a bit late for that by the sound of things.'

'But there's no way we can let Mallory and the others know what we know, right?'

Berriman's confidence in Hooper who, up until about two hours ago, he had thought of as a possible future Director General, was beginning to take a severe pounding and he allowed his temper to get the better of him.

'No, of course we fucking can't. This is between you and me. And it'll stay that way. The last thing we need is someone like Mallory screwing everything up.'

'Look, I'm going to have to go,' said Hooper in a strained voice. 'We might have something coming through from the train.'

'Listen, Mark, make sure you keep me up to speed with everything, OK?'

Berriman didn't bother saying goodbye, just hung up and reached into the desk drawer for another Nurofen.

10:19 AM

Northern Line Train 037, rear cab

Belle loved the way he spoke. It was so measured and thoughtful. Of all the times he had told her the story, this was the best telling of all. As of course it had to be. Today of all days. The way he had to whisper too. It sounded intimate. For no one else's ears but hers. He looked so good. So tall and handsome. They would be together for ever. He might not know it yet but she did.

She watched his mouth moving, his soft almost feminine lips and his straight teeth, so white and clean against his skin. She imagined her lips on his, their flesh moving together.

Simeon told her of his time in London. She knew this part of the story off by heart, and she wasn't listening to it so much as admiring its delivery. He lived on the streets after his ex-wife had refused to allow him to see his son. Then he had an epiphany and remembered the name of a place he had once heard about that helped people like him.

'And the rest you know,' he told her and she was back

there – was it only four months ago? – meeting him for the first time at Madoc Farm and him looking at her with that self-same expression he wore now. At that moment she knew there was something between them, some sort of psychic bond.

The walkie-talkie crackled into life and there was her brother's voice from the front cab of the train: 'Belle, can you hear me?'

She put down one of the Glocks, picked up the radio and pressed the 'talk' button.

'Yeah, Tom. We're just talking, me and Sim.'

'Quietly, I hope.'

'Yeah.'

'Everything all right?'

'Good as gold.'

'No one else tried to reach the train?'

'Nope, not since those two earlier.'

'It won't be long now.'

'Absolution, right?'

'That's right, all our sins will be gone for ever.'

'So even if we do bad things today, well, that's all right, isn't it?'

'Whatever we have to do today is what has to be done. Remember that. And our rewards will be in heaven.'

'I love you, Tommy.'

'I love you too. Now let's keep it nice and quiet, and nice and calm. We're nearly there.'

'OK, Tommy.'

Belle put down the walkie-talkie and the other pistol on the top of her holdall. Smiling at Simeon, she stood up and moved towards him.

Surely she could allow herself a moment's sin? Tommy would never know.

He had hoped this moment would come. As she put her hand on the back of his neck and pulled him towards her, her head slightly to one side, he should have said to her, 'Belle, we mustn't.' Better still, he should have taken out his gun and shot her there and then. But two men had died for this. He could have shot her at any time since they had boarded the train. Instead, he had chosen to wait. He hadn't reckoned on her complete moral ambivalence about killing the two men. She seemed to thrive on the violence and, as hard as he tried, he couldn't help but find that attractive. It was so hot down there. As hot as Helmand in the summer. He craved a release from it but, if he was being completely honest with himself, he also craved her. So what if the authorities found out? He would say that it was all part of his covert mission, he could tell them that she had pulled a gun on him or something. It might even enhance his heroism in their eyes.

'Belle, what are you doing? Think of Tommy. Think of the Lord.'

'You heard Tommy on the radio.' She pulled his head closer and he let her. 'He said that whatever we have to do today is what has to be done, and that our rewards will be in heaven.'

Their lips brushed together. 'You know this is not what he meant,' said Simeon. 'If we sin so badly now, we may never make it to heaven.'

Her grip wavered, loosened; immediately Simeon felt regret. His mouth was saying one thing but his body was screaming another. He needn't have worried; whatever thought process had made her doubt the wisdom of her actions, lust had overpowered it and she pressed her lips against his. He would kill her straight afterwards. Maybe he'd snap her neck as he came – or when she did. She'd die happy and he could get on with the task of being a hero. In a few minutes it would all be over. The dark world that he had entered when he walked into Madoc Farm would become a distant memory. But first he needed to do this.

She had imagined this moment so many times. She used to watch him during evening prayers. He was so good-looking. She knew that his praying was a fake but it didn't bother her. Cruor Christi attracted all sorts. She had imagined what it would be like to undress him, run her hands over his muscular body, take him inside her.

When Tommy told her that Simeon was part of End Time, she knew that this was the fulfilment of her destiny, a marriage of sorts. Simeon was different from the rest. He saw something in her – he told her he did – and she loved him with all her heart. And now, they would be together in eternity.

10:23 AM

'This is George Wakeham, driver of train number zero three seven out of Morden to Mill Hill East via Charing Cross.'

The voice from the speaker commanded instant silence in the control room. Ed Mallory spun around in his swivel chair.

'Can someone let me have the handset?' asked Ed, his voice maintaining its even tone. Calvert pressed it into his hand and, depressing the 'talk' button, Ed held it up to his mouth.

'This is Ed Mallory in the Network Control Centre in St James's.'

A short pause before the response came back: 'What's your position?'

'Please repeat the question. My position in terms of?'

'Your job, what's your job?'

There was no point attempting to lie. Ed knew that he needed to initiate a mood of honesty and openness. An untruth at this stage might prove awkward down the line.

He wanted the subject to trust him right from the start.

'I'm a Detective Inspector at Scotland Yard. I'm also a crisis negotiator.'

Ed could just make out a whisper in the background, proving what he suspected, that Wakeham was being told what to say.

'Are you in charge?'

'Am I in charge of what?'

A pause as further instructions were relayed to George Wakeham. 'Are you in charge of dealing with this situation?'

Ed knew there was no point painting himself as merely a single cog in a much larger machine. It was clear that whoever was speaking through George Wakeham wanted to feel that they were communicating with someone at the sharp end.

'At this present moment in time, yes. But can you please clarify exactly what your understanding of this situation is?'

There was a longer pause than before.

'What's your position within the hierarchy of the negotiating team?'

It was not the sort of question one would expect from a train driver who was experiencing technical difficulties with his train.

'There is no negotiating team, George. Should there be?'

A pause, then: 'Yes.'

Ed felt the muscles in his abdomen tighten. He knew the answer to the question before he asked it but asked it anyway: 'Can I ask, are you being told what to say by someone else?'

'The two men you sent down here to retake the train are dead.'

Ed's stomach muscles were wound tighter still. Calvert muttered, 'Oh Jesus,' under his breath.

Ed knew that pushing his line of questioning might be dangerous but he decided to try one more question as to the authorship of the words he was hearing.

'OK, George, would it be possible to speak to the person who's telling you what to say?' A long pause this time. 'George?'

'Be aware that any further attempt to make physical contact with the train will result in dire consequences for the passengers. The carriages have been rigged with high explosives which will be detonated if anyone is seen in the tunnel or any physical contact is made with the train.'

'George, please ask the person you're with to speak to me directly.'

As the seconds ticked away, Ed knew he was not going to get a response.

'George?' he said but he was talking to himself.

10:28 AM

Northern Line Train 037

The temperature in central London was ninety-two degrees Fahrenheit, making it the hottest day of the year so far. This information would feature in many morning news bulletins but only as a secondary item after the lead story that the entire London Underground network was closed due to a security alert and a section of the West End had been evacuated.

News crews and outside broadcast units were scrambled to points in front of the police lines on the outer perimeter of the evacuation area. No statement had been issued by police, which aroused much speculation in the media, fuelled by the presence of bio-chemical units at the evacuation sites, that London was under threat from a 'dirty bomb'. Other news sources reported that the Underground network closure and evacuation in the West End were due to a tube train being hijacked.

With so few hard facts to report, news crews were forced to interview members of the public who had witnessed the massive police deployment. A no-fly zone was put in place over central London, the only aircraft allowed over the West End being police helicopters hovering low over Charing Cross Road and providing a mechanical thrum to the soundtracks of the outside broadcasts from the scene.

On the MI5 website the security threat level had been raised to critical, a fact that did not go unnoticed by the media, although no accompanying explanation was given. Everything pointed to the government and security services being caught unawares by a threat about which they had no foreknowledge. They were having to react as swiftly as possible to events as they unfolded on the ground.

On the train, the temperature was a little over a hundred and four degrees. Eleven passengers had succumbed to heat exhaustion and dehydration and were receiving treatment from other passengers with medical training. The apparent mood amongst many passengers was one of anger – many spoke of London Underground's lack of regard for the health and safety of its customers – but all were afraid. For over an hour and a half they had been stationary in the tunnel. Whatever was going on, it was serious.

In the sixth carriage consumer affairs columnist, Hugh Taylor, was convinced he could hear voices from the rear cab of the train. But for the time being he decided to stay quiet about it. He had managed to keep a lid on his panic now for over twenty minutes. An attempt to meditate for the first time since he had gone backpacking around Asia over thirty years before had seemed to do some good. The voices he heard could be his paranoia playing tricks on him, and even if he could hear voices they probably belonged to the engineers that the driver had said were in the tunnel.

In the second carriage, a man in his mid-thirties with no history of heart problems was complaining of shooting pains in his chest and was being made comfortable on the floor of the carriage by a porter from Guy's Hospital.

Empty water bottles and lunchboxes were used to urinate in. People stood in the corners of carriages and shielded one another. Two adults and four children on the train had by now soiled themselves.

In the first carriage a Greek woman who ran a restaurant in Brighton and was visiting London to meet an old friend from school decided that she wanted to speak to the driver. It was at least fifteen minutes since his last announcement that they would be evacuated from the train imminently and she wanted to find out what was going on. She banged on the door to the front cab.

'Driver!' she shouted. 'Open the door! Driver!'

George Wakeham was heartened by the sounds of potential insurrection from the other side of the bulkhead. Denning told him to make another announcement.

'This time, George, sound a bit more convincing, will you? Sound heartfelt. Tell them you're doing all that you can. Don't worry, they'll believe you. They still have no reason not to. And get the woman on the other side of the door to shut her mouth while you're at it.'

George picked up the handset.

'This is George, the driver, again. I'm really sorry about this extended delay. I've spoken to the controller and I've been assured that we will have you out of here soon.'

If he was a hero, he would tell them the truth; he would quickly tell them that the train had been hijacked and they should try and escape. Some of them would manage it. Their sheer weight of numbers would make it a mathematical certainty. But George was not a hero, not in his own mind. All he wanted was to see his wife and children again and he would do nothing to jeopardise that.

'I'm really, really sorry about this, everyone, I've been assured that we're being kept here for safety reasons. I realise that it's incredibly hot and stuffy but I'm being advised that we have to stay put. So please just sit tight and I'll keep you posted. Oh and to the lady who keeps banging on the door here and shouting: can you please stop because it's giving me a headache?'

'I like it,' said Denning as George replaced the handset. 'You're getting better at this.' Denning's amused little smile, the wry curl of his top lip, was really beginning to bug George. He had never thought of himself as a violent man but how he longed to banish Denning's smile by driving his fist into it.

'Can I ask you a question?' said George.

'Looks like you just did.'

'Why are you drawing this out? Why not just do whatever it is that you've come here to do?'

At least the question put a stop to the smile.

'Don't you know anything about theatre? Performers

don't just walk on stage as soon as the audience arrives. That's not how it works. You have to build up the audience's expectation; you have to let them get high on the anticipation of your performance. You have to make them wait. It's all about showbusiness. Before Adolf Hitler arrived at his rallies, he kept the crowds waiting and then finally he would arrive by helicopter. He literally came down from the sky. That's powerful symbolism. Don't get me wrong, I'm not a fan or anything, but the man knew a thing or two about how to make an entrance. And, anyway, I'm waiting for the media to "set up" as the expression goes. I don't want anybody to miss anything and it's barely even breakfast time in New York.'

George felt like asking him, if Hitler's symbolism was that he came from the sky, what was Denning's? Emerging from underground – was his symbolism that he came from the sewers?

It seemed to George as though Denning was becoming more confident as time went by, as though he was feeding off the power that the situation had given him and drawing strength from it.

'Now I want you to get on the line to that Ed Mallory bloke and tell him that you've got the first of your demands.'

'*My* demands?'

'You know what I mean.'

'And what is my first demand?'

'You can tell him that I want a wireless router installed in the mouth of the tunnel at Leicester Square station so that the entire train will have access to the internet. There must be no passwords required, nothing. It must be internet for all. I want everyone on this train connected to their loved ones. I'll give them until eleven-thirty to put it in place and then I'll start killing the passengers, one for every minute I'm kept waiting over the deadline, in the accepted Hollywood manner.'

10:41 AM

Network Control Centre, St James's

'George, you need to ask the person you're with to speak to me directly otherwise we're not going to be able to sort this out.'

'That's not possible. You need to put the router in place by exactly eleven-thirty, at the latest, otherwise the passengers start to die.'

'I can't promise that I can do that. I have to speak to the powers-that-be. I'm not sure if it's even feasible, technically speaking.'

'It is and it needs to be open access. Any attempt to limit the signal in any way will be taken as a failure to comply and the passengers will start to die at a rate of one a minute.'

'George.' Ed lowered his voice to make it sound as conspiratorial as possible, knowing full well that whoever was with him would be listening in. 'You need to tell the person you're with that it's extremely unlikely that I'm going to be able to fulfil their request. Getting a makeshift Wi-Fi signal along the tunnel to the train is going to be difficult. If I can speak to this person directly then it's more likely that I can find out exactly what it is that they want and I can set about trying to do what I can to help.'

It was all bluster, anything to get the subject on the line. Ed knew that his confidence would be boosted immeasurably if he could hear a voice, hear the words and their delivery. Without them, there was no way that he could build up a profile, no way to deconstruct the perpetrator's personality and start working on him.

'You've got until eleven-thirty and then someone dies.'

'George?'

It was too late. Ed was talking to a dead line. He took off the headset and put it down on the desk. He rubbed his hand across his face, his fingers sliding across the ridges of scar tissue.

'Ed, this is Laura Massey,' said Calvert. 'She's going to be the negotiating cell's co-ordinator.'

Ed was pleased it was Laura. They had worked together once before on a siege in the East End. Four days they had spent together, locked up with the rest of the negotiating team in a council high rise, trying to talk down a crack-addled father of seven who had taken his wife hostage after finding out that she had been having an affair with his brother for the past five years. It was a gruelling negotiation but he had found Laura to be fiercely professional and also human. In addition to her skills at running a successful negotiating command centre, she was also an excellent negotiator in her own right.

Ed held out his hand and Laura shook it. Her hand felt

soft and dry. She didn't wear perfume, her aroma came from a combination of deodorant and moisturiser. Ed liked it.

'Hi, Laura. Are we going for a standard cell?'

'Yes, Ed, you're the number one, Calvert and White here are numbers two and three respectively.'

'I understand we're staying here for the time being,' said Ed.

'That's right, we can set up the console and plug it straight into the London Underground system so we can have direct access to the radio in the driver's cab on the train. We'll look at moving to the stronghold later on if we need to.'

'Presumably Serina Boise is Incident Commander.'

'That's right. She wanted me to reiterate to you that MI5 must be kept in the loop on everything.'

'Yeah, right.' Ed didn't care if his displeasure at this was apparent to Mark Hooper, who was standing nearby, or to anyone for that matter. There was no point wasting time thinking about it but conversely there was no getting away from the fact that the constant affirmation of MI5's involvement was just plain odd.

'Any news on the Wi-Fi?' asked Ed.

'They'll have to employ some heavy-duty hardware to get the signal far enough into the tunnel to reach the train. But it should be possible.'

'Good,' said Ed. 'We'll turn it on just after the deadline has passed. I realise we've got hundreds of people down there in extreme conditions but we must still play for time. The normal rules apply. We slow this thing down. There's no rush. We've got all the time in the world.'

'And what happens when they've got internet access down there?' asked Hooper.

'Well, unless we can restrict it in some way, then they go live to the world. With just a shop-bought laptop, they can broadcast sound and vision anywhere they like. They've got their very own reality TV programme.'

'That can't be a good thing,' said Hooper. He said it in such a way that it felt to Ed as though he was taking this situation personally, as though it made him resentful in some way.

'What's the alternative?' asked Ed.

'Well, we have no control over the internet. Signals can be made; messages sent to accomplices.'

'It's a risk we're going to have to take for the time being. It could even work in our favour. They'll have a communication link but so will we. We should find out the identity of as many passengers as possible. You never know, we might find there is a person – or persons – who has the knowledge and expertise to launch a counter-attack from within the train. Failing that, we should still be able to harvest valuable intelligence. The passengers can act as our eyes and ears. Just as much as the hijackers want to use the internet to broadcast their message, we can use it against them. We need to have GCHQ analysing all communications, every single word that is spoken in a conversation, every email. We must be constantly updated on everything going into and out of that train.'

'I'm still not sure.' Hooper again.

'We have no alternative,' said Ed. 'If what we are being told is true, they've already killed two men. And anyway, the Wi-Fi also provides us with bargaining collateral. We give them that then ask for something in return. What do people think?'

'Children out?' Hooper suggested.

'We'll try if we get the chance but I have a feeling we won't succeed.'

'Why not?' asked White.

'If they want to freak us out, which is what I think is going on here, then keeping the kids in there is going to do just that.'

Over the years, Ed had tried to condition himself to think that the number of hostages in any given situation was immaterial. But it was difficult. A big number was always scary. Like the RAF Brize Norton hijack of 2003 in which a squaddie on his way to Iraq for Operation Iraqi Freedom kept sixty-four fellow troops and crew hostage for a day and a half, threatening to blow himself and the plane up with a couple of hand grenades. It never made the news. The authorities wanted it that way but it didn't make it any less stressful. When Ed had managed to talk down the squaddie – a nineteen-year-old with mental health problems – it was an achievement for which he felt some pride. Although that pride had soon turned to frustration when the Gold Commander on the incident had suggested that it was his blindness that had provided him with his abilities, as though anyone who was blind would be able to resolve an extremely complex hostage situation.

He'd always been good at listening to people. It was instinctive. Even as a young child, he seemed to have a natural understanding of people's moods and feelings. He had an aunt, his father's sister, and it was clear to Ed that she was troubled. Others didn't seem to see it. He didn't mention anything to his parents. How could he? He was a child. But his suspicions were confirmed when she had a nervous breakdown and was admitted to a psychiatric hospital from where she never returned to normal society. But whenever he visited her – and sadly it wasn't often – the nurses would tell him that it was in his company that she was at her most calm and contented. It was this natural ability to communicate with people and make them feel comfortable that had proved a crucial asset in his professional life. And it wasn't just with hostages on the other end of a phone line. It didn't matter who it was: he had the ability to put people at their ease. It was as though he didn't have an agenda. And maybe that was because he didn't, not at the moment that he was speaking to someone. He could focus on another person's point of view; he could empathise. Other hostage negotiators he had come across – most of them – never allowed the purpose of the hostage negotiation to slip into the background. It was always there, like the elephant in the room. But Ed could create a relationship with a subject and even if only momentarily, the subject could forget about their often desperate life-or-death situation. With one subject in a crisis situation in Nigeria, he had discussed Manchester United's UEFA Cup chances. 'Keeping the channels open,' he had heard it called by psychologists. This skill, whatever it might be called, could not be taught. Ed had it – had always had it – and it helped.

But everything that had gone before in his career now paled into insignificance. He was faced with a gang of terrorists of an indeterminate number with hundreds of hostages and no apparent motive other than a desire to achieve communication with the outside world. It was this desire for communication, however, that gave Ed some hope. If they wanted to harm the passengers, they would have done so already. It appeared that what they really wanted was media exposure and once they had that, it was possible they would let the passengers go. He could exert control over them by threatening to cut off the communication. The apparent enormity of the hijack and the potential loss of life might just be a smokescreen for something else; and if he allowed his optimism to have free rein then maybe the two CO19 guys were not dead either. Perhaps they were being held hostage and their demise being reported only as a means to give the impression that the hijack was a deadly serious venture. The thought that this might just be some sort of crazy publicity stunt allowed Ed comfort. Misguided theatrics he could deal with. It was terrorism that made him nervous.

11:02 AM

Northern Line Train 037, sixth carriage

Despite the intense heat, Hugh still had his sports jacket on. Maggie couldn't decide whether she wanted him to suffer another panic attack or not. Part of her wanted something – anything – to happen, a situation to develop that would force the truth on her fellow hostages, make them realise that they *were* hostages. Another part of her, however, wanted nothing, least of all some loose cannon jeopardising whatever chance she still had of seeing her family again.

Why them? The question came to her once more. Of all the train drivers who worked for London Underground, what twisted confluence in the random streams of chance had led these people to their door?

Whatever thoughts she could muster that were not concerned with Sophie and Ben, and where they might be and what might be happening to them, were a welcome relief from the crushing despair. When they had told her that she was to be separated from the children, she had tried to scream and shout out to passers-by – they were in the street at the time – but the Asian man had put his hand over her mouth and told her that if she continued to shout he would personally kill the children himself. She hadn't seen the other man – the white man with the shaven head – or Sophie or Ben after that. She fired questions at the man and woman who accompanied her into the tube station but all she was told was that the more questions she asked and the more protestations that she came out with the worse it would be for her.

'If you don't shut up, we'll kill them.' The woman had said it a couple of times. By the time they were on the train and the two hijackers had gone into the rear cab, Maggie knew she had to keep quiet, play dead, until such time as she could work out if there was anything she could do.

Hugh was on his feet again. He looked across at Adam opposite, as though willing him to calm him down like he had done the previous time.

'There are people in there having sex.' Hugh gestured at the door to the rear cab. 'They're in there screwing. Can't you hear them?'

Maggie had heard them; Adam must have heard them too. They weren't loud, but it was unmistakable, the meaty rhythm, the breathing and the muted gasps.

Adam stood up. 'It's OK, mate. It's all right.' He placed his hand on Hugh's shoulder but before his attempts to soothe could take effect, Hugh had broken free of his grasp and taken a run at the door to the rear cab, charging at it with his briefcase held up in front of him like a battering ram. The case crashed against the rear door and as it did so, he started to shout, 'I can hear you. Stop it! Open the fucking door!'

His leg was pressed against Maggie's and she could feel him trembling through his trousers. Adam was close behind him: 'It's all right, mate, calm down.' But Hugh managed to take another swing at the door with his brief-case before Adam could restrain him.

11:07 AM

Northern Line Train 037, rear cab

On the other side of the door, Simeon and Belle heard the commotion but as they were both reaching orgasm at that moment, it was all they could do to refrain from crying out. Sweat came off them as though they were in a sauna. Belle relished the feeling of their bodily juices co-mingling. It felt as though they were both made of liquid. It might have been the forbidden nature of the situation, it might have been because it was today of all days but Belle was certain that she had never experienced an orgasm as intense as that before. She leant up and pressed her lips against Simeon's, her tongue writhing against his. She wanted to savour this feeling. He placed his hands around her neck. His thumbs dug into the flesh; she loved his strength. He was still hard and he pushed himself into her one final time before their hungry grinding came to an end.

'I knew this would happen,' she said. Simeon still had his hands around her neck. He stared into her eyes. She said, 'I love you Simeon.' There was a strange intensity to his gaze. His fingers dug into her flesh. She adored his physical strength. It felt as though he could crush the life out of her in a moment. She placed her hands on his and whispered, 'We can do it again before, you know ... But maybe now we should make ourselves known to the people on the train.' He let her pull his hands from her throat and she placed them on her breasts as she told him again, 'I love you Simeon.'

Dressing was difficult, the slick on their bodies made their clothes stick to them. She kissed him again before she picked up the walkie-talkie, raised it to her mouth and pressed the 'speak' button: 'Tommy? Can you hear me?'

The walkie-talkie crackled into life: 'Hi, Belle, what's happening?'

'The passengers are getting uppity. Shall I give them a scare?'

'Hold on for the time being,' said Tommy. 'I'll get the driver to make the announcement.'

Should he kill her now? Now would be as good a time as any, before anyone actually got hurt, before she could 'give them a scare'. He would give her a double tap – two from the Browning 9mm – into that pretty face. She wouldn't be giving anyone a scare after that. Then he would release the passengers and prepare for his debriefing. But the fear kept nagging away at him. Why had they gone a week early? Who was to blame for this? Or, more importantly, who would they choose to blame for this? He should shoot her straight away, get it over and done with. He had had his fun. It was one of the most intense sexual experiences he had ever had. That was part of the problem he now faced. He knew he must kill her and put a stop to the madness but he also wanted to repeat the pleasure of lifting her up, pulling her legs around him and relishing that sweet, runny feeling of having her slide down upon him. Could he not do both?

'It's going to get good now.' Raising the two Glocks, she aimed them at him. 'Pow! Pow!' she said and giggled.

There was a faint hum from the public address system before the driver said: 'Right, I've got some good news and I've got some bad news. The bad news is that the power to the train has slumped so we can't proceed to Tottenham Court Road under our own steam, but the good news is that I've just had word that we're going to be towed out of the tunnel by another train which is going to be with us in a moment. Now, as a safety procedure, I'm afraid I need all those passengers in the first and last carriages to move down towards the centre of the train because we need to evacuate them. I repeat, passengers need to evacuate the first and the sixth carriages and move towards the middle of the train.'

On the other side of the door Simeon could hear movement. People were doing as they were told. But the man continued to shout despite the voices attempting to placate him. 'Open the fucking door,' he kept shouting. There was a scuffle. It sounded like he was being restrained. Simeon watched Belle. She was excited, like a child waiting to go on a scary fairground ride. The thought of killing her didn't bother him. He could live with it. Any pangs he might feel as he shot her would be as nothing to what he felt after he had killed the family in Helmand. Having sex with her again before he dispatched her was greedy, lustful. There would be other women, other times, other places. He had to do what he had come here to do. She might fuck like a porn star but she was also a murderer. Scum. He reached into his pocket and his fingers closed around the grip of the Browning. He clicked off the safety catch and watched her as she said, 'I'm going to enjoy this.' She was intoxicated with the thought of shooting more people. Aside maybe from her brother, she was the sickest person he had ever met. Whatever childhood she might have had to endure, however much her mind might have been screwed up by religion, there was no excuse for this. She had to die. There was no alternative. Now was the time to bring all this to an end. He had the Browning out of his pocket in one fluid motion and placed the barrel only inches from her face.

'I'm sorry, Belle.' He waited perhaps half a second while she turned to look at him, not enough time to allow her to raise up one of the Glocks, but enough time for him to see the flash of realisation on her face that she was about to die. But it never came. She just stared back at the gun impassively. What the hell. He pulled the trigger. Two squeezes one after the other – a double tap – two clicks, metallic, inert, dead. Instead of the slurry of brain matter on the wall of the cab and the slumping body with that facial expression – that strange gasping expression that people wear as they die – there was silence as Belle continued to study him. He squeezed the trigger again, twice. But there were two more mute clicks.

'I don't know, Simeon. We have beautiful sex together and then you go and try and shoot me in the face. You really don't know how to treat a lady.'

Simeon frantically pulled the trigger over and over but Belle had a Glock in her right hand and pointed it at him. 'I knew you'd feel the weight difference if I just left it empty so I disarmed the bullets myself.'

When MI5 had come knocking after his return to the UK, he had had a bad feeling about the mission that he'd been assigned. But he couldn't turn them down, not a man in his position.

'Come on, Belle, I'm just messing with you.' It sounded pathetic and he knew it wouldn't work. He knew she knew, and as though to confirm it, she said, 'You're a terrible actor, Sim. Me and Tommy knew about you all along.'

She was glad she didn't have to use the Pulveriser – the Heckler & Koch PSG1 sniper's rifle with the dum-dum bullets. She didn't want to make a mess. Not that she would ever have shot him in the face. She needed his face. So she shot him in the heart. Twice. Double tap, just as Tommy had told her. Simeon slumped back against the driver's console and then down onto the floor of the cab, staring into her eyes all the while just as she had hoped he would.

'It's all right, Sim, I know you can't talk right now,' – the air was leaving his lungs in a long sigh – 'but we'll

be together again soon enough. Wait for me and before
you know it, I'll be there with you.'

When he stopped blinking and his final breath petered
out into a gurgle, she bent down to him and kissed him
on the lips. They were still warm, still sensual and alive,
at least for a few moments more. She forced her tongue
into his mouth and tasted him as he died.

Today kept getting better and better, just as Tommy had
promised. Today was the day she could do whatever she
wanted. She put down the Glocks, picked up the Pulveriser
and checked it over before she opened the door to the
carriage.

11:11 AM

The flow of passengers from the sixth carriage into the fifth was stemmed by a group of men coming in the opposite direction. Hugh Taylor was not the only passenger at the rear of the train who thought that the information they were being given by the driver was suspect. Coming through the door from the fifth carriage was a group of five men who'd got talking. They'd had nothing else to do for the last two hours. Potential interpretations of the information they were getting from the driver had been analysed and processed. Their suspicions had been aroused. They saw no reason for evacuating the sixth carriage. Why, if the train was going to be towed to Tottenham Court Road station, would they need to evacuate the first and last carriages of the train? It made no sense. They were coming to sort things out. No one was going to stop them. They were professionals. Two were in IT, one was a metals trader. One was on garden leave from an insurance broker's prior to joining another one. One was studying for a MBA at a private American college in London.

The driver was clearly deluded or incompetent. He should be telling the authorities to get the passengers off the train before someone was taken ill. It was time to take matters into their own hands. There was no point fighting their way through the train to the driver's cab. They would just go to the sixth carriage, open the door and make their way into the rear cab and from there down onto the track and off down the tunnel, making sure to avoid the live rails as they went. They had missed meetings; their schedules were all messed up. But problem-solving was a key component of their busy lives. They found it challenging. They were born to it. There were five of them. Five men varying in age between twenty-seven – the MBA student – to fifty – the insurance broker. Their collective endeavour had provided them with an official air. Some of the passengers they asked to stand aside to make way for them found this reassuring. These men were here to help.

At the other end of the carriage Adam was trying to pull Hugh away from the door when there were two loud bangs from behind the door to the rear cab. They didn't register with Hugh and Adam, so absorbed were they in their difference of opinion.

'I'm going to carry you, if you don't move now,' said Adam.

'Don't fucking touch me,' shouted Hugh. 'They're lying to us. Can't you see that? It's all bullshit.'

Adam had decided to try and carry Hugh in a fireman's lift into the fifth carriage. If he tackled him hard enough

– jabbed his shoulder into his solar plexus as he did so – he might wind him enough to prevent him struggling until they were safely there.

As Adam bent down to carry out this manoeuvre, two things happened, one closely followed by the other. Firstly, the five men from the fourth carriage arrived at the door to the rear cab. Pumped up by the zeal and fervour of their mission, they were about to explain their intentions when the second event unfolded.

The door to the rear cab was opened and in the doorway stood a pretty young woman holding a gun, an automatic rifle. To Hugh, this was unequivocal proof of his worst fears and suspicions. The five men were momentarily paralysed by the sight of the armed woman. It looked so incongruous, almost as though she were an actress in an alternative theatre production, in which the players mingled with the audience. The men were expecting London Underground bureaucracy; they were ready to puncture the petty laws of health and safety in order to get on with their busy lives. They were not expecting an attractive woman with a gun.

Even as she turned the muzzle of the rifle towards them, it felt as though it was some sort of elaborate hoax, play-acting, make-believe. A smile began to form on her lips. Two of the men in the group of five found themselves smiling back. She was good looking after all. She looked great in her tight vest and black combat pants.

Shooting from the hip, she opened fire.

The sound the gun made was like a series of muffled thuds, as if the entire carriage was being squeezed in the tunnel. It was as though a piledriver was hammering chunks of flesh from bodies. Blood sprayed from gaping wounds. The five men on their mission were cut apart by the exploding lead, which tore through one body and into another. By the time the shooting stopped, of the seven men who had been crowded around the door, six of them were on the floor of the carriage. Five of them were dead or dying and one of them, Adam, was beginning to scream. His left leg was severed at the knee. His lower leg – what remained of it – had skidded in its own bloody lubricant along the floor of the carriage.

'Now move,' shouted the woman in the doorway. She looked straight at Hugh and for a moment, as colours danced across his field of vision, he thought he might pass out. She raised the gun, pointed it at him and with Adam's screams reverberating around the carriage, he turned around. As he did so, he reached down – it was an instinctive action – and he grabbed hold of Adam's arm and started to drag him along the carriage through his own blood and over what remained of his lower leg towards the door to the next carriage.

11:13 AM

Network Control Centre, St James's

Who was he? What did he want? Presuming that it was a he. The few whispered words that Ed had heard over the radio from the train sounded as though they were spoken by a man. His motivation had to be terrorism. He was employing terror as a tactic in a negotiation. By anyone's definition he was a terrorist. He hadn't put a foot wrong so far. His planning and reconnaissance were meticulous. He had accomplices, which hinted at a common cause. At this moment in time he had the upper hand.

Ed listened to the setting up of the makeshift negotiating cell all around him. The voice of Laura, the cell's co-ordinator, was a constant as she ensured that everyone in the room had what they needed. Ed had asked for fans and air conditioning. The heat was intense and, due to his heightened heart rate, he was feeling it more than he might otherwise have done. Excessive sweat had a tendency to irritate the scar tissue on his face.

'Ed, I've got Howard Berriman for you,' said Mark Hooper.

His voice was devoid of its earlier surfeit of emotion; it was subdued as though attempting a sort of intimacy. Ed had managed to compartmentalise his concerns regarding the involvement of MI5 in the negotiation but this development dragged it into his conscious thoughts once more. What did Howard Berriman want with him? It would have been understandable if he had wanted to speak with the Incident Commander, Serina Boise, but why would he want to speak to the number one negotiator? Ed didn't have the time to ponder on this before a BlackBerry was pressed into his hand.

'This is Ed Mallory.'

'Hi, Ed. This is Howard Berriman.'

'Hi. What can I do for you?'

'You're no doubt aware that we're involved in this?'

'Everyone seems to want me to know that.'

'I'm sorry if it's creating any problems, it's just we've had some recent intelligence.'

'Anything that you want to share with us?'

'It's nothing that's going to help you with any ongoing negotiation so it's probably not worth discussing at this stage.'

'You're sure about that?' Ed didn't care if he sounded difficult. There was no reason for this heavy-handedness from MI5 and he didn't like the way that Scotland Yard and his superiors appeared to be grovelling. If he was going to attempt to talk to the perpetrators of this scenario and try to find a solution then he could do without the politics.

'It's nothing that's going to help you in any way, but I wanted to get an update from you personally as I know you've been speaking to the driver of the train. What's the current situation?'

Standard negotiation protocol was being bulldozed on all sides. This was a bizarre situation by anyone's estimation but this added layer of weirdness compounded it.

'The driver's just been on the radio issuing statements from an unknown party. He says the two CO19 officers we sent into the tunnel are dead and if anyone else approaches the train, explosives will be detonated. A demand has also been made for Wi-Fi access to the train with an accompanying threat to kill passengers if it's not in place by 11:30 am. But I'm guessing you know all this.'

'And still no demands other than the wireless connection?'

There was no reason why Berriman would need to get this information from Ed but he played along with the charade. 'No, no demands as yet other than we keep away from the train.'

'And you think that allowing them Wi-Fi is a good idea?'

'It works in our favour as much as theirs. We can gather intel from the passengers and possibly initiate their mobilisation if required.'

'Do you think it might be al-Qaeda?'

'It's not exactly their MO.'

'Home-grown crazies like 7/7?'

'Could be – it's too early to say.'

'Listen, Ed,' said Berriman. 'I realise that the last thing you need at this stage is further pressure but I want to ask that, either directly or through Mark Hooper, you keep me informed of what is occurring at all times. We cannot allow anything to happen to the people on the train. Whoever it is who is holding them, we cannot allow them to threaten our freedoms.' Berriman sounded like he was rehearsing a sound bite.

'Right you are, Howard,' said Ed.

'I'm told you're the best negotiator we've got.'

'I couldn't possibly comment on that,' said Ed with enough mock seriousness to make Berriman chuckle.

'Bye, Ed.'

Ed's day was getting stranger. Now he had the head of MI5 phoning him up and treating him as though he was going to be on his Christmas card list. There was no apparent reason for it. Berriman's and Hooper's motives were difficult to read but they both clearly had an agenda. Of that there was no doubt. But Ed had more important things to think about. As a blind man, he couldn't be provided with relevant research and intel in written form and it would take too long to have the material transcribed into Braille. So all he could do was ask questions. A lot of questions.

'What sort of exclusion zone have we got around the stronghold?'

It was Nick Calvert, now Ed's operational number two, who answered. 'We've got two inner perimeters containing Tottenham Court Road and Leicester Square tube stations and then the outer perimeter takes in an area that extends approximately one hundred yards either side of Charing Cross Road and an area of the same distance radius around each respective station. The evacuation is now complete and there is an SAS unit on standby at each station.'

'Is Laura here?'

'Yes, Ed.'

'What's the situation with comms from the stronghold?'

'We're trying to get visual and audio from the tunnel but everyone's jumpy after what happened with CO19 earlier.'

'Do we have a rapid intervention plan in place?'

'They're working on it,' she replied. 'You know they like to work on a simulation first before attempting anything real world so it might take some time. Boise will be speaking to the relevant co-ordinator.'

Whereas at other times and in other places, special forces back-up might have made Ed feel reassured, now it gave him little comfort.

11:15 AM

Northern Line Train 037, first carriage

Terror follows no rules. It is anarchy, pure and simple. No one knows how they will react to it. Aside from a small number of specialist military personnel – a minute fraction of the population – no one is trained to deal with it. Scientific studies – other than those that deal with purely physiological manifestations of terror such as the secretion of pheromones – are pointless. Terror is impossible to simulate, roleplay is ineffective. Nothing can re-create terror other than terror itself. The passengers on train 037 out of Morden – the adults at least – felt terror. It passed along the length of the four carriages in which they were now gathered like an electrical charge.

This was news transmission in its most basic human form – word of mouth – and all the more horrific for its immediacy. There had been shooting in the rear carriage of the train. Men had been killed. The train had been taken by terrorists. They were hostages, victims of a hijack.

Some prayed to their gods; others cursed them. Some

became silent, withdrawn; others talked, ranted, pleaded, wept.

By the time the news swept through the train to the second carriage, which now contained the evacuees from the first carriage, a collective escape impulse was activated in the passengers. But before this could become a coherent surge back along the empty first carriage, the door to the cab was thrown open and a slim man in his twenties, Tommy Denning – Brother Thomas of Cruor Christi – stepped through it and walked purposefully between the empty seats to the adjoining doors to the second carriage. In his hand was an automatic pistol with a silencer attachment.

A markets analyst, newly married – a really decent man – as the newspapers would subsequently describe him, was not alone in thinking that Tommy Denning was someone official, a member of special forces perhaps who had stormed the train and would now set about securing the passengers' release.

As the one nearest to Denning, he took it upon himself to speak to him, asking, 'What the hell's going on?' Denning raised the Browning automatic and shot him straight through the forehead, leaving a small perfectly round entrance wound in the middle of his well-moisturised skin, a neat wound in comparison to the gaping butchery of the exit wound, which distributed skull and brain matter across a wide radius of passengers. The screaming started as the man slumped to the floor and a tide of bodies recoiled from the horror.

Denning slammed the two doors shut between the carriages and, taking a chain from his pocket, looped it around both handles and pulled it tight before securing it with a padlock just as he knew that Belle had done on the doors between the fifth and sixth carriages at the other end of the train. George was in the cab. He could make a run for it. He could open the door in the front of the train and set off down the track. Denning knew that, but he also knew that George wouldn't try it.

'Remember, George,' he had said to him before he left the cab, 'if I don't achieve what I've come here to do, then you'll never see your family again. So it's up to you.' It wasn't necessary to say any more than that. Denning knew he would behave himself, and if he didn't then Denning would shoot him. It wasn't as though he was important any more. Although Tommy had to admit that he rather liked having someone speak for him, issue his demands. He liked the power.

'George,' he shouted along the carriage, but the hubbub of voices – the shouts and screams – made it inaudible. 'George!' he shouted louder this time and got a response.

'Yes.'

'Make the announcement to the passengers, just like I told you.'

Tommy Denning turned back to the adjoining doors between the carriages. The man he had shot lay in an expanding pool of blood. Other passengers cowered further along the carriage. For a moment, Tommy thought he might shoot another one. Just for effect. But the moment passed. This wasn't about senseless murder.

The PA hummed and there was George's voice. Good old George. He was glad it was George, someone spiritually empty. It made it easier somehow.

'This is George, the driver. As some of you may have realised by now, I've been lying to you. The train has been hijacked by an armed gang and wired with explosives. But so long as everyone remains calm and makes no attempt to interfere with the hijackers then no one will be harmed. I've been told to tell you that anybody – including women and children – who attempts to escape will be killed. In the event of a sustained escape attempt, explosives will be detonated.'

'OK, that's enough,' said Denning. He didn't need to shout, the people on the train were quiet as George switched off the PA. He knew that the passengers wouldn't remain quiet for long. But for the time being they were cowed by the knowledge that their lives were in danger. Their self-survival instincts were being activated as they processed the unsettling news.

Denning walked back along the first carriage towards the cab.

'Come on, George,' he said as he stepped into the cab and slammed the door behind him. 'We need to take a walk.'

George watched Denning, whose excitement was almost childlike. But he didn't seem to be mad, or psychopathic, or suffering from anything that would compel him to hijack a tube train for no apparent reason. And now he wanted to go for a walk in the tunnel. What could that mean? Was Denning going to kill him? If so, why not kill him here? Denning pulled a package from his canvas bag, opened the door in the front of the cab and gestured for George to go first.

George climbed down from the cab, making sure not to stand on the trainee driver, who was lying where Denning had let him fall, his lifeless eyes staring up at the roof of the tunnel. George had never been in a tube tunnel outside a train before. Only scant light was thrown from the cab and, as he stared into the darkness up ahead, he wondered if there was anyone there, watching them, lining up their rifle scopes. Denning must have been thinking the same because he made George walk in front. They didn't go far, ten yards at the most. Denning flashed on a torch and shone it at the wall. He found what he was looking for, a set of flimsy metal steps up the side of the curved wall, which disappeared inside a hole in the ceiling about two feet in diameter.

'You stay here. I'll hear you if you try and make a run for it. We're friends now, so don't make me kill you.'

Denning looked at him and smiled, like a boy who has watched some violent gangster movie that he shouldn't have and wants to act out the dialogue for the benefit of a friend. But behind the juvenile posturing there was a violent unpredictable energy.

'OK?'

George returned Denning's stare and nodded.

With the agility and precision of a gymnast, Denning

was up the ladder and swallowed by the narrow hole. His ascent was accompanied by the creaking of the old metal struts. George looked up the tunnel and then back at the train. Whatever escape plan he could conjure up, he knew he wouldn't put it into practice. He had to believe that what Denning had told him was true, that if he did exactly as he was told then he would see his family again. He had to cling to that. Without it, he knew he would go to pieces. Just like it sounded some passengers on the train were doing. There were loud voices, most of them male. One man was shouting something that sounded like a biblical incantation, a prayer perhaps, and another man was shrieking a string of obscenities. A baby was crying. A woman screamed, then a man.

The ladder started creaking as Denning descended.

'All done, George,' he said. 'It's out of our hands now.' As he jumped down onto the track, George noticed that he was unravelling a reel of red wire which led up into the bolt hole. They walked the few yards to the train with the wire trailing behind them. As they climbed up into the cab, Denning passed the reel through the window in the cab door, before closing the door behind him and pulling up the window, leaving an inch gap at the top for the wire.

'You might want to cover your ears and open your mouth,' he said as he fiddled with a large powerpack battery. George looked confused. 'It'll protect your ears.' George felt a sense of rising panic and as Denning said, 'Don't say I didn't warn you,' he covered his ears and opened his mouth. Denning touched the wires against the electrodes on the battery and there was an explosion in the tunnel which cracked the glass in the cab windows. Even with his hands over his ears, George could feel the air displacement punch his eardrums as the sound of eviscerated brickwork and masonry raged in the confined space. As a gritty wind blew down the tunnel followed by wafts of dust, the passengers remained silent for a moment as a pulse of fear was transmitted through the carriages. Then the shouting – more urgent and frantic than ever – started up once again. But as George took his hands away from his ears, he heard something else, something wholly unexpected. It was the sound of running water.

11:16 AM

Network Control Centre, St James's

'All messages and web activity can be directed into a cache which we can analyse,' said Laura. 'But what concerns me is if the hijackers realise that we're tampering with their web access.'

'I doubt they will,' said Ed. 'They'll have more important things on their minds, like staying alive long enough to get out their message.'

'But if they do realise, Ed, they might start killing hostages.'

'We should only revise our negotiation if we have intel that proves conclusively they're killing people. Without that, we keep negotiating. How long have we got until the deadline?'

'Twelve minutes,' said White.

'And the router is in place in the tunnel?'

'Yes. Just needs turning on.'

'OK, well I guess we're going to have to let them speak. Without any communication whatsoever, there's no way of resolving this. We give them this. We get them talking and we take it from there.'

'How long after the deadline do we leave it?' asked White.

'Let's leave it forty-five seconds.'

'You're sure about that, Ed?' asked Laura.

'Absolutely,' replied Ed. 'We have to use every opportunity we can to claw back some control, however minute. When they see the time go to exactly eleven-thirty and there's no wireless, they're going to be afraid. Yes, they can kill a hostage but they're not going to straight away. Like everyone else on the planet who has ever used a personal computer, they're going to think that there's something wrong with their connection. They're also going to have a niggling doubt in the back of their minds that we're not going to be as compliant as they want us to be. We inject a little drip of fear into their brains. We unsettle them.'

'OK, OK . . .'

Ed could hear the indecision in Laura's voice. 'Laura, this is the only way we can play it. We have to start chipping away at them from the start. We have to make out that everything they want is a problem and it's going to take time. We own time, they don't.'

'All right, Ed, I don't need a lesson in hostage negotiation. I'll see what can be done.'

Ed turned to Laura, attempting a fix on her exact location and directing the lenses of his Ray-Bans at it. 'You mean to tell me that we haven't actually got clearance to switch on the wireless connection yet?'

'No, I need to phone it through to Commander Boise. Only she can sign off on this.'

'Laura, you'd better do that fast. We've got – how long have we got?'

'Nine minutes thirty seconds,' said White.

'OK, let me make the call.'

Ed baulked at the old negotiating maxim that 'the negotiators negotiate and the deciders decide'. He wanted to be closer to the sharp end of the decision-making process. He knew standard procedure dictated that in a negotiating cell everyone had their one specific job and there should be little overlap but, while he could see the reasoning behind this, he also found it frustrating.

When Laura returned, she said, 'They're calling back.' Ed could tell that she shared his frustration about this from the way that she said it and he couldn't prevent himself from feeling a flash of anger.

'This is fucking ridiculous.' Ed didn't raise his voice, didn't give any indication that he was angry aside from his choice of words. 'We should have more autonomy to make strategic decisions related to the negotiation. If they don't give us the go-ahead, we might as well pack up and go home. What was the point of getting all the Wi-Fi equipment down there in the first place?'

'Ed, there are enormous implications here. We've got an armed gang with hundreds of hostages and they want a media link to the world. Politically, this is extremely sensitive.'

'So we wait.'

'Everyone knows the time frame.'

They sat and waited. Ed thought about throwing out some deflective chatter in an attempt to diffuse the tension but his mind kept racing elsewhere. They had to allow the connection. It would be madness to deny it, although nothing would surprise him now as the usual rules of the game seemed to no longer apply. On the positive side, however, the setting up of the negotiating cell was complete. All the equipment was in place. They all had their headsets, their coffee and water. A fan had been set up on the desk in front of Ed and cool air was blowing across his scarred face.

At three minutes to the deadline, Ed heard the door open and a whispered conversation between Laura and one of the support staff.

'OK, Ed,' said Laura. 'We've got the go-ahead.'

'Good, so when we get to deadline plus forty-five seconds, we switch on the juice. Not a second before.'

11:17 AM

Northern Line Train 037, driver's cab

'What's that sound?' asked George.

Denning smiled. He pulled down the window in the M door in the front of the cab and cupped his ear theatrically. 'That, my friend, is holy water.'

'What do you mean, holy water?'

'Have you ever been baptised?'

George's mind flashed to the framed photograph that his parents had on the table in their hallway, a picture that despite his protestations, remained there to this day. It showed a one-year-old George wearing what looked like some sort of white silk shroud. It was taken at his christening and his mother always said he looked like a little angel in it. But George had never shared his mother's religion, much preferring his father's strong religious scepticism. This didn't, however, stop him getting confirmed when he was fifteen. All his friends were doing it and there were presents, so he was told, although all he received was a book called *Words for Worship*, which ended up in the back of a cupboard somewhere. It wasn't really the sort of present that he'd had in mind.

'Yeah, I was christened,' he said.

'Good,' said Denning but his mind was elsewhere, focused on the sound of footsteps in the tunnel. Pulling down the window in the N door in the side of the cab, he leant out. He saw something further up the train and, drawing his gun and grabbing his bag, he said, 'Come on, follow me.' Denning opened the door and George followed him into the first carriage, where a man in his forties, red faced and sweating, was trying to make his way down the outside of the train. As soon as he saw Denning move towards him, he pitched forward to try and get below the level of the window but a 9mm bullet was already on its way towards him and, having punched a hole in the window, it struck him in the left ear, exiting in a crimson flower-like wound on the right side of his neck. As the man slumped dead against the side of the train, Denning was on the move again, walking towards the end of the carriage.

'There goes another one,' he shouted. He stood at the door and looked through the window at the terrified passengers. 'I've got a lot of bullets. I've got enough for every one of you if need be. So if you want to die like this then keep on coming.' He turned away from the door and walked back along the carriage opening up his canvas bag and taking out a laptop computer. Then he took out extra batteries wrapped in clear plastic. In the middle of the carriage, between the two handrails set into the ceiling of the train, he stretched a piece of doubled-over bed sheet and pulled it tight, using a staple gun to secure it. In the middle of the sheet, he placed the laptop and opened it up.

George watched Denning as he worked. He could tell this was something he had rehearsed many times. Once the laptop was up and running on the makeshift hammock, he connected a webcam to it and after tapping on the keyboard for a few moments, a window appeared on the screen in which there was a real-time image of him. He smiled when he saw himself.

'Isn't technology miraculous, George?'

11:30 AM

Northern Line Train 037

At exactly forty-five seconds past the deadline, a minia-
ture symphony of pings, chimes and other electronic alerts
greeted the switching on of the wireless signal. The compulsion to communicate would not be denied. The tension
and fear had to be relayed above ground to friends, family
and loved ones. Social networking, emails, web-based
phone and video calls, the communication stream began
to flow from Train Number 037 and soon the flow became
a torrent and doubled back on itself in a swirling parabola
of news. This was media of the masses, naked expressions
of human emotion, unedited, uncensored, the raw material over which the media industry could now scavenge for
highlights, moments of drama and narrative continuity.
This was an unfolding tragedy brought to the people of
the world in the international language of the day's
top story.

There were journalists on the train, two freelancers and
a features editor for the *London Evening Standard*, but their
professional status meant little; there were amateur jour-

nalists all along the train, reporting from the front line of their own experience. The images and film footage radiated from the stricken train, to be consumed by a hungry global audience eager for an opinion to take.

Militants seize London tube train.

Terrorists attack London.

Tube hijack: terrorists take commuter train.

Hundreds of hostages on the London Underground.

Londoners' courage on day of terror.

Stacey's makeover: pictures.

11:31 AM

Network Control Centre, St James's

As the train driver came through on the radio once more, Ed Mallory thought he could detect a greater degree of fear in his voice.

'This is George Wakeham, the driver of – well, you know who I am.'

'George, this is Ed Mallory.'

'You were late switching on the wireless connection. Any further delays in carrying out demands will result in passengers dying.'

'George, I need to speak to the person who is telling you what to say.'

'That's not possible. You need to write down this web address.'

'OK, but can you tell me why we need this address?'

The frequency of the hiss relayed into Ed's headphones changed as the radio connection cut out momentarily and then George's voice came on the line once again. 'You need to shut up, write it down and then connect to it.'

Ed knew that George was merely relaying the words of

one of the hostage takers but he noted the element of anger and impatience in his delivery.

'OK, let's have the address, George.'

'It's denning23.co.uk. Have you got that?'

'Denning23.co.uk,' repeated Ed and he heard White tapping on a keyboard nearby.

Calvert squeezed Ed's arm. This was the sign they had decided on for when Ed should enable the mute facility on his microphone.

'We've got a visual on a white male in his mid-twenties,' whispered Calvert. 'He's standing in front of a webcam in the middle of a deserted tube-train carriage. He's got short cropped hair and he's wearing black. He's of medium build—'

Calvert was interrupted by a voice coming out of the computer speakers, clearly the voice of the man on the train speaking into his webcam and microphone: 'Check they can see and hear me, George.' It was the voice of a young white male, a Londoner or long-time resident of south-east England. The voice was calm, measured, confident.

George's voice came through Ed's earphones: 'Can you see and hear him?'

Ed clicked the mic back on and replied: 'Yes we've got visual and audio. Tell the guy you're with that he's coming through loud and clear.'

'That's a yes,' said George, shouting to the man.

Calvert squeezed Ed's arm and Ed clicked off the mic again to hear him say, 'The perp's looking straight into the camera like he's about to read the news.'

Ed slipped his earphones forward on his head and listened to the voice as it came through the speakers.

'This web link has been sent to all major news organisations,' said the man in a tone that made no attempt to hide an underlying sense of excitement. 'A group mailing has gone to everyone from Al Jazeera to CNN. It'll probably take a short while for the emails to filter through and for the journalists to realise what's going on, so in the meantime, I need to lay down some ground rules. High-explosive charges have been rigged throughout all six carriages and any attempt to make physical contact with the train will result in me detonating them. Now I reckon there's about – what? – three hundred and fifty people on this train and with a series of explosions in such a confined space, everyone will die. That's a lot of bodies, so let's not have any heroics.'

If the guy was lying, he was a good liar. Often Ed could pick up something in a hostage situation even when those around him could see the subject on a visual link and detect nothing in their body language or behaviour. But this guy gave off no 'tell' in his vocal inflexion.

'My name is Tommy Denning and I am leading a team of heavily armed hijackers who are positioned throughout the train.'

As soon as the perp had said his name, Ed could hear the activity in the negotiating cell as it was typed into keyboards and the process to construct a full character profile of him was set in motion.

'I have a message for the world,' said Tommy Denning.

It sounded to Ed as though he was enjoying himself. It was as though he had rehearsed this moment in the bathroom mirror a thousand times.

'At exactly twelve noon, I will broadcast my message. If any attempt is made to prevent me from doing so, I will detonate the explosives on the train. Please do not be under any illusions: we are all fully prepared to die and to take everyone on the train with us.'

The ensuing silence was unbearable for Ed while the rest of the team watched the video link to the train.

'What's he doing?' he whispered.

Calvert said, 'He's walking away from the camera back towards the driver's cab.'

Ed could just make out the sound of distant shouts and screams on the train. He felt his tactile watch. It was 11:35 am. Twenty-five minutes until Denning's message. Plenty of time for the world's media to focus on this solitary webcam deep beneath the streets of London.

All of the crisis negotiations that Ed had been involved with over the years had involved one-on-one communications with the subject. Conversations were invariably taped and covert audio and visual connections were always attempted. This situation, however, was totally different on account of the subject's ability, thus far, to control the flow and direction of the communication. What the hell was it that this Tommy Denning had to say? Did he have some great secret to impart? Or was his message going to be the typical ramblings of some delusional paranoid? The three types of psychological profile assessment – either mad or bad or mad and bad – were difficult to apply in this case. From the way Denning presented himself to the world he didn't easily fit into any category.

The more Ed thought about Tommy Denning's announcement, the more he thought that they hadn't fully evaluated the implications of allowing him a voice and one that all the news media would be only too happy to trumpet from every rooftop. But that was an intangible and now he had to focus on those aspects of the situation that he could control.

'Try and raise the driver on the radio,' said Ed. 'Denning might be so pumped up by the fact this whole thing is going better than in his wildest dreams that he might let us through.'

A moment later, White said, 'Ed, you're on.'

Ed slipped on his headset. 'George? Are you there? This is Ed Mallory from the Network Control Centre. Can you hear me?' There was nothing for a few moments, just radio static before George's voice came through the speaker.

'Hi, it's George.'

'Can I speak to Tommy Denning?'

There was a muffled conversation in the background before George came back on the line.

'No, he will only communicate via the webcam. You must wait until twelve noon.'

'Please tell him that it's essential that I speak to him because we've got a problem fulfilling his request.'

Another pause. There was a crackle on the radio connection before another voice – Tommy Denning's this time – came on the line.

'Listen, Mr Mallory, I know you'd like to get into a conversation with me and try to talk me down but you've got to realise that I'm not up for a chat, OK?'

Hearing his voice again, Ed guessed that he was definitely a Londoner but the accent wasn't strong enough to allow him to hazard a more specific origin.

'Mr Denning – can I call you Tommy?'

'You can call me what the hell you like, it's not going to do you any good. Although I have to say that I rather like the fact that we're calling each other "Mr Denning" and "Mr Mallory", it sounds very refined. Now don't take offence from this – it's nothing personal – but I'm not going to be talking to you, OK? All you need to know is that if anybody tries to stop me making my announcement at twelve o'clock then I'll kill all the passengers on the train.'

'The problem I have is that the wireless access is very unstable. Our technical people are struggling to keep it going. It may pack up before twelve noon.'

'You're lying, Mr Mallory. You know it and I know it. If the connection is so unstable then you'll get some backup. What's that compared to the deaths of hundreds of people?'

Ed could hear something in the background. He had heard it on the computer, on the link to the webcam, but on the radio it was louder. It was a rushing sound, like wind blowing through trees.

'Tommy, if we're going to resolve this situation, we're going to have to create some trust here. We're giving you the internet connection so we're going to need something in return.'

'You are getting something in return – you're getting the lives of the passengers on the train.'

'We're going to need something more tangible than that, Tommy. I'm thinking that it would reflect really well on you if you were to release the children.'

Denning chuckled. It was unforced. It sounded like a genuine expression of goodwill, as though he was enjoying their conversation and felt confident he was in complete control of it. He sounded like no other hostage taker Ed had ever come across. He was calm, collected and thinking clearly, behaving as though this was something he was born to do.

Denning clearly wasn't going to respond to his line about the children so Ed thought he would try another tack. 'What exactly is it that you want, Tommy?'

'You'll find out,' said Tommy and the line went dead.

'He's enjoying this,' said Ed to the occupants of the negotiating cell. 'He's having a ball.'

11:36 AM

Northern Line Train 037, driver's cab

Through the cracked window, George could see that the puddles in the tunnel were merging, lapping at the rails. Soon there would be a continuous expanse of water in front of the train. How long the power supply through the rails would continue was difficult to say but, once it had gone, the battery on the train would continue to provide electricity for a while until it ran down and the entire train would be thrown into darkness.

The negotiator, Ed Mallory, was trying to keep Denning talking. But it was never going to happen. There was no way that Denning was going to respond to any sort of conversational psychology. It sounded like Mallory was probably aware of that. George chewed his gum as he listened to the attempted negotiations. It was Juicy Fruit. Denning hadn't wanted any when George had offered him a piece.

'All you need to know,' said Denning into the radio handset, 'is that if anybody tries to stop me making my announcement at twelve o'clock then I'll kill all the passengers on the train.'

Why the water? Why flood the tunnel? By asking the questions, George hoped he might be able to find an answer other than the one that kept offering itself to him and made his claustrophobia flare up and steal the breath from his lungs. There was no avoiding it; there was only one answer – the water was a threat. And as the driver of the train, George knew that he should try to do something about it. The passengers were technically still his responsibility. There had to be something that he could do. Something that would not jeopardise his family.

He had been trying to avoid looking down at the floor of the cab – he was never very good with blood – but as he glanced down, he saw that stuck to the drying blood was a plastic bottle of Diet Coke about half full. It had fallen out of the trainee driver's jacket pocket when he slumped to the floor. The fact that it was Diet Coke made its owner's death even worse somehow. It personalised it. The poor bugger had been a little overweight – like George – and maybe he had wanted to slim down, through health reasons or possibly vanity. Whichever it was, it didn't matter now.

Then it came to him. If he drank the Coke, in addition to quenching his thirst – it was so damned hot, the chewing gum felt like rubber in his mouth – he would have an empty plastic bottle in which he could place a letter, a message in a bottle.

Could he scribble a note on a piece of paper to the effect that Tommy Denning was flooding the tunnel? It was clear that Denning had no intention of telling the authorities the full details of the hostage scenario that he was engineering, otherwise he would have done so already. It obviously served his purposes not to. So if George could let it be known some other way, provide some forewarning of what was going on down there then the authorities might be able to put in place some evasive procedures. There was clearly a small amount of current in the water caused by the deluge cascading down from the bolt hole in the tunnel roof where Denning had set off the explosion. It might be just enough to carry the bottle past the train to where it might be found by someone. But no sooner had the idea come to him and he had embraced what scant hope it offered than he rejected it out of hand. It was a stupid idea. Quite apart from the fact that Tommy Denning would have been alerted to what he was up to when he started writing a letter, even if he could manage to put his message in the bottle and cast it into the water, the chances of it actually reaching anybody in time for them to do anything were infinitesimal; the risk far outweighed any possible benefits.

Despite the plan's failings, the idea of alerting the outside world to the exact nature of what Denning was up to was still sound.

The radio handset, there it was. There was his mouthpiece to the world. But it would take more than just speaking into it. This would take ingenuity.

'What exactly is it that you want, Tommy?' asked Ed Mallory through the speaker console.

'You'll find out,' said Denning taking his finger off the push-to-talk button on the side of the handset and passing it back to George. The chewing gum was already out of George's mouth and in his hand. He kept the talk button pressed down and packed the chewing gum around it tightly to hold it in position. The channel was still open.

But as soon as George had done this, all he could see was the piece of chewing gum. There it was on the mouth-piece hanging in its cradle on the radio console. It looked enormous. It might as well have been red and throbbing. What was he thinking? He wasn't a hero. His recent attempt to snatch the gun from Denning had very nearly got him killed. This was far more reckless. An open channel would sometimes – often – hiss and crackle. Denning would only need to hear this, look across at the handset and see the chewing gum on the talk button. He wouldn't think twice. It would be George's turn to be thrashing around the cab, blood pissing from a hole in his head. This time he really was going to die.

Talk, George. That's all he could do. He would have to try and mask any sounds from the handset. And for Christ's sake, George, stop looking at it.

Denning stared through the cracked window at the water in the tunnel. He looked confident, like whatever his sick plan was, it was all going smoothly.

Say something, George.

'So, what's with the water?'

Denning glanced at him – disaster – before returning his gaze to the tunnel.

'Think of it as an egg-timer,' he said, smiling, pleased with his explanation.

George glanced at the radio console. The gum around the button was beginning to stretch as the spring behind it forced it away from the main body of the handset. The channel would not stay open for long. He had to describe the situation more clearly, at any moment the radio might crackle and he would be found out.

'So you're trying to drown us by flooding the tunnel, is that it?'

Had he overdone it? Had he killed himself? Had he killed Maggie? Had he killed his children?

Denning looked at him. He would only have to glance a little to one side and he would see the handset and the gum on it. In his peripheral vision, George could see the talk button straining against the sticky tendrils.

'It's not a matter of drowning. This is much more important than drowning. This is a blessing.'

The last of the gummy tethers was about to give way, allowing the press-to-talk button to snap back into place, closing down the channel and emitting as it nearly always did a crackle of static.

Say something. Anything.

'It's so damned hot.'

When it came, it was more of a hiss than a crackle and it coincided with the 'want' as George said, 'Do you want a drink?'

George stooped down and picked up the bottle of Diet Coke, prising it away from the congealing blood. If he looked up and saw Denning pointing the pistol at him then he knew it would be the last thing he would ever see. He couldn't bear to look so he focused on the top of the bottle as he unscrewed it. There was no avoiding it now, he had to look at Denning. What would his expression be? Had he heard? The hiss from the radio might as well have been church bells to George. It was loud and unmistakable. But when he managed to look at Denning again, he was met with an expression of disgust. Was it disgust at his woeful attempt to communicate with the outside world? Was it disgust which could only be banished by pumping a bullet into his head? It was impossible to say. George's thirst felt terminal. If he was going to die, he wanted to have a drink first. He raised the bottle to his lips and took a sip. The fizzy liquid was warm and not as fizzy as it should have been. It probably contained a few millilitres of its former owner's saliva.

'How could you?'

George felt like sobbing with relief. He took another gulp and held out the bottle to Denning.

'Want some?'

'No.'

Denning watched him as he took another gulp.

'Drinking a dead man's drink,' said Denning with disgust.

'Well, you killed him.'

George didn't know where it came from. Suddenly he was a comedian, joking about the darkest and sickest subject matter imaginable. And Denning was smiling at him, amused. But this wasn't the time for complacency. There was still a big sticky bolus of chewing gum on the radio handset and the implications of Denning's reply to his question regarding the running water had now filtered through his mind and made him feel sick.

'So what are you after, what are your demands?'

'Look, I don't want to spoil it for you. If I told you, it wouldn't be a surprise now would it?' The smile was gone as he took out the walkie-talkie and spoke into it: 'Belle?'

The woman's voice on the other end crackled back: 'Yeah, Tommy?'

'Everything's as it should be. I'm going to make my speech at twelve noon, so sit tight, not long now.'

'OK, Tommy. Oh and Tommy, Simeon's dead.'

'You did what you had to do. Remember, today is the day. This is our time.'

'I love you, Tommy.'

'I love you, Belle.'

As Denning pocketed the walkie-talkie, George caught his eye. 'She your girlfriend?'

'Sister.'

'She's at the other end of the train, right?'

'Got it in one.'

'Who's Simeon?'

'He was a false friend.'

'So he had to die?' Denning said nothing, just nodded while watching George, who decided to capitalise on this moment of openness to question him further: 'So what now?'

'We wait.'

'You haven't really wired the train with explosives, have you?'

Denning's expression changed.

'What is it with you? Doesn't it worry you now I've made myself known and established my link with the outside world that I might not need you any more? That maybe you could be surplus to requirements.'

George knew it might sound desperate but he didn't care. 'You promised that so long as I did as I was told you would spare me and my family. That's the truth, right?'

Denning nodded thoughtfully. 'Of course it's the truth. Why would I lie to you? You're my friend. But now you're going to have to keep quiet because I've got a speech to rehearse.' He took some sheets of foolscap paper from his canvas bag and flicked through them.

George returned his gaze to the water in the tunnel up ahead, avoiding the handset and the piece of chewing gum. With sideways glances, he watched Denning as he pored over the sheets of paper, reading the words written in blue biro. The handwriting was small and neat and there were numerous crossings out and words underlined. Denning muttered to himself as he read, pacing in the confined space.

His guard was down. Both his hands were on the pieces of paper and the gun was in his pocket. If George hit him as hard as he could, smashed his fist into his face, he would be debilitated for at least a few seconds. Enough time perhaps to land some more punches and prevent him reaching for his gun. Enough time possibly for George to get his hands around his neck and squeeze the life out of him. As the thought came to him, he clenched his fists, his fingernails digging into his palms. His murderous thoughts kept his claustrophobia at bay. There he was, a man who had never thrown a fist in anger, not since he was a child, and yet he knew with a cold dispassionate certainty that if he got the chance, he would kill this man and feel nothing, no remorse, nothing. It would feel good. It would feel liberating.

11:39 AM

'So, what's with the water?'

As soon as Ed heard the train driver, George Wakeham, say the words – they were faint but clearly audible through his headphones – he knew it was significant. Wakeham had managed to keep the radio channel open.

Everyone in the negotiating cell – White, Calvert, Hooper and Ed Mallory – listened to it and behind it there was that sound. It was unmistakable now. Flowing water. Falling water. 'What's with the water?'

'Think of it as an egg-timer,' said Denning. His voice sounded different. The tone was more subdued, more conversational. This was how he spoke when he wasn't grandstanding and Ed could tell straight away that he had no idea that he was being listened to.

Ed willed George to ask another question, and he did. 'So you're trying to drown us by flooding the tunnel, is that it?'

Ed winced. Was that too exclamatory? Would Denning realise that he was being steered?

'It's not a matter of drowning, George. This is much more important than drowning. This is a blessing.'

A blessing? What the hell did that mean?

'It's so damned hot.' George Wakeham sounded nervy, he was speaking too loudly. Was his ruse about to be discovered?

'Do you w—'

The radio cut out. It was the start of a question; what was George about to ask him?

'Can you play it back?' asked Ed. 'The bit about flooding the tunnel.'

White clicked away on a computer nearby and there were George's words again: 'So you're trying to drown us by flooding the tunnel, is that it?'

'Again,' said Ed.

'So you're trying to drown us by flooding the tunnel, is that it?'

'Laura?'

Laura spoke to him from the direction of the doorway. 'Yes, Ed?'

'I've got a really bad feeling about this. We need to put a whole new strategy in operation. And we need to move fast.'

11:43 AM

Northern Line Train 037, driver's cab

Father Owen had turned towards him as he had approached with the knife the night before. It had felt as though God's hands were guiding him as he pushed Owen back into the bath and pressed the tip of the blade against his throat.

'What ... what are you doing?' Stripped from Owen's voice was the assured confidence that he employed for his interminable sermons, preachings that had become so tiresome of late. What did he know about washing away the sins of the world, about rebirth?

Like everyone whom God had seen fit to accompany him on this journey, Father Owen was a prophet. Tommy's was the task of beginning the End Time but others were to play their part in the great unfolding of the end of days. He felt a strange sense of love for them. It was God's love shining through him.

When he had sacrificed the old man, he had stood so close to him that he could smell the whisky on his breath. As the arthritic old hands struggled with his in a vain attempt to prevent the inevitable, Tommy leant forward against the knife. It burst through Owen's throat, squirting blood as the gristle crackled.

It was a line that Tommy had heard the old man use many times before, a line taken from the Book of Revelation, although Owen and all the other members of Cruor Christi had mistaken its significance and meaning. Their foreheads were touching, sweat mingling; they were so close that Tommy's words as he had spoken them were inhaled by the old man as he breathed his last: 'And the waters shall rise.'

And now was Tommy's final opportunity to get all those other precious words straight in his mind. There would be no notes when he went live. Christ didn't have notes. Great words, great speeches, came from the soul. God would guide him. Just as he had guided him here. Everything came from the Almighty Father and he had never felt so close to him as he did now. God had always been with him, even on that day all those years before. Especially on that day. Although it had not been possible to know it at the time. How was he to know that what he felt was God's presence in the room when his father picked up the bread knife off the chopping board and pushed it into his mother's stomach right up to the handle?

At first it had felt like a joke. Time stopped. Everyone in the room looked at the wooden handle of the knife sticking out of his mother's floral-patterned apron. It looked absurd. He was about to laugh. But before the laughter could reach his lips, his mother started gasping and slumped to the floor, where she whimpered and then lay still. He remembered when they used to play cowboys and Indians. His dad never joined in but his mother, who had been interested in amateur dramatics as a younger woman, had thrown herself into the childish roleplay with a vengeance. Tommy had killed her. He had drawn his gun, shot her and she had rolled onto the carpet and pretended to die. Her dying when they played cowboys and Indians and her dying on the floor of the kitchen as her family watched – it felt the same. It always felt the same every time he thought of it, and he thought of it a lot.

The feeling was there then and it had never really gone away again since. The feeling was God and God had stayed with Tommy and Belle in the kitchen when their father walked calmly out of the room as their mother's blood pooled on the cracked linoleum by the breakfast table.

They could hear him banging about in the garage next door, then it went quiet. When Tommy went through after a few minutes – he wanted to know whether he should call an ambulance – he found his father hanging from a metal roof beam, the flex from the power drill around his neck. Remembering it now, God was there in everything, from the urine that dripped from his father's trouser leg into the puddle on the floor to the faint rubbery creak of the flex as the body slowly turned a quarter circle and then back again. Before they dialled 999, Tommy and Belle watched *The Terminator*, which their dad had taped a couple of nights before when it was on television but their mother had said they were too young to watch. The film gave Belle nightmares for weeks.

Tommy opened the door to the first carriage. At the other end of it there was movement on either side of the train. Despite the public executions he had carried out earlier and the threat of detonating explosives, people were trying to escape again. They wanted to take their chances. Tommy raised up his pistol and emptied the magazine in two bursts, the first at one side of the carriage and the second at the other. There were cries, screams, the splashing of bodies into water. That would give the others pause for thought and it would buy him some more time.

The laptop was in position on the makeshift hammock slung between the handrails. Another few minutes and he would stand in front of it and address the world.

With the pistol reloaded and holstered in his pocket, he closed the door to the cab and turned his attention to the speech once again while George, the driver, sat in the driver's seat and stared out into the tunnel. But however hard Tommy tried to concentrate, thoughts kept forcing themselves into his mind, memories from childhood, and one memory in particular, of his father telling him about the River Lime.

His dad might have been a hard bastard but he told a good story. He had worked on the London Underground in the early seventies before he met Tommy's mother. An engineer was what he said he was, but knowing how he exaggerated, he was probably involved in little more than track maintenance. He regaled Tommy with stories of secret tunnels and forgotten stations, and one of the stories that he told him was about London's underground rivers, tributaries of the Thames like the Walbrook, the Fleet, the Tyburn and the Lime, that had once flowed on the surface but had been boxed into culverts by the encroachment of the city. It was the story of the River Lime that particularly interested little Tommy. Rising from the same springs on Hampstead Heath as the Fleet River, it flowed down through Camden Town and under the eastern-most section of the West End to rejoin the Fleet in Holborn and from there into the Thames at Blackfriars Bridge. When the Charing Cross, Euston and Hampstead Railway – later to become the westerly branch of the Northern Line – was being built in the late 1890s and early 1900s, it was necessary to house the River Lime in a tunnel for a two-mile section from Goodge Street in the north to Covent Garden in the south to prevent flooding in the newly constructed underground railway line. It was a major feat of engineering. The flow of the river could not be described as fast but still constituted thousands of gallons per hour.

Following a major survey of the London Underground carried out in the early seventies, it was decided that the tunnel housing the River Lime should be shored up to prevent any danger of leakage. One area in particular was considered to be most at risk and that was the section beneath Charing Cross Road, where the Lime ran very close to a section of train tunnel, which was itself in a low level area between the stations either side of it – Tottenham Court Road to the north and Leicester Square to the south. The survey report had said that in the event of the River Lime flooding in this section, the Northern

Line tunnel would fill with water in a matter of hours.

Tommy's dad was part of the engineering team that reinforced the tunnel carrying the water, and he had told Tommy how he and his fellow workers had joked that if someone like the IRA – the main purveyors of terrorism to Londoners in the seventies – wanted to pull off a spectacular attack, they could flood the northbound Northern Line tunnel and any train that happened to be in it. And there it was, a seed in little Tommy Denning's mind. Almost exactly halfway between the two stations in the northbound tunnel – that's what his dad had told him. A flight of metal steps. A maintenance access shaft to all that remained of the River Lime, the forgotten river. Tommy never forgot.

After his father died and Tommy grew older, this random piece of information took on greater significance. It was secret knowledge. It was a gift. When he found Christ and was born again, the gift became more precious and significant as did other events in his life. Like the attacks on the Twin Towers.

He watched it all on television, right from the moment when United Airlines Flight 175 went into the South Tower. At the age of fourteen, suddenly his life had meaning. The lines were drawn. The army was his only option. He was going on a crusade. But then came Afghanistan and everything got confused. It wasn't the crusade he had hoped for. The Afghans weren't the enemy. For a time even his faith in Christ was shaken but he did what he had to do. Even when his friend, Jed, was blown up by a roadside bomb, he could not bring himself to hate, as so many of the men he fought alongside did. He bided his time and he got out when he could. During his time in Afghanistan, he managed to avoid killing anyone. That wasn't to say that he didn't see people get killed – he did, plenty – but God had decided that it wasn't right for him to kill. Not yet.

When he came home, Belle was living in Wales, in Snowdonia, in an old farm which was now the monastic headquarters of an evangelical sect called Cruor Christi. Typical Belle. She never did things by half. Bored and frustrated after years in foster homes around London, she had written to him to tell him she wanted to move to the country. But he never expected a farm converted into a monastery on the side of a mountain.

It was good at first. They seemed like decent people. But as Tommy's faith grew stronger, it also changed, and he found it difficult to share his new brothers' and sisters' convictions, grew tired of their blinkered attitudes, particularly those of Father Owen. To Owen, Christ was the only way, and all other religions – even those who interpreted Christ differently – were wrong, sinful. The strength of the old man's faith was admirable but it was misguided. The same went for Brother Varick. They were fighting the wrong battle. The lines were drawn but not where they thought. 9/11 was a call to arms but not for believers to fight one another as some deluded souls believed. It was a rallying cry.

The Muslim brothers and sisters were in pain but no one was listening to them. God allowed 9/11 to happen because he wanted to send a message to the world. But mankind, as always, and particularly in the West, misunderstood the symbolism and poured oil on the flames.

9/11 was like a diamond bullet. The strength of will that it required, its pure crystalline simplicity. The World Trade Centre became an epic metaphor beamed into homes across the globe. So too the Pentagon and, as for United Airlines Flight 93 going down in that field in Pennsylvania, this offered humanity hope. Destiny can be changed. Man can make a difference.

And the more he thought about 9/11 and what it meant, particularly after the lunacy of Helmand, the more he thought about the River Lime and his secret knowledge. He knew it was no accident that he had been given this information. The hand of God was guiding him. It felt as though everything was coming to a head. The pressure was building. When Simeon Fisher arrived at Madoc Farm and his true identity became apparent, it was a sign to begin preparations.

Like Mohammed Atta before him, Tommy decided he would utilise existing hardware and infrastructure and turn it against the enemy. It was what God wanted, he could feel it, and the true gold of this psychic alchemy was the discovery that a great battle had once taken place on an ancient bridge over the River Lime between Boudicca and the Romans. Before the battle, the river was blessed by one of the first Christian missionaries to visit Britain, Matthew of Parnassus, an old man who when he was a child had met Jesus. All of which meant one thing. The River Lime flowed with holy water.

11:44 AM

Morden Tube Station car park

The heat was intense as Brother Alistair retraced his steps yet again between the rows of cars. It didn't feel like England. It felt tropical. When he closed his eyes, the sun beat down on him, coming through his eyelids in a reddish brown. Opening them slightly, he looked away from the sun into the blue sky streaked with the vapour trails of airliners. Then he looked at the cars all around him. What were the odds of him finding the children? If he was a betting man, which he supposed he probably was being a former junkie, then he might have thought it was about a ten-to-one shot. Those were good enough odds for him, worth taking a punt on. And the likelihood of his finding them was in direct proportion to the amount of time that he spent looking. The trouble was the number of cars. After living in the countryside for so long, it was almost too much for his mind to compute that there could be so many people and so many cars all crammed together in one place.

But as time dragged on, he could feel the odds of finding

the children safe and sound lengthen. He had been in the car park since just after nine o'clock and apart from a short break when he had gone to the shop to buy a bottle of water, he had wandered between the cars, both in the car park and in the streets surrounding the station.

It bothered Alistair more than anything else, more than the hijack of the tube train, more than what Tommy Denning intended to do to the passengers. It was the unthinking cruelty of it that was so much more shocking than all the other aspects of his sick plan. In the car that morning, as they made their way along the motorway towards London in the milky early morning light, Varick had told him about the contents of the notebook Father Owen had found in Tommy's room. Varick had looked for the notebook before they left but he couldn't find it. Tommy must have taken it back before he had driven the carving knife through the old man's neck. But Varick could remember the contents and, as he had told Alistair what the plan entailed, he mentioned the children only in passing. Clearly, their part in the whole thing was just one atrocity out of many, but Alistair couldn't get the image out of his head, just as he couldn't banish the memory of how he had found Owen thrashing around in the bath with his neck impaled on the knife's blade.

'In order to make sure that the train driver does exactly as he says,' Varick had said as he drove the car, 'Tommy's going to tell him that he has taken his children hostage and any attempt to raise the alarm or release the passengers from the train will mean that they'll be killed. In his notebook, however, it says that the children will be locked in the boot of the car they use to get to the tube station.'

Varick had gone on to explain the other aspects of the planned atrocity but Alistair wasn't paying much attention. The thought of two children locked in the boot of a car on a day as hot as this haunted him. As they had parked in a public car park just off Piccadilly Circus, Alistair could keep his thoughts to himself no longer.

'We should try and find the children,' he had said as they walked through Soho.

'It's more important that we find Tommy.'

'But we can't leave the children in the boot of a car. They'll die in this heat.'

Varick frowned as he said, 'Let me think about it.'

By the time they reached Leicester Square tube station, Varick had reached a decision and he put his hand on Alistair's shoulder as he said, 'We both have a mission here, Alistair. I'll find Tommy, you must find the children.'

They had bought tickets and taken the escalators down to the Northern Line. But whereas Varick took up his position on the northbound platform to begin his wait for Tommy, Alistair had taken the first train southbound.

When he had arrived at Morden station a member of London Underground staff, a man in his fifties with grey hair and a belly grown from too many years seated at a desk, was taking questions from members of the public who had arrived at the station expecting to be able to travel into central London. Brother Alistair joined the crowd of people and listened to what was said. There had been an incident on the Underground and the network was closed down. Tommy had clearly managed to put his plan into operation. Whether Brother Varick could stop him from taking it to its ghastly conclusion was something that was in God's hands now. He felt bad about leaving Varick to try and save the train passengers all by himself but he felt confident that he would succeed. Besides, Alistair now had far more pressing concerns. If he didn't hurry up, the children would be dead before he found them.

11:48 AM

About certain events in his life George had almost photographic recall and his first date with Maggie was one of them. She had worn a striped Breton top with jeans and a leather jacket. Her hair was much shorter than it was now. They both smiled a lot; both had lasagne and drank far too much wine because they were nervous. He had toyed with the idea of asking Maggie if she wanted to come back to his place but decided that if he really was serious about her – and the butterflies in his stomach were testament to the fact that he was – the best thing would be to show a bit of gallantry and make sure that she got home safely in a taxi. When she sat in the back of the cab, he leant in to give her a goodnight kiss on the cheek and she had pulled him close and kissed him on the lips. He knew then that it was more than just drunken affection. It was obvious that she liked him as much as he liked her. He walked home that night, all the way to Muswell Hill from the West End; he just wanted to keep walking, enjoying the warm summer night and his thoughts of Maggie.

Ever since that night, Italian restaurants had held a special resonance for them because they were reminded of their first date. Like all couples, he and Maggie had developed their own little conversational rituals and traditions. Whenever the bread rolls were delivered to the table in an Italian restaurant, George would often take two pieces of bread, pop one in each cheek and do his 'Marlon Brando in *The Godfather*' impersonation: 'You come into my house on the day my daughter is to be married and you ask me to do murder for money.' She groaned every time he did it but she still laughed all the same.

They had passed their affection for Italian restaurants on to Ben and Sophie. Mr Pizza, or Mr Pieces rather, had become a family favourite. Would they ever go there again? Not if Tommy Denning saw the chewing gum on the handset or if the threat of flooding the train didn't force the authorities into succumbing to his demands.

'OK, George, I want you to kneel with me and pray.' Denning had that expression on his face – the little smile and the raised eyebrows – as though he was a child goading his friend into a dare.

'I er, I don't pray.'

'I know you say you don't believe but try to open your mind for a moment. Didn't the psalm that you recited earlier mean anything to you?'

'It might have meant something to me when I said it.'

'It might have meant something to you when you said it.' Denning spoke like a barrister, repeating the words of a witness in an attempt to make them sound ridiculous.

'Yeah, I don't know.'

'Well maybe another prayer might mean something to you now.'

'Maybe.'

'The thing is, I want to pray now and I don't want to pray alone. I think you're very important to this whole—' He looked around the cab trying to find the word. Please God don't look at the handset, don't see the chewing gum. George was praying already. Denning found the word: '—occasion, this moment in time. Do you understand what I'm saying?'

An idea was forming in George's mind. Praying would involve kneeling; it might even involve Tommy's eyes being closed. What better time to launch an attack on the bastard than when he was in congress with whichever imaginary being he had chosen to believe in? He would be vulnerable. This might be George's best chance to disarm him. All it would take would be a lucky punch. If he hit him as hard as he could then it might buy him a few seconds, might allow him to hit him again, kick him, grab the gun even. He wouldn't need to worry about the chewing gum on the radio mouthpiece then.

'Your faith means a lot to you, doesn't it?'

Tommy chuckled at the absurdity of the question. 'Of course, it means everything. Can't you see that?'

'Yes, I can and . . . I envy you. I've struggled to believe in the past. I've tried but something just always held me back. Until now.'

'Until now?'

He shouldn't overplay his hand but he needed Denning to know that he was serious about his intention to pray. The more relaxed Denning was the better. In addition to being his motivation, religion was also his weak spot, his Achilles heel.

'In a weird kind of way, I guess I respect you.' Was that too much? He didn't have time to judge. Denning looked convinced – so far. 'I've spent my whole life compromising my real feelings and beliefs. And look where it's got me? I'm forty, I'm messed up, I'm in a job that I can't stand, all my hopes and dreams have turned to dust. Today for the first time in years – and despite the fear that I feel for myself and my family – I actually feel alive.' Denning was watching him, expressionless. Could he tell that he was lying? Was he lying? It didn't matter, he was engineering an opportunity for himself. A choice had been made – it might not be the right choice but it was a choice. He was going to keep coming at this freak; he was going to keep testing him. He was going to find a moment of weakness and he was going to stop him.

'You're serious, are you? You can really feel God's love?'

'I don't know what it is but I can feel something. I feel different.'

'I thought it would be more difficult than this. I thought you would fight against it harder. You've made me so happy.'

George had not anticipated Denning's next move. He reached out to George and put his arms around him, hugged him, their cheeks pressed together. Before George could decide whether this might prove a better moment to launch his attack than later on, Denning had released him, put the gun down on the driver's console and was kneeling.

'Come, George, let's pray together.'

Tommy Denning raised his hands up to his mouth and closed his eyes. George knelt too and did the same – except he kept his eyes open, watching, waiting.

'Dear Lord, our heavenly father, this is your humble servant, Thomas ...'

11:48 AM

Ed could hear the distant sound of helicopters as they hovered over the West End. The wailing of sirens on the streets below was a constant. For a moment, it felt as though the barrage of sound was taunting him. Ed was trained to deal with pressure – he trained others how to deal with it too – but this was something else. No one in the negotiating cell could fail to feel it. These people were experts in hostage negotiation. They were experts in establishing psychological profiles and doing so rapidly so that negotiation tactics could be tailored to those profiles. But none of them had been faced with such a meticulously planned and executed scenario involving so many hostages and with so little apparent motive; none of them had come across someone like Tommy Denning before. In every hostage negotiation that Ed had been a part of over the years, he had gone into the negotiation knowing with an unwavering certainty that he had the upper hand psychologically speaking, that he was the one in control. But in this situation Ed knew he wasn't. Tommy Denning was shrewd, resourceful, calm, confident, and seemingly possessed of an innate understanding of the negotiation process and an ongoing refusal to be drawn into it. What Denning had created here couldn't help but make all the other situations that Ed had worked on seem low key, trivial almost, in comparison. The sheer scale of this situation and the numbers of people involved elevated it into a different realm.

Ed's negotiating team, Des White, Nick Calvert and Laura Massey, were feeling the pressure – he could hear it in their voices – but they were responding to that pressure as the professionals that they were. Hooper, on the other hand, was an unknown quantity. His responses to the psychological pressure of the crisis were inconsistent. Ed couldn't read him. To Ed, the pressure felt like vertigo. He used to suffer it when he was sighted; when blind it seemed to go away. Now it was back. It felt as though the negotiating cell was perched at the very top of a skyscraper of security infrastructure.

The whole area around the hijack was locked down, the stronghold was secure. Special forces were on standby while the rapid intervention plan was being devised. The police, the military and the government – not to mention the victims and their families – were looking to Ed and his team to make the right decisions. Storming the train was always an option but the risks were clear. Over three hundred passengers stood to die if it went wrong, not to mention the SAS soldiers themselves who would have to undertake the operation. One thing he knew for certain

– even if he was uncertain of anything else – was that when Tommy Denning said that he would kill everyone on the train if anyone tried to stop him making his announcement, he meant it. The conviction in his voice when he made his threats – whether articulated through George the driver or from his own lips – was unequivocal.

Without an immediate intervention, Ed and his team were faced with a negotiation with a subject that was going to be about as difficult as they came. To add to that, there was now the issue of the water in the tunnel. 'Think of it as an egg-timer,' Denning had said over the radio link. George had then said, 'So you're trying to drown us by flooding the tunnel, is that it?' Even though the radio link had been broken for some reason before George could tease any more from his captor, Denning's intentions were clear. He was going to ensure that everything was stacked in his favour. He held all the cards. Whatever his demands were, he fully expected them to be met. He had set in motion a series of events that could not be reversed. Either the authorities complied or the passengers would end up dead. It was as simple as that. Denning knew enough about hostage negotiation to know that the negotiators' premium commodity, time, was the one thing that he could turn against them to make it play to his advantage.

So, what the hell were his demands going to be? What could this evangelical ex-soldier possibly want? As soon as Ed knew what it was, the psychological balance of power in the negotiation would shift. Knowledge of what those desires were would allow Ed to manage them and use them to manipulate Denning and begin the process of securing a positive outcome.

Laura entered the room – he could tell it was her from her footsteps – and she was pulling pieces of paper from an envelope.

'We've got an interim profile and background on Thomas Denning,' she said.

'Thanks, Laura,' said Ed. 'Can you paraphrase as we've only got a few minutes until he's going to make his speech?'

'Yes, let's hear it,' said Hooper. It was clear to Ed that he was trying to reassert himself as a key player within the negotiating cell. He didn't seem to care about the protocol; you didn't bark orders at the negotiating co-ordinator, particularly one with the experience of Laura Massey. She didn't say anything in response to his comment and nor would he but it was yet another sign that Hooper was working to a different agenda.

'He's twenty-five years old,' started Laura. 'One of non-identical twins. His sister's called Belle. When they were nine years old, they saw their father murder their mother with a bread knife before he hung himself. After that, Tommy spent most of his childhood in various foster homes in London and the south-east. Lots of petty crime, shoplifting, anti-social behaviour.' Laura flicked over a sheet of paper then continued. 'Did time in Feltham Young Offender Institution, where it appears he found God. He's got a high IQ but was diagnosed with a borderline case of dissociative behaviour although it was not considered bad enough to prevent him from joining the army. He ended up fighting in Afghanistan. Did two tours there, one in 08 and one in 10. And then it looks as though he dropped out and, still big on God, joined up with an evangelical Christian sect located in a remote part of Snowdonia in Wales. The sect is called Cruor Christi. It means the "blood of Christ", blood as in blood spilled in battle, bloodshed, rather than "sanguinis" which is the Latin for blood which is used in the communion. They've been under investigation by the local constabulary following reports of gunfire.'

Ed said, 'I take it the place is being taken apart as we speak?'

'Welsh Special Branch are on their way there. It's very remote. What we do know is that in addition to the core members who number about fifteen or twenty brothers and sisters as they call themselves, there's an ex-New Orleans police officer called Varick Mageau who is under suspicion of having fired on looters after Hurricane Katrina. It seems that Cruor Christi specialise in taking in people who have personal problems, mainly drug or crime related.'

Laura flicked onto another sheet of paper. 'So amongst the flock we've got a guy who did eight years for armed robbery, another one who burned down the family home but got off because of diminished responsibility and another one here, Brother Alistair Waller, who is a former heroin addict.'

'Sound like a nice bunch,' said Ed. 'So are we assuming until we have further intel that this hijack is the work of Cruor Christi collectively or do we think that Tommy Denning is a rogue element?'

'In my opinion, he's a rogue element,' said Hooper.

'You sound very sure,' said Ed. 'And we also have to bear in mind that he has accomplices. This isn't a lone-wolf operation.'

Hooper didn't have an opportunity to respond before Laura Massey said, 'Ed, I'd like to introduce Professor Frank Moorcroft.'

Ed held out his hand and it was taken in the weak grip of a hand that was old and leathery. Ed breathed in the aroma of the man to whom he was being introduced. The main components that he managed to isolate were books, paper and the still air of fusty offices and classrooms. It was the smell of a man who has spent his life within the confines of academia. He had also failed to shower or bathe that morning.

'Hello, pleased to meet you.' It was the voice of a man who felt nervous and awkward, guilty even, as though he had been caught in the act of doing something shameful.

'Professor Moorcroft', said Laura, 'is an expert on the London Underground's architecture, construction and rolling stock.'

'Glad to meet you, Professor. I'll get straight to it. As you have no doubt been briefed, we've got a hostage situation on the London Underground. Terrorists have taken a train with over three hundred people on board. We also think that they're trying to flood the tunnel. For the purposes of our negotiation and our understanding of the perpetrators' psychological profiles, it's essential that we understand whether it's possible that they could genuinely flood the tunnel to such a degree that it would threaten the lives of the people on the train.'

'Well, the thing is, you see, there are numerous water sources in and around the London Underground – water mains, underground rivers.'

Professor Moorcroft was a man whose opinion counted for a lot in his world. But he was clearly feeling a degree of culture shock to find himself in a situation so raw and urgent. He masked his trepidation with a tone and manner which he might have employed with a student, one in which the respective roles of intellectual and sub-intellectual were accentuated. It was a common trait of academics, Ed had found, but he was happy to indulge it – play the 'sub' – if it meant that Moorcroft would give him the information that he required as quickly and efficiently as possible.

'This particular incident is in the West End I believe?' asked Moorcroft.

'Between Leicester Square and Tottenham Court Road in the northbound tunnel.'

'Ah, now you see that will be the River Lime. It's little more than a big water pipe at that section but if it was breached in any way then, of course, you're looking at quite substantial flooding.'

He might have come across as something of a weird fish but Ed was grateful for Moorcroft's clarity and focus. What he said next was confirmation of Ed's fears that Tommy Denning was a fierce adversary.

'The trouble you've got at that specific location is that there's a section of tunnel at a particularly low elevation with respect to the stations on either side of it and, to make matters worse, the ground is very unporous. The tunnel will fill in no time. I'd say these people knew exactly what they were doing when they chose the location for their er, erm ... attack.'

'When you say it'll fill in no time, what are we talking?'

'Well, I'd have to put together some figures, which I'm happy to do if someone can let me have access to a computer.'

'Absolutely, of course, but in the meantime, can you give me a ball park? Will the tunnel fill in a day? Half a day? An hour?'

'Oh gosh, I really couldn't hypothesize to that sort of degree ...'

'Nearer to which?'

Ed suspected that Moorcroft was shaking his head, not realising that he was blind.

'I really need to press you on this,' said Ed. 'It really is very important.' He couldn't hide the desperation and urgency in his voice.

'Well, one would have to say that in the worst-case scenario you're looking at maybe two hours from the start of the flooding. In the best case, I don't know, three or four?'

Ed felt strangely light-headed as Professor Moorcroft said this. It was as though the sheer enormity of what they faced had finally been confirmed. In a typical hostage negotiation, Ed was comforted by the knowledge that he could settle in and wait, allowing the minutes and hours to tick by, knowing that with every moment that passed, the perpetrator's resolve would be weakening and the balance of power inexorably tipped in the direction of the negotiators. He had felt that same comfort earlier in the day. It had been something to cling to when there was no other information coming through from the stronghold. But now it was gone, snatched away by the realisation that they were faced with a situation that was going to worsen rapidly. When Denning had advised George, the driver, over the radio link to 'think of it as an egg-timer', he knew exactly what he was saying.

'OK, we need to stay completely focused now,' said Hooper stating the obvious. He sounded anything but focused. His voice was imbued with a shrill note that whispered fear to Ed.

'This guy's clever,' said Calvert. 'He certainly knows how to pile on the pressure. He's got over three hundred people down there with a train that's wired with explosives and a tunnel that's filling up with water. He sure as hell wants to ensure that we give him what he wants.'

'Professor Moorcroft, how long do you think it might be until the power to the train goes down?' asked Ed.

'Again, it's a question that's almost impossible to answer with any degree of accuracy,' said Moorcroft.

'Try,' said Ed.

'Well, what you have to consider is that just because there's water on the track doesn't mean that the power won't continue to function for some time. And once the power does indeed fail, the trains that are used on the Northern Line also have a battery that may keep the lights on for anything up to an hour longer. It really depends in what state the battery's in.'

'Ed,' said Laura, 'I'm going to have to butt in at this point. Commander Boise wants you to take part in a conference call with COBRA. As the only person who has spoken to the perpetrator of the hostage-taking at this time – and as lead negotiator – she wants you to discuss the situation with the committee.'

Ed was about to express his immediate thoughts and say that it was crazy that he should have to be taken away from the front line of the negotiation with Denning so close to issuing his demands, even if it was only for a moment, but he decided against it and said, 'Sure.' He stood up and Laura took him by the arm and led him from the room.

They walked along the corridor – the same corridor he'd walked along earlier that morning with Hooper when he had arrived at the Network Control Centre – and Laura said, 'They don't know about the water in the tunnel.'

'So I guess I'm the messenger? Let's hope they don't shoot me.'

Laura emitted a humourless chuckle as she led Ed into another office and placed a telephone receiver in his hand.

'Hi, this is Ed Mallory, lead negotiator.'

'Ed, this is Malcolm Walker. I'm chairing this meeting of the COBRA committee. Can you please give us an update of where we are with this situation? Our last piece of news was about the internet broadcast.'

There was no point considering that this was the highest level briefing that he had ever been party to; no point even considering the deeper significance of his inclusion in this discussion.

'We're obviously treating this as a major terrorist incident due to the sheer scale of the hostage-taking, the possible death of the two CO19 officers and the claim that the train is wired with explosives. We've also had some alarming news in the past few minutes. The train driver managed to keep the radio channel open so we heard some extraneous conversation between him and the main hijacker, Tommy Denning. This has led us to believe that there is some sort of flooding taking place in the tunnel which might be coming from a water source, namely the River Lime, which is an underground river that was boxed in adjacent to the Northern Line tunnel during the construction of the Underground rail network. We're worried that the intention is to flood the tunnel, thereby placing the passengers in further jeopardy, by way of a bargaining tactic.'

Ed felt relieved; he sounded like a man in control even if he didn't feel like one. The members of COBRA were clearly stunned by the audacity of Denning's attack and, for a moment, there was silence on the line as they all hid behind the faint hiss of the multiple connection on the conference call. When they had turned up for work that morning, they could never have imagined they would be faced with an attack from such an unlikely source, and one that would gain such overwhelming media attention.

Because despite the scene of the hostage-taking being hundreds of feet underground, the grainy, almost ghostly, video feed from Denning's webcam was replete with all the iconography of the World Trade Centre as it had billowed smoke in the sunshine of that September morning.

The voices that filled the silence were imbued with palpable tension. In the absence of any coherent plan to counter the threat, talk in newsrooms throughout the world had already turned to intelligence failings and the apportioning of blame.

Taking advantage of a break in the chatter, Ed said, 'From what we have gleaned so far from intelligence relating to Denning and his sect, it would appear that we are faced with religious psychopathy here. Despite his accomplices, I'd say this is very much of Denning's own devising and, let's face it, he's not come all this way to go away again. I can hear it in his voice; he's going all the way. In that respect, he's very much like a classic spree killer and once a spree killer has started his killing spree it's almost impossible to talk him down, even if a dialogue can be established. In the space of a couple of hours Tommy Denning has gone from being a nobody to being the most talked-about person on the planet. He has created his own myth. Nothing I can say is going to compete with that.'

'So where does that leave us?' Head of MI5 Howard Berriman's booming upper-crust voice on the conference call was unmistakable. It was less than an hour since Ed had last spoken to him, after all.

'As lead negotiator in the cell, it's not really my place to offer thoughts on that.'

'I'm just asking your opinion as someone who has much experience in this area,' said Berriman.

'Well, we have a few options open to us. We can send in special forces to storm the train. We can inject gas into the tunnel that will overcome the hijackers and hostages alike. We can send in special forces under cover of a simultaneous gas dispersal. We can even drive another train into the tunnel and possibly tow or push the train into a station where it can be stormed more easily. Lack of options is not the problem. Clearly the most efficient option in bringing this scenario to a close is also the most difficult.'

'And that is?' asked Berriman.

'Killing the hijackers simultaneously before they can set off any explosives. We could put snipers in the tunnel at either end of the train but what we don't know is whether there are further accomplices along the body of the train who might have the capability to detonate the explosives.'

'And you really think there are explosives?' asked Berriman.

'We have to believe that there are.'

'How long until the tunnel fills?'

'It could be no more than two hours.'

Another unmistakable voice Ed had heard numerous times on radio and television news programmes, that of the Home Secretary, chipped in with, 'Do you think there might be someone down there on the train, like a policeman or a member of the armed forces, who might be able to try and take action?'

'It would be great if there was,' said Ed, 'but it's unlikely.'

'Are you sure that it's wise to allow the hijackers the publicity they want?'

Ed understood the protocol well enough to know that he would need to show deference to those higher up the chain of command, police being thought of as lower than spies and politicians.

'This is not really my call as lead negotiator and I know this is being discussed in detail between the Incident Commander and the relevant co-ordinators, but my thinking on it is that the internet access provides us with valuable intelligence from the passengers on the train. It is possible that there is someone who could intervene, someone who we may be able to mobilise. Denning has ensured that it's the only way we can find out his demands, and we need to know what they are in order to tailor our negotiation accordingly.'

There was silence on the line. He didn't have much first-hand experience of politics but he knew enough to know that the fear of doing the wrong thing was all pervasive. He could feel that fear emanating down the wire. But it was three minutes to twelve by his tactile watch and he needed to be elsewhere.

'I'm afraid I need to get back to the negotiating cell because Denning is due to issue his demands at twelve.' Ed didn't wait to hear confirmation from his superiors, just passed the phone back to Laura and said, 'We'd better go.'

11:54 AM

Northern Line Train 037, driver's cab

George watched him as he prayed. Denning's eyes were shut tight as he concentrated on the words – lots of Dear Lords and Our Heavenly Fathers, lots of requests for blessings for the 'dangerous task ahead'. They were facing each other, kneeling in the cab, knees tacky against the treacly blood on the floor. George didn't rate his chances. He had never been in a fight before. The only punch he had ever thrown was at a school bully when he was twelve years old. When the taunting had got too much, he had snapped. He'd broken the bastard's nose, which had got him into lots of trouble and nearly led to expulsion from the school. It had, however, made him feel a whole lot better. The difference between that moment and this one was that, when he punched the bully at school, he was driven by pure rage. He felt rage now but it was twisted and neutered by the ever-present fear that sapped his strength, leaving his muscles soft and trembling. Denning was young and athletic. A half-hearted attack could be fatal both for George and his family.

'And Dear Lord Our Father, bless my sister, your humble servant, Belle. Her heart is pure and her will is strong.' It sounded as though the prayer was coming to an end. If George was going to hit him, it would have to be now otherwise his chance would be lost. Denning's eyes remained closed as George pulled his fist back and lashed out, punching him in the middle of the face. It wasn't a bad punch but it wasn't enough. Momentarily shocked and blinded by pain, Denning slumped backwards. George was torn between hitting him again and making a grab for the gun. He decided on the former and took another swing but this time, he missed and his fist crashed into the side of the driver's seat. Denning was regaining his composure. George aimed another punch and managed to connect but it was a glancing blow against Denning's jaw and had little effect. In a last desperate attempt to land a knock-out blow, George started to rain punches down on Denning but his mad flailings came to an abrupt end as Denning pulled his left knee hard up against his chest and kicked his foot out, his boot connecting with George's throat.

George felt as though he had been hung. He fell back against the train wall. It was as though something in his neck that had resided there quite happily for the past forty years had been permanently dislocated. Breathing was an impossibility as he clutched his throat and coughed and gagged. Denning was on his feet, picking up the gun and spinning around. He aimed it at George's face and pulled the trigger. As the shot was fired, George's existence was reduced to pain and darkness and the metallic stench of smoke. If he was dying, however, he was oblivious to the wound that was about to kill him. The pain remained located solely in his throat and his senses were otherwise unimpaired. As he opened his eyes, he could see through the watery blur of his tears that Denning remained standing over him. Scrambling to his feet, George turned and looked at the bullet hole in the train wall, inches from where his head had been moments before.

Instead of the fury that he expected, Denning looked sad and troubled. The gun remained pointed at George but his anger of earlier was absent.

'You lied to me.'

George tried to speak but his trampled voice box would make no sound.

'You lied to me. You said that you were ready. You made me think that you had accepted your destiny and you were happy to come with me. George, we were *praying* . . .'

George tried again and this time managed to get out a whispered groan: 'I'm sorry.'

'You're sorry? What do you mean, you're sorry?'

'I was confused.' His throat was throbbing and every syllable ached but his voice was gaining in strength. 'Maybe I'm not ready yet. But I'm trying. It's hard for me. I can't stop thinking about my family. I'm afraid. I want to do the right thing but I don't know what the right thing is.'

Denning must have realised that he was lying. The gun was raised once again and this time the end of the still-hot barrel was pressed against his forehead. This really was the end.

'Dear Lord, bless George' – George didn't want to be blessed; this bastard could stuff his blessing – 'a good man, confused by the journey on which he has embarked yet still worthy of your grace. This your humble servant Thomas commends his soul to your mercy.'

George shut his eyes waiting for the bullet.

'Let me be strong during these difficult and testing times, let me be strong enough to carry out your will as you see fit. Amen.'

George opened his eyes to see that Denning was staring straight at him with an expectant expression on his face. Was George meant to say something? And then it occurred to him and he said it: 'Amen.' Ironic if this was to be the last word he ever uttered that it should be a word born of religion, a form of salutation to a god in whom he did not believe.

But the bullet didn't come and George knew that he was going to live for a few more minutes at least when Denning lowered the gun. The look that he gave George was one of affection, warmth even.

'You've made a terrible mistake. I think you know that.'

'I do. I'm sorry, Tommy.'

'You're my disciple.'

'I know.'

'Promise me you won't betray me again.'

'I won't, I promise. Thank you, Tommy.'

Denning stepped back and George glanced across at the

chewing gum still throbbing, singing, screaming out to be noticed on the radio handset. Should he attempt to ride the wave of Denning's forgiveness and own up to what he had done? Before he could come to a decision, Tommy folded up his dog-eared pieces of paper, turned to him and said, 'Come on, I've got a speech to make and I want you by my side.'

He opened the door and George followed him, relieved to be out of the cab and on the move, even if it was only to enter the first carriage and sit, as instructed, on the row of seats by the laptop hanging in its hammock swung between the handrails. Denning approached it as though he was approaching a pulpit in church, about to read the lesson and, in his own mind at least, that's exactly what he was doing.

11:59 AM

Network Control Centre, St James's

As he re-entered the negotiating cell, Ed took advantage of the silence to ask: 'Do we have a list of passengers yet?'

'It's not definitive,' said White. 'Those passengers whose identities we have been able to confirm appear to be drawn from a typical London cross-section. Professionals, clerical and admin staff, students, academics, tourists, school-children unfortunately; no one who looks like they might be able to intervene.'

'Here he comes,' said Calvert as Tommy Denning emerged from the driver's cab on the video feed. Ed could only take a seat and listen as the other members of the negotiating cell watched the images from the train.

'That must be George Wakeham following him,' said Calvert. 'Do you think he might be involved? Like he might be on the inside?'

'No,' said Ed. 'You've only got to listen to his voice to know that he's shitting himself. He's doing whatever he can to stay alive.'

'He also appears to have blood all over his clothes,' said White.

'Tell me what's happening,' said Ed, failing to disguise the impatience in his voice.

'Denning is gesturing for the driver to sit down,' said Calvert. 'He's sitting down and staring at the floor of the carriage. He looks pretty freaked out.'

'Well, I think you would be,' said White.

'Denning's looking into the webcam,' continued Calvert. 'He's looking at his watch.'

'OK, so it's one minute until noon,' said Denning. 'I'm just going to check that you haven't stuck me on some secure link and I'm not going global. We wouldn't want that now, would we?' The sound of Denning's fingers tapping on a keyboard came through the speakers.

'I knew he'd check that,' muttered Calvert.

'That's fine,' said Denning. 'Good to see that you haven't tried to censor me or do anything stupid. By my watch it's noon, so I guess it's time for me to explain what we're all doing here.' As he said this, there was a series of screams from a woman in an adjoining train carriage as she succumbed to a fit of hysteria.

'Another of London Underground's happy customers reacting to today's unfortunate disruption of the Northern Line service,' said Denning, smiling. He was as calm and composed as ever. The circus he had created was nothing to do with two-way communication; it was a performance, a well-rehearsed and carefully scripted performance, and one that he had looked forward to for some time.

'For those of you who don't already know, my name is Thomas Robson Denning. Tommy. I'm a twenty-five-year-old ex-soldier. I'm also a British subject. My mother and father were British and their mothers and fathers before them. I don't make the point because I'm obsessed by racial purity, it's just to show you what I'm not. I'm not a Muslim fundamentalist from Africa, Asia or the Middle East. I'm not the accepted archetype of a modern terrorist.'

Denning's roundabout admission that he was indeed a terrorist served to twist the nerves yet further in Ed's stomach.

'I come from a country of supposed democracy, freedom and peace, a country opposed to oppression and cruelty. But when I look around me, that's not what I see. What I see is a society that feels the need to lie and cheat and deceive. There is a war going on in the world, a war between good and evil played out in a series of ongoing battles for hearts and minds. Wherever you look, propaganda is at work. The news networks pedal lies and untruths in order to further the aims and goals of the people in charge. The only way that I can broadcast this message is by utilising the internet, for many lost souls a den of filth and yet also the last bastion of free speech. Propaganda serves not to make an objective study of the truth but to incite. So I want believers everywhere to see that what I am doing here today is an act of incitement. I say this as a Christian and not a Muslim but I say it, standing shoulder to shoulder with my Muslim friends. I call on all Muslims and Christians to see beyond the lies of their governments and rather than fighting between each other, unite and fight the one true enemy. This is a war between believers and non-believers and standing here today, in front of the peoples of the world, I am igniting the spark.'

Denning's voice was rising. His London accent was becoming more pronounced. The image he had cultivated at the start of his speech, that of a reasoned, well-balanced individual with a message to impart, was beginning to fade as a firebrand preacher took its place.

'Make no mistake about this, I am a global insurgent, and I stand alongside my brothers and sisters to fight for what I believe in, a spirituality based on Christian and Islamic values, the belief in one God, prayer, peace, quiet contemplation; and I fight against the enemy, the forces of hypocrisy, greed, corruption and war.

'Our so-called freedom represents destruction and deceit in the name of commerce and business, while resistance to this insidious plague is painted as terrorism and intolerance. But every action has a reaction and the truth is that democracy and capitalism afford us no more freedom than the world's most repressive regimes.

'My authority comes from one place and one place only, the Bible. "For the Lamb which is in the midst of the throne shall feed them and shall guide them into fountains of waters; and God shall wipe away all tears from their eyes." Revelation chapter seven, verse seventeen. I, Tommy Denning, am that lamb. And here beneath the London streets, I am about to guide the world to the "fountains of waters". I stand alongside my fellow believers and say that it is time for an eye for an eye – or rather – a terror for a terror. Vengeance is a simple motivation but it is also pure and just. It is something that people can understand. Know this: I'm not some outsider, I'm just a normal guy who leads a good and spiritual life and wants to make a difference. And as long as there are people in the world who are downtrodden and exploited and feel no security then their oppressors will feel no security either. The longer the godless oppressors can keep us divided, the longer they will keep us down-trodden. The war starts today between believers and non-believers. All those who believe, have faith, all those who have God in their hearts, must rise up behind me and prepare for battle.'

As Ed listened to Denning's words, just as millions around the world were doing, he felt fear creep through his innards. He had never felt it so acutely before. Not just for all the passengers on the train but for himself. He knew as he listened to Tommy Denning saying the words that, unlike every other subject he had come across in his years of crisis intervention and hostage negotiation, he was afraid of him.

12:06 PM

Northern Line Train 037, second carriage

Varick moved towards the doors between the second and first carriages. The passengers were now tightly packed together following the shooting by the hijacker and their nerves were shot to pieces. No one knew exactly how many people had been killed; numbers varied from between five and ten. Whatever the truth, Tommy had crossed the line and now it was up to Varick to stop him. He felt no fear, God was with him. There was no rush. It was important that Tommy made his intentions clear to the world before Varick finished him.

Although he was moving against the tide, people were only too pleased to let him through as his displacement meant that there would be just that little bit more space behind him. And as he approached the first carriage, there was a collective assumption that he was there to help them, save them even, and he did nothing to dispel it. He *was* there to save them.

'I wouldn't get any closer,' said a heavy-set man in his late thirties, who looked almost drunk with trembling nervous energy. 'He's already killed lots of people.'

'I'm here to help,' said Varick.

The man stepped aside and muttered, 'Thank God.'

Varick kept his head down as he moved along the now deserted section of carriage. Up ahead, he could see Denning through the windows in the connecting doors.

There was a body by the door, a man in a suit with his head resting in a puddle of congealing blood. But Varick remained focused on Tommy in the first carriage, who stood in front of a piece of bed sheet slung between the handrails set into the ceiling of the train. On it was a laptop computer into which he spoke. Varick stepped over the body and crouched down behind the door to wait. It was essential that the authorities had a full understanding of what Tommy was going to do before he acted. Tommy wasn't the only one mindful of his own publicity.

Varick listened as Tommy revelled in his new-found celebrity. It was the rambling of a fantasist but he had to admit that it was more coherent and rehearsed than he had expected. He'd seen him around Madoc Farm for the past few weeks, brooding, deep in thought, scribbling in his notebook. What he said was more cogent than the ranting of your average religious fanatic – although he knew that religious fanatic was what both he and Tommy would be seen as by the vast majority of people. But if he could only stop Tommy carrying out his mission, turn the tide, and make the world see that Cruor Christi were saviours and not aggressors, then he might succeed in changing people's perceptions.

Whether Tommy had managed to achieve the global media saturation that he hoped for was immaterial. This was a big enough event in its own right to make the news across the world. Varick's mother and father, elderly as they now were, sitting in their home in New Orleans – what would they make of this? What would they make of their son if he managed to save the lives of hundreds of people? He would be a disappointment no more. At last his mother would be able to speak of him with pride.

Tommy spoke about freedom and democracy. What did he know about freedom and democracy? Twenty-five years old and thought he knew it all. Varick hoped that in his last sentient moments as the bullets tore into him from the Smith & Wesson that there might be some realisation that he was wrong, that he had chosen the wrong path. And although he knew that he should also hope with all his heart that Tommy might offer himself up to God's mercy and be saved, there was another part of him – there was no denying it – that hoped that Tommy's pleas would be refused and God would turn his back on him and damn him for all eternity.

His geo-political diatribe at an end, Denning talked about the underground river, the River Lime that he had redirected into the tunnel with his explosives. But as Varick listened to the words, it occurred to him that it was not Tommy Denning who was speaking them but the devil himself.

It was up to Varick to carry out an exorcism.

As he looked back down the carriage behind him, the people cowering at the end of it stared at him, mesmerised. He nodded once, a simple gesture that conveyed so much: they must be patient, he would act, all in good time. He chanced a quick glance through the window in the door. Tommy was less than twenty feet away. He couldn't miss.

12:13 PM

Northern Line Train 037, first carriage

George watched him as he spoke into the webcam. Denning was nervous at first – almost fluffed his lines a couple of times – but now George could tell he was building up to the money shot. When he came to the part about the River Lime, and how the holy water would fill the tunnel in a few hours, George understood the twisted genius of the situation that Denning had engineered. It was indeed an egg-timer. Unless the authorities did exactly what he wanted them to do, the passengers – however many hundreds of them there were – would drown. The authorities were clearly reluctant to storm the train on account of Denning's threats about explosives rigged in the carriages, threats which, just like the boast of there being multiple hijackers throughout the train, George suspected were untrue.

Denning was reflected in the little black eye of the webcam. How many people were watching him? How many more would watch the recording of this in the coming weeks, months or years? George had to hand it to him, it was an audacious concept. George and his family were part of a historical moment, but one he would have traded his life to be excluded from. No, that wasn't true; he wouldn't have traded his life. Anything, even this, was better than losing his life. He didn't want to die; he had never wanted to die less than he did at that moment. All he could console himself with was that he would know soon enough whether this was a situation that could be resolved or not. It all came down to Denning's demands. Whatever they were. If he wanted something mundane and domestic, something like the release of a relative from prison or even something political that might be negotiated then there might be a possible resolution. But George had a sickening feeling that Denning was not a man who wanted to pursue anything straightforward or reasonable. This was not a straightforward or reasonable way of getting the world's attention. Whatever he wanted, it would be something complex and difficult. George hoped the authorities would give in to it – lie if they had to – tell Denning that they would do what he wanted, even if they reneged on the deal later. They would have to do whatever it took. That was their job.

Listening to Denning, he could tell that he was building up to a finale. There was a relaxed manner in his tone, an acknowledgement that he was almost finished.

'You're wondering why I'm doing this. You're asking yourselves: what can possibly be worth all this? You want to know what my demands are. There are always demands, aren't there? People don't just do something like this for the sake of doing it. Do they?' Denning smiled and stared into the camera. 'Well, I'll tell you what my demands are. At present, there are thousands of gallons of water flowing into this tunnel, a tunnel which is beginning to fill up. So, it's very simple. I have just one demand and it is this: that the people of the world should see my sacrifice and watch while everyone on this train, myself included, drowns.'

12:16 PM

Through the windows in the adjoining doors, Varick could see Tommy standing in front of the hammock slung across the carriage on which there was a laptop computer. The hammock was fashioned from a bed sheet from Madoc Farm. The thick bluey grey cotton was unmistakable. Varick had bought a job lot when they first moved in. They had money for more expensive sheets but he and Father Owen had agreed that a house of God was no place for fancy linen.

Tommy tapped away on the keys and the mouse pad, his head visible from the chin upwards above the back of the laptop lid. The hammock and the computer concealed his upper body, Varick's preferred target. A bullet in his lower abdomen would be debilitating and excruciatingly painful but would not kill him. Not quickly enough anyway. It would have to be a head shot. The lower part of the face would be best, the site of the ideal entry wound being between the top lip and the nose so as to ensure that the exit wound destroyed the top of the spinal cord, leading to instant death.

All those years of target practice with this very gun, now they meant something, now they had value. And he knew that he mustn't forget to aim slightly to the left. Not that it was a matter of forgetting; it was second nature, automatic.

There it was through the adjoining doors, the bullet's ideal entry point, Tommy's moustache of thick stubble. As Tommy continued to tap away on the laptop, Varick glanced back at the people behind him, cowering. Nearest to him was the large man who had spoken to him when he had made his way through the carriage. Their eyes met and Varick nodded to him: now was the time.

Turning back to the carriage up ahead, Varick stepped back from the window and raised the gun up in front of him. With the sight just over Tommy's right cheek, when the gun kicked right, the .38 calibre bullet would strike him just below the nose punching a hole clean through his head, rendering him dead even before his body hit the floor of the carriage.

Heavenly Father, please steady the aim of this your humble servant as he consigns his fellow sinner, Tommy Denning, to your flock and begs forgiveness on his behalf, for he knows not what he does.

That would have to do. He didn't have long. Tommy might look up at any moment.

He pulled the trigger and his hands braced the explosive kick which sent the bullet on its God-given flight. And as the smoke cleared, he knew that it had reached its target when Tommy fell heavily to the floor. Evidence of the head wound was provided by blood spattered throughout the carriage and what his former NOPD colleagues might have referred to as 'facial debris' which included a tooth that slid down a crimson slick on a window and then dropped to the floor with a faint click.

12:16 PM

Network Control Centre, St James's

The information that Denning was going to flood the tunnel had come as no surprise to Ed thanks to the driver's ability to keep the radio link open. To hear him voice it in such a reasoned and clearly thought out way, however, was chilling. Ed Mallory could feel the pressure mount in the negotiating cell. The helicopters overhead had grown louder, the thrum of their engines and the thwok-thwok-thwok of their rota blades had become more insistent than before. The government and the security forces were naked in the glare of the media arc light. Whatever the outcome of the scenario down there in the tunnel between Leicester Square and Tottenham Court Road stations, blame would be apportioned and the appropriate necks would be on the block once the necessary excuses and buck-passing had been attempted. Ed was part of the process. His was one of the necks in waiting.

After Denning's diatribe had finished, Laura came into the room to say that the members of COBRA were watching the live feed and the consensus was beginning to swing behind the notion of closing down the Tommy Denning Show. Hooper felt the same.

'Serina Boise is getting a lot of pressure on this,' said Laura.

'If you're asking me what I think,' said Ed, 'I think we keep the line open. You heard what Denning said, if the link is broken or compromised in any way, he will start killing passengers. There is every possibility that if he is denied the oxygen of publicity then he will set off further explosives. His instant celebrity appears to be as important to him as his desire to kill all the passengers on the train. So faced with the option of killing those passengers either slowly as a piece of sick television, or quickly at the push of a button, he might take the latter option if denied the former. So my opinion, if it's being sought, is that we take the option that buys us the most time and that is to let him keep talking.'

'Ed, I have to say that I don't agree with you.' Hooper sounded more argumentative than ever and Ed toyed with the idea of telling him that he didn't give a shit what he thought but decided that such an open demonstration of hostility would be bad for the morale of the team.

'Then we'll have to agree to differ,' said Ed. 'As far as I'm concerned, the line should stay open. It's the only way that we can communicate with the hostage takers and the hostages.'

'Denning could be signalling to others above ground to set off further attacks.'

'He could be but I don't think he is. Denning has his stage, this is all he's ever wanted. There's no way he wants anyone else to come along and steal the limelight from him. It's all about him and his twisted hunger for celebrity.'

Hooper tried to butt in but Ed kept on talking: 'As with the most cravenly ambitious reality star, Tommy Denning hungers for fame and recognition, and while he's set on getting that he's less dangerous. Take it away from him and he's going to flip.'

Ed knew that as soon as he finished speaking, Hooper was going to come right back at him. When he did, the animosity in his voice was unmistakable.

'All we've done since he stopped the train in the tunnel is act like his facilitators. We're like a bunch of television producers. We're giving him everything that he wants.'

'I'm not arguing with you, Mark. My vote is that we keep the line open. Until we know more, I don't think it's a good idea to antagonise him any further. We need to negotiate ourselves into a better position before we start taking away his toys.'

When the sound of a gunshot came through the speakers and headphones, it made them all jump.

'What the hell was that?' said Calvert.

'Someone's shot him,' said White in a tone of voice that he might have used to comment on a particularly spectacular run at goal in a football match.

'What are you seeing?' asked Ed.

Calvert responded: 'Because of the angle of the webcam, it's impossible to see him but, before he disappeared from view, a speck of blood splashed onto the webcam lens.'

Ed waited, sick with anticipation, listening intently just as countless others around the world did the same.

12:19 PM

Northern Line Train 037, second carriage

A man cheered behind him in the carriage but Varick didn't look back, didn't acknowledge the growing hubbub of hope. The lead hijacker was shot; it was a message that spread through the train. Varick pulled the window down as far as it would go in the two adjoining doors and dragged himself through the gap to drop down onto the floor of the first carriage. Hunkered down on his knees, he looked along the row of seats. He could see Tommy's legs on the floor but, due to his angle of vision, the remainder of his body was concealed behind the laptop and its supporting bed sheet. He aimed the Smith & Wesson at the computer and squeezed off a shot. The bullet ripped through the back of the screen and sent it crashing to the floor. Now he could see that Tommy's head was marooned in a puddle of blood. The driver was watching it, motionless.

'Friend,' Varick called to him, 'is he dead?' There was no reply, or none that he could make out. It was difficult to hear above the voices in the remainder of the train that were growing in volume and excitement. He shouted louder. 'Friend, is he dead?' Still no reply. There were gurgling sounds but nothing specific that he could make out. Tommy's head was moving. It could be nerve activity. An armed robber he'd seen killed back when he was in the NOPD had trembled for minutes after he'd been shot. The human body often behaved in curious ways following massive trauma.

Varick pulled himself to a standing position and made his way down the carriage, pointing the gun in front of him according to the standard police procedure he had learned almost thirty years before.

His eyes flicked from the body on the floor of the carriage to the driver sitting in the row of seats. Perhaps the driver was catatonic with fear. Perhaps he had passed out with his eyes open. He kept the gun sight aimed at Tommy's chest. The slightest movement and he would squeeze off another shot. Should he squeeze one off anyway, just to make sure that Tommy was on his way to the Lord? It was a question that he didn't get to answer as his attention was drawn to a strange sound. It could be the hissing of pressure in the train's pipes. It was rhythmic, breath-like but inhuman. As he stood not ten feet from the body on the floor of the carriage, he realised where the hissing sound was coming from. It was Tommy's ruptured face; it was his breath whistling through the shredded tissue of his right cheek as he held a walkie-talkie radio to his mouth and muttered into it.

Movement in his peripheral vision made Varick look up. It was the driver. He was shaking his head. No, not shaking – there was less movement than that – it was more of a tremble. The man's eyes were wide and unblinking, imploring, as they bored into Varick's. His face conveyed the message as well as if he had shouted: *it's not safe.* Varick's eyes flicked back down to Tommy – who was watching him.

'Varick,' he said. But the voice wasn't human. It was uttered from a shattered face, gurgling blood. Varick could see everything now with infinite clarity and as Tommy raised the gun in his hand and fired the shot which speared his thigh, shattering the bone and sending him sprawling to the floor, he couldn't help himself. Despite being faced with an immediate and urgent need to avoid death, he couldn't prevent the thought forming in his mind. In all the years he had fired the Smith & Wesson, this was the one and only time that it had not pulled to the right. That had to mean something. That had to have come from somewhere. That had to have come from God.

The pain was intense but the fact that it emanated from his leg was a source of hope. He was still alive and one shot away from achieving what he had set out to do when he hurried from Madoc Farm in the early hours of the morning.

Dragging himself onto his front, he pointed the Smith & Wesson. The bullet would have less than six feet to travel. It wouldn't matter whether the gun pulled to the left or to the right. But as his finger began to squeeze the trigger, a bullet from Denning's gun struck his wrist, severing all the tendons that wired his fingers around the revolver and sending it thudding to the floor of the carriage. The pain and trauma from his bullet wounds – his very own stigmata – rendered him mute. Was this how it had felt that day at Calvary?

A force composed of pure animal rage crashed into him and slammed him against the floor, knocking the air from his lungs. What remained of Tommy Denning loomed over him, gasping and slathering blood.

Varick had failed; he had tried to be a good man, tried to do the right thing at all times but he couldn't fight this. It was too much for him. It was God's will. He would surrender himself to it.

As the demon began to strangle him, he closed his eyes and shut it out.

'In sure and certain hope of the resurrection to eternal life through our Lord Jesus Christ, I commend my soul, the soul of your humble servant, Varick Mageau . . .' But the words in his head petered out as the electrical activity in his brain came to an end.

12:19 PM

Northern Line Train 037, first carriage

The bullet had ripped off half of his right cheek, taking with it a large quantity of gum tissue. It was a vicious wound that had shattered all the teeth on the right-hand side of his upper jaw. George could see the place where the teeth should have been through the hole in Denning's cheek from which blood sluiced across his face. An expression came to mind: 'That's got to hurt.' He had used it a few weeks before when Maggie had stubbed her toe on the corner of the coffee table. 'That's got to hurt,' he had said and smiled. But it hurt too much for Maggie to find it funny. She scowled at him and hobbled off. But here it was again: 'That's got to hurt.' He wanted it to hurt. He wanted it to hurt so much; he wanted it to be the most debilitating physical pain that anyone had ever felt. A bullet in the face. That's got to hurt.

These bizarrely jovial feelings had a dark flipside of agonising indecision and cold paralysing fear. Denning lay still on the floor. There was so much blood on his head that it looked as though he had been dipped in crimson and it took a moment for George to realise that from out of this bloody mess, Tommy was staring straight at him.

From the end of the carriage came the sound of someone climbing through the window in the connecting doors. A quick glance confirmed it. A middle-aged man with a strong build was approaching with certainty and purpose. Here he was, the saviour, the man who would make them all safe. Denning must have known this but all he did was stare into George's eyes with no hint of the extreme shock and pain that he must have been experiencing.

Shoot him again. George nearly said it. But the way Denning looked at him stopped him.

There was another shot – for a moment George felt certain that his sub-vocal request had been answered but the laptop computer crashed to the ground and Denning continued to stare at him. George had to do something; he had to act. Denning was on his way out. This was the end for him. There was no way that he could survive this.

'Friend, is he dead?' It was an American accent, deep south if he wasn't mistaken. Answer him, George, tell him the truth. He isn't dead; he needs another bullet. Put one through his heart this time or right between his eyes; it wouldn't really matter which but whatever you do, shoot him again.

Denning fumbled in his pocket and pulled out the walkie-talkie radio. Holding it to his mouth, he said, 'If I don't get back to you in five minutes, kill the train driver's kids.'

George froze.

'Friend, is he dead?' Louder this time, more urgent. George had to answer him, had to say something, had to *do* something, had to shout, 'No, get back,' and rush from his seat. Denning was less than six feet away from him. If George threw himself on him there wouldn't be time for him to pull the pistol from his pocket. The distraction would allow the man to put another bullet into him. Denning couldn't shoot two people at the same time, could he?

But George couldn't move. His would-be saviour had become his children's potential murderer. If George had had a gun, he would have shot the man himself.

'Varick.'

Denning said it just before he took the gun from his pocket and shot the man in the leg. What did it mean? Was it some sort of twisted salutation or was it a name? It didn't matter. The man slumped to the floor but he wasn't going to give up without a fight. Even as his leg gave way he pointed the revolver in his hand. But Denning managed to squeeze off a shot first, a shot that struck the man's wrist and the revolver dropped from his hand.

Denning was in control once more and George felt relieved. He watched motionless, frozen, paralysed, as Denning hurled himself at the man and closed his hands around his neck. Denning could have shot him, the gun was in his hand, he could have shot him in the stomach or the chest or the head but he had shot him in the leg. His intention was not to kill. Not yet.

Denning straddled him, knees pinning his arms to his side as he drove his thumbs into the man's throat. The gun was back in his pocket and he stared at the man – at this Varick – with the same blank expression with which he had stared at George only seconds before.

'This is meant to be,' he said, spitting blood onto the man who struggled beneath him. 'Can't you see it? No one can stop me. This is the will of God. Look, you tried and you failed. You did well, Varick, I'll give you that. You did your best and you got close. You are a prophet and you'll join me on the other side. But you have to know that this is meant to be. I am meant to be. And you can't stop me. No one can.'

Varick. A man's name. Named by his proud parents all those years ago and now about to die. George thought that he still might be able to save him if he tried. If he rushed Denning now, hit him with as much force as he could muster, he might be able to knock him off balance. But it was a straight choice now between Varick's life and his children's. Which meant that Varick was a dead man.

There was a gristly tearing sound as Denning crushed Varick's throat. Varick's legs kicked out and his final breath was a sigh that sounded almost contented in its finality.

Denning pulled himself to his feet and looked at George.

'Do I look pretty?' His pained smile was one of two openings in his face through which his bloody teeth were visible. It was like he had two mouths, one on the front of his face and one on the side. George was unlocked from his paralysis.

'That's got to hurt,' he said.

One of the mouths closed.

'You bet it hurts. It hurts like crazy. But only on the surface. On the inside, I don't feel a thing.'

The laptop had been destroyed by the bullet that had struck it. It lay on the floor of the carriage. Putting his head to one side, Denning looked at it dispassionately.

'My kids . . .' George's voice trembled.

'In a minute.'

Pulling the gun from the pocket of his jacket, he aimed it down the carriage through the adjoining doors and into the second carriage. George couldn't tell how many shots he fired, they came one after the other so quickly, the brass bullet casings clattering to the floor. He only took his finger off the trigger when there were no more bullets, at which point, he released the empty clip from the handle and let it drop to the floor before he stabbed in a full one and locked and loaded. There were shouts and screams from further up the train; people were shot. There were injuries, deaths.

'Never underestimate the power of indiscriminate killing to instil terror in people. It's a winner every time.'

'My children,' said George again, more urgently this time.

For the first time since he had received his wound, Denning raised his hand up to his face and ran the tips of his fingers around the rim of the crater that the bullet had created.

Denning raised the walkie-talkie to his mouth: 'It's me. What I said about the kids – forget it. For the time being.'

Movement in George's peripheral vision distracted him and he looked down to see water seeping from between the cracks in the doors and racing along the floor of the carriage in rivulets that rapidly merged with one another. As though in recognition of this invasive flow, the lights in the carriage flickered and dimmed.

12:20 PM

Network Control Centre, St James's

'We've lost the feed,' said White. 'And there's no response on the radio.'

'Someone must have taken him out,' said Hooper. He sounded more hopeful than he had done all day but Ed wasn't ready to share his optimism.

'Let's hope someone has because, if they haven't, it could mean that he's set off the explosives.'

'I'll get straight on to GCHQ,' said Laura. 'Let's see if it's just him we've lost or whether there's any other chatter from the train.'

Despite his suggestion that the news might not be as rosy as they all hoped, Ed could feel the mood in the room change. Gone was the doom-laden tension and in its place was a buzz of nervous expectation. Could this really be the end? Had someone managed to get at Denning? If so, how would the other hijackers on the train react? Without their leader, their figurehead, there was every chance that they would throw in the towel. The train passengers could be out of the tunnel in under the hour. Maybe the biggest and potentially most difficult hostage negotiation that he had ever been involved in would also turn out to be the most quickly resolved. Ed, however, couldn't share his colleagues' nervous optimism. Of course it was possible that someone might have got lucky and taken Denning out – all the evidence pointed that way – but Ed couldn't help but feel with every second that passed that Denning was still very much alive.

Just from the sound of Laura's footsteps on the floor as she entered the room, Ed could tell that the news wasn't good. If it had been, she would have been in more of a hurry. Her tone of voice as she started to speak was enough for Ed to know that the situation was very far from over.

'Messages and internet calls from the train indicate that there have been further shots fired in the first carriage and people in the second carriage have been hit and injured, some of them fatally. It would appear that the person doing the shooting is a wounded Tommy Denning. Whoever it was that managed to attack him in the first instance has failed and been killed.'

'Shit!' Hooper smashed his fist down on the desk. It was a golden rule of hostage negotiation that personnel within a negotiating cell should keep a check on their emotions. That Hooper was failing to do that was further testament to Ed that he was allowing personal feelings to trespass on his professional behaviour. If he had been a copper and Ed his superior, Hooper would have been long gone.

'OK, let's concentrate,' said Ed. 'Is this now the right

time to send in the special forces to storm the train? Do we hope that Denning is hurt badly enough and so rattled that he can be taken out?'

'I'm not sure that sending in special forces at this moment in time is even a possibility,' said Laura. 'Boise tells me that they're working on potential scenarios at the moment but, with the water rising, they're having to send for specialist equipment. We do now have the train driver George Wakeham's mobile number but our technical co-ordinator tells me that with only wireless access we're not going to be able to get to him because his phone isn't Wi-Fi compliant.'

'Can't we arrange for phone reception in the tunnels?'

'We had enough trouble getting the Wi-Fi sorted out,' said Laura. 'It's going to be impossible to get phone network reception down there in the time necessary for it to make any difference.'

'What about the passengers? What are we telling them?'

'Generic emails are being sent to those we've managed to make contact with, reassuring them that we're doing all that we can to get them out of there.'

'Maybe we should be telling them to do whatever it takes to try and escape.'

That no one even deigned to respond was all the proof Ed needed that this was never going to be a viable plan. It felt as though the temperature in the room had jumped a few degrees. A portable air-conditioning unit had been wheeled in and was humming away in the corner but it was having little effect, and a couple of desk fans that churned up the air only accentuated the heat by providing the occasional waft of cooler air against which the hot air was contrasted. Ed took off his sunglasses and dabbed at his face with a handkerchief before covering his eyes once again.

'Well, of course, there may be a way to drain the water out of the tunnel.'

Ed had forgotten about Professor Moorcroft, who was sitting at a nearby desk, and he suspected that everyone else in the room had as well. By rights, he shouldn't have been in the negotiating cell. But the situation with Denning's speech and his subsequent attack had rendered him invisible.

Ed turned towards him. 'How?'

Moorcroft's can-do demeanour of a few moments previously took a knock from the sudden attention that it attracted. He cleared his throat nervously. 'Well, I was looking at the plans and charts for that section of the Northern Line. I was hoping that the southbound tunnel might have been adjacent to the northbound tunnel, or at least close to it, but sadly it's not at that point, they're set quite well apart.'

Ed fought the urge to tell the professor to get to the point.

'However,' continued Moorcroft, 'there is a tunnel that runs near to the location of the train. It's one of a number of service tunnels that were built in the 1930s. It runs just to one side and slightly below the Northern Line from Leicester Square station up to Tottenham Court Road.'

Ed couldn't help the impatience in his voice. 'Frank, just tell us what we can do.'

Ed listened as Moorcroft stumbled over the words, this man who had spent his life in academia. Never spent a day in the real world – that's what people probably said about him. Ed wanted to shake him.

'Well, I suppose the thing is, er, well yes, from the outcome of my calculations – rough though they clearly are without concrete data – I should say that at its closest point, the absolute closest point, there is about three metres, let's say, ten feet, between the two tunnels.'

'Ten feet of solid earth,' said Ed.

'That's correct but it might well be that a controlled explosion that worked in conjunction with the weight of the water might open up a fissure – that is to say hole – which might facilitate substantial drainage.'

'Enough to stop the Northern Line tunnel from filling up.'

By the time the professor said, 'Exactly,' Ed's feelings for him had undergone a transformation. Now he felt like kissing him.

'The only problem, of course, is that the sort of blast that would be needed to breach the two tunnels might also bring down a large section of the surrounding infrastructure. It would be a tricky explosion to judge.'

Here was hope. This eccentric man with his curious aroma had presented them with a possible solution, a dangerous one – a mad one even – but one that had to be worth exploring.

'Laura?'

'Yes, Ed.'

'We must get back to Boise with this. She needs to speak to COBRA and get it sorted out. This might buy us some time. Denning specifically said that he would only detonate the explosives if we tried to make contact with the train. Well, we're not going to. We're just going to slow down the flood. If we can re-establish contact with Denning then I might be able to work on him, try and make him believe that it's a sign or an act of God.'

'I'm on it,' said Laura and he heard her walk back to her office along the corridor to talk to the powers-that-be, away from the negotiating cell and any chance of allowing the negotiators to become too closely involved in the decision-making process. That was against the rules.

Ed turned back to Professor Moorcroft. 'So, Frank, you really think we could drain some of the water from around the train?'

'Well, of course, it's impossible to say with any degree of confidence without all the hard data to hand.'

'You're not changing your mind, are you, Frank?'

'It's not that I'm changing my mind, I'm merely responding to the limited facts that are being presented—'

'You did say it was possible.'

'No, let me be very clear. I said it may be possible. *May* be.'

'I realise that what I'm asking you to do is completely unfair and compromises your professional ethics but for a moment I want you to try and forget if you can about the human life involved here. All I need to know from you, Frank, is whether, if this were just a purely hypothetical exercise, you think that blowing a hole in the tunnel would be able to prevent it from filling with water.'

'Well, the point at which the two tunnels are at their closest and the point that marks the location of the train are far enough apart that if an explosion was judged well enough – neither too large to compromise the safety of the passengers nor too small to create enough of a breach – then with the limited information we have at our disposal at the current time, I would have to say that it *may* be possible. But I'm no explosives expert. It would require someone with knowledge and expertise in that field.'

'Thanks, Frank.' Ed turned towards Calvert and White and said, 'Guys, we should arrange for the military explosives people to speak to Professor Moorcroft here and put together the fastest feasibility study they've ever done. If we get the go-ahead for this, we need to make sure that everything's in place. This is the best shot we've got.'

12:34 PM

Northern Line Train 037, sixth carriage

Whatever it was that had struck Adam, the black man in the sharp suit who had tried to calm Hugh down – was it only a bullet or was it some sort of explosive? – it had taken his left leg off at the knee. Maggie didn't want to look at the wound, the stump, but she couldn't help herself as Hugh tied his belt around Adam's thigh to try and stem the flow of blood. Adam drifted in and out of consciousness. Maggie preferred it when he was unconscious because when he was conscious, he shouted, shrieked. His cries were high-pitched, incongruous with his demeanour which until a few minutes before had been so calm and controlled, so eager to maintain order and bolster morale.

The rear half of the carriage was deserted; passengers had tried to get as much distance as possible between themselves and the female hijacker. Some of the schoolgirls were crying but the younger of the two teachers with the group, who didn't look as though she would have the emotional strength to prevent herself from succumbing to the terror everyone felt, was the only voice in the carriage which did not betray the horror of the situation. She spoke to the little girls about the British Museum, their intended destination when they had set out that morning. To listen to her, you'd think that everything was fine. You would never suspect that she was a hostage of terrorist hijackers. Her steady narrative about Egyptian treasures gave the children something to focus on aside from the harrowing sounds of distress. Whatever terror the woman felt, she repressed it. Her tone of voice displayed no other emotion than a warm willingness to engage. It was some performance.

The desperate voices were like nothing that Maggie had ever heard before. All social restraint had gone from them and the sound of crying denoted an emotional incontinence that was unnerving. The lights flickered on and off. They weren't going to last much longer. Maggie was surprised they had lasted as long as they had. The water in the tunnel had already started to enter the carriage, seeping between the doors, and was now an inch deep on the floor.

In the last carriage, the female hijacker paced around and Maggie could hear her talking to herself as her boots splashed in the water. She might have been reciting some sort of prayer. Maggie could make out the occasional 'Jesus' and 'Christ' and they weren't used as expletives; she was talking to him – whatever her idea of him was.

The woman's footsteps came closer and there she was, framed in the open windows in the two adjoining doors. People cowered, crouched down, tried to find any form of cover, even if that cover was the bodies of other passengers. The hijacker stared through into the fifth carriage, her eyes surveying the terror she had created, and she smiled to herself as though happy that everything was absolutely as it should be. Whereas the people in the carriage who were closest to her tried to keep quiet, the young teacher kept on talking to the children and it appeared that the hijacker was listening to her words until Maggie had the sickening realisation that she was looking around the carriage, searching for her. The woman didn't even seem to register the man whose leg she had spontaneously amputated with her gun and Maggie's fears were confirmed when the woman looked straight at her.

12:35 PM

Network Control Centre, St James's

'Ed,' said Laura. 'I've got Commander Boise on the line. I'll patch it through to your headset.' Ed didn't have time to ponder on the significance of why he was allowed to take this call in the negotiating cell, just slid his headphones forward onto his ears and said, 'This is Ed.'

'Ed, it's Serina Boise. Laura's told me about the explosives option. I can see why you like the idea of buying some more time in which to negotiate with Tommy Denning but it's extremely unlikely that we would ever get clearance.'

'But we've got to at least try.'

'You know I'll discuss it at the highest level but an explosion on the Underground network goes against everything that the police and security services are employed to prevent. There are numerous issues that have to be taken into account, not least the possibility that with so little time in which to plan and devise such an explosion, we might actually be putting the passengers on the train in more danger than they are already.'

'Listen, Serina, I've got an expert in the construction of the tube who's telling me that he thinks it's a possibility.'

Serina Boise's tone suggested that she wanted to get off the line as fast as possible rather than waste her time with some outlandish scheme to let off explosives underground. 'Ed, there's no way it's going to be even possible to run all the necessary computations that would be needed to work out where the explosive charge should be placed and the quantity required. It's just not going to be possible. I'm sorry.'

'I still think we need to look at it.'

'No, Ed.'

'Why not?'

'Because even if we could suss out the feasibility in time, we'd never get the go-ahead. It's not as though this is a small controlled explosion we're talking about. We'd need something big enough to blast through ten feet of solid brick and earth. The whole tunnel could collapse.'

'I appreciate that, Serina, but there are over three hundred people down there. We have to look at every eventuality, don't we?'

'Ed, you're a great negotiator. You need to do all that you can to make contact with Denning and talk him down.'

'I'm doing that but he's a religious psychopath. I've heard it in his voice, there's no way we can stop this guy through psychology alone. Drastic situations require drastic measures.'

'I'm going to have the conversation, Ed. You know I'll

do whatever I can but you also have to understand that it's never going to happen.'

So there it was. The authorities would rather present the image that the passengers on the train had died while they battled an evil and audacious enemy rather than risk having to take the blame for killing the passengers with a highly controversial pre-emptive measure. Ed could understand that but it didn't make it any easier for him to accept.

As Ed's conversation with Serina Boise came to an end and he passed the phone back to Laura, he turned to where White and Calvert were sitting at their computers. 'Keep trying the radio on the train. We've got to try and keep talking to Tommy Denning.'

12:36 PM

Northern Line Train 037, first carriage

Tommy paced up and down between the two opposing rows of seats, his boots splashing in the water. He held up his hand to his face and the blood streaked down his arm and dripped into the rising water in the carriage. George considered speaking to him but Tommy was deep in thought, locked in some form of meditation or prayer. His muttered indecipherable words were interspersed with groans that George supposed were borne purely of pain. The steady flow of blood from the wound made George hope that perhaps it might be enough to make Tommy lose consciousness. The human body held eight pints of blood – Tommy had to have lost at least a pint or two already. But if that didn't finish him off then George knew that he would have to launch another attack. Unlike his previous attempts, this one would have to be successful. George had been lucky last time inasmuch as Tommy had forgiven him for what he'd done. Prior to his speech to the world and his subsequent wounding, Tommy had been in a benevolent mood. The adrenalin was pumping, everything was going according to plan. But now events had taken a turn for the worse. He resembled nothing more than a twitchy psychotic and if, as he had stated during his speech, he wanted everyone on the train – himself included – to die, then George supposed he was happy to suffer the excruciating pain in his face for a little while longer before the rising water snuffed them all out. Another failed attack from George would almost certainly be greeted with a bullet.

In Tommy's left hand he held his pistol. Every couple of minutes he would fire a shot in the direction of the second carriage, either at someone whose desperation had reached such a level that an attempt to escape and almost certain death was preferable to remaining on the train, or indiscriminately through the windows in the connecting doors. Both side pockets of his black combat trousers were bulging with spare clips of bullets which he clicked into place as required. Whatever brotherly affection he might have felt for George earlier on would be long gone; it would be so easy for him to do to George what he was only too happy to do to those trying to escape. So George remained silent until the radio in the cab crackled into life once more. Tommy had ignored it previously but now he stopped pacing and turned to look at him.

'Well, George, it looks as though they're not going to leave us alone. Do you think we should talk to them?'

George shrugged as though he couldn't care less but all he could think about was the chewing gum on the handset. If Tommy decided to go to the radio he would see it and know that he had been tampering with it to keep the radio link open. Would it matter? Would Tommy even care any more? Or, would he see it as yet another betrayal by George – the final straw perhaps – and retaliate accordingly?

'You'd better answer it,' said Tommy, his tongue slurring against his shattered gum.

12:38 PM

Northern Line Train 037, fifth carriage

'Ah, there you are,' said the female hijacker, her face framed in the window between the carriages.

Maggie tried to pull herself even closer around the bulkhead behind the row of seats in the centre of the carriage but there were people crushed against her on all sides and short of trying to push someone in front of her, she was in the hijacker's direct line of sight.

'You were supposed to stay up here with me but what with all the commotion with them blokes I completely forgot.' She didn't sound like a woman who had only so recently committed multiple murders. Maggie was torn between staying completely silent and trying to engage the woman in conversation. Perhaps if they could open some sort of dialogue, she might be able to find out more information about Sophie and Ben. But before she could ask what had happened to them, the woman pre-empted her train of thought. 'Sorry about your kids.'

'Where are they?'

Maggie was shocked by how angry she sounded. She didn't feel angry. Broken with fear but not angry.

'They'll be pretty hot by now.' The woman said the words like she might have said, 'They'll be having a lovely time.'

'Please tell me where they are.'

'They're not on the train if that's what you're thinking.'

'Tell me what you've done with them.' The voices in the carriage, even the formerly hysterical ones, were subdued as people listened, trying to glean some meaning from what they were saying, trying to wring some hope from it.

'They're in the boot of the car at the tube station,' said the hijacker.

Maggie couldn't speak. The woman's words gouged at the terrible burning wound that Maggie felt inside and, for a moment, she thought she might throw up. Of course they were in the boot of the car. It all made sense. As she had been marched across to the entrance of the tube station at Morden that morning, she had looked back to see if she could see the children. As she did so, the woman had pushed something hard, like a gun barrel, into her kidneys and told her that if she didn't keep moving, 'The kids will die.' Maggie carried on walking but as she did so, she had heard the boot lid being slammed.

'They'll die in this heat.' Maggie's words were automatic, spoken with no conscious intent, and as she said them, fury radiated through her body like iced water. She had slapped George across the face once during an argument but, that aside, she had never felt violent towards another human being. Violence was something that she left to men. But when the bitch responded by saying,

'Most probably,' she felt like gouging her eyes out. For a moment, Maggie weighed up the logistics of launching an attack, of throwing herself at her, lunging through the open windows in the adjoining doors and trying to get her hands around her throat. The normal rules of humanity no longer applied. She would kill her if she could. For a moment, the violent urge was such that it managed to blot out Sophie and Ben and their horrific predicament. But then it passed and the vile truth emerged once more.

Was it a lie? Could it be? She knew it wasn't.

She had to move. She knew how George felt when he had to wait in tunnels at a signal and became claustrophobic. Now it was her turn.

'Please, I need to get through.' She stood up and turned back towards the scrum of people in the second half of the carriage. She had to move and if she was shot then so be it.

'Please,' she said with more urgency this time, as though she was hurrying for a closing door on a crowded train. Like she was late for work. Like all that was going on was normal.

If the bullet was going to come, it was going to come now.

'There's nowhere to go,' said the hijacker behind her, but she was wrong.

Maggie made her way between the people, picked her way through the children sitting on the floor as the lights flickered once again and dimmed.

'Ain't gonna do you any good,' the woman shouted after her. The schoolteacher was still talking to the children and keeping them calm – she was telling them something about the tombs of the pharaohs – and Maggie could see the open doors to the next carriage up ahead. She had to get through them. She had to try and raise the alarm. She couldn't just sit there and let her children die.

She was through the doors and she was still alive. She was moving. That was all that mattered.

'I need to get through,' she said as she tried to insert her body into any gap that she could find in order to move forward up the train. She knew she had to get a message to the outside world. Maggie looked at all the people clutching their phones, computer tablets and laptops as though they were sacred objects. The mood was one of emotional anarchy as people wept and shrieked and prayed whilst others tapped out messages or spoke to relatives. Their communication with the outside world had become a precious lifeline.

'Please,' said Maggie to a woman about her age who was clutching her BlackBerry and staring at its screen as though it held some profound significance, 'I need to get a message to my husband.' The woman looked up at her with tears in her eyes.

'I'm almost out of battery.'

'He's the driver of the train and they've taken our children and locked them in the boot of a car. They'll be dying in this heat.'

'I managed to send an email to my mother,' said the

woman with a faraway look in her eyes. 'She'll be trying to contact me.'

'My children might be dying,' said Maggie.

'You can't make an ordinary phone call. It's just Wi-Fi.'

'Please, let me send a message.'

'Be quick,' said the woman. 'Try not to use too much battery.'

She held out the BlackBerry to Maggie who took it and opened up the browser on the screen and stared at it. Who was she going to contact? Who could she send an email to who might conceivably be able to get a message to George in time? She could send it to her sister but she couldn't remember her email address. The police, that was it, she should contact the police.

'Please, have you finished yet?' The woman wanted her phone back.

'How do I call the police? Can I do that?'

'I don't know. I know others managed to make a call but I don't know how. I don't know, OK?' The woman was teetering on the edge of hysteria. Maggie returned the BlackBerry and muttered, 'Thanks.'

Maggie looked at the people crowded all around her. Messages were being typed and sent, people were making calls. There was a heavy-set man standing next to her whose pink business shirt was stained with sweat. He was shouting into his phone, 'Well they've got to fucking do something, they're trying to drown us down here.' He was speaking to the outside world. Whoever he was speaking to could get word to the authorities about the children.

Maggie put her hand on his arm to get his attention. As he looked at her she made her pitch.

'I need your help. I need to get a message to the police.'

The man looked at her with blank staring eyes and said, 'They can't leave us down here. Someone's got to come.'

'Can you help me? Please.'

This second attempt at getting through to him was greeted with an angry expression and the man turned away from Maggie and shrugged her hand off his arm. She turned around and looked to others. A middle-aged woman with a calm impassive expression was standing with her back against a yellow vertical pole. She had her eyes closed and was clutching a mobile phone to her chest. As Maggie said, 'Please, you need to help me,' the woman opened her eyes and she snapped, 'No!'

Everyone was so possessive of their phones and computers – their lifelines to their families – that to try and borrow one was going to be almost impossible. Even if she could, she didn't know how to make a call using the Wi-Fi link; she didn't know who she was meant to be phoning and even if she did manage to get a message out, there would be so many messages and calls from the train that it would take too long to filter through the system to save Ben and Sophie. A few hundred feet along the train was George. If he knew the truth about the children then he would be released from his enforced compliance and he might be able to do something. If she couldn't get through the train itself then she would go down the side. If she didn't make it – if she was shot or attacked by a hijacker – then so be it. At least she would have tried. The thought of Ben and Sophie locked in the boot of the car in the blazing heat of the hottest day of the year was too much for her. All the time she might spend trying to work out how to send a message from one of her fellow passengers' phones – a message that might not even be read – was time wasted. She needed to get to George, now.

She splashed through the water on the floor of the carriage. When she managed to squeeze her way through the people in the fourth carriage and made it into the third, she could see the water in the tunnel through one of the sliding doors that had been partially wedged open.

An American man in a polo shirt and slacks stood by the doors, his fear manifesting itself as a jittery excitement. When he saw Maggie contemplating the water, he told her that the track might still be live. The lights in the carriage were still on, dimmed considerably, providing only a yellowy almost sepia tint, but on nonetheless. If she went into the water in the tunnel, the electric current might kill her.

But there was no way that Maggie could proceed any further within the train itself. The bodies in front of her were packed too tightly together, crushed together in the centre of the train where people had fled to from the scenes of violence at either end. Maggie looked through the open door, at the dim flickering lights reflected in the dark water.

As she moved towards it, the man who had warned about possible electrocution said to her, 'They're shooting at people if they try to go down the side of the train.' He said it as though he expected it to dissuade her. But her trajectory didn't waver and she pushed her way through the gap in the doors and dropped into the water. It was cold enough to make her breathless but as soon as she had found her footing on the uneven floor of the tunnel, she started wading down the side of the carriage, a space narrow enough in places to force her to press herself against the side of the train. Inside the carriage she could hear crying and raised voices; there were faces contorted into masks of pain and a smell of excrement came through a broken window. Some faces were blank, as though in acute denial of the reality of the new world they found themselves in. Some faces reflected a weird sort of acceptance as though they knew this was meant to happen, as if they'd dreamt it, as if it was meant to be. But Maggie thought of nothing beyond her children, roasting in the boot of a car.

She lost track of the shouted warnings. 'Don't go down there . . . They'll shoot you . . .' Over and over. Maybe they would shoot her. But she couldn't stop herself. She had to get to George.

There was a man in the tunnel up ahead. He was trying to climb onto the roof of the train but he couldn't get a steady footing from which to lever himself up. He turned to face Maggie as the lights in the carriage flickered and for a moment he flashed up as a green negative on her retina.

'It's all over,' he said.

'What is?' said Maggie.

'It was only a matter of time. It was bound to happen

again. We brought this on ourselves.' He wore a suit and tie; the side parting in his hair was still in place. But his mind had gone.

'I need to get to my children,' said Maggie, hoping that her heartfelt mission might resonate with him. He looked like a father.

'You can get in there,' he said.

'Thank you,' said Maggie and following his direction to the carriage door that had been levered open, she climbed back onto the train in the semi-darkness, the lights fading fast. It was easier to move amongst the passengers here. She was going against the flow. At the end of the second carriage there were bodies, their blood colouring the water in which they lay. There were muttered warnings behind her but she paid no attention and moved forward towards the door at the end of the carriage, picking her way through the arms and legs.

She looked through the window into the first carriage and there was a man's body halfway down. The door to the cab beyond it was open. There was movement from inside and she could hear someone speaking. The doors between the first and second carriages were chained together. She toyed with the idea of squeezing through the open windows in the doors but she decided against it and crouched down.

'George, can you hear me? George, it's me.'

Any worries that she might have had that she hadn't shouted loudly enough disappeared when she heard George's shaky voice: 'Maggie?'

She had to speak fast. She might not have long. She couldn't even stop to think of what sort of extra danger she might be putting George in. She just knew that she had to tell him about the children.

'Sophie and Ben have been locked in the boot of a car at Morden station. We've got to do something otherwise they'll die. You've got to use the radio.'

A shot was fired. She would have worried for George if it wasn't for the metallic thud of the bullet striking a part of the train carriage near to her. It wasn't George that was being shot at. She ducked down below the level of the windows.

'Did you hear me, George?'

There was no reply.

'You've got to do something, George. You've got to do something or they're going to die.' Another shot and the bullet struck the door behind which she sheltered. She could hear footsteps approaching. If she stayed where she was, she was dead. In a running crouch, she made her way back to the first set of double doors in the carriage and ducked down behind the row of seats. When she chanced a glance, she could see a figure framed in the window in the door. It was the man who had held the gun to Sophie's head that morning. But there was something wrong with him. He clutched his face and his entire arm was red and shiny with blood. When she saw him raise up the gun, she ducked down once again and a shot thudded into the seats inches away from her head.

12:42 PM

Network Control Centre, St James's

The radio connection to the driver's cab on the train was relayed through all the headsets in the negotiating cell. Ed listened intently. His breathing quickened as the radio was answered.

'Hello?'

'George, it's Ed Mallory. I need to speak to Tommy.'

The radio link crackled with white noise for a moment and Ed could hear a whispered conversation in the background before George came back on the line and said, 'Tommy wants to ask you a question.'

'Tell Tommy that he can ask me the question himself. It's essential that I speak to him.'

George's voice trembled as he said, 'Tommy wants to know whether you'd like him to shoot me.'

'Tell Tommy that we don't want him to harm anyone on the train. And tell him that I need to speak to him as a matter of urgency.'

A pause and then, 'He wants to know what you want to talk to him about.'

'Tell him that I want to talk to him about how we're going to resolve this situation so that the innocent men, women and children on the train can be released.'

Another pause before George said, 'No deal, it's God's will that they must all die.'

'George, tell him that there's some information that I need to give him related to that and I can only do it if I speak to him.'

Ed listened to the muffled conversation in the background.

'He says no.'

As long as the line was open, Ed would keep going, keep pushing, keep thinking. There had to be something that would make Tommy speak to him. There was clearly a degree of playfulness, however perverse, in the way that Tommy was fielding his requests via George. Ed had to keep believing that there was a switch in Tommy's psychological make-up that once thrown would compel him to communicate. Ed knew he didn't have long. He needed to find that switch before the line went down or Tommy tired of the game.

'Tell Tommy that I have information regarding the flooding of the tunnel that he's going to want to hear.'

Ed waited.

'He says that he knows what you're trying to do. You're going to tell him that something is going to prevent the tunnel from filling up.'

Tommy had got it in one. Ed was going to tell him that he had spoken to an expert in the construction of the tube who had stated quite unequivocally that once the water had reached a certain level, it would start to drain away and rise no further. His intention was to try and make Tommy think that his mission was futile. Even if it was a lie.

'No, it's something that I need to tell him directly.' Ed had no idea what it might be but that didn't matter. He needed to get Tommy on the line. Once he had managed that, he would worry about what he was going to say.

'No deal,' said George.

Ed needed something that would jolt Tommy out of the game he clearly felt he was playing.

'Tell him I want to talk to him about his parents.'

Ed waited for his words to be relayed to Tommy. Silence over the line. Had the connection been broken? Before he could ask the question, he heard a voice that he hadn't heard before coming through his headphones.

'Ed Mallory.' The words were pained and seemingly spoken with great difficulty.

'Is that Tommy?'

When the voice said, 'Yes,' Ed clenched his fists. He was through.

'Tommy, we need to talk.' To people with no experience of hostage negotiation, the 'we need to talk' line might appear corny but Ed knew that many perpetrators of hostage crises – Tommy included – had spent their lives being marginalised and shut out by family and wider society. No one had ever solicited their opinion on anything. No one cared what they had to say. The situation that they found themselves in was sometimes the only time they had been the focus of any attention. Ed was convinced that Tommy was enjoying his new-found celebrity; he was enjoying being famous, even if the fame and notoriety were only ever going to be short-lived.

'You might need to talk, Mr Mallory, but I don't.'

'Please, call me Ed.'

'Aren't you guys meant to find someone from my past who means something to me like an old teacher or a former girlfriend?'

'Who would you like to talk to, Tommy?'

'No one, least of all you.'

'Why least of all me? Are you afraid that I might persuade you to stop what you're doing?'

'Come on, Ed, you can do better than that.'

'Tommy, you're sounding different from before. What's happened?'

'I've been shot in the face.'

Ed didn't think that Denning would back down now just because of an injury, even if it was excruciating, but Ed was heartened by his growing willingness to communicate. This represented something of a sea change in his behaviour but whether it would make negotiation any easier remained to be seen. It was impossible to verify his injury but if he hadn't been shot in the face then he was doing a good impersonation of someone who had been.

'Who shot you, Tommy?'

'Varick.'

'Who's Varick?'

'Cruor Christi. Varick's the main man.' The words tailed off into a gasp.

'What's wrong, Tommy?'

'It hurts.'

'We could have you out of there in a few minutes and get you some medical attention, painkillers.'

'Why would I need painkillers?' The antagonism that Ed could hear in his voice made him realise that Denning's outlook had changed from earlier.

'Tommy, if you put a stop to this now, you're going to earn a lot of respect.'

'Don't insult my intelligence. That sort of shit might work with some of the losers that you have to deal with but do you really think that it's going to work with me?'

The negotiation wasn't taking the course that Ed might have hoped but at least Denning was asking questions of him, seemingly keen to perpetuate their dialogue. Time for a different approach. Ed softened his tone in an attempt to remove any sense of a superior speaking to a subordinate. This was man to man.

'Why don't you give it up, Tommy?'

There was a thin chuckle. 'Just like that?'

'Just like that.'

Silence, then: 'Don't be ridiculous, Ed. You don't seriously think that's going to work, do you?'

Tommy's questions were telling. However rhetorical they were, he was still asking Ed's opinion. He was looking for reassurance. Now was the time for the ego massage.

'You're on every single news report in the world. What you've achieved here is extraordinary. Everyone will respect you if you show compassion and release the passengers.'

'We both know that's never going to happen.'

'I don't know that, Tommy, and I don't think you do either. If you let the passengers go now you'll be a folk hero. People will respect you for it. You'll have bought yourself a platform. You can tell the world about your thoughts and beliefs and the world will listen.'

Tommy sucked at his shattered teeth and gums. 'They're listening now, aren't they?'

'They are, Tommy. Everyone's listening to you now. And they'll listen to you even more if you let the train passengers go.' Tommy remained silent, so Ed pressed on. 'Don't do this. Think of all the people. Think of the children. Think of their parents, think of the families of all the hostages and what they must be going through.' It was a tack that Ed rarely took, the emotional angle. He found that being rational and dispassionate was usually the best option; listening was as important as talking but he could hear something in Denning's voice. He was at a low point. After all the time spent planning and anticipating this moment, the reality of what he was going to do was upon him and a vicious counter-attack from this Varick person had clearly shaken him. He was feeling the pain that he had planned to bestow on others. He was the cocky young soldier no more. If there was any way of talking him down, now was the time. It was almost certainly the last chance that he would get. The power to the train would have died by now and what light remained would be coming from the battery. This, however, would last for only a few minutes more and then all communication with the train would cease apart from the occasional message from those passengers whose laptop computers and handheld devices were dry and still had power.

Perhaps that might mean something to Denning. Here was a man who had contrived to get his face on every television screen in the world – he had come close – but now he was about to go off air for good. For ever.

'Tommy, you owe it to all the people all over the world who are watching what is happening here now. You need to show them the sort of person you really are.'

It was a sound that Ed did not expect to hear during a hostage negotiation. Laughter was a commodity in short supply in situations like this, especially emanating from someone who has been shot in the face. But it was coming through his headphones. It was pained and awkward but there it was, Tommy was laughing at him.

'Come on, Ed, let's not go through this charade,' he said. 'You know as well as I do that I'm not going to walk away from this. This is more than just a piece of terrorism. It's more than just an attack. This was prophesied: "For the Lamb which is in the midst of the throne shall feed them, and shall lead them unto living fountains of waters: and God shall wipe away all tears from their eyes." Revelation, chapter seven, verse seventeen.'

'But they're only words, Tommy. They could mean anything to anyone. That's just your interpretation.'

'This will probably be our last chance to talk.'

It was almost the exact same line that Ed was planning on saying to Denning. He hadn't expected to hear it said to him.

'You've done your best, Ed, but you never really stood a chance.'

'Why didn't I?'

'Because I'm an honest man. I tell the truth. People like you can have no effect on me. You deal with fuck-ups, weirdos, losers, desperate men who are backed into a corner. I'm not like that. I know what I'm doing and I know that what I'm doing is right.'

Tommy Denning was a religious psychopath and, as such, he represented the most difficult psychological character type with which to negotiate. Ed decided that there was only one thing to do now and that was to revert back to what had made Tommy speak to him in the first place.

'I want to talk to you about your mum and dad, Tommy. I suspect they have quite a lot to do with this.'

Ed frowned at the slurping, gurgling sound that came through his headphones before he realised that Tommy was laughing again. 'Listen to you, Ed, you sound like a shrink. Give it up, OK? This has nothing to do with my father and what he did. I was chosen to do this. The fact that this is happening, the fact that you and me are here talking like this says it all. It was meant to be.'

'Maybe it wasn't meant to be, Tommy, maybe you're just making it happen.'

'It's happening because I'm being allowed to make it happen.'

'Come on, you know as well as I do that the authorities can't let you drown everyone on the train. They'll send in special forces before they'll let that happen.'

'In which case, I'll set off the explosives. It can be baptism by water or baptism by fire, it's all the same to me. We are all of us God's children and for me and my flock down here beneath the streets of London, this is our end of days.'

'This is wrong, Tommy. You say that you're a Christian but this goes against all of Christ's teachings. Do the right thing, Tommy.'

'I am doing the right thing.'

'At least let the children go.' Damage limitation. Standard negotiating procedure. If you can't get them all out then at least get some of them out.

'The children are coming with me, Ed. They've been chosen too.'

'They haven't been chosen. They're innocent. Let them go.'

'I'm in a lot of pain, Ed, so I'm going to say goodbye now.'

He had to keep him on the line. Without that, they had nothing.

'I know all about pain, Tommy.'

'Oh yeah?'

'I was blinded in a hostage negotiation a few years ago.'

'You're blind?'

'Yes, there was an explosion and breaking glass cut my face and took my sight.'

'Bless you, Bartimaeus, I shall pray for you.'

'If you want to do something for me, Tommy, then let the passengers go.'

'I can't do that, Ed. This is God's will.'

'It isn't God's will.' He said it with much more force than he had intended but his frustration could only be suppressed for so long.

Calvert was squeezing his leg. It was a pre-arranged signal that he was – in the terminology of hostage negotiation – 'falling in', becoming too absorbed in the negotiation and beginning to lose perspective. Tommy picked up on it as well.

'Don't be bitter, Ed. I know the authorities have been made to look very silly by all this.'

'Why, Tommy?'

'Two words: Simeon Fisher.'

'Who's he?'

'He's one of yours, or he was. He's dead now. You're lucky that my webcam and laptop were broken otherwise I would have announced it to the world, told everyone how dumb you all are.'

'Tommy, I don't know who Simeon Fisher is.'

'Then perhaps you're not far enough up the food chain but I'm sure you can find out.'

There was a crackling on the radio. The sound faded in and out.

'Tommy, the radio link's not going to hold out much longer. You've got to release the people on the train.'

But instead of a reply, there was further crackling followed by the sound of a woman's voice in the background. She sounded desperate. She was shouting about 'the boot of a car'. There was more shouting followed by the sound of a gunshot.

Silence. The woman started up again but it was impossible to make out anything over the white noise which whined and spluttered as the radio lost power. Another shot was fired then nothing, just crackle and hiss.

There was a break in the squall from the speakers and there was a sound like movement in the train cab.

'Tommy? Tommy, can you hear me?' Ed's questions were greeted by a crescendo of radio static and then silence once more.

Ed could hear White turning switches and clicking away on a computer keyboard before he said, 'He's gone.'

After Ed had dropped his headphones onto the desk in front of him, he took off his sunglasses and squeezed the bridge of his nose between his thumb and forefinger. He'd read somewhere that it eased tension. It didn't seem to help much now. Tommy Denning was so whacked out on God and religion that he had actually come full circle and sounded more sane and reasoned than Ed did. He was never going to release the passengers. No one was coming to save them.

'Shall I try and get through again?' asked White.

Ed said yes but he knew that it wouldn't be possible and the continued silence from White was confirmation. The thought of what was going on all those hundreds of feet beneath the London streets tortured him. If the lights in the carriages were still working, they wouldn't be for very much longer. And then the people on the train would experience the same darkness that he had for all these years.

'Why did he call you that name?' asked Calvert.

'Bartimaeus?'

'Yeah.'

'It's the name of the blind man that Jesus cures on the road to Jericho.'

There was no point in asking Laura if she had heard anything back from Serina Boise about clearance for the use of explosives to drain the tunnel. That was never going to get the green light. Yet the plan possessed an appealing logic and his mind kept returning to it. There was a man who might be able to help. He was a man who Ed thought about every day – couldn't help it – and as the idea started to take shape, he worried for his sanity that he should even consider it. The fact was he had run out of alternatives. This had to be considered. Nothing was off the table. Not in his mind at least. The plan that he was about to put in motion would almost certainly mean the end of his career. But this was bigger than one man's job and it was probably the only conceivable hope he had to resolve the situation. But when he started to say the words, they sounded all wrong. He said them anyway, turning in the direction of Calvert and White as he did so.

'I need you to find someone. He was the IRA's leading explosives man back in the day. He subsequently did some work for the secret service.'

'OK, Ed,' said Calvert. 'Who is it?'

'His name's Conor Joyce.'

12:53 PM

'Tommy, I don't know who Simeon Fisher is,' said Ed Mallory on the radio.

'Then perhaps you're not far enough up the food chain but I'm sure you can find out,' replied Tommy Denning.

As Mark Hooper watched Detective Sergeant White tapping away on his keyboard, running the name through the database, he had that feeling again around the back of his ears. It had a certain heat to it. He had felt it when he was a boy and he had got in trouble at school – and now he had felt it twice in one day, once when he spoke to Berriman earlier and now here with Ed Mallory. Was this the moment when he was meant to throw his hands up and admit that Simeon Fisher was his man on the inside and he had known about Denning all along? No, that moment would never come. He would never allow anyone the pleasure of knowing that he had fucked up and there was no way that Ed Mallory, the blind bastard, would be able to tell that his attitude was anything other than that of a man under pressure.

Was this the end of the line? His whole life had been leading up to his career in the service. He had made sure he did everything right. That he was unpopular with colleagues on account of his naked ambition didn't bother him. He wasn't in the job to be popular. If people didn't like him then that was their problem. What he wanted was to prove that he had what it took. During his time at a minor public school in Cheshire, he had always been made to feel second best. Never good enough at sport to make the first teams and not quite bright enough to shine academically, he had been told by some crusty old careers advisor that he should aim for business management. But what did he know? By the time Mark was the rising star in G Unit, he knew that he had found his vocation. Not for him the boring middle-of-the-road life mapped out for him by his upbringing. In the service, he was pulling down jihadis, disrupting the rise of Islamic terrorism in the wake of 9/11, honourable work, and work that suited him. There was no way that he was going to throw all that away.

If only things hadn't played out like this. A month from today he was due in Whistler in Canada with his girl-friend, Anna. It was all planned. If Denning had moved a week later when he was supposed to then it would have given him three weeks to soak up all the plaudits within the service for preventing a major terrorist atrocity and then two weeks of skiing and quiet nights in with Anna, maybe even popping the question. There would have been no better time to do so than when he was at the top of his game and flushed with the confidence that would give him. But Denning had spoiled all that.

If he could just make it through these next few hours, however, then everything might still be all right. This was a test, a big one. The people who made the difference were the ones who could not only adapt and strategise but also keep their heads when the unexpected happened and turn a situation to their advantage. This whole operation looked bad, very bad; it would be difficult to make it right but he knew that, so long as he dug deep enough and drew on all his reserves of courage and determination, he would be fine; he would prevail. It was all about self-belief.

01:01 PM

Northern Line Train 037, first carriage

A few minutes earlier his priorities had been so different. He had wanted to stay alive, he had wanted to protect his family; he had hoped that Tommy wouldn't notice the sticky pieces of gum on the handset that he had attempted to pick away as he had answered the radio to Ed Mallory. Now that he had heard Maggie calling to him from the next carriage, everything had changed. As the water lapped at his ankles, George looked at Denning, who met his stare, blinking nervously.

'Is it true?'

'Is what true?'

'You know exactly what I fucking mean. You heard her. What have you done with my kids?'

'Is that the wife?'

'Tell me!'

'I'm sorry, we didn't know what to do with them.' He said it as though he was a child himself, one who had been caught out, discovered committing the very deed he had denied for so long. He was cowed. He might be the one with the gun and the mission from God but he was also a guilty little boy. And now he wanted to explain: 'They may have aroused suspicion. They'll be all right. Someone will find them. We thought: what the hell?'

'What the hell? What the hell! I thought you were supposed to be a Christian. What about suffer the little children, eh, Tommy? You're not the new Messiah, you're the fucking devil.'

'Don't worry about your kids, worry about yourself. We come into this world alone and we leave alone. You're going to be part of something the likes of which humanity hasn't seen for two thousand years.'

George's rage was all the more acute for having been kept in check for so long. It felt like every feeling of anger and frustration that he had repressed since his first sentient moment was summoned up and brought alive.

'Think of them as a sacrifice,' Tommy went on. 'Abraham was prepared to sacrifice his son; you should be prepared to do the same. You are a prophet too. I've seen you in my dreams, George. You're one of mine and you're coming with me.'

If what he was about to do would cost him his life, then so be it. George Wakeham had spent a lifetime swallowing his pride, suppressing his true self. No more. He threw himself at Denning. Clutching his mangled cheek with one hand, Tommy was caught off guard. He tried to bat George away with the pistol, striking him across the temple but George was bigger and heavier than him and his coiled energy was not going to disperse at the first sign of a counter-attack.

Perception is everything, and in that explosive moment George's perception of his tormentor had changed. No longer was he the hard young soldier whose brain was scrambled by war, a killing machine whose wiring had gone. Now he was a potential conquest. George's sudden impulse to fight came from somewhere primeval. He was doing what he should have done all along – all creatures are at their most dangerous when their children are put in peril – he was saving his children.

By the time Denning was pulling the gun back for a second swipe at him, one with some more spirit-crushing brutality to it, George had his hands around his throat. His momentum and weight pushed Denning backwards and he slammed him down into the water on the carriage floor. He forced his thumbs into Denning's throat, grinding them together. But he knew what was coming. All he had was impulse. There was no strategy. He wanted to kill; left to his own devices, he would crush the life out of Denning. But he was never going to get a free run at this. The first of Denning's strikes with the gun felt as though someone had taken a hammer to his head. But he felt it; he felt the skin open up and the blood spray. The pain was real. It was excruciating, but he was still conscious, still strangling the man who thought it acceptable to lock children in the boot of a car on the hottest day of the year. He was still killing him. He didn't feel the second blow.

All the lights went out.

01:02 PM

Northern Line Train 037, fifth carriage

When the water came through the doors, they lifted Adam onto one of the seats. Someone had said something about trying to prop up what remained of his leg; the blood flow was still heavy despite the belt Hugh had managed to tie above the wound.

Hugh's panic had gone. For how long he didn't know. But while his thoughts remained lucid, he channelled them into exploring a possible escape plan. He couldn't remember which of those torturous away-day management seminars it was that his magazine publisher bosses had seen fit to send him on but one of the numerous point-less aphorisms he'd been subjected to had stuck in his head. The exact wording of it he had forgotten but the meaning remained. In order to solve a problem, you've got to keep making choices and decisions. The moment you stop, you're sunk. It was clear to Hugh what had to be done. No one was coming for them. If they did nothing, they would die. The driver had relayed the information from the terrorists that if there was a mass escape attempt then explosives would be detonated. So they could either be blown up trying to escape or do nothing and drown. It wasn't a difficult decision to make.

The lights were dim. They had cut out altogether a couple of times. As terrifying a prospect as it was that in a few moments they would be cast into pitch darkness, it was also a situation which presented them with opportunities. Just as they would be rendered blind so would their hijackers, making an attack more difficult to repel.

That these thoughts came to Hugh so soon after his earlier panic attack gave him pause to think. Was this sudden clear thinking just another manifestation of his panic and, as with all the other stages that it had gone through, it would pass and something else would take its place? It was a distinct possibility. But he knew with a clarity of which he would not have thought himself capable that there was only one solution to their situation. He felt the need to voice it, to articulate it and thereby make it real. Even if it was real for no one but him.

'We need to try and retake the train.' The words were whispered; he didn't want the female hijacker in the next carriage to hear but, as he said them, it was clear that he was clothing in words ideas that others had been mulling over for some time. Daniella, the attractive woman from New York who had helped him tend to their wounded co-hostage, looked at him and nodded. The faces of others who peered at him from the yellowy sodium glow of the fading lights were in agreement.

'It's going to be dangerous,' he went on. 'But it's the

only chance we've got. If they let off the explosives then so be it.' It came out like a line from a film and for a moment the absurdity that he, Hugh Taylor, should be articulating it was not wasted on him. Here he was planning and co-ordinating an attempt to retake the train. It was insane. He had to keep on speaking, if for no other reason than to repel the doubt that was firing missiles at his resolve.

'Does anyone have a weapon of any sort?' A penknife was passed forward. He had a sudden impulse to laugh. Someone trapped in this metal tube with him felt that a penknife was a suitable weapon against a psychotic hijacker with some sort of mobile cannon. But he took it and said thanks.

'I got this.' It was a man's voice with a heavy London accent. Its owner stepped forward. He was dressed in regulation street gear, white trainers – now underwater – track-suit trousers and T-shirt. In his hand was a large hunting knife. No one took it from him.

Hugh asked, 'You know how to use it?'

'Not really.'

'Are you going to come with me?' There needed to be a group of them. They needed to play the numbers game. The hijacker could pick off a few of them but so long as enough of them ran at her, some would get through and they could kick, punch, strangle, stab – whatever it took to finish her off. All that stood between them and freedom was a slight woman with a big gun. Hugh looked down the carriage and could see her framed in the window in the adjoining doors. So, which way would his potential recruit go?

'No, man. You take it, though.' As Hugh heard the words and he took the knife that was offered to him, all the lights went out. There were screams and shouts from further up the train but in the fifth carriage, people remained quiet. The darkness wasn't complete, however, as light shone from media players, mobile phones and computers, as further voices both male and female volunteered to join the attempt to retake the train.

'So what we need to do', whispered Hugh in the half-light, 'is make our way down either side of the tunnel and try and find a way into the carriage. Whatever it takes, we just need to get in there as quickly as we can and try and kill her.'

01:03 PM

'Ed, we're going to move you all down to the stronghold in Leicester Square,' said Laura. 'We've got a dedicated negotiating cell on the back of an artic within the perimeter. We can get the radio signal from the train patched through there.'

'We're not going to get to speak to Tommy Denning again.' Ed didn't care how pessimistic he sounded. He didn't need to think of the morale within the cell. It didn't matter what anyone else thought, the negotiation with Tommy Denning was at an end. Of that he was certain. And if he was being brutally honest, he knew that there never had been a functional negotiation.

'You may be right, Ed,' said Laura. 'We may not get through to him again. But we need to keep the negotiating cell up and running just in case. I've taken this cell off-line while we all relocate to the stronghold. There's another team of negotiators manning the radio link until we're ready to get down there. Serina Boise is going to conduct a review of the situation then.'

'Still no plan for special forces to go in?'

'A strategy is being drawn up but there are issues with the water and the explosives on the train.'

'Is Frank Moorcroft still here?' Ed asked the question knowing full well that he was still there; he could detect his musty aroma from across the room.

'Yes, I'm still very much here, Ed,' said Moorcroft.

'Where do you think we are with the water level at this stage?'

'Again, incredibly difficult to gauge with any degree of accuracy but my calculations would suggest it's up to people's knees, possibly, maybe higher.'

'GCHQ intelligence from all the communications into and out of the train confirm that,' said Laura.

'So, Frank,' said Ed turning towards the old academic, 'how long have we got until the carriage fills?'

'It's very difficult to be exact as there are so many variables—'

'Imagine I've got a gun to your head.'

'I'm a professor, not a hostage.' He sighed. 'Very very approximately, I'd say we've got about an hour.'

'Are they going to get special forces in by then, Laura?'

Ed could detect something in Laura's voice. As far as she was concerned, Ed had crossed the line between being a talented hostage negotiator whose often unconventional methods should be indulged due to his ability to talk down crazies, and become a loose cannon who might at some later stage need to be sidelined. 'I can only go on what I'm getting from Commander Boise.' Laura's use of

Boise's rank in terms of the situation meant that the shutters were beginning to come down. 'Any intervention faces unique problems. They're having to revise their plans as the situation progresses.'

As much as Ed had respect for Laura's abilities as a negotiating co-ordinator, she was part of the infrastructure now and as the seconds ticked by, Ed realised that if this situation was going to be resolved with the minimum loss of life – if the passengers on the train had any chance of survival – it wasn't going to be the authorities who were going to bring about the resolution. But not all the options had been exhausted. There was still one person who might be able to cut through the bureaucracy and make a difference.

Once Laura had told the members of the negotiating cell to reconvene at the stronghold as soon as possible where they would be required to remain on stand-by, Ed turned to the epicentre of Mark Hooper's aftershave cloud and said, 'I need to speak to Howard Berriman. Immediately.'

01:05 PM

Northern Line Train 037, first carriage

It was as though George could watch and appraise his efforts to regain consciousness from some other realm. It felt as though the core of his being was still there, still alive, but it had withdrawn to the furthest reaches of his mind. Silence, pain, the side of his head felt as though it had a heart of its own beating beneath the torn skin, each beat performing a sharp almost unbearable stabbing pain. Someone was groaning. When he realised that it was him, he didn't stop; somehow the process of emitting the sound helped him to deal with the pain. When he opened his eyes, someone was shining a torch into his face.

'I'm sorry, George, I think I may have cracked your skull there. I didn't want to shoot you. You're important to me.'

It was a voice that he recognised. It was an old friend. It had to be. What was he saying? Something about not wanting to shoot him? What was all that about? George was sitting down in a row of seats in a carriage. Why wasn't he in the cab driving the train? The train was flooded with water. And where were the passengers? Why were the lights out? He couldn't move his leg. Or, rather, he could but only so far. It didn't hurt but it wouldn't move. Looking down at it, he could see there was a chain and padlock securing his ankle to one of the yellow upright poles. What did it mean? As his eyes got used to the light, he could see the face of the man who was holding the torch. He had a hideous wound on his right cheek and his neck was bruised. George knew him from somewhere.

'Are you with me? I really don't want you to miss this. You probably thought that I'd shot you, like you'd never wake up. That's probably what you thought when you passed out. Or maybe you thought nothing. Didn't have time. I'm sorry about that. And I'm sorry about your kids too.'

Kids?

The download was complete and the programme was running. It was all there, instantly, and George was out of his seat and diving straight at Denning once again, hands outstretched. As he did so, the chain snapped tight around his ankle and he fell, flailing around in the water.

'Are you totally insane?' George remained on all-fours in the water as he stared at Denning. For a moment, his ankle bettered his head wound in terms of pain. 'You can't lock children in the boot of a car when it's a million fucking degrees. What kind of animal are you? You can't kill people for no reason, murder people and say that you're doing it for God.'

'I'm not doing it for God, I'm doing it for us. I'm doing it for you as much as anybody. We all have so much to learn.'

'What are we learning here?' George maintained eye contact and registered a minute victory when Denning looked away. 'It's all in your mind. It's a delusion. There is no God.'

'Not even you believe that, George.'

'Yes I do. So do you, if you're honest with yourself. You know there's nothing there. Everyone knows there's nothing there. Deep down, in those moments when you are alone in your head and you're forced to put a bet on your own existence, you know. You know!'

'I forgive you for your blasphemy.'

'I don't want your forgiveness. This isn't blasphemy, this is truth.'

'I forgive you.'

'Let my wife go. Let her save our children.'

'I can't do that.'

The water was cold and for the first time all day, George shivered. 'Tommy, it's not Christian to murder.'

'Don't tell me what is and isn't Christian.'

'But I'm right, aren't I?'

'It's Christian to baptise . . .'

'Please let my wife go free.'

George pushed himself onto his haunches and sat back on the seat. Tommy watched him and George thought that he looked like a man who was genuinely sorry.

'Let her go. If you let her go she'll be able to release the children. That's the Christian thing to do, Tommy.'

Denning stood and watched him. Deep welts on his throat were visible from where George had tried to strangle him but it was clearly the missing parts of his face that bothered him the most and he continued to press his hand against the channel of excavated flesh as blood dribbled and spat from the wound.

'I can see what you're trying to do and I respect you for it but you're wrong. This is about metaphor, it's about symbolism. If I let her go, then what am I saying? I'm saying that I'm not committed to this, that this is not an act of love.'

'Let her go, Tommy.'

'It might seem hateful and vile to you but I'm doing this out of love. You must accept that and you must be baptised with love in your heart.'

'They're children, Tommy. Their names are Ben and Sophie. Ben's five and Sophie's two. Ben likes pirates, he has a little wooden pirate ship and it's the centre of his world. And Sophie, she's obsessed with her dolls. She's got four of them and she talks to them and has tea parties with them. Does God want you to kill them? Does he? Does God want you to kill children? Is that the role that he's specially picked out for you?'

'I know you think that you can test my faith. But you can't. There are plenty of children on this train. If I was going to waver then I would have wavered already, wavered before I'd even made this journey. What you have to realise is that your children are part of this too. They've been chosen as well. Can't you see? Two thousand years after Christ, another man has arrived to show the world the way to go. I am baptising my flock; I'm washing away their sins. This was meant to happen. Just as it was meant to happen that a man called Simeon Fisher would come to betray me. I could have disposed of him before but, no, I brought him with me. Now he is dead. But he is as much a part of this great journey as you and I. Can't you recognise me, George? You must have seen me in your dreams.'

Tommy stared at him, smiling, and George felt a moment's déjà vu. For a flash, it felt as though Denning was right, that he had always been there in some dark corner of his subconscious.

'What about your parents, Tommy? What happened to them?'

He had heard Ed Mallory, the negotiator, on the radio to Denning earlier and he had mentioned something about Denning's childhood and his parents. It wasn't much but it was something.

'They abandoned me.'

'How does that make you feel?'

'Don't bother. I've spent years talking to people who were only too keen to make me answer that question. The fact of the matter is God decided what should happen. It was all part of my journey. But this isn't about my family or my upbringing.' He met George's stare and held it. 'This is all about sacrifice, George, all about sacrifice.'

01:06 PM

How could something that had felt so right suddenly feel so wrong? The ongoing COBRA conference calls were torture. He had never felt so guilty in his life. Hooper was toast for this. The little shit was putting Howard's entire career in jeopardy. This thing needed wrapping up as quickly as possible one way or the other. It was meant to be a triumph for the service and him as its Director General. The media would have been all over it like a cheap suit. It would have been a badge of honour for the security service under the leadership of its dynamic new Director General. The Home Secretary and by extension the government as a whole could have basked in reflected glory and known who it was who had kept the country safe. The knighthood might have come earlier than expected.

But then came Hooper's news. A tube train parked up in a tunnel exactly as he had told him it would be. Right place, right time of day, right everything, except for one detail. It was one week early.

Hooper told him it was impossible to say conclusively that it was the work of Tommy Denning because he had had no intel from Simeon Fisher – their man on the inside – and he wouldn't be able to confirm anything until demands were issued. There was a small chance it was all a coincidence, a possibility that the train driver had suffered a heart attack or been otherwise incapacitated. Berriman had hoped to God that that's what it was. Anything but Denning one week early.

But he knew it was a false hope even while he clung to it and, sure enough, there was Denning on the bloody internet feed spouting his madness. At least he hadn't mentioned that the service had infiltrated his group. Maybe he didn't know? But Berriman knew that that was probably a false hope too. Why go a week early unless he realised they were on to him?

It wasn't as though the media could paint it as a black op or anything like that, although given half a chance they would no doubt try. All that he and Hooper had – all that could be proved they had – was a little fore-knowledge. They were monitoring Denning but they didn't have any specific intelligence. They might just get away with that. He and Hooper had been careful. Nothing was in writing. And nothing existed to tie him to it apart from Hooper.

As he reached into his desk drawer for another couple of Nurofen to try and combat the sciatic ache down the backs of his legs, his phone rang. It was Hooper.

'Mark.'

'I've got Ed Mallory for you. Wants to speak to you urgently.'

'OK, put him on.'

Ed Mallory's reputation as one of the best negotiators in the country had been built on his ability to construct psychological profiles of subjects through active listening. His blindness had given him increased sensitivity to speech patterns and verbal expression. Would he be able to tell that he was lying? Had he already done so during their previous conversations?'

'Hi, Ed.'

'You need to know that our negotiation is effectively at an end. There's no way that anyone's going to be able to talk Tommy Denning out of that tunnel. The only hope we have of getting those passengers out now is a rapid intervention by special forces.'

'Listen, Ed, I've spoken to Major Burroughs, the SAS squadron OC, and there's no way he's sending his men in under the current conditions. There's been a direct and specific threat that the train will be blown up if there's any attempt to storm it.'

'If we can't put together a rapid intervention at this time, we have to consider using explosives to drain water from the tunnel.'

The only way that Howard was going to survive this was to keep his head down, play everything by the book and in the event that anyone started making accusations that he had prior knowledge then he would deny everything.

'A controlled explosion is even less likely to happen, Ed.'

'You've seen Tommy Denning on the internet feed – he's got no demands. All he wants is to die and take hundreds of people with him. Even if we could get through to the train, we're not going to be able to talk him down. We need to blow a hole in that tunnel wall. I have a professor here who thinks it can be done.'

'I know, Ed. I've spoken to Serina Boise. But we're never going to get clearance for that either.'

'So what are we going to do? Are you telling me that we're going to allow upwards of three hundred and fifty people to die on this train? Is that what you're saying?'

'I'm not saying anything, Ed. We need to keep thinking of alternative resolutions. You're asking me and I'm telling you that, at this moment in time, special forces with or without explosives are not a possibility.' Howard didn't care whether Ed could detect the frustration in his voice. Maybe it would mask his deceit. 'Look, Ed, I'll do what I can, OK? Leave it with me. There's another COBRA meeting scheduled for later. I'll discuss this with everyone then.'

'OK, you do that. Oh, and one more thing: who's Simeon Fisher?'

The question punched him in the guts. But he couldn't show it.

'Simon Fisher?'

'Simeon.'

'Doesn't ring any bells. Why?'

'Denning mentioned him, said he was "one of ours" – whatever that means.'

'No, never heard of him. Ed, we'll speak later.'

He finished the call before he could be drawn into further conversation. Taking Ed's call had prevented him from having a drink of water to wash down the Nurofen and now he could feel the tablets moving slowly – and painfully – down his gullet. There was a cup of coffee on his desk that Yates, his assistant, had made him earlier and he had left to go cold. Picking up the cup, he took a big gulp but it didn't manage to shift them. His day just kept getting worse.

01:11 PM

Network Control Centre, St James's

Ed passed the phone back to Mark Hooper. As he did so, his fingers touched Hooper's palm, which was moist. The smell of the young spook's aftershave was fading as a faint smell of sweat began to break through it. And his hand was shaking.

'Ed, we've found Conor Joyce,' said Calvert. 'He lives on a houseboat on the canal in Camden.'

Part of him had hoped that they wouldn't be able to find Joyce. He could have been dead; he could have emigrated to Australia. But no, he was living not five miles away in Camden. Ed could either use this information and explore its potential or he could do the right thing and put his crazy idea out of his mind. Over three hundred people were facing death beneath the London streets. If he had found a way to save them – even if it was acutely hazardous – was it not right at least to investigate it? The situation was changing by the minute as the water rose in the tunnel. Howard Berriman's words were fresh in his mind. Neither storming the train nor blowing a hole in the tunnel was an option.

Ed didn't even know that Laura Massey was in the room. But when she spoke, he could tell she knew exactly what he was thinking.

'Ed, you need to switch off now. You need to try and relax and make your way down to the stronghold. The cars are ready outside.'

There was no point arguing with her. She was right. If he was still part of the negotiating team, if he was still honouring his oath to the force, then he would do what was expected of him and make the trip down to the stronghold and wait while the other negotiating cell tried to make contact with Tommy Denning and failed. But in the time it had taken for him to process the information that Conor Joyce was nearby, his priorities had changed and he knew that he couldn't do what was expected of him because he knew that, if he did, everyone on the train would die.

'Sure, Laura, we're on our way.'

As he listened to the others gathering their things and making for the door, he put his hand on Nick Calvert's arm and it was enough of a sign for him to hang back. As Ed listened to the footsteps leaving the room, he turned to Calvert and said, 'You need to do something for me.'

'Oh Jesus, Ed, you can't be serious about this.'

'All I want to do is meet him and talk to him.'

'Why?'

'I just need to know that it can't be done, that's all. You need to get me to Camden now. We can say we got stuck in traffic or something on the way to the stronghold.'

'Ed, you could cost me my job.'

'Nick, under normal circumstances, I'd deem that enough to pull back but not today. There's too much at stake. If it's not possible – and let's face it, it probably isn't – then you can drive me to Leicester Square and we'll sit and wait for them all to drown.'

'Ed . . .'

'You're going to do it, Nick. I know you are. I can hear it in your voice.'

Calvert emitted a bitter chuckle. 'Oh shit. Look, I'll get you there, you can talk to him. But that's it.'

'I want Frank Moorcroft with us and no one else.'

'Jesus, Ed. You don't want much, do you? How am I going to insist that it's just us three in the car?'

'I don't know, we'll think of something.' But just as Ed said this, his mind was elsewhere, diverted by the mention of a car. Since he had heard the woman shouting on the train when he was trying to negotiate with Tommy, something had been niggling at his subconscious and the mention of the car was enough for it to suddenly make sense. She had said something about *the boot of a car*. The woman was Maggie Wakeham, the train driver's wife. Her children weren't accounted for. Tragically, in the scheme of things, they were low down the list of priorities.

As he took Calvert's arm and they made their way from the room, Ed said, 'I think I know where the train driver's kids are.'

01:27 PM

Northern Line Train 037, first carriage

'Listen to me, Tommy. What you've done here. Well, it's not your fault, right? You're ill, you need help. If you let us go now, the authorities can treat you. You'll go to hospital and, when you're better, they'll let you out. You can get on with your life. You can get yourself a wife and have some kids.'

'Sounds nice.'

'Come on, Tommy, just put down the gun and let us go.'

Denning had hung the torch by a piece of string from a handrail set into the ceiling of the carriage. The light shone downwards onto the surface of the water that was now above their knees. Watery reflections bounced and danced around the ceiling of the train. Tommy stood just outside the cone of light that shone down onto the water but there was enough peripheral light for George to see him raise up the pistol and fire more shots down the carriage, from where the desperate cries of the passengers were emanating. Bullets struck metal, pinged and clanged, and George thought of Maggie out there in the darkness in the next carriage.

'Listen to them, George. Just listen to them.'

George didn't need to listen for the sounds; they were a constant torture all of their own. Sounds of desperation: shrieks, screams, bursts of manic shouting, sobbing, praying, children crying.

'Tommy, it doesn't have to be like this. Just let Maggie go. Let her save the children.'

Denning was little more than a shadow in the darkness. As much as George tried to add whatever impact he could to his words, he couldn't make eye contact with him.

'I don't expect you to understand.'

'But that's it, Tommy, I do understand. I know what it says in the Bible. I learned the Ten Commandments at school. I can't remember all of them but I can remember the most important one: "Thou shalt not kill." It's there in black and white in your holy book. "Thou shalt not kill." Doesn't that mean anything to you, Tommy?'

'It means everything to me. It's the word of the Lord.'

'So let us go.'

'You know I can't do that. This is God's work.'

'But "Thou shalt not kill", Tommy. "Thou shalt not fucking kill!"'

01:31 PM

Camden Town

Calvert was so tall that Ed could hear his shaved head scratching against the vinyl interior of the car as he steered them through the streets. Professor Moorcroft sat next to Ed in the back seat while Ed fired questions at him regarding the logistics of a controlled explosion in the service tunnel near to the location of the train. Knowing that what he had said to Ed regarding his hypothesis had set in motion a sequence of events that appeared to be rapidly running out of control, Moorcroft was modifying his original hypothesis with numerous caveats. When Ed asked him questions regarding the amount of explosives that might be required to open up a fissure between the tunnels, Moorcroft stonewalled him and refused to be forced into hazarding a guess.

'Really, you have to believe me when I say that it would be a dereliction of duty if I were to allow you to cajole me into even offering an estimate.'

'Come on, Frank, when you told us about the possibility earlier on, you were sounding a lot more positive.'

'It's really not a matter of being positive or negative per se. All I can do is respond to empirical evidence as it presents itself to me at any given stage. At this moment in time, I have to say that, having reflected on the logistics of the situation, I feel neither more nor less positive than I did before as to the feasibility of—'

'OK, sure.' Ed couldn't face further bluster from the professor. It was getting them nowhere. The plan might possibly work. That was the best he was going to get from him.

Nick Calvert had been silent since they had set off from the London Underground Network Control Centre earlier. He had insisted to the uniforms that it was an operational necessity that he commandeer a squad car for just himself, Ed and the professor. Ed had been able to hear in Calvert's voice his hatred of the deceit implicit in doing so. Ed knew that he was pressurising Calvert and Moorcroft into taking part in something that they didn't feel happy with. But unless he was seriously deluding himself, he could also hear something in both their respective demeanours that meant that as crazy as they thought he was for even contemplating this course of events, they didn't think that a positive outcome was completely unfeasible. Ed concluded his questioning of the professor and settled back in his seat. He didn't want to use up all of his co-conspirators' goodwill just yet. If he was going to do what he was planning, he would need as much of it as he could get.

As for Conor Joyce, he had no idea what he was actually

going to say to him when they met. What could he say to the man whose wife had died as a result of his negligence? No, it wasn't negligence. Ed was all for self-laceration regarding the events of that day but it wasn't entirely negligence that had made the Hanway Street siege turn out so badly. It was more like over-confidence. His failure to talk down the IRA hitman and his resultant death alongside Conor's wife, Mary, had – aside from the lifelong disability that it had caused Ed himself – made him more diligent and cautious in subsequent hostage situations, something that had perhaps saved many other lives. Or was that just a way of making himself feel better about the whole thing? Perhaps there was some sort of ironic symmetry to the fact that today of all days he was going to come face to face with the man who represented his single worst professional failure to date.

All Ed knew was that Conor Joyce might offer him a solution to the situation, a solution that was almost certainly illegal and most definitely went against all forms of relevant protocol.

'Here we are,' said Calvert and Ed was snapped out of his thoughts as the car swerved to a halt.

'You stay here, Frank,' Ed said to the professor. 'We won't be long.' Frank murmured in the affirmative and Ed opened the door and stepped out of the car onto the pavement, where Calvert offered him his arm. Ed took it and they made their way down the steps onto the canal towpath.

As the first smell of the oily water reached Ed's nostrils, Calvert said, 'The uniform who's with him said he was pretty pissed off to be detained with no reason given.'

'I can imagine.'

'Apparently he's threatening all sorts of legal action.'

'I can't blame him. Now listen, Nick, you just get me in to see him and then leave me to it. You don't need to be involved in this.'

'I'm already involved, Ed.'

'You can cut me loose any time you want, Nick, you know that.'

'I know.' It was a tone of voice that Nick Calvert probably employed with his children when they had disappointed him. It was not the tone of voice of a man who had reached the end of his tether and Ed was thankful for that. He was only moments away from meeting the man whose destiny had become so cruelly tangled with his own thirteen and a half years ago. It would have been so much easier if he had lived hundreds of miles away or had died some years previously. Ed would have known then that there was nothing that could be done. But with Joyce alive and living nearby, Ed's hand was forced. There was no way that he could allow a chance like this to pass him by.

They walked along the towpath and Calvert spoke to a police officer, before ushering Ed onto the deck of a canal boat.

'I'll be right out, Nick.'

'OK.'

Ed listened as Calvert stepped back onto the towpath and struck up a conversation with the uniforms. The hatch into the cabin was open. Ed ran his hand along the wood and rapped his knuckles against it.

'You'd better come in.' It was the same voice that had told him, 'You fucking let her die,' all those years before. Now it sounded calmer though still possessed of an acute antagonism born of mistrust. Ed had never seen Conor Joyce in the flesh but remembered seeing a photograph of him. He had a short muscular figure with a square jaw and short hair, already grey by his forties. He had to be in his fifties now.

'Hello, Conor.'

Ed stepped forward into the cabin. Conor wasn't going to provide him with directions or take his arm. There was an aroma on the boat that was unmistakably male. This was the home of a single man who had let things slide. The air was stale and inert. Tobacco smoke competed with greasy cooking and the odour of a man who didn't pay as much attention to his personal hygiene as he might once have done.

'They fixed your face up pretty good, all things considered. You were in a right state when I last saw you.'

'They did their best. I wish things had turned out differently that day.'

'You're telling me.'

'I'll get straight to the point.'

'You do that.'

Conor's tone was combative. He was conceding nothing. The police had invaded his home as they probably had done on a number of occasions over the years. He had constructed a wall around himself. Whether it could be broken down was something that Ed needed to establish. Fast.

'I take it you've seen the news?'

'Yeah, hottest day of the year. Might go sunbathing later.'

'We've got a major terrorist hijack on the Underground. An armed gang has taken a tube train, they're holding the passengers hostage and threatening to drown them by flooding the tunnel.'

'Ah, I saw something about that. Nasty business.'

'The hijackers are religious psychopaths.'

'Islamic?'

'No, Christian.'

'Christian? Jesus.'

'We think you might be able to help.' We? There was no we, it was his crazy plan and his crazy plan alone but maybe it would sound more convincing if there was an air of consensus to it.

'Really?'

'The tunnel's filling up with water. We've got less than an hour before the passengers drown. It appears that there's a service tunnel that runs close to the tunnel in which the train is situated. If we can let off an explosion that will break through the adjoining wall then we might be able to drain off some of the water and buy ourselves some time.'

It sounded totally ridiculous but there it was, it was done. The pitch was made. He wasn't going to plead or beg; either Joyce would help him or he wouldn't.

Joyce chuckled to himself but it was a form of laughter entirely devoid of humour. Ed listened as he opened a packet of cigarettes, took one out, put it in his mouth and lit it with a lighter that had to be a Zippo – the click the lid made when opened and the smell of the flame were unmistakable. He blew smoke around the cabin and Ed waited, knowing with every second that passed that the water would be getting higher in the tunnel and the passengers would be getting that bit closer to oblivion.

Would he help them? Was he even able to help them?

Ed battled his impatience, wrestled with an urge to prompt Conor for an answer. Fate had decreed that the paths of these two men should converge after all these years. But what outcome would fate decree for this furtive, desperate encounter? Joyce could so easily say no. Ed would be powerless as his final chance of saving the train sank beneath the water in the tunnel along with all those hundreds of people.

'There are children on the train. Chances are there'll be quite a few.' The emotional blackmail was heavy-handed and Ed winced at his own unsubtlety.

'Children you say?'

'Yeah, we don't know how many but we've had reports there's an entire class of them on a school trip.'

'Mary and I were going to have kids. She was pregnant when . . . You remember that?'

'There's not a day that goes by when I don't think about what happened.'

'Me neither.'

Joyce's voice was measured and devoid of emotion as he said: 'I'd love to help you, Mr Mallory, but the thing is this is your war, not mine.'

'This is everyone's war.' Ed's voice was weak, almost childlike. 'This is just a group of isolated religious lunatics and we need to stop them from murdering hundreds of innocent people.'

'The same was said about me and my lot once upon a time.'

Silence. Ed felt sick, numb. This was his last chance; it was their last chance – and it was slipping away.

'If you're not going to help me, Conor, I need to know now so I can try and figure out some other solution.'

'It was good of them to keep your job open after what happened to you.'

'I don't think they wanted to. It hasn't been easy.'

'What I don't understand,' said Conor after a deep lungful of cigarette smoke, 'is why me? You need an explosion but instead of calling on the might of the British army, you come and see – sorry – come and *find* me. Me! Are you fucking mad?'

'Maybe I am but the truth is I can't get the go-ahead for the explosion. The powers-that-be say no. They can't get the SAS into the tunnel in time. So if I don't try and do something, there are going to be hundreds of dead bodies down there. So, there it is, I thought of you.'

'You need a big fucking explosion on the London Underground and you want me to do it? And it's unofficial. So even if we can save the people on the train and the explosion doesn't kill them, I still go to prison.'

'We can worry about your defence later. You can tell them that I made you do it. All I know is that we've got less than an hour to try and save those people.'

Conor Joyce rubbed his forehead with the flat of his hand whilst he thought. Ed waited, his innards feeling empty and tremulous.

'It was never me that set off the explosives. You do know that, don't you?'

Ed didn't and he suspected that Conor didn't either. He said it in such a way that Ed could hear a state of denial shrouding the words. But if that was his way of dealing with the past then so be it. It was unimportant now.

'I just got them for others. I know that none of you lot believed that but it's the truth. I was a sort of fixer, dealer if you like. I've got a vague knowledge of how to make the stuff go bang but that's it.'

Ed felt sure that Conor had much more expertise than that but he dodged the issue, not wanting Conor to lose the train of thought.

'There's no one else I can turn to.'

'You're not setting me up here, are you?' The antagonistic tone had returned. 'I try and find you some explosives and you lock me up?'

'No, you have my word.'

'And that's meant to count for something, is it?'

'Right at this moment, it's all that I've got.'

Conor sighed. 'OK, well, let's give it a shot. It's not like I've got anything else to do today.'

01:33 PM

Morden Tube Station car park

Thinking about the children made him feel suffocated. The thought of them roasting to death in the boot of a car was sickening, abhorrent. When he was a little boy, maybe five or six, his sister had locked him in a cupboard for what felt like hours but was probably no more than about twenty minutes. He never forgot it. The heat, the darkness, that sense of terror that he would never escape, never breathe fresh air again, never be free. He had shouted and screamed for the first few minutes of his incarceration but after that he had become silent, traumatised. If the train driver's kids behaved in the same way then he would never find them.

He walked along slowly, hands by his sides listening all the while, waiting to hear sounds from the cars. Children's voices, knocking, tapping. They would be thirsty after their ordeal. He would buy them cold drinks, he would pay, he was thirsty himself. His treat. They would be frightened. They would want to know what had happened to their parents. They would need comforting.

Up one row of cars and down the next. Up another row and around the corner. They were here somewhere. If the police had found them already then there would have been some evidence of that. But there were no police other than a couple of community policewomen he had seen by the tube, who were just standing there looking bored, watching the world go by.

Could the children have passed out already from the heat? Were they too traumatised to even make their presence known? Those poor children; Tommy Denning had so much to answer for.

Alistair walked between the rows of cars, listening, straining to hear anything, any movement that might betray the children's whereabouts. As he began yet another circuit of the car park, he became nervous that perhaps his continuing presence might alert the authorities. Varick had told him that London was under constant scrutiny via CCTV cameras. So Alistair decided to leave the car park and go to the corner shop he had been to earlier to buy another bottle of water. There was a small portable television on a shelf behind the counter. On the screen was a blurry image of Tommy Denning standing in a tube carriage. There he was, broadcasting to the world. The news reader explained that due to a wireless internet connection that had been installed in the tunnel to allow negotiation with the hijackers, people on the train were able to send emails and photographs; some could even make calls. But it was the image of Tommy staring into the camera that the TV channels kept returning to, like an itchy wound they couldn't help but scratch.

Time was ebbing away. If Alistair didn't find the children soon, they would be dead. He took a swig of water as he left the shop to carry on searching. It was while he was walking past a row of cars he had already passed a couple of times before that he heard faint crying and muffled knocking. He needed to establish exactly which car it was. Another couple of passes and it was obviously the dark blue Vauxhall. The car wasn't even locked. He pressed the button on the boot, the lid flipped up and there they were, hot and frightened but otherwise unharmed. They blinked in the harsh sunlight as they climbed out and stood looking at him. The little girl was crying and the boy took her hand as he turned to look at Alistair and said, 'Where are my mummy and daddy?'

'They'll be back soon,' he said. 'They just had to take a trip. They asked me to look after you until they get back.'

'What's your name?' asked the little girl between sobs.

'I'm Alistair, I'm your friend.'

'I'm thirsty, Alistair,' said the boy.

'Let's go and get a nice cold drink then.'

Slamming the lid of the boot, he ushered the children in front of him. He didn't hear the cars pull up at the entrance to the car park; he didn't hear the footsteps. He was thinking about the children, he was thinking about the cold drink he would buy them and how he had saved their lives.

As soon as he heard a voice through a loudhailer, he knew the ensuing words would be directed at him.

'You, in the jeans and the grey T-shirt. Stay where you are.' There was no one else in jeans and a grey T-shirt; there was no one in the car park besides him and the children. He turned around and there they were. They weren't the usual ones; this was all to do with Tommy Denning. They were crouched down behind a row of cars on the other side of the car park. They had guns; he couldn't see them but he knew they were there. It wasn't as if he'd done anything wrong. All he had done was rescue two children who otherwise might have died. But no one would ever see it that way. He was involved. He was implicated. They would look on their computers and they would see who he was.

'Alistair? What's going on?' asked the little boy, but he didn't get to answer before the loudhailer cut through the hot air once again.

'Sophie! Ben! Walk towards us, keep walking towards this voice.'

'You'd better do as he says,' said Alistair. The little girl was crying again. She was so young, so innocent, she didn't deserve this.

'Don't worry, Sophie,' he said, 'everything will be all right. Go on now, you'll be fine. Just go over there towards those cars.' And she did, she started walking. So did her brother. Alistair was all alone now. He hadn't done anything wrong. But that didn't matter. Not any more.

They wouldn't understand, they never did. They would make it their business to misunderstand. They would twist his words, make it appear that he was trying to hurt the children. They would make out he was in league with Tommy Denning when, in fact, he was doing everything in his power to save two innocent children from Tommy's madness. They would want to know why he hadn't gone to the police in the first place. In his desire to help the children, they would see subversive desires at work. They would probably suggest that he was in the process of abducting them. He would never be able to make them understand. They would create their own phoney confusion. Throughout his life he had spent so many hours in police stations, so many hours in cells, he couldn't face any more.

He knew what he had to do. It was play-acting. When he was a little boy, he had been in all the school plays. Over-acted terribly. But it didn't matter. Just as it didn't matter now. He started to shout as he ran, screamed, heading straight for the kids, putting his hand in his pocket as though he might be pulling a gun. Today of all days, it would be enough. They couldn't allow him to hurt those children.

The voice through the loudhailer was shouting at him but he couldn't hear the exact words above his screams. It took longer than he thought it would. He was almost upon Sophie as the first bullet hit him. It hit him low down, in the stomach. It might not be enough so he carried on running, hurling himself forward and the second one hit the mark. Middle of the chest. He wasn't going to hospital. He would be all right; he was flying straight into the arms of Jesus.

01:49 PM

'He's walking across the road and approaching some railway arches. He's knocking on a door set into the timber facade.'

Ed sat in the back of the car with the professor while Calvert commentated on Conor Joyce's movements.

'The door's being opened by a white male in his forties, thick set, about five nine. They're talking to one another. Joyce has gone inside and the door's been closed.'

Ed slid down on the upholstery. Conor Joyce's involvement was providing him with a whole new set of problems. While he had proved easier to persuade than Ed had feared, it was his seemingly compliant attitude that worried him. It didn't take much psychological intuition to realise that Conor had an ulterior motive and it wasn't difficult to conceive of what that motive might be. Ed knew all about frustration and how it could brew and fester. On that day over thirteen years ago Ed and Conor had both lost something dear to them. Wounds like those didn't heal. Now Ed had given Conor a shot at revenge and he had to accept that Conor might very well take it.

The air conditioning struggled to combat the hot air baking the car. He tried to empty his mind, knowing that even if he could do it for only a few seconds it would help. Ed's use of meditation had no spiritual angle to it, nothing more ritualistic than trying to cleanse his mind for a few minutes each day. It helped him think clearly. It was difficult to do knowing what he knew of the passengers on the train but he needed to try and get a perspective on what he was about to attempt. He knew that if he asked Calvert and Moorcroft their opinion, they would construct their answers based on their perceived professional obligations. Although they were very different, one a dedicated street-wise copper and the other a lifelong academic, they both had a strong sense of duty. But in this instance, it was misguided. Ed felt certain of it. What the situation needed was someone who didn't care about his career or his place in society, someone who sometimes found himself dangerously uninterested in his own personal safety.

'What's he doing in there?' asked Calvert.

'He's collecting something,' replied Ed and just as Calvert was about to ask him – as he knew he would – exactly what it was that he was collecting, Ed asked him, 'You got any children, Nick?'

It was two boys if Ed remembered correctly. Calvert had mentioned them one time during a coffee break at a counter-terrorism seminar at which they had both been speaking. The voice of the big fearsome-looking special branch officer softened as the connections were made and he thought of his children.

'Jack and Felix. Jack's eight and Felix is five.'

'Where are they today?'

'They're both at school. Ed, we need to get going—'

'I never had kids. It just never seemed to happen. Shame really. My younger brother's got three. They're beautiful.' Ed could hear Calvert turn to look at him as he spoke about his brother's children and how, in the absence of children of his own, he had tried to be the best uncle to them that he could possibly be. He reminisced about Christmas the year before and how his brother's youngest, Jasmine, had staged her own song-and-dance routine – anything to avoid the subject of what they were doing there outside a railway arch in King's Cross. But he was interrupted when Calvert said, 'He's on his way back. He's carrying an old cardboard box. Oh shit, he's putting it in the boot.' Ed listened as Conor slammed the boot lid and climbed into the passenger seat. His story having served its purpose and, with Conor Joyce and his provisions now on board, Ed remained silent while Calvert started the engine, swung the car around and set off.

01:50 PM

Northern Line Train 037, first carriage

'If there is a God, you'll burn in hell for this.'

'You don't know what you're saying, George.'

'Stop talking to me like I'm your friend. Stop calling me George. You can kill me, but you can't befriend me.'

'You've got spirit, I'll give you that.'

The water was now over George's waist, higher on Tommy, who continued to fire his pistol down the carriage every few minutes as though compelled to do so by the distant sounds of desperation from the passengers.

'Why don't you just kill yourself?' asked George. 'Why do we have to die with you? Just put the gun in your mouth and pull the trigger. It'll be over in a second.'

'I wish you people would stop wishing me dead,' said Tommy. 'All my life people have been trying to keep me alive. In Afghanistan, blokes were getting shot at all the time. Me? Not once. But now everyone wants me to die. Am I not going to be dead soon enough?'

'Don't be a prick,' said George. 'Don't delude yourself. You're a murdering psychopathic scumbag. That's why people want you dead. You're no prophet. You're about as much of a prophet as that David Koresh or Jim Jones.'

'Bless you, you're doing what you think is best.'

George pulled against the chain that bound his leg to the pole even though it sent shooting barbs of pain up his shin. The pain was a distraction from his agonising frustration.

'Maggie?' George shouted into the darkness.

'Yes, George, I'm here.' She sounded distant, further away than the twenty feet or so that he knew it to be.

'You've got to get as many people together as you can, and you've got to come down here, and if there are enough of you and you're determined enough, you'll be able to overpower him and kill him.'

'Yes please, Maggie,' shouted Denning. 'Bring them here. Once I've shot poor George here, I'll shoot them too.'

'Do it, Maggie,' said George. 'Do it for Sophie and Ben.'

George could just make out Denning watching him, shaking his head slightly, like a father might, disappointed at the behaviour of a child.

'You know she won't do that. She's terrified. You're all she's got to cling to, and besides they're going to start coming for me soon anyway.'

He left the statement hanging there; George didn't want to give him the satisfaction of asking him to qualify it but curiosity got the better of him.

'They?'

'The passengers. Back in the old days, it was possible to do something like this and they'd stay put, wait, hope that you were sincere when you told them that they would be all right so long as they did as you said. But United Airlines Flight 93 changed all that. They're going to come for me and I've got to be ready.'

Denning reached into the holdall that he had slung around his neck so as to keep it above the water. His arm glistened in the light from the torch, varnished with blood from the wound in his face that he had been pressing his hand against. As he retracted his arm from the holdall, he was holding a semi-automatic rifle.

'I'm ready for them,' he said. 'I'm prepared for all eventualities. But what about you? All this shouting to your wife that she should bring some bigger boys to duff me up, well, it makes me think that perhaps you want to die.'

'I'm going to die soon anyway, isn't that right?'

'You're going to die and you're going to be resurrected to eternal life. But maybe you don't want to wait.'

George watched as Denning pointed the gun at him.

'If you'd rather, I can baptise you now and send you on your way. Would you like that? After all, you suffer from claustrophobia, right? Those two or three minutes in the water while your lungs give out, that might not be a very pleasurable experience. Particularly if you go into it with the wrong frame of mind. So, as a special concession to you and because I like you, I'm going to give you the option. If you'd rather go here and now then tell me.'

What had George got to live for? Just another few minutes of horror knowing that he was going to die and being powerless to stop it, tortured with the knowledge that he might have been able to do something if only he had tried harder, made different choices. And then at the end of it, drowning – something that had terrified him all his life.

Why not go now? If he was a coward – and he felt like one – then why not die like one? Why not just make things easier for himself for once in his miserable life?

'Just say the word, George. I know you're thinking about it.'

'No, he's not!' shouted Maggie from the next carriage.

'Don't listen to her, she'll try and dissuade you.'

'George! If we have to die then we have to die together.'

'See? I told you. Ignore her. I'm prepared to do you a favour.'

'*George.*' It was a tone of voice he had heard Maggie use a thousand times. It said, 'Don't you dare.'

'What do you say, one little squeeze of the trigger and all that pain goes away, just like a sweet little pill, only quicker?'

'Go fuck yourself.'

Denning lowered the gun, chuckling as he did so.

'What's so funny?'

'You are, George. You really crack me up. I wasn't going to shoot you. Even if you'd pleaded with me. How many times do I have to tell you? You're coming with me.'

01:55 PM

Northern Line Train 037, fifth carriage

Hugh Taylor, consumer affairs columnist, his sports jacket now long discarded, waded through the water towards the doors between the fourth and fifth carriages. His way was lit by the screens of phones, tablets and laptops. For the first time in hours there was a sense of hope amongst the passengers at the rear of the train. They knew there was going to be an attempt to retake the train by a group of men. Hugh was one of those men. He was more than one of those men, he was their leader.

He didn't know where it came from. For all his life he had felt excluded, left out, a watcher, a spectator, a nerd, a joke, and now here he was captaining the team. It felt surreal although the fear itself was real enough. He was afraid, not so much that he would die – he had resigned himself to the fact that he probably would – but afraid that he would revert back to the man he had been for the sum total of his forty-seven years. He enjoyed this new version of himself. Hugh Mk 2. This was the man that he wanted to be, even if it was only for the last few moments of his life. He believed in destiny, perhaps this was his.

Recruitment choices had not been difficult. He took every person who volunteered. There weren't many but there was no question of shaming people into making the journey with him; he could hardly sit in judgement over others with regard to their potential bravery or cowardice. It wasn't that long since his last panic attack and, although he was no psychologist and didn't hold with all that analytical self-help bullshit, he knew with an unwavering certainty that his panic attacks were born of fear and more than a little cowardice. But the need to take a stand had forced him into action. It didn't feel like bravery. It didn't really feel like much of anything. It was just the right thing to do. The water was up to his middle. The schoolgirls had to stand on the seats. They were frightened. Everyone was frightened. The expressions on the children's faces, lit by the glow from electronic equipment, were what drove him on. He couldn't just stand by and let the children die.

First out of the door, he squeezed himself between the end of the fourth carriage and the fifth and down into the cold water, up to his shoulders, and along the side of the carriage towards the rear of the train. The plan that they had hatched in urgent whispers only minutes before was that they would divide themselves into two groups and make their way along the tunnel wall on either side of the train and up to the sixth carriage. There they would attempt to draw fire from the hijacker to allow opportunities to enter the train and, once inside, try and kill her.

The plan was weak: he knew it, they all knew it. But what choice did they have? Hugh had never even been in a fight before but he knew, if he could reach the woman, she was dead.

The others followed him; he could hear them climbing down from the carriage and into the water. They didn't look like heroes. They looked like what they were, frightened desperate people doing whatever it took to try to stay alive. Of the four of them who had sat together at the end of the carriage and introduced themselves to each other that morning, Maggie had set off along the train – God alone knew why – and Adam had lost half his leg, which meant that he and the New Yorker, Daniella, who had insisted on joining the attempt to attack the hijacker, were the only two remaining.

As far as the others in the team were concerned, Hugh knew that he couldn't think about who these people actually were. They were all of them someone's son, father, mother or daughter. A strictly adults-only policy was his only hard-and-fast rule but other than that anyone could take their chances with the crazy bitch.

When Daniella dropped down from between the carriages, the water came to just over her shoulders. She pulled herself along the side of the train but, after a couple of footsteps, she lost her footing on the uneven ground and as she steadied herself – one hand on the side of the train and the other on the cables mounted on the tunnel wall – she took a mouthful of water. It tasted sour and muddy and she spat it out, gasping.

There was more light the nearer she came to the last carriage. The hijacker stood in the glow from a battery-powered lantern hanging from a handrail, its light reflected in ripples on the ceiling of the train. Standing with her legs apart, she had her rifle rested across her shoulders, her arms hanging over it in the classic James Dean pose. She looked as though she was acting.

The plan was simple, to draw fire from the hijacker and through the resulting shattered windows, gain entry to the carriage. Once inside, the idea was to choose a moment when she might need to reload – or even better run out of ammunition – and then attack her, kill her if need be. Daniella had been wrong about Hugh. He might have been an unworldly guy with a panicky demeanour but he had somehow discovered untapped reservoirs of courage under pressure. The plan to retake the train had been his and it was impossible to know why Daniella had said yes when he asked for volunteers. Wherever the impulse had come from, it had made her feel better than she had since this entire nightmare had begun. There were moments back there when she feared she was cracking up. It was the inertia, the helplessness. Now she had something to do, something to focus on over and above the crushing despair. The fear didn't get any less but at least this was something positive. Now she had hope.

Hugh was the first to try and draw fire from the hijacker. The others pulled back behind the end of the fifth carriage, leaving him standing by the window, banging on the glass, waiting for the woman to shoot at him. As she did so, he jumped back and the dum-dum bullet smashed into the window of the sliding door at the end of the carriage, creating a hole the circumference of a large dinner plate. The exploding glass fragments ricocheted in the tunnel stinging the back of Hugh's head and when he dabbed at the cuts with his hand, his fingers came away wet with blood.

As they had planned, a young Iranian man banged and shouted on the other side of the carriage, and the resulting shot from Belle slammed into the metal carriage wall blasting a ragged hole in the metal. Another shout from Hugh and this time he stood his ground as the woman raised the gun. For a moment, their eyes met along the barrel and he threw himself back as she pulled the trigger. Blinking away the muddy water, he saw a hole in the window in the door. It was big enough. He waited for more shouting from his co-conspirators and, glancing up over the lower edge of the window, he could see the woman taking aim at the opposite side of the train.

He had to move fast. Finding a foothold on the tunnel wall, he pulled himself up and threw himself against the hole in the window. The shredded glass snagged against his back and chest as he clambered into the carriage. Holding his breath, he curled up in a ball underwater behind the row of seats as the thump of a large calibre bullet struck metal nearby.

He was in.

Pushing his head above the surface of the water, he sucked up a lungful of air. He looked across at the young

Iranian, who hammered on the side of the carriage to try and distract the hijacker. But he mistimed his evasive manoeuvre and as a gunshot thumped the air half his head came away.

Hugh managed to turn around in the water and crouching on his haunches, he leant back against the end of the row of seats. With his eyes just above the level of the water, he could see another team member, a man in a black suit, as he squeezed between the side of the train and the tunnel wall. The man was about to beat on the side of the train but the hijacker had spotted him and fired off a shot which splintered the metal in the door and he was hit by something, some sort of shrapnel from her diabolical weapon. Slumping down in the water, Hugh could hear him gasp and cry out but he was still moving and clearly audible as he retreated, making his way back down the side of the train.

Daniella Langton knew that she was probably level with the hijacker now. She had to climb over the young Iranian's body. His limbs were solid and heavy in the water. If she gave herself away, a shot through the side of the train would mean the end. But the carriage was tight against the tunnel wall. She would have to force herself through the narrow space. There was nothing else she could do. Once again, she had over-estimated her abilities. It was something that her mother – who never failed to miss an opportunity to put her down – had said to her often enough. It was even said to her in her work appraisals until she reached a position in the company where she didn't need to care what others thought of her. And now she was going to die for it.

There was another gunshot. This was her moment, this was her chance. She pushed herself through the gap, her clothes scraping against the side of the train, and threw herself forward into the water trying to go as deep as she could until her fingers dug into the gravel on the bottom of the tunnel. Explosive gunshots above her head were muffled by the water, their impact against the side of the train punching her eardrums. She dragged herself along, her lungs aching for air. As her fingers curled around the end of the carriage, she pushed her head above the surface, drew a deep breath and plunged back into the water.

Further sounds of gunfire came from the train. Maybe the second wave of people had begun their attack. Perhaps they would succeed. She wouldn't get to find out; she couldn't stop herself even if she tried. The impulse was irresistible. She just had to put as much distance between herself and the train as was humanly possible.

As the train receded behind her, Daniella felt safe enough to take another breath and do the front crawl as she swam along the tunnel towards a faint light in the distance.

Hugh's strangely beatific mood of confidence of only a few moments before had taken a pounding. He felt his bravery ebb. It was essential that he maintain his momentum. But he couldn't help but feel that rather than gaining entry to the carriage through his own guile and ingenuity, the hijacker had allowed him to do so. The thought unnerved him. Perhaps throwing himself forward blindly was not the best strategy. He worried that perhaps this reasoning was the onset of a resurgent cowardice and the thought filled him with more fear than he had felt all day.

Someone else tried to make their way into the carriage on the other side of the train. Hugh couldn't see who it was. As a shot was fired, another man clambered through the window through which he had come before a shot threw him backwards against the tunnel wall and he slumped forward into the water.

It was time for Hugh to move but just as the torture of his indecision began again, two men managed to gain entry to the carriage through newly broken windows but he didn't rate their chances. It was obvious they were being allowed entry – just as he had been – and the ensuing shots and the splashing of their bodies in the water were confirmation of this.

No one else was going to try their luck. It was all down to him now.

It was dark in the carriage – the only light came from the single bulb in the hijacker's lamp swinging from a handrail. The water was dark too. If he could move cleanly beneath it without breaking the surface, he might reach the end of the row of seats and hunker down once again by the first set of double sliding doors. Could he pull himself along between the seats without giving himself away? There was nothing to be gained from pondering on the logistics of his plan, so he took some deep breaths to oxygenate his blood and set off towards her. He remembered from when he was a little boy playing soldiers with his brother in the garden that they always used to say you'd never hear the bullet that killed you. It was something they must have read in a comic or seen in a film. And here he was all these years later about to find out whether it was true.

She was only about ten feet away from him now. With the hunting knife in his hand, he pulled himself along under the water towards her.

MI5 Headquarters, Thames House

'We both own this, Howard, but I'm the one who's been left to make the big decisions. If it all falls apart because one of us loses our nerve then we'll both be held responsible.'

'Is that some sort of threat?'

'We both agreed that this could work. You can't walk away.'

'Mark, there are hundreds of people down there. Special forces think it's impossible to get in there without exposing their men to Denning's threat to let off more explosives. Number Ten, the home office, COBRA, the media – at the moment, they're paralysed. But once this is resolved either way, they're going to be all over us. It'll be impossible to contain.'

Berriman's sciatica felt like a burning wire being held against his buttock. How could something so tiny as a nerve cause so much pain?

'What you seem to have forgotten,' said Mark Hooper with that whiny hiss to his voice that he seemed to have developed in the past few hours, 'is that if Denning succeeds then it is contained.'

'If Denning succeeds, hundreds of innocent people will die.'

'That's not something that we have any control over now.'

'What about Ed Mallory and his idea about draining the tunnel by deploying an explosive charge?'

'His judgement's completely gone. He's trying to find some old IRA bomber.'

'Have we considered what happens if he does manage to find a way to drain the water out of the tunnel?'

'You know as well as I do, Howard, that he's never going to get clearance to let off explosives on the Underground.'

'None of this alters the fact that we were handling someone on the inside. We had clear provable foreknowledge of a potential attack.'

'No, Howard. That's not how it was. We had an ongoing intelligence timeline. We interpreted it as best we could.'

'We could have stopped the attack but we didn't because we were too preoccupied by the media and how the project would play with them.'

'No, we made an error of timing, that's all.'

'Mark, if this is going to leak then we need to manage it.'

'We can't manage it, Howard. We just bury it. There's no paper trail. Simeon Fisher went AWOL in Helmand, he returned to the UK, moved to Wales and got involved with Cruor Christi. There was no intelligence. We're as shocked about what's happened as everyone.'

'I'm not sure, Mark.'

'You are sure, Howard. Believe me, you are.'

Howard started to respond but he realised he was talking to a dead line.

02:03 PM

Northern Line Train 037, first carriage

George had often wondered what it would feel like to be famous. What was his constant yearning to find some talent in himself that he could nurture, if not a fascination with fame and its transformative effects? When reality shows had first started on television, he had often found himself wondering what it would be like to be suddenly catapulted into the public eye. He liked to feel that it was intellectual curiosity that fuelled his interest; he hated the thought that he might actually be part of the target demographic for the increasingly vacuous shows. He would never have actually joining the queues of hopefuls trying to take part in the tawdry carnival. But it was snobbery that held him back – of course it was – and within a couple of years of the first *Big Brother*, he had added his voice to the chorus of derision, so much of it hypocrisy, hypocrisy he was equally guilty of, seeing that he still watched the shows avidly.

What did it say about him – that he had a secret longing for fame? Why wasn't being himself ever enough? Maybe it was loneliness. He had always felt lonely but it wasn't the sort of loneliness that could be cured by the company of family or friends. If anything, they accentuated it, enhanced its potency by making him realise that even they couldn't save him from it. But just as he knew that having a crush on fame was all part of his desire to cure his loneliness, he also knew with stone-cold certainty that if he ever – for whatever reason – achieved even a modicum of public recognition, he would still be lonely, if anything, more so. And he could see that same loneliness in so many others around him. Mostly in men, of course. Men are good at being lonely, despite their inevitable packs and tribes.

The irony was that he would be famous now, fleetingly, as the driver of the doomed train – but he would be famous for only one thing, and that was dying. George would be reduced to just a statistic in the ensuing news story.

In these last few minutes of his life, he didn't feel lonely. His sense of bereavement was all-consuming. His wife and children were dying and they had never felt more precious. He thought of his own parents; how they would cope with this. His mother, his poor mother – from this day on, any mention of his name and the tears would come to her eyes. His dad too. What a burden they would have to bear – their only son, their daughter-in-law and their two grand-children, dead. All killed on the same day. Facing such trauma and at their age, they might never recover. He couldn't think about it, it was too much, like thoughts of Sophie and Ben and what had been done to them – what was still being done. His family was being violated and he could do nothing to stop it. But they were still his family. Whatever sick horror was being visited upon them – and this felt about as sick and horrific as it could get – no one could take that away from him. As he thought of them, he could conjure up their aroma, the soft, nutty, almost honey-like smell of the children; Maggie's smell – feminine, reassuring, alluring. He could smell the house, that homely smell of carpets and clothes, humanity and food cooking in the kitchen.

He was turning the key in the lock now, returning from his shift and there was the smell. What he wouldn't give for that smell now. Sophie ran towards him and hugged him around the legs. Benji came thundering down the stairs and standing on the second step, flung his arms around his neck. There was Maggie, framed in the doorway to the living room, smiling as he shouted, 'Group hug!' and they all came together on cue, as they had so many thousand times before, he and Maggie scooping up one rascal each and all of them grabbing hold of each other. Afterwards, laughter and games, playtime, bathtime, bedtime stories, kisses, 'Night night, I love you,' sleeping children, then down for supper, glasses of wine, feet up, television and talking, a night in the Wakeham house. No more frustration, no more loneliness. Nothing else mattered. This was *his* god. Denning could keep his.

The water was up to his chest now. George would be dead soon. There was nothing he could do about it, not physically at least; he couldn't reach Denning now, not with his leg chained to the pole. His gaoler stood there in the middle of the carriage, looking around at the havoc he had created with a look of wonder and pride in his eyes. This was Tommy's proof – if proof were needed – that he was doing God's work.

George knew there was no god; and he knew too that in a very short time, unless he could figure out some way of saving himself, he would be returning to the unknowable primordial hum from which he had sprung. This was his last chance.

02:05 PM

Northern Line Train 037, sixth carriage

It was like playing a video game. Not that she had ever played more than one in her life. *Kill Fire* it was called. She loved it. It was a 'first person shoot 'em up'. Jason, a boy she had been fostered with, had let her play it in return for hand jobs. They were a small price to pay. The graphics were amazing. That's what Jason said anyway. So that's what she said as well.

You walked down a street in some desert town shit-hole. Iraq or somewhere like that. And rag heads came at you, ran at you from buildings, tried to shoot you and you had to take them out. Some of them didn't even have guns. They were just armed with knives, and the nearer you allowed them to get to you, the higher their score value when you drilled them. She played the game a lot, which meant plenty of hand jobs for Jason.

It was a buzz when they came for her. In the space of just a few hours she had become hooked on killing. She had a need, a hunger. Tommy had said to her that she should only kill people if they tried to stop them carrying out the baptism. So that meant that what she was about to do was fine. It was OK, it was allowed. They were trying to make her smash the windows with gunshots so they could get into the carriage and try to rush her. It felt as though she was playing *Kill Fire* all over again and it was up to her to try for the highest score possible. So she allowed one of them into the carriage with her. She could have shot him easily as he clambered through the broken window but she wanted him to get closer.

Another one came down the opposite side of the train and she shot him in the head. It was almost too easy, like shooting fish in a barrel. That was an expression that Tommy came out with when he was playing video games. She only ever played *Kill Fire* with him once and even though she had played it hundreds of times more than he had, had practised and improved, he beat her best score on his first attempt. And that's what he kept saying every time he killed someone: 'Like shooting fish in a barrel.' She loved Tommy. He had engineered all of this. He had the intelligence and understanding to realise that he had been chosen. A lot of people might have missed it, might have gone through their lives without realising that they had a mission. She knew in her heart of hearts that, without Tommy, she would not have realised that she was special too, chosen to carry out God's work. She was lucky. She was blessed.

She and Tommy had spoken about this moment for so long and now here they were just as Tommy had said they would be. Tommy talked to God a lot and told her about their conversations.

'God loves you, Belle,' Tommy told her. Of all the millions of people on earth that God had created, he was thinking of her. More than thinking, he loved her. She was special to him. And it was Tommy who had made her realise it. Tommy might have been at the other end of the train but she could feel him; he felt as close as if he was standing next to her.

'Not long now.' He had said that to her so many times in the past few weeks. And it really wasn't long now. There was no death. Not for her. She would be resurrected to eternal life and she would sit alongside God and Tommy and Jesus. She would sit alongside the disciples.

Some more of them made their way down the side of the train and she shot at them. One of them ducked down beneath the window and she shot him through the carriage wall. Evidence of her inch-perfect aim was plain to see as part of the man's skull, complete with hair, slapped against the window. Another one she shot as he climbed through the broken window through which she had allowed the skinny bloke to climb a few moments before. She let the other two make their way into the carriage as well, let them think they were going to be able to reach her. She even pretended to reload the gun and swore as though she was having problems, enticing them ever closer. She thought she might try and take them both out with one shot. That was a triple bonus score. But she settled on shooting them one by one. The first one wasn't very satisfying. The shot hit him in the chest and he was thrown back against the seats, dead before he even hit them. But the second one was choice. Took his head clean off.

Where was he, the skinny one who she had allowed into the carriage first? She knew he was crouched down behind the end of the row of seats. He'd probably lost his bottle and who could blame him after what the Pulveriser had done to the others? He must have known he was going to die. Brave of him really. She could respect that.

She waited. When he made himself known – made a run at her or whatever he was going to do – she would let him get close. But where was he?

She took a step forward and there he was, rearing up out of the water straight in front of her. He was too close, way too close and he had a big hunting knife in his hand with which he slashed at her. She could feel the air displacement from the blade against her cheek. Another inch closer and he would have taken her face off. They struggled; he might have been skinny but desperation made him strong. Another swipe with the hunting knife which nearly caught her throat and she managed to push him backwards and manoeuvred the Pulveriser into position.

The bullet almost tore him in half. Only a short section of his midriff, just a few inches of flesh, remained after the dum-dum bullet had done its work. He dropped the knife into the water but with one final supreme effort, he managed to get his hands around her throat. His face looked up at hers as his intestines flopped into the water from his gaping abdomen. And then he did the strangest thing. As his fingers lost their strength and he began to collapse into the water, where he would drown in a soup of his own guts, he managed to fight against his impending death long enough to spit in her face. She wiped the spit away with the back of her hand and kicked him away from her. That had to be a triple score. If he was close enough to spit in her face, it had to be. But she didn't like it that he had got that close. It was too close. It unnerved her.

Belle reached into the side pocket of her jacket that was now below the level of the water in which she stood. She felt for a fresh magazine but there wasn't one. Not to worry, there were plenty more. She waded through the water back to the rear cab. By the light of her torch, she could see that Simeon had tipped forward from where he had slumped after she'd shot him. Blood hung from his wounds in big clouds in the water. She considered kissing him again but decided against it. Feeding the Pulveriser was more important. And besides, he would be cold by now.

Somewhere in the water was the bag that contained the ammunition. She tried feeling for objects with her feet. She felt something by the door, it wasn't a bag, it was something small and hard – it was one of the Glock pistols but as she reached down into the water, she knocked it out of the open doorway.

Never mind, there was another one around here somewhere and she had plenty more bullets – food – for the Pulveriser. She just had to find the bag. She stepped over

Simeon's body and explored the other side of the cab with her feet. Nothing. There was only one place that it could be – under Simeon. Rolling him over, she reached underneath his body and felt the reassuring touch of the canvas bag against her hand. She pulled it out of the water and opened it up. It wouldn't matter that the bullets had got wet. She had applied wax sealant to them to ensure they were waterproof. She reached inside the bag. It was empty. Her fingers frantically scoured the bag's interior and finally she turned it inside out. No magazines, no bullets.

But Simeon had packed them . . .

And there it was – Simeon had packed them.

She felt sick. She held the torch between her teeth and went through his pockets. She knew they weren't there. Just as she had loaded his gun with dud bullets, so he had disposed of her ammunition. But as she straightened up, God saw fit to throw her some small consolation. There on the driver's console, now half in and half out of the water, was the other Glock. She stepped over Simeon and picked it up. A Glock would fire when wet; it would even fire under water. It held seventeen rounds. Being the one from which she had fired the two shots into Simeon, there would be fifteen rounds left. Hopefully that would be enough if there were any further attempts to attack her. There was also one bullet left in the Pulveriser. One of her holy bullets with the cross carved into the end. She wouldn't tell Tommy about losing the other bullets. He would think she had been sloppy in her preparation and he would be right. She wouldn't tell him but she needed to speak to him. The water was rising fast. She might not have another chance.

She took the walkie-talkie from her top pocket and pressed the switch. When he answered it, he sounded different, almost like it wasn't him.

'Tommy? What's the matter? You sound really weird.'

'I've been shot. It hurts but I'm OK.'

'How did it happen, Tommy?'

'It doesn't matter. It's not important. We must stand firm. They'll keep coming for us right up to the last moment. But once the baptism is complete then we will have accomplished God's work. Just remember that no one will ever forget the name of Belle Denning.'

'I love you, Tommy. I'll see you on the other side.'

'I love you too, Belle, always and for ever.'

02:11 PM

Northern Line Train 037, first carriage

His sister's voice was so full of hope. It gave him strength when he heard her speak like that. The pain in his face had settled down into a series of stabbing jolts that kept time with his heartbeat. It felt as though someone was kicking him in the face with a sharp, pointed boot, a silver-capped cowboy boot perhaps. Over and over again, almost every second, and some kicks were worse than others. At times it felt as though the person doing the kicking had taken a run-up. He needed the end to come quickly now to stop the pain. Sometimes the frequency changed. Instead of deep and thudding, it would be high-pitched and the cowboy boot would be replaced by a handful of needles jabbed mercilessly into his gums.

But he knew this for what it was and he could take it. It was a test. If he could pass the test and carry out the baptism then all the angels in heaven would sing his name. He hadn't come this far to fail. God was with him. God was with his sister too. Tommy could hear God in his sister's voice. Belle was a prophet.

'Bye, Tommy.'

'It's not goodbye, Belle. This is not the end but the beginning.'

'I know, Tommy.'

'Be strong, Belle.'

'I will, Tommy, I will.'

He took his finger off the switch on the walkie-talkie and let it drop into the water. He didn't need it any more.

His bond with Belle was more than just spiritual. They had great sex. They fitted together perfectly. Maybe it was something to do with being brother and sister, twins. They could go for hours but they would always come at the same time. And in a funny sort of way, today would be the same.

02:19 PM

Unmarked Police Car, Leicester Square

Ed listened to Nick Calvert as he showed his ID to the police officers manning the perimeter of the evacuation zone on the edge of Leicester Square. As Calvert spoke, his voice was imbued with a frequency usually absent from it. In amongst the masculine low notes was a screech that betrayed his inner conflict. He and Ed hadn't spoken as the car had made its way through the West End traffic. They didn't need to. Ed knew that Calvert was torn about what they were doing. Nick Calvert was a career cop. He did everything by the book. You could never wish for a more reliable colleague in a negotiating cell. Ed was asking him to compromise his most cherished principles. If Ed could have carried out his mission without enlisting Calvert's assistance then he would have done so but they both knew that it wasn't possible. So here they were, entering one of the most heavily secured and policed locations on the planet, and doing it with an illegal cache of Semtex and a former IRA bomber in the car with them.

With their credentials confirmed, the uniformed officer

said, 'OK, you can park up. The negotiating cell's on that artic over there.'

'Thanks.'

Calvert pressed the button to raise the window and it slid back into place with a faint hum. He drove on for a few yards before swinging the car around and cutting the engine.

'Ed, we're here. I'm presuming you're not coming to the negotiating cell so I need to know what to tell them in there.'

Ed could hear the fear and confusion in Calvert's voice. Ed had no doubt that when he answered, his own voice would contain the same emotions. Calvert was the gatekeeper of his plan so he knew that he must maintain an air of self-confidence. It was crucial that Calvert felt that what he was doing was right and that Ed's plan was the product of serious tactical considerations and not a panicky act of desperation. In reality, it was somewhere between the two.

'Here's what I think we should do, Nick. I'm going to stay here in the car with Conor and the professor. I think you should go to the negotiating cell and collect as much information as you can. What's the intel from GCHQ on the communications going into and out of the train? That goes for passengers and terrorists. We need to know how high the water is; we need to know if there is any movement on the rapid intervention plan. And, finally, you need to get back here as fast as you can.'

'What if I don't agree to this, Ed?'

It was a question that Ed was hoping Calvert wouldn't ask but he had his response ready nonetheless.

'If you don't agree to it, Nick – and you're perfectly entitled not to, all things considered – then there's nothing else we can do. We just sit and wait.'

'For them to die, right?' Ed remained silent. Calvert had answered his own question. 'Oh, what the hell am I doing?' He muttered the words and Ed couldn't read them. Was this Calvert backing out, throwing in the towel? He didn't get a chance to decide before Calvert was out of his seat and slamming the door.

Ed turned to Frank Moorcroft sitting next to him. 'Frank, as briefly as possible, how long until the tunnel fills?'

'It'd have to be very approximate because there's no way of judging exactly how porous the masonry and earth around the site of the flooding is. But taking into account the flow of the River Lime, the level of the Thames, the water table, the amount of potential seepage . . .'

'Please, Frank, give it your best shot.'

Robbed of his potential variables, Frank fell silent for a moment before he said, 'About twenty minutes, half an hour? But of course—'

'Do you think it's possible it might be more than that?'

'It's possible but unlikely.'

'It's more likely to be less?'

'More likely, yes.'

'How high do you think the water might be now, Frank? I know it's painful that you can't be exact in your answers but just give it your best shot. Whereabouts would it be on a man of average height – midriff, chest, shoulders?'

'Chest? Possibly.'

'And the explosives in the service tunnel, Frank, do you have any thoughts on the optimum location to place them in the event of an attempt to drain water from around the train?'

'I have to say that this is most improper inasmuch as I am being asked to provide opinions on incomplete data—'

'Frank, none of the responsibility for this is going to rest with you. You have my word on that. I want you to give me your opinion. That's all. What I do with that subsequent information is my responsibility. Ultimately all I'm trying to do is save the lives of some – if not all – of the passengers on that train.'

Frank's reservations were eased a little by Ed's pep talk but his verbosity was uncowed as he explained that, based on the location of the train, the ideal location for the attempted breach was approximately twenty yards from the rear of the train.

Ed attempted clarification: 'And that's not so close to the train that we're going to do the terrorists' job for the them and blow up the passengers?'

'One would feel that it would be far enough away from them, taking into consideration that the main force of the blast would hopefully be taken by the stone and rock between the two tunnels. That would have to be the general idea anyway.'

The driver's door was snatched open.

'There's nothing from the train,' said Calvert as he climbed in and closed the door. 'Serina Boise has been talking about ways of getting a line of communication to Denning. My guess is it's not going to happen. Word from GCHQ is that the level of chatter from the train has dropped considerably in the past hour as batteries on phones and laptops have given out. From what they can make out, the water's rising fast.'

'Any talk of special forces going in?' asked Ed.

'Sub-aqua equipment is being sent for but, even if it can be got there in time and we can get a consensus from COBRA, it's unlikely to make much difference. And, Ed, they're looking for you.'

'Why?'

'You're the only one who's spoken to Denning. They think if they can get him back on the line, it should be you at the other end of it.'

'It's not going to happen.'

It needed saying again. It needed reinforcing within this cell that comprised Ed and his three conspirators, this post-negotiating cell, this unofficial covert intervention team. 'If we don't try and do something, then there's nothing else that can be done. With that in mind, each of you needs to tell me now whether you're prepared to help me or not.'

The interior of the car fell silent. The upholstery creaked as the men shifted in their seats. Conor spoke first.

'I'm in.' There it was again – Conor's mysterious enthusiasm for the job in hand.

'Well, I suppose, all things considered, I am too,' said the professor.

'Fuck you, Ed Mallory.' Calvert's sudden venting of frustration was accompanied by his hand slamming down on the steering wheel with such ferocity that it sent a tremor through the car. 'Let's do it.'

02:33 PM

Northern Line Train 037, first carriage

'Don't you think that London has suffered enough, after last time?'

Denning watched him by the light of the torch hanging from the handrail in the ceiling of the carriage. George could see two of him; his head and shoulders and their reflection in the rising water. It was up to their shoulders now.

'London is the most important city in the world,' said Denning. 'It is a cultural and spiritual crossroads. It's the perfect place to start a war.'

'It didn't happen before.'

'It's different this time.'

'Why?'

'Because it's me that's doing it.'

'Do you have any conception of how delusional you sound?'

'I'm not the one who's deluded, George.'

'There is no God,' said George. 'Religion was made by man. It was a primitive attempt to make sense of the world before science came along. It's a superstitious relic from the past.'

Denning said nothing, just smiled. Whatever George said, he couldn't help but betray his animosity. If he had any chance of saving the people on the train and his children, he had to think clearly; he had to find a key to unlock Tommy's mind. Faced with imminent death and physically immobilised – his leg ached within the chain that bound it to the pole – all he had was his voice and his mind.

'So your parents abandoned you, did they?'

'Not this again.'

'Go on, tell me.'

'If you really want to know, my father knifed my mother over the breakfast table and then he hung himself.'

'So what did you do?'

'I carried on eating breakfast.'

'I don't believe you.'

'Believe what you like. It means nothing to me what you believe. You can come out with as much heresy and blasphemy as you want. Nothing will change the course of your destiny now.'

George didn't know where he was going with this but he knew that he needed to keep him talking. Denning's mood had changed. Faced with imminent death, perhaps his resolve was weakening.

'If you could turn back the clock, would you try and stop your dad from doing what he did?'

'Whatever for?'

'He killed your mother. Didn't you love your mother?'

'She was all right, I suppose.'

'How can you say that about your own mother? Jesus loved his mother. Jesus preached that everyone should love their mother.' George was winging it. He had no idea whether Jesus preached any such thing – he had failed his religious studies O level – but his comment made Denning think for a moment.

'Maybe I would.'

'Maybe you would what?'

'Have stopped him doing what he did but it doesn't matter now. Nothing matters.'

'It matters now more than ever, seeing as in a short while you're going to be meeting up with your mother and father again.'

'I don't think so.'

'Why not?'

'I just don't.'

'But you're going to heaven, aren't you?'

'They won't be there.'

'Your mum and dad will be in hell, will they?'

'Maybe.'

'Have you thought that if you kill hundreds of innocent people, you'll probably meet them there?'

'I'm just doing what I was destined to do.'

'Have you ever stopped to think for just one moment,' said George, trying with all his might to sound measured and thoughtful when his natural instinct was to hurl obscenities, 'that perhaps this is not what God wants, that perhaps you've misread the signs? Every nut job that carries out an atrocity like this thinks they've got God on their side.'

'Why are you talking to me about God when you don't even believe?'

'Because I'm trying to show you that what you're doing is wrong. By every law of humanity or religion or whatever you want to believe in, this is wrong. This is cold-blooded mass murder.'

'No, George, this was prophesied two thousand years ago.' Suddenly alert, Denning stopped talking and listened. Someone was trying to make their way down the side of the train, trying to make their way between the side of the carriage and the tunnel wall. He raised his assault rifle, fired off a burst of rounds and the sound of movement outside the carriage stopped.

'Can't you see?' said George. 'Can't you comprehend for even one moment that what you're doing is wrong? If there is a God, you're going to be judged and damned. Don't you see that?'

Denning turned and pointed the rifle at George.

'Stop.'

'Am I getting to you?'

'I want you to be baptised, I want your sins to be absolved but if you have to die a sinner then so be it.'

George held his stare and said nothing. Denning broke eye contact when he heard more movement but this time it wasn't coming from the side of the carriage as before but from above. Someone had climbed out of the doors between the carriages and managed to make it up onto the roof and was now crawling along it, trying to be as quiet as possible. Unfortunately, the sound of his or her clothes dragging along the metal was impossible to hide. Whoever it was – and George would never know – they were struggling to stay alive. When Denning looked up and George could see him calculating in his mind the exact angle and trajectory of the shots that he would fire into the ceiling of the train, he couldn't help the tears that came to his eyes. After a short burst of gunfire, the sound of crawling stopped.

'These people just don't want to learn. They are so close to salvation and yet they keep trying to throw it all away.'

He turned to George and holding the rifle in one hand, he pressed his other hand against his ruptured face and said, 'I like you, George, please let me save you. Don't let me have to kill you, not after all that we've been through together. You'll thank me when you see what lies in store for you and your family. You'll be reunited on the other side. You are all prophets. I am leading you into the promised land. You'll see.'

At the moment that he spoke, George didn't care whether Denning shot him or not. 'Fuck you,' he said, 'and fuck your God too.'

02:42 PM

'Nick, do you think you can get Conor and I down into the ticket hall?'

'I don't know, Ed.'

'Come on, we're coppers. They're going to let us down there.'

'It's what we're going down there with that worries me.'

'You think there'll be dogs?'

'Yeah, bound to be. They're going to start howling when they get a load of what's in that cardboard box.'

'Well, we just need to make sure that we keep away from them.'

The four men made their way towards the Underground entrance on the west side of Charing Cross Road. Ed didn't dare think what they must look like to the massed ranks of police and special forces milling around the empty streets around the tube station – the blind man with the tall shaven-headed man holding his arm, the crusty academic and the stocky Irishman carrying the cardboard box. They would look strange and incongruous under normal circumstances – what the hell would they look like now?

'There are two CO19 officers at the Charing Cross Road entrance to the tube,' whispered Calvert.

'Dogs?'

'None that I can see. But what are we going to tell them we're doing?'

'Leave it to me. All you need to do is point me at them.'

Calvert led on, while Ed held his arm and thought about what he was going to say.

'Hi,' he heard Calvert say to the CO19 guys. 'This is DI Ed Mallory from Special Branch.'

Ed took his ID card from his pocket, showed it to them, and said, 'We're going to need to get access to the tube station. This is Professor Frank Moorcroft and Dr Conor Joyce from Imperial College London.' Ed pocketed his ID. If they were going to challenge him, ask to see ID for Joyce and Moorcroft, then they would do it now and his plan would be foiled.

'OK, Gov,' said one of the armed officers and as soon as Ed heard it, he knew they were in.

'We're going to need a member of London Underground staff with a pass key to allow us access to where we need to go.'

'The station manager's down there in the ticket hall.'

'Thanks.'

Calvert steered him through the doorway and down the steps towards the ticket hall. Ed heard Joyce's and

Moorcroft's footsteps as they followed them down.

Calvert called ahead to someone – the station manager – and while Professor Moorcroft explained where they needed to go to, Ed listened to the stillness of the tube station. There were a couple of subdued voices far off to his left, uniformed police most probably, and he was certain that he heard the whine of a dog.

'Conor?'

'Yeah.'

'Who's down here with us?'

'There are some paramilitary looking fellas over there.'

'Have they got a dog with them?'

'Jesus, yes, they have. Spaniel.'

'We need to move. Nick, come on.'

'Hold on a sec,' said Calvert.

Ed tuned in to the conversation between the professor and the station manager. They were taking too much time.

'Frank? Frank, listen. Do you have the key and do you know where you're going?'

'Well, er—'

'Yes or no.'

'Well, yes to the key and, I'm afraid, no to—'

'Let's go. Now. Down the escalators. Bring this guy with us.'

The dog barked again. Its behaviour could attract attention at any moment if it hadn't done so already. Ed took hold of Calvert's arm and almost pushed him forward, trying to set the pace. They made their way down the static escalator. Ed listened for footsteps behind them or the clicking of dog's claws on floor tiles. He heard neither but a distant bark set his nerves jangling.

'I think it's down towards the Northern Line,' said the station manager.

'Show us where you think it is,' said Ed.

'I know I've been there. We used to use it for storage.'

'It's extremely important that we find it now.'

All the supposed might of the British government, all the security forces, all the committees, all the counter-terrorism strategies and the fate of the passengers on the train was in the hands of this unlikely group of men.

Ed struggled to contain his frustration as they all came to a standstill once again and the station manager said, 'No, I just can't seem to . . . No.' Ed was about to give free rein to his boiling impatience when the man said, 'Oh, hold on. Here we go.' They were moving again. Twenty feet further along a pedestrian tunnel and then they stopped. Keys jangled. A lock was turned. A door opened – heavy, metal, hinges creaking.

'OK, Conor. It's just you and me now,' said Ed.

'Great.' Ed couldn't miss the Irishman's sarcasm.

'Nick, you need to go back and scope out the ticket hall, make sure that if anyone comes looking for us you delay them as long as you can. Frank, you just need to tell us how far we have to go into the tunnel.'

'I'd be happy to come with you.' For once, Frank had got straight to the point.

'No, Frank, I can't ask you to do that. Just tell us where you think we need to be.'

'By my calculations, the best place is about two hundred and thirty-two yards from the mouth of the tunnel. Here, use this.'

'What is it?' asked Ed.

'It's a laser measuring device – all the estate agents use them. You press the button on top and it tells you the distance between the device and whatever surface you place the laser dot on.'

'Give it to Conor, it's no use to me.'

'And I'll need a torch too,' said Conor.

'Here, have this,' said the station manager.

'OK, let's go,' said Ed, taking hold of Conor's arm as he made his way into the doorway and down the steps. Before the professor was out of earshot, Ed could no longer put off asking the question he had been so afraid to ask for the past few minutes.

'How long do you think we've got, Frank?'

'Impossible to say, I'm afraid. I'd just be as fast as you can.'

As they reached the bottom of the steps, the air became cooler. Ed listened to Conor's laboured breathing. He listened as he put the cardboard box down on the ground.

'You're not going to like this,' said Conor.

'What's the matter?'

'We're never going to make it.'

02:47 PM

Northern Line Train 037

Those children tall enough to keep their heads above the surface of the water stood on the seats; those too short to do so were held by adults and clung to the handrails in the ceiling of the carriages. Adam did the same, his arms aching as he struggled to remain conscious despite his increasing blood loss. The guide dog paddled around in a tight circle. Her owner, a man who knew all about perpetual darkness, kept pulling on the lead that was looped through a handrail as the water level rose, maintaining the tension to alleviate the strain on the dog's tiring legs.

In the second carriage of the train, Maggie Wakeham stood on the seats, clinging to the handrail, straining her head up into the apex of the ceiling, sucking at the air in the thin gully that remained, the only space that the water had not yet filled. All but the most water-resistant of the electronic devices that had provided some tiny points of light from the people further down the carriage were now extinguished; they had either run out of power or been doused in water. But if she could see nothing, she could still hear plenty and there were sounds that she would rather not have heard. The prayers, shouts, wails, cries and pleas had gone and all that remained were the sounds of people desperately trying to stay alive, thrashing around in the water, fighting to find those last few inches of warm, oxygen-depleted air.

02:55 PM

Leicester Square Tube Station, service tunnel

'What is it, what's the matter?' Ed couldn't disguise the fear in his voice. Just when he felt as though they had a real shot at trying to save the passengers on the train, Conor's words had him rattled.

'The tunnel's blocked.'

'What with?'

'Shelving units, filing cabinets, office shit.'

'Well, we need to get them out of the way.'

'You should see it.'

'Wish I could.'

'Yeah, right.'

'Come on, give me the box, you start shifting it.'

Ed held his hands out and Conor dumped the box into them. It was heavier than he had anticipated. Conor was muttering and swearing as he pulled at metal objects that scraped and screeched across the stone floor.

'How deep into the tunnel do you think they go?' asked Ed.

'There's no way of guessing.'

'Conor, I can't tell you—'

'Don't you fucking dare. Jesus!' It sounded as though a metal shelving unit had slipped and fallen onto Conor. He swore and cursed but he continued pulling at the metal obstructions. Whatever they were, they had clearly been down there for some time because when moved, they threw up clouds of dust that caught in the back of Ed's throat and made him cough.

'OK, stay with me.'

Ed pushed the cardboard box against Conor's back as he forged a path. Conor threw himself forward, pushing his way between the metal obstructions. Ed's arms ached under the weight of the box. The air was warm and gritty. Ed's shirt began to stick to him as he fought his way through; his shins and ankles cracked against metal, making him wince and curse. A piece of shelving slid back from where Conor had pushed it away and caught him on the side of the forehead. The pain made him cry out and he could feel a lump form and start to throb. But at least it distracted him from the time they were wasting, time that might mean the difference between life and death for hundreds of people.

'OK, we're going to have to climb over this,' said Conor.

'What is it?'

'Just a load of – oh fuck it, you don't need to know. Give it to me.'

Conor took the cardboard box from him and lifted it upwards. Ed reached out to feel the obstruction. It felt like a wall of individual metal shelves stacked one on top of the other. He felt for the top one which was at chest level. Ed pulled himself up and started to crawl along the top of the shelving after Conor, who was doing the same, pushing the box of explosives in front of him, the cardboard scraping against the metal.

'OK, we're getting down here, it looks like it's clear from here on in.'

Ed heard Conor jump down to the floor ahead of him as he moved as fast as he could, his shirt snagging and tearing against the sharp corners of the metal objects over which he dragged himself.

'How far do you think we've come?' asked Ed as he jumped down onto the tunnel floor.

'I have no idea.'

'Do you think you can use the measuring device that Frank gave us?'

'No, I don't.'

'He said it was two hundred and thirty-two yards from the start of the tunnel. Let's say we've done the thirty-two, we need to go the other two hundred yards.'

'If you say so.'

'Come on, give me the box and you hold the torch. Watch out for me, if I'm heading for a wall.'

Conor said nothing, just emitted a derisory snort as though the thought of Ed running full pelt into a tunnel wall rather appealed to him.

They ran. It was hard going with the box of explosives in his straining arms. But his thoughts weren't focused on his discomfort as he tried to guess the distance they had travelled and how much further they needed to go. At this rate, even if they did succeed to rupture the tunnel wall, they might very well be draining the water away from a train full of corpses.

When running on his treadmill at home, Ed always finished off his jogging with a short sprint. He reckoned it was roughly about two hundred metres. He imagined himself at home now, pushing himself to the limit as he forced himself onwards. Occasionally, he could feel the tunnel wall snag against his shirt sleeve and he recalibrated his trajectory. Conor's heavy breathing and footsteps provided him with a sound source that he could focus on and plot his course by.

'How far do you think we've gone?' asked Ed.

'It's got to be about two hundred yards now. My vote is we go for it here.'

They stopped running and Ed put the cardboard box on the ground.

Conor's knees emitted a faint cracking noise as he knelt down to the box and started opening up its cardboard flaps.

'I'm going to use all of this.' It wasn't a question. Conor had made a decision.

'If that's what you think.'

'Yeah, I do.'

The insolence was still there in Conor's voice but it was tempered by urgency. Objects were being unwrapped from polythene. Conor muttered and cursed as he went about his work.

'What are you doing?' asked Ed.

'I'm baking a fucking cake, what do you think?' Conor sighed then muttered, 'I'm moulding the Semtex against the wall, then I'll use some electrodes to connect it to the detonator.'

'Are you nearly done?' Ed made no attempt to conceal his impatience.

'Shut your mouth.'

Ed stood and waited as Conor went about his work. It had to be ten minutes they'd been down there, possibly twelve. Their estimation of where the point of the blast should be was wholly inexact and Conor was clearly uncertain regarding the quantity of Semtex needed to get through the tunnel wall. But somewhere, just a few feet away from where they stood were thousands of gallons of water pressing against the brickwork.

03:07 PM

Northern Line Train 037, first carriage

Water had dribbled into his mouth through the wound in his face. Amidst the earthy, oily flavours was a sweetness. It was something he had tasted before although he couldn't remember when. It was comforting; it made him know that this was how things were meant to be.

'When you got up this morning,' he said in George's direction, 'you were just a tube driver. A simple man, doing a simple job. And now you will die a prophet and rise again to sit with God.'

'Don't,' said George. 'I don't want to hear it.'

'Feel the water, it's cleansing you. It's making you pure and whole. This is holy water, George.'

'No it isn't. It's just water. Cold, dirty water.'

George was afraid; he was suffering. Tommy forgave him. The water was up to his neck and it felt good. The pain in his face had begun to subside and he was filled with the glory of God. He knew the end to his suffering, to all their suffering, was close at hand. He felt a oneness with himself and the world and when he looked at George, he knew that he was his brother. They were fellow travellers on the same journey. He and George, his sister Belle, and everyone on the train. They would all die together and rise again.

03:11 PM

Leicester Square Tube Station, service tunnel

'Come on, let's clear off.' As soon as Ed heard Conor say the words, he started moving back along the tunnel. But Conor was slower than him as he unspooled the cable. Ed felt sicker with each passing second. Aware of what the people on the train might be going through, he felt as though he was succumbing to some sort of phantom suffocation all of his own. The air was thin and stale and it felt as though there just wasn't enough of it to fill his lungs.

'Can't we move any faster?'

'We mustn't pull the wire out of the Semtex. It's not like we've got time to go back and fix it all up again.'

They carried on walking. Conor had managed to speed up but then he came to a standstill.

'What's the matter?' asked Ed.

'Oh no. Oh shit.'

'Conor, what is it?'

'The wire's come to an end.'

'What does that mean?'

'Well, we're only about fifty yards from the Semtex. If I rig up the detonator here and set it off, we might not survive.'

'Just set it up, get it ready and give it to me. I'll do it.'

Conor hesitated. He was clearly thinking about it. Ed held out his hand.

'No way,' said Conor. 'You'll only fuck it up, you blind bastard.'

'Conor, I was responsible for your wife's death. Don't make me responsible for yours too.'

'It's too late for all that now. It won't be the first time I've been blown up, will it?'

Ed listened while Conor busied himself with the detonator.

'I'd turn around, crouch down and cover your ears, if I were you. It probably won't save you but it's worth a go. Ready?'

'Do it.'

Conor flicked the switch on the detonator. Nothing happened. He flicked the switch again.

Silence.

03:12 PM

Northern Line Train 037, first carriage

The surface of the water slapped gently against George's chin as he stood on the seat, the top of his head touching the ceiling of the carriage. The chain made his leg ache. He had managed to slide it up the pole; it was the only way that he could keep his head above the water. The pain fuelled his anger and his anger was the last thing that kept him together, held back his final despair.

'You murdering scumbag. Come on! This is your last chance to do the right thing.' George only had a few moments left before the water closed over his nose and mouth. He couldn't help but think about all the time he had wasted earlier in the day. All those opportunities that he might have taken to disarm Denning or kill him, but here he was, immobilised as much by his own inadequacy and failure as he was by the chain around his leg. He had failed himself, he had failed his family and he had failed all the people on the train.

He turned towards the few remaining inches of open window in the adjoining doors through which somewhere, his wife, the mother of his children, was clinging onto a handrail in the darkness and the filthy water.

'Maggie?'

Her voice came through clearly above the sounds of desperation in the distance. 'Yes, George.'

He had never heard her sound so afraid. It made him want to cry. What should he say to her? What could he say that would mean anything at a moment like this? There was only one thing, but just as he had decided to say it to her, she said it to him: 'I love you.'

'Oh Christ, I love you too, Maggie. And I'm sorry.'

'Don't be sorry, George. This is not your fault.'

'I'm just sorry for bringing this on us.'

'We were in the wrong place at the wrong time.'

'The right place at the right time,' muttered Denning. Maggie's voice was stronger than before, more emotionally robust as she said, 'Whatever delusion or madness is causing these people to do this, if there is a god, they'll rot in hell for what they've done.'

'I baptise thee in the name of the father, the son and the holy ghost.'

George had wondered when Denning would start in on the religious bullshit again. Even if a deity were to make itself known to George now, during the final few moments of his life, he would curse him. Damnation would be infinitely preferable to some sort of union with an entity that thought that Denning's pointless mass murder might in some way be a good thing.

'Dear Lord, our father, accept these humble souls into the kingdom of heaven.'

George looked at what remained of Denning's face caked in semi-congealed blood, his head tilted to one side, sucking at the last few inches of warm fetid air through his nose, mouth and the wound in his cheek, as he spoke to 'the almighty'.

'There's no one there, you stupid bastard,' said George. 'No one's listening.'

But Denning kept right on, talking about the 'sure and certain resurrection to eternal life', and George put his head back in the water, so his ears were beneath the surface and he didn't have to listen. This was how a condemned man must feel, thought George, waiting for the moment of death and fearing the pain that precedes it.

Any hope that the authorities might be able to do something was fading fast and the sounds that were coming from along the train were the most gut-wrenching he had ever heard. Hundreds of people were about to die – and they knew it. George was about to die. His nose was pressed against the ceiling of the train. He had to time his breaths to coincide with those moments when the water dropped away from the ceiling before rising up to slap against it once more.

No one was coming.

George took a mouthful of water as he tried to suck up some air from the tiny pocket around his mouth. He choked, coughed, spluttered. More water entered his mouth. He choked again. He pressed his mouth against the ceiling and managed to suck up some air before the water closed over his mouth. It would be his last breath. The water he had swallowed made him choke once more but he fought the urge to spit out the air. He kept his mouth crushed against the ceiling preferring the sharp pain that it caused to the dull sickening ache in his oxygen-starved lungs.

No one was coming.

As though in recognition of his final breath, the torch that Denning had hung from the handrail which had flickered and fluttered underwater for the past couple of minutes, finally gave out, throwing the submerged carriage into total darkness. The words echoed in George's head as Joe Strummer sang 'London Calling' for the final time.

03:19 PM

Northern Line Train 037

There was silence along the submerged train. Spots of light from mobile phones and handheld computer devices – those whose light had survived the water – illuminated desperate faces, cheeks bulging, as men, women and children held their breath, in final seemingly futile attempts to delay the inevitable.

It is common knowledge that the person who panics uses more oxygen than the person who keeps calm. But who could keep calm when confronted with a single lungful of air and no apparent hope of another one? Panic reigned on the train and panic squandered all those lungfuls – all those hundreds of pockets of air – in those hundreds of bodies.

Every single living passenger felt the agony of oxygen starvation, knowing that it was merely a prelude to oblivion. Most of the passengers clung to the rapidly depleting lungful of air that they had sucked in before the water reached the ceiling of the carriages. But there were some, like those who had chosen to jump from the twin towers rather than face the flames, who roared the oxygen from their lungs, hoping to reduce the torture and die more quickly.

No one was coming.

03:20 PM

Leicester Square Tube Station, service tunnel

Conor pressed the switch a third time. Still nothing.

'What's the matter?' Ed sounded scared.

Conor didn't reply, just threw the detonator against the wall of the tunnel. Plastic splinters and pieces of circuit board clattered to the stone floor.

'Tell me what's happening, Conor.'

'I'm sticking the wires straight onto the battery.'

Ed listened to Conor's troubled breathing as he fiddled with the detonator's components. Then he exhaled, long and hard. Ed didn't have a chance to ask him what this meant. He felt the explosion before he heard it. The vibration in the ground travelled up through his feet and into his legs. Then came the sound, a deafening crack followed by a low rumbling thunder which swelled as it moved along the tunnel. The blast knocked both of them off their feet and sent them crashing to the floor turning over and over amidst the smoke and billowing brick dust.

Ed lost consciousness for a moment and he came around as though waking from a dream, unsure whether he was asleep or not. His sunglasses had been knocked off in the blast. As he sat up, he started feeling for them. He did it automatically, without thinking.

'Conor?'

No reply. His hands scrambled around through the brick dust and pieces of rubble all around him.

'Conor?'

His fingers touched a warm liquid which he raised to his nose. It was blood, either his or the Irishman's.

'Conor?'

He got lucky. His fingers closed around the sunglasses and he put them on. The lenses were cracked but still in place, still providing a barrier between his sightless eyes and the outside world.

'Conor?'

'Jesus, my feckin' head,' muttered Conor in a pained voice. And then Ed heard something else. It was slapping against the walls of the tunnel as it picked up speed and momentum. Conor's words had allowed Ed to ascertain where he was. He moved towards him and managed to grab hold of his arm as both of them were engulfed in a tide of cold muddy water.

03:21 PM

In the band of air in the apex of the train carriage ceilings, mouths opened up like flowers. Gasps erupted from the surface of the water as it dropped from the ceiling of the train and the passengers on Train 037 coughed and spluttered the first breaths of their new lives. There were some ruptured eardrums caused by the shockwaves of the explosion in the water and many heads ached, but everyone who had gone under had come out alive and they brought back with them hope that somehow their collective nightmare might now begin to recede.

George sprayed out the stale air from his lungs and breathed in the new. Never had a breath tasted so good.

'Maggie?'

It was a struggle to keep his mouth above the water and his voice was tremulous and weak and unlikely to reach her in the next carriage. Fear made him desperate and the desperation made him shout louder.

'Maggie!' He heard a voice but he couldn't be sure if it was hers so he called again. This time when she responded he knew. She was alive.

And so was Denning, close by, somewhere in the darkness. George reached out and the fingers of his right hand touched Denning's face. He could hear him sucking air into his lungs, breathless from oxygen starvation.

'George?' He sounded confused, disorientated. This wasn't in the plan. George said nothing but as his hand brushed against the wound in Denning's cheek, he curled his fingers around the bottom edge of it as though it were a handle and gripped tightly. Denning emitted a scream of acute pain and rage but George was not going to let go and he pulled Denning's head towards him by his mangled cheek. With his other hand, he tried to find his eyes but Denning started flailing at him, lashing out at the source of the pain. A fist caught a glancing blow against George's forehead but it lacked power and precision and George brought his left hand around and approximating the target in relation to the position of his right hand, he started firing punches at Denning's head. The water dulled his fist's trajectory and there was another blow from Denning, this time more powerful and desperate but still not enough to stop him.

The chain around his leg, anchoring him to the vertical pole tore at the skin around his calf muscle but no amount of discomfort was going to stop him. Denning's next strike, however, was altogether more brutal and well-equipped. The square barrel of the Browning automatic whipped across George's nose. He couldn't contain his reflexes which made his hands retract and paw at his bleeding face.

Denning flailed around in the water swinging the gun at George, trying to hit him again. They struggled as a sound grew louder outside the train, a sound made incongruous by its location in the flooded tunnel. It was getting closer. It was the sound of a boat's outboard engine.

03:23 PM

Leicester Square Tube Station, Northern Line Tunnel

Andy spent a lot of time thinking about the types of operation that he might find himself involved with. Much of it was just day-dreaming. There was plenty of waiting around in this job after all. But he had never envisaged this. A hijacked tube train was one of the scenarios they had discussed at a seminar only recently. No one joined the SAS to sit around in rooms listening to people talking and pointing to things on blackboards but he did enjoy devising resolutions to hypothetical crisis situations. And he felt that most of the potential situations had been covered during his ten years on the job. When the call came through that the terrorists were flooding the tunnel, he knew that this was something new, something that had never entered the collective mind of the security services and the powers-that-be. As with 9/11, the terrorists' imagination was one step ahead.

It had been decided that there would be two teams, one in Tottenham Court Road station and one in Leicester Square station at either end of the tunnel. When news of the flooding arrived, word came from on high that those with advanced diving skills were to make up two patrols of four. But by the time all the operational necessities had been seen to and all the equipment put in place, including one IRC, inflatable raiding craft, for each team, they were informed that the possibility of further explosions meant that an attempt to storm the train could not be sanctioned. Both teams were told to take up positions at a safe distance, far enough away to avoid any potential sniper fire. There they were told to wait while ongoing negotiations were made with the terrorists.

Andy was given operational control of Group A, the team to the south of the train operating out of Leicester Square station. He and his three men – Pat, Todd and Smithy – waited in the water holding onto the inflatable as the level rose.

When Pat had said that he could see someone swimming towards them through his night scope, Andy had felt nervous. Was this some sort of ambush? He picked out the swimmer with his torch and shouted, 'Make yourself known.' The swimmer stopped and trod water while she explained that she had escaped from the train. Having checked that she was unarmed and free of explosives, Pat and Smithy escorted her back to Leicester Square and returned a few minutes later smiling about some private joke. Andy envied them their nonchalance. The flooded tunnel had him spooked.

But just when it looked as though the water would reach the top of the tunnel and they would be forced to use their newly supplied breathing apparatus, there was a huge explosion that sent waves slapping against the tunnel walls. Almost immediately, the water level began to drop and the radio crackled into life as Andy's operations officer gave them the green light to go in.

As they made their way towards the train in the inflatable, he felt that buzz of excitement and adrenalin that he always had when a mission was under way. The water was still high enough to force them to duck to avoid cracking their heads against the top of the tunnel. The scream of the outboard engine was almost deafening in the enclosed space but it was the thought of the explosives that bothered Andy the most. All he could hope was that, by now, all the pieces of detonation equipment would have been given a good soaking and might not be in the best shape to do their job.

Pat sat in the prow and shone a portable arc light to try and dazzle anyone intending to shoot at them. As he had expected, the shots started when they were about a hundred feet out from the train. There were a series of muzzle flashes from a handgun. Bullets ricocheted around the tunnel and one of them struck the arc light making it shatter in Pat's hands scattering debris throughout the boat.

'All right, Pat?' shouted Andy above the sound of the engine.

Pat shouted back a 'Yeah!' but Andy could see by torchlight that he was bleeding from a minor head wound. If nothing else, the gunfire proved that they wouldn't be

MAX KINNINGS | 445

confronted by a train full of corpses. If one of the hijackers was still alive then the chances were that some of the passengers were too.

'Cut the engine!' he shouted and Todd killed the outboard motor but the IRC's forward momentum propelled it towards the train. If whoever was firing at them had a night-vision scope, they would be easy targets.

The men hunkered down in the boat as more rounds were fired, two of which struck the inflatable hull, pitching them forward into the water. Smithy tried to keep his Heckler and Koch G36 level as the torch attachment on the end of it lit up a figure with a handgun standing in the doorway set into the cab. Smithy positioned the red dot reflex sight on it and started shooting but the deflating IRC made it impossible to hold his line of fire and the bullets struck metal. Forced to swim as the IRC sank, Andy and his men were left facing an enemy that had seized the upper hand. They needed to regain the initiative – and fast.

03:25 PM

Northern Line Train 037, sixth carriage

Belle saw the red dot just in time and stepped back into the cab out of the way of the burst of automatic fire. This wasn't the first time that she had been forced to deal with attackers and, while the men making their way towards her now were far more of a danger than the passengers on the train had been, she felt sure that she could repel them just as easily. Whatever it was that had happened, whatever it was that had caused the explosion that had made the water level drop, Tommy would think of something. Tommy always thought of something. All she had to do was to stand firm, maintain her position and counter all attempts to enter the train. Tommy had told her that it wouldn't be easy, that the journey would be long and perilous. As always, he was right.

She could hear them in the water coming closer. If only she had more holy bullets in the Pulveriser then she could have truly shown them the wrath of God. But there were – how many? – about seven or eight bullets left in the Glock. She had lost count but there was no way that God would forsake her now. Not after she had come this far. Tommy had told her that despite the journey being long and difficult, the outcome of their crusade would never be in doubt. The water from the holy river would never stop flowing. The tunnel would fill up with water once more and she would feel it close over her head just as it had done before.

Belle stepped back into the doorway and fired two shots into the water. Another burst of automatic gunfire was returned but once again she had already stepped back into the cab when it came. She felt invincible. She was doing God's work.

They came closer and she allowed them. The darkness made it impossible to aim with any degree of certainty but, just as it made things difficult for her, it did the same for them. Let them come closer, let them believe that they were going to kill her. It would do them no good. People had underestimated her all her life. So let them do so now. Let them see the truth of God's work; let them see how his wrath was channelled through his servant, Belle Denning.

They were close now, she could hear them. Despite the clamour of voices from the passengers on the train behind her, she could hear their every movement in the water. Stepping out into the doorway, she fired the Glock down into the darkness once more.

The first round that struck her shattered her thigh bone, the second bullet hit her just above the vagina, smashing her pubic bone; and the third entered through her navel, passed through her abdomen and severed her spinal cord. Belle slumped back into the cab, floundering in the water before she came to rest against Simeon.

It hurt. It hurt so much but it had happened, clearly it was meant to be. She had been baptised, born again. She would never die. Pointing the Glock into the doorway, she kept her finger on the trigger until it stopped bucking in her hand and she let it drop into the water. She reached for the Pulveriser and by the torchlight in the tunnel making its way towards her, she could just make out the silhouette of Simeon's face in the darkness. She leant forward, kissed his cold dead lips then spun the Pulveriser around in her hands and put the end of the barrel in her mouth. It was there in the chamber, the last holy bullet. The cross had been carved into the lead by her own hand, steadied by the hand of God. That same hand of God was steadying hers now. This was how it was meant to be.

The pain from the bullet wounds was receding and being replaced by a warm feeling, a feeling of love and peace. This was God's glory; he was reaching out to her to pluck her from this dark place and take her in his arms.

The light was getting closer now. She could hear voices. One of the men in the tunnel said, 'I think we got her.' He was wrong. They would never get her. Never. She caressed the Pulveriser's trigger with her forefinger and as the light came closer still, she pulled the trigger and launched the last holy bullet, that blessed little lump of heavy metal with the cross carved into it that would send her on her way to heaven.

As the four SAS soldiers made their way on board the train, they were confronted by the sight of two corpses. One a man, and the other a decapitated woman. As they hurried through in the semi-darkness towards the voices further along the train, none of them noticed the blood, brain and bone fragments that dripped down on them from the interior of the cab.

Northern Line Train 037, first carriage

The engine was getting closer and with it, an increasingly powerful light which shone through the windows into the carriage. George could make out Denning's silhouette standing in the water nearby. He readied himself to dive under the water at the first sign of the gun being pointed. But he need not have worried; Denning took his Browning automatic and pressed it against the bottom of his own chin. He started muttering something, some sort of valediction, and anger propelled George forward once again. He had to try and stop him. As the chain snapped tight around his ankle, he swung a fist at the pistol, managing to knock the barrel away from Denning's face as he pulled the trigger. The shot clanged into the ceiling of the train. Denning tried to pull the pistol back into position but George had his hand around it now and they struggled with it, face to face.

'Let me die, George.'

Legs waded through water in the cab. Torches flashed in the carriage. Denning looked George in the eyes. The vicious pain in his face had sapped his strength and he looked broken, like a frightened child.

'You have to let me die. This is God's will.'

A gloved hand reached out and grabbed hold of the pistol, pulling it from their collective grasp.

'Where are the explosives?' said the soldier who took the gun. 'Tell us now!' Denning was pulled to his feet. There were four of them in total and all pointed their automatic weapons at him.

'Where are the explosives?'

Denning suddenly became calm. He caught his breath and staring back into the eyes of each of the soldiers in turn, he said, 'They're just about to blow.'

Frith Street, Soho

'Clearly, Simeon Fisher has failed to prevent the attack,' said Berriman.

'Clearly,' said Hooper into his phone as he walked along the pavement, not even bothering to mask his sarcasm.

Any respect that he might have felt for his boss had evaporated in the past few hours. In reality, he knew he was running the operation alone. That's the way that it had to be if it was going to succeed. And it still could. Choices, that's what it was all about. He had to keep making them. So long as he did that and those choices were good ones, based on the best intelligence he could gather, then he knew he was still in with a fighting chance.

'Mark, it sounds to me as though we should resume this conversation at another time. You're sounding rather agitated.'

'I'm fine. This whole operation can still work.'

'How can it work, Mark? You don't seem to understand. The cat's out of the bag. Or it soon will be.'

'What do you mean?'

'I've just heard that the water level in the tunnel has dropped. It could be that Ed Mallory's plan that you told me about has been put into operation. It doesn't mean that we're out of the trees. But hopefully it means that the passengers won't drown.'

Hooper felt the heat of guilt burning behind his ears again. This spelt trouble. He had never thought for one moment that Ed Mallory's idea of using some IRA dinosaur to blow a hole in the tunnel wall would actually work. But if he had succeeded, as Berriman suggested, then this changed everything. With potentially live witnesses and – even worse – live terrorists, the truth about the service's and most notably his, foreknowledge, would almost certainly be discovered.

'Well, we'll just have to make sure that some people don't make it out alive.'

'You are joking.'

Berriman's perpetually negative tone was infuriating but he knew that he had to keep a lid on his temper. If he lost control, he was more likely to make mistakes. He couldn't afford to do that. There was too much at stake.

'All it means is that anyone who knows the truth does not survive the evacuation.'

'This is insane, Mark. The hijackers of the train know. The driver of the train probably knows. I know. You have to face it. This is impossible to contain.'

'You're not going to tell anyone. The terrorists are going to die. And as for the driver—'

'Mark, you're not making any sense. You need to stop. You need to stand down.'

'No, Howard, you're the one who's not thinking straight. I can still make this work. We do whatever it takes. This is a war.'

'What are you talking about? These aren't Islamic fundamentalists. They're Christians, Mark, Christians.'

'They're all the same,' said Hooper as he walked across Charing Cross Road. 'What's it matter where they come from? What's it matter which god they believe in? There is a growing tide of lunatics and extremists who are driven by a belief that they are doing the work of a supernatural figure. We have to fight them; we have to stop them.' Hooper flipped his ID at the police line and made his way towards the steps down into Leicester Square station. 'You've got to trust me, Howard, it's all going to be fine.' He could hear Berriman call his name a couple of times as he took the phone from his ear and hung up.

It was true what he'd said. This was a war. This was about right and wrong, however simplistic that might sound. So what if operational procedure wasn't being followed? At a certain stage, pragmatism had to come into play. That was the nature of the job. So long as the good guys won, that was all that mattered.

Hooper knew that if he failed today, it would mean the end of his career. There would be shame, not only for him but for his family too. All those privileged jerks at school who had said he would amount to nothing would be proved right. They would have won. He couldn't let that happen. That's why before he had made his way down to the stronghold in Leicester Square, he had gone home and made sure that he had the right tools for the job.

03:29 PM

Northern Line Train 037, first carriage

'He's lying,' said George. 'There are no more explosives as far as I can see.' He spoke to the soldier nearest to him, who was doing all the talking and appeared to be the one in charge.

'When he caused the explosion that started the flood he had wires and a detonator but I haven't seen anything to suggest that he's rigged up anything else.'

George could feel Denning's eyes burning into him but he had more important things to consider. 'Someone needs to find my children,' he said as Maggie clambered through the window from the adjoining carriage and waded through the water towards them.

'Your children are safe,' said the commanding officer. 'They're at Leicester Square tube station, waiting to see you.'

'You're sure?' asked Maggie, her voice trembling with emotion.

'Yes, I was told to tell you. They're fine.'

Maggie fell against George and they threw their arms

around each other. But their joy at being reunited was interrupted by Denning as he lunged forward and made a grab for one of the soldiers' automatic weapons. It wasn't a serious attempt to launch a counter-attack; his actions were clearly nothing more than an attempt to incite one of the soldiers into shooting him.

'Do me a favour,' said George. 'Keep him alive, will you?'

The soldier fixed George with a nervous stare. 'You're sure about the explosives?' he asked.

'As sure as I can be. The only wires I saw him use were for the first explosion.'

The soldier nodded at one of his colleagues and muttered something. Denning was roughly spun around and his hands secured behind his back with a plastic tie.

A crackle of short-wave radio and the commanding officer received word from the SAS team at the other end of the train that all the carriages were now secured and they were going to begin the evacuation.

As the chain that Denning had used to shackle George's leg to the pole was severed with bolt croppers, Denning looked up at him and their eyes met.

'See you,' said Denning blankly.

George hesitated for a moment before he said, 'I don't think so.'

Never usually the most demonstrative of couples, George and Maggie clung to one another as they were led through the train towards the rear carriage. The water they waded through was a soup of discarded clothing, bags, books, newspapers, cell phones, music players, notebook computers – all the accoutrements of the urban commuter – now discarded, rendered obsolete and lifeless by the water that had swallowed them.

As the water level dropped yet further, people climbed down from the rear of the train and waded along the tunnel towards Leicester Square station. But the mood was sombre; the bodies of those cut down by the terrorists' bullets both on the train and in the tunnel were a brutal reminder of the carnage that had taken place.

George and Maggie with their special forces minder, a stocky bulldog of a man with a ginger crew cut, brought up the rear of the trail of refugees. When they arrived at the northbound Northern Line platform at Leicester Square, the soldier led them away from the others and up a flight of stone stairs to a low narrow corridor. George's and Maggie's shoes squelched as they walked along, their clothes dripping. They were shown into a room which had chairs and a table in the middle of it, at which a police-woman in uniform was seated playing a board game with Sophie and Ben.

The hallucinatory sheen through which George had watched the day's events unfold was at its most intense as Maggie scooped up Sophie and he picked up Ben and they fell into a group hug.

'Daddy, you're stinky,' said Ben, and George and Maggie laughed through their tears.

03:31 PM

Leicester Square Tube Station, service tunnel

The return journey back through the filing cabinets and metal shelving frames was marginally less difficult than before – Ed and Conor's outward trip had cleared a path of sorts. The water slowed them down; it was up to the tops of their thighs but they weren't in a hurry any more. Ed's ears were ringing from the explosion. The skin on his face, despite the fact that he had turned away from the blast, felt leathery and scorched, as though he had been lying in the sun for too long. Conor complained of a headache and concussion but his mood had been transformed. When Ed asked him whether he thought the blast might have secured the desired outcome of draining the Northern Line tunnel, there was no disguising his confidence. 'I can feel it in my bones,' he said.

'I hope you're right,' said Ed.

'Well, I guess we'll find out soon enough. And at least we didn't blow the whole of Leicester Square off the map. Funny, cos thirty years ago, that's exactly what I would've wanted to do. That and to kill you. In fact, that's what I intended to do when you came knocking earlier on.'

'What stopped you?'

'I guess I wanted to try and save the people on the train more.'

Calvert met them at the top of the escalators. 'We heard the blast. The special forces in the tunnel have reported that the water level has gone down. They've secured the train.'

'Survivors?' asked Ed.

'We don't know numbers or details but yes, it looks like there are.'

'What about further explosives?'

'Seems there weren't any.'

'Weren't any?'

'Looks like Denning bluffed us.'

'Jesus.'

'Ed!' He could recognise the voice – it was Frank's – but it was the product of an altogether different disposition than before. The professor's footsteps approached. 'Ed, well, what can I say? It looks like we got it right.' Ed held out his hand but Frank ignored it and gave him a hug. He hadn't taken Frank as the hugging kind but he reciprocated and patted him on the back.

'Well done, Frank. We couldn't have done this without you.'

'Sorry to break up your romantic moment,' said Conor, 'but I think I'll be getting on my way.'

'Ed?' Calvert had lowered his voice to a conspiratorial whisper aimed at Ed's ear. Ed leant towards him. 'We're going to need to have a pretty serious debrief about all of this. We may need Conor.'

Ed didn't care who overheard what he said, Conor included: 'Nick, I need one more favour from you and then we're done. I need you to get Conor outside the cordon. And Frank. If it wasn't for what these two have done – and you – we'd have a train full of dead bodies on our hands. Whatever fall out there is from this, I'll deal with it.'

'Sure.' Conor's wasn't the only demeanour that had changed after the blast. The tension and reticence had gone from Nick Calvert's voice. He clearly knew that explaining the nature of what they had conspired to do – and the legality of it – would take some doing, but the mission had succeeded. That should be enough to swing official opinion their way.

'Good on you, Conor,' said Ed.

'Don't get soppy on me, I don't think I could take it.'

'What you did here today will probably never be known for obvious reasons but you've saved a lot of lives.'

Ed felt Conor's hand slide into his and squeeze it.

'You'll need to get yourself a new pair of sunglasses. Those ones are fucked.'

'I will,' said Ed. 'And thanks.'

As Nick Calvert ushered Conor and Frank away, Ed heard footsteps making straight for him.

'DI Mallory?' It was a young woman's voice. 'I'm WPC Holland. I've got a call for you.'

03:49 PM

Leicester Square Tube Station, ticket hall

The circular ticket hall was busy. Passengers from the hijacked train were being brought up the escalator from the Northern Line. Hooper watched a group of little girls, their pink dresses wet and muddy. The sight of them was like an emotional punch. Right there in front of him was evidence that what he was doing was right. He was saving children from the clutches of radical lunatics.

Near to where he stood, a group of paramedics administered first aid to those with gunshot wounds and other injuries. One man had lost his left leg at the knee. He was clearly in shock but was being stabilised. The place was hectic with police and special forces. It felt like a war zone. It *was* a war zone. And sometimes in times of war, it falls to one man to clean up the mess.

The logistics of what he was going to attempt made him feel sick with trepidation. How exactly was he going to clean up after his failed operation? How would he explain to the powers-that-be that his actions amounted to an operational necessity? It haunted him. He was stepping over the line. But he had no choice.

There were some junior service personnel loitering about outside the control room in the centre of the ticket office. They were beneath him in the pecking order; he could pull rank. He sidled up to a guy called Johnstone. He was a low-grade wannabe. A no one in the scheme of things. They nodded a mutual greeting.

'Where's Denning?' asked Hooper.

'They've just put him in there.' He gestured towards the control room in the ticket hall.

Hooper knew that if White or Calvert were there, he was in trouble. But if they weren't, if it was just some grunt who was watching over him then he would be able to do the job. He stepped inside.

He was in luck. There was just the one CO19 officer standing in the room. Hooper flashed his MI5 ID at him. Denning sat on a chair at a table pressing a large piece of bandage against his bloody face.

'I just need to ask him a few questions,' said Hooper.

'You're going to have to be quick,' said the grunt. 'He's off to St Mary's with Special Branch to get his face patched up before he goes to Paddington Green.'

Hooper nodded. He *was* going to be quick.

'Who are you?' asked Denning looking up.

'MI5,' said Hooper.

'Oh dear,' said Denning. 'Not one of your better days.'

'Why's that?' Hooper tried to keep a flat measured tone to his voice. He pulled out the chair opposite Denning and sat down, listening for footsteps outside the door.

'I should think there'll be a few job cuts after this little lot leaks out.'

'Why should you care, Tommy? I thought this was all about God and your need to wipe out hundreds of people in his name.'

'This was prophesied in the Bible.'

'Listen, Tommy, you need to tell me how many people know about Simeon Fisher.'

'Who's he?'

'Don't play games, Tommy. How many knew?'

'You knew. I knew. My sister knew.'

'Who else?'

'Why are you so interested all of a sudden?'

'Did the driver know?'

Denning turned and looked at the CO19 officer and then looked back at Hooper. 'George was such a disappointment to me. I thought he was one of us.'

'Tommy, I haven't got time for this. Does he know about Simeon Fisher and MI5's involvement?'

Denning looked Hooper in the eyes and said, 'Yeah, he knows. George knows everything.'

'No one else?'

'No one.'

It was old school and he loved it for that. A Walther PPK with a silencer. Bond's gun. Iconic. He had bought it on the black market. It couldn't be traced back to him. It could just as well have been Tommy Denning's as his. And now it would be Tommy Denning's. For all time.

Beneath the table, he pulled on the surgical glove and drew the gun from the holster on his ankle.

'What are you waiting for?' said Denning.

Hooper raised the gun and shot over Denning's head. Two bullets, straight into the CO19 officer's face. He fell heavily but not loudly enough to arouse suspicion outside the door.

'Bless you,' said Denning. He looked up and had just enough time to say, 'Father, into your hands I commit my spirit,' before Hooper forced the gun into his mouth and pulled the trigger. A bloody spray peppered the wall from the exit wound in the back of his head before he fell forward onto the desk.

He had to move fast. Taking off the holster from his ankle, he strapped it to Denning's. He wiped the surgical glove on Denning's right hand to provide the necessary firearms' residue before he curled his fingers around the Walther PPK.

And there it was. Denning had managed to keep a concealed weapon about him and when the time had come he had killed his guard and shot himself in the mouth. Regrettable of course.

Hooper walked from the room and pulled the door closed after him. When interviewed, he would say that when he left the room, everything was fine. And it was. Absolutely fine.

But he would worry about that later. Now he would update Berriman, then he would find the train driver.

Leicester Square Tube Station, station manager's office

WPC Holland was struggling to keep a lid on her nerves during a scenario for which she was mentally ill-prepared. As Ed took her arm, he could feel a slight tremble through the starched cotton of her blouse. Once they were inside the station manager's office, she pressed a telephone receiver into Ed's hand and he raised it to his ear.

'DI Mallory.'

'Ed, there you are. I'm so glad to have located you.' Howard Berriman's tone was radically altered from their previous conversations. He sounded solemn, contrite and more than a little panicked.

'What can I do for you?' asked Ed. He was expecting some sort of congratulation or at least acknowledgement of what he had succeeded in doing to drain the water from around the train. He received neither.

'I need to talk to you about Mark Hooper. Have you spoken to him?'

'Not since we were at the Network Control Centre in St James's.'

'Do you know where he might be?'

'No idea.'

'The thing is, Ed, I think today's events have conspired to make him suffer some sort of breakdown.'

'He seemed OK earlier. He was very guarded about things but I figured that it had something to do with professional friction between our two departments.'

'Well, since then, things haven't panned out as he'd envisaged and I think it's pushed him over the edge.'

'What things, Howard?'

There was silence on the line and Ed had a curious feeling. His subconscious was stirring. Thoughts were forming, thoughts that he didn't even realise he had been having. And once they had started to form, his enlightenment was rapid. Everything tumbled into place and when he said the two words, he said them as a statement, not a question.

'You knew.'

There was relief in Berriman's voice when he said, 'Yes.' Guilt was Howard Berriman's burden and he was only too pleased to offload it. But there were caveats – of course there were.

'We only knew the vaguest of details. All we knew was there was going to be a hijacking on the Underground. We thought it was going to be next week.'

'And you only tell me now when they're evacuating the train?'

'It wouldn't have helped you to do your job.'

'Shouldn't I have been the judge of that?'

'Look, I'm sorry, Ed. All we knew was that Tommy Denning was going to try and hijack a tube train. Hooper was handling someone on the inside who told him it was going to be this time next week.'

'So why weren't we doing all we could to bring them in?'

'Look, Ed, I can't deny that it wasn't a politically motivated decision. I thought if I delivered a result on the day with maximum news and media coverage then everyone would come up smelling of roses – the government, the service, me . . .'

'And Hooper was your boy.'

'He was the one who brought it to me but they moved early. Denning must have found out about our man on the inside—'

'He wasn't called Simeon Fisher was he, by any chance?'

'Yeah, how did you—'

'Denning.'

'Right, well, it allowed him to catch us off guard. There was no point you knowing. It wouldn't have helped.'

'And now you think that Hooper has lost the plot.'

'Ed, I think he might try and kill Tommy Denning.'

'What?'

'When we last spoke, he said he was going to try and take out anyone who knew about the operation.'

'Jesus, Howard.'

'He thinks he can clean up the mess and we can all walk away.'

'I take it you've put a call out for him to be stopped on sight?'

'We're speaking to Commander Boise.'

'Let's hope they can bring him in straight away.'

'I'm sure they will.'

'And what about me, Howard? How do you think what I did will go down with the grown-ups?'

'You got the passengers out, Ed. You'll be fine.'

'That's easy for you to say. There are still going to be a lot of questions to answer about the methods I employed.'

'I'll be fighting your corner, Ed, you know that.'

Berriman's words offered little reassurance. Ed knew that Berriman would have too many problems of his own regarding his prior knowledge of the attack to spend time trying to save some copper's skin. Ed's feelings towards the Director General of MI5 had gone through various twists and turns during the day but now they felt as though they had resolved themselves in his mind. It was straight-forward enough, he just didn't like the guy.

'And Ed? What I've just told you about this operation remains between the two of us for the time being, is that clear?'

'Sure, Howard.'

'We'll talk about this later.'

'If that's what you want.'

'I do, Ed. I really do.'

The line went dead.

Howard had lied to Ed Mallory; he hadn't put the call in to Serina Boise. He wanted to find out whether Mallory knew where Hooper was first. As he put the phone down, he snatched it up again, his finger poised over the keypad. He would make the call now.

But what if Hooper did manage to make it all go away? If the train driver did know about the service's complicity and he didn't make it out alive then perhaps they would be in the clear. He could blame Hooper for what had gone on. He could blame it on his mental state. Tragic that a young man like that should crack under pressure but it happens. That's life. Who else was there? Only Ed. And what possible advantage or benefit could he have in raining on his own parade? What he had done was unconventional, foolhardy maybe, but because of the outcome for many he would be perceived as a hero. Maybe Hooper was right. Maybe the shit storm could be averted. There was no harm in just leaving it a few minutes. Wait and see. If he got a call from Hooper to say that it had all been taken care of then what was the point in rocking the boat? He could still have him taken out of the game. And as for Ed's safety down there, well, if he didn't make it out alive either then that would be tragic too. He'd say nice things about him, make sure he got some sort of posthumous award.

Hooper had sounded disturbed when he'd phoned just before he spoke to Ed but that was only to be expected. Perhaps he sounded unbalanced because what he was proposing was, by anyone's estimation, insane. But that didn't mean that he might not be able to see it through. Howard needed to look at the big picture. As the Director General of MI5, he needed to make the big decisions.

Howard Berriman took his finger away from the telephone keypad and drummed it against the top of the desk as he thought.

Wait and see. It was definitely the best course of action.

Leicester Square Tube Station, ticket hall

Ed took WPC Holland's arm as she walked him across the concourse in the ticket hall towards the offices where Denning was being held.

'What's your first name?' asked Ed.

'Jessica. Jess.'

'Well, listen, Jess, you may not like what you're about to see.'

'What am I about to see?'

'Two dead men.'

The angle of her delivery changed as she spoke to someone up ahead. 'This is DI Ed Mallory.'

Ed held out his ID and said, 'I'm here to see Tommy Denning.'

The officer opened up the door and Ed and WPC Holland went inside the room. The air smelled of blood and aftershave. Mark Hooper's recent presence there was confirmed when WPC Holland lost her composure and muttered, 'Oh my God.'

Ed let go of her arm and putting his hands on the table

top, made his way around it to Tommy Denning's corpse slumped in the chair. Ed ran his fingers over Denning's face, feeling the massive wound in his cheek and the shattered teeth and lacerated gum tissue within it. He touched the stubble on Denning's head that would grow for a few more hours at least. He felt the ridge of ruptured skull at the back of his head – the exit wound – then he reached down and felt for Denning's right hand. He lifted it up and held it between his own. It was still warm. Holding it to his nose, he took a deep breath. There was blood of course, oily water from the flooded tunnel, the smell of gunpowder residue from all the shooting he had done but beneath all of that was the smell of human skin, the smell of Tommy Denning.

Within seconds, WPC Holland had raised the alarm and the room was full of police officers. But Ed didn't intend to hang around to explain the intricacies of the situation. Ed said to Holland, 'You need to take me to the train driver and his family.'

04:04 PM

Leicester Square Tube Station, admin office

'Everything's going to be all right now,' said George and Maggie smiled at him. It was a corny line but he didn't care. They had survived the storm. They were alive. Everything came into focus now. Every moment was precious.

There were footsteps in the corridor outside followed by a muttered conversation on the other side of the door. The door opened and a policewoman entered the room followed by a slim man dressed all in black. His face was scarred and he wore cracked sunglasses, clearly the prop of a blind man. The state of his filthy soaking clothes made it appear as though he had been on the train with them.

'George Wakeham?'

'Yeah, that's me.'

'I'm Ed Mallory. We spoke earlier.'

George recognised the voice. Mallory held out his hand and George shook it. But the mood was anything but convivial.

'Thanks for all your help,' said George.

'Don't worry about that now. What happened to your security detail?'

'Well, there was someone with us earlier who brought us up from the train but—'

'George, I need you and your family to follow us.'

'Is something the matter?' asked George. Ed Mallory's tone and demeanour had taken the shine off his celebratory mood.

'You need to come with us. Now.'

George felt his fear return but he needed answers, he needed to know the nature of this new threat.

'What's going on?'

'You and your family are in danger.'

George felt the moment wrap itself around him like clingfilm. He sucked at the air but it was hot and devoid of oxygen.

'Please, we need to move fast.' George and Maggie gathered the children together and they followed Ed Mallory and the policewoman out of the room towards the top of the escalators.

'What the hell is going on?' asked Maggie in a frantic whisper.

'I don't know,' said George. 'But we should trust this guy.'

'How do you know?'

'I just do.'

Ed held onto the arm of the policewoman, who looked around nervously as though searching for someone in amongst the crowds of paramedics, police, special forces and evacuated train passengers. She gestured for George to follow them down an escalator. While Maggie held the children's hands, George caught up with Ed and said, 'Do you want to tell me what this is all about?'

'Soon. Let's keep moving,' said Ed.

They came to a red steel door which stood ajar set into the side of a pedestrian tunnel. Ed said to WPC Holland, 'Make contact with DI Calvert and tell him where we are.' She hurried off, leaving him standing in the doorway.

'Inside quickly and close the door,' said Ed, and George ushered Maggie and the children into the dark interior and pushed the steel door shut on its screeching oil-free hinges. 'I'm sorry about this,' whispered Ed in the pitch darkness behind the door. 'The problem is we have a rogue MI5 agent who's had some sort of breakdown. He may be dangerous. Armed police officers are on their way but we're going to have to wait for them. Here's as safe a place as any for the time being.'

'OK,' whispered George and pulled Ben, Sophie and Maggie close to him as they waited.

04:07 PM

Leicester Square Tube Station, ticket hall

It was the policewoman holding his arm that did it. If it hadn't been for that, Mark Hooper might not have recognised him. Ed Mallory was dripping wet and his formerly pristine black clothes were soaked in muddy water. After Mark had seen to Tommy Denning, he had gone to the office in the ticket hall where the train driver had been reunited with his family, but there was a special forces soldier on duty. He had been forced to wait. But clearly believing that the driver was no longer in danger, the soldier had obviously been instructed to stand down. Just as Hooper was about to move in, however, Mallory had arrived with a policewoman. Now, they were leaving, heading down the escalators with the train driver and his family. Where the hell were they going? It didn't matter. He had come too far to turn back now. With the train driver taken out of the equation, the intelligence leak was contained. It was a tough call. An innocent man who had already gone through so much was going to have to die. Possibly his family too. Possibly Ed Mallory. A cover story would be difficult but not impossible. Ed Mallory had already gone rogue. What was employing an ex-IRA bomber to blast a hole in the tunnel if not evidence of a mind gone awry? Mark would try and pin the train driver's death on him. So he was blind, that didn't mean that he couldn't go berserk with a gun. If only the blind bastard had just stuck to the script and accepted that his negotiation had failed then everyone on the train would have died and no one would have been any the wiser as to the service's foreknowledge. That was all that had needed to happen. But now Mark was exposed. All roads led back to him, and Berriman would be only too happy to hang him out to dry. Well, if he was going down, he was going down fighting.

At the bottom of the escalators, Ed Mallory and the others turned into one of the pedestrian tunnels leading to the train lines. Keeping them in a clear line of sight, he followed them and only hung back when he saw them turn into a doorway. Ed Mallory spoke to the policewoman. He couldn't make out what was being said but he knew that he had to take cover as she turned and made her way back towards him. Near to where he was standing were some stairs providing access to the two Piccadilly Line platforms. He descended the stairs taking two steps at a time and waited for the policewoman to go past. When he could hear her footsteps recede, he climbed up the steps and reached into his pocket, his fingers closing around the handle of the Glock. It wasn't his favourite handgun. That accolade went to the Walther PPK he had left in Tommy Denning's hand. But this would do its job well enough when the time came.

04:11 PM

Leicester Square Tube Station, service tunnel entrance

Ed could hear footsteps on the other side of the door. The person making them was walking on tiptoes, trying to be as quiet as possible. There was only one person who would see fit to try and keep their approach a secret. The footsteps stopped but Ed could smell Hooper's aftershave. They needed to move fast but he didn't want to alarm the children in case they cried out and gave away their position. He put his hand on George's shoulder and was about to steer him towards the steps down into the flooded service tunnel when the door was kicked open, the hinges screeching, the air displacement brushing against his face.

'No!' George's voice was charged with fear. The threat to which it referred was implicit. Ed threw himself forward, fists clenched. Hooper wasn't big; if Ed could reach him, he might be able to restrain him long enough for George and his family to escape into the service tunnel. But before his hands could find Hooper, his shoulder was speared with a pole of agony as a muted gunshot made a flat echo in the enclosed space and he was thrown backwards, staggering into George and his family. He struggled to maintain his balance and realised that it was futile to do so when his foot reached out for the floor and found nothing. He was pitched backwards; his shoulders, one of them shattered by the bullet that had, only moments before, passed through it, smashed against the stone steps as he fell. Ed's head made contact with a stone riser and just before he blacked out, he felt himself falling into water, sinking deeper and deeper.

Leicester Square Tube Station, service tunnel

The man with the gun looked around the dark enclosed space. Ed Mallory wasn't his only target. He was searching for someone else. Looking at Maggie first, he raised his gun, finger on the trigger, then he looked at George. Their eyes met. The man was going to kill him. George had never been so sure of anything in his life. He threw a reflex punch that made contact with the man's abdomen and with his other hand, he made a grab for the gun, pushing it back, cracking it against the wall. Lunging forward, George's forehead connected with the man's nose. He battered the gun against the wall again and he heard a reassuring clatter as it fell to the floor. The man was dazed but there was plenty of fight left in him. He lashed out and his fist made contact with the side of George's head. It was a powerful blow and George knew that he was in trouble. This guy was in the secret service; he had probably been trained in unarmed combat.

'George!' Maggie was shouting at him. The children were crying. The two men struggled at the top of the steps.

Another punch struck George's jaw. Before the man could draw his fist back once more, George pushed him backwards, past Maggie and the children to the top of the steps and over, the two men falling, the stone edges providing far more painful blows than either of their fists ever could. The cold water into which they fell brought some clarity back to George's perception. He appeared to have survived the fall in better shape than his attacker and seeing the man rise up out of the water in front of him, flailing around, George threw his head forward into the man's face for a second time. His forehead cracked against the man's nose and as he heard his gasping pained exhalation, George held him at arms' length, his hands closing around his neck as he forced him down into the water. George was bigger than him, his arms were longer; he had a whole lot more to lose.

The man lashed out with everything that he had, kicking and punching, but the impact of the blows was reduced by the water and George could cope with the pain as he drove his thumbs into the man's neck and forced him downwards. George pulled his head back so the fingers that desperately scrambled around for something to hold onto fumbled across his face but could find no purchase.

George dragged the man towards the tunnel wall and cracked his head against the brickwork, once, twice, three times. The kicks and the flailing arms became more desperate but weaker now and George pressed even harder against his neck. The man's hands picked at his fingers, trying to prise them off, but they lacked the necessary strength and finally they dropped away. George felt the life go out of him and he flopped back into the water.

'George!' Maggie shouted from the top of the steps. 'George, are you OK?'

'I'm fine, it's over.'

But this wasn't enough for Maggie. She had been through too much that day to accept a vague reassurance.

'What happened? Where is he?'

'He's down here,' said George. 'But stay where you are.' Sophie and Ben were still crying after their shock and fear of moments earlier but were consoled by the sound of George's voice.

It was a struggle to unclench his fingers. They were locked in a stone grip and he had to concentrate to relax them. He looked down at his victim. He didn't look like a bad man, just an office drone with his smart shirt and his tailored slacks, someone who wanted to get on; someone who had ambition. He had seen the type at school. You knew they were going places; but you also knew that whatever they did, it would never make them happy. But happiness didn't come into it now. This guy would never be happy again, would never be anything.

George turned to where Ed Mallory lay in the water, slumped against the side of the tunnel. A cloud of blood hung in the water around his neck. The bullet had entered through the top of his back by his shoulder blade breaking his collarbone. He was semi-conscious, groaning and struggling to keep his head above the water. George dragged him to his feet.

'You're going to be all right,' he said.

George had no idea whether this was true. But from the amount of bleeding, it looked as though the bullet had missed any arteries or major blood vessels and the wound was far enough away from the spinal cord and the heart so he would probably make it.

'You killed him,' said Ed, looking down at the body in the water.

'I had to stop him,' said George.

'It was self-defence,' said Ed. 'I can attest to that.'

Blood seeped between Ed's fingers as he pressed down on his shoulder and George helped steady him as they climbed the steps to join Maggie and the children. As they made their way towards the escalators, Ed stumbled and George put his arm around him to hold him up.

'Do you want me to go and fetch someone?' George asked Ed as they started climbing up the static escalator with Maggie and the children following behind.

'No, it feels as though I'm losing blood so we'd better keep moving. But you need to remember this. Think of it as an insurance policy. Two names: Howard Berriman and Mark Hooper. Berriman is the head of MI5 – you've probably heard of him – and Hooper is, was, the guy in the tunnel just now. They knew all about Denning's intended hijack, but they let it happen because they wanted the kudos of appearing to have stopped it right at the last minute. The trouble was that Denning got wise to what they were up to and he moved the attack to a week earlier. That's what all that was about down there. Mark Hooper thought that you knew the truth and he could save his skin if he took you out.'

'But what about Tommy Denning?'

'Hooper killed him.'

George didn't have time to explore his feelings about the death of the man who had engineered the horror that he and his family and so many others had been forced to endure. He had wanted him to live, had wanted him to suffer for what he had done but it was not to be.

'So what will happen to Howard Berriman?' asked George.

'His career's over,' said Ed. 'I'm going to take great pleasure in bringing him down.'

They made their way into the ticket hall and seeing Ed Mallory limping, clutching his bleeding shoulder, a tall man with a shaven head rushed forward.

'Ed, I only just got the message, what happened?' he asked.

'It's all right, Nick, I'll explain later after I've got some medical attention,' said Ed. 'In the meantime, I need you to look after these people.' Ed explained who George and his family were and introduced them to Detective Inspector Nick Calvert.

'I'll be in touch,' said Ed to George. 'Don't worry, it'll be fine.' Ed held out his right hand that he had been holding against his bullet wound and George shook it, their palms both wet and sticky with blood.

As Ed was helped onto a stretcher by a paramedic, Nick Calvert ushered George and his family up the steps leading from the ticket hall to ground level. As they emerged into the daylight, George thought that the London air, so much maligned under normal circumstances, tasted cleaner and fresher than ever before.

George saw the reflection of a man in a shop window on the opposite side of Charing Cross Road. He was filthy, marinated in sludge and his face was swollen, bruised and bloody. It took a moment for him to realise that he was looking at a reflection of himself. He looked like a refugee from a nightmare. His outward appearance, however, belied his state of mind. His hands had stopped shaking; his breathing had steadied. Despite his recent ordeal on the train and his even more recent explosion of violence, he felt calm, strangely uplifted, somehow new and cleansed.

George heard someone call his name and then someone else did and then more voices were calling to him. He looked towards the perimeter of the evacuation zone to the news crews and photographers that had gathered behind the barriers.

'George! How are you feeling?'

'George! Over here.'

They knew him; they had seen him on Denning's video feed from the train. The media had processed him and now he was part of their story. After all those years of craving recognition for something other than driving a tube train and now here it was, a direct response to doing exactly that and nothing he could do to prevent it.

News of who had just emerged from below ground had spread fast. Cameras and camera phones were pointed from the growing crowd as George held Maggie and the children close. People jostled to catch a glimpse of them as the shutters clicked and the sun shone down from the cloudless London sky.